FIRST THERE WAS THE BOMB IN HIS CAR, NOW...

Michaelis unlocked the door to his apartment, opened it, and flipped the light switch.

"Don't you ever go to bed, Professor?"

The voice came from his favorite easy chair. In it sat Horace Strang. Michaelis remembered him well from the long hours in the jury room. He had a Walther machine pistol propped on his lap, the barrel pointing directly at Michaelis's midsection.

"Shut the door."

FRANKLIN BANDY

ATHENA

TOR
A TOM DOHERTY ASSOCIATES BOOK
NEW YORK

This is a work of fiction. All the characters and events portrayed in this book are fictitious, and any resemblance to real people or events is purely coincidental.

ATHENA

A TOR Book
Published by Tom Doherty Associates, Inc.
49 West 24 Street
New York, NY 10010

ISBN: 0-812-58050-8 Can. ISBN: 0-812-58051-6

Library of Congress Catalog Card Number: 86-51489

First edition: July 1987
First mass market printing: December 1987

Printed in the United States of America

0 9 8 7 6 5 4 3 2 1

Dedicated with love to my wife, Beth,
for making our marriage of many years
a happy one, for giving us two sons we're
proud of, and for her unswerving
confidence in my writing.

My many thanks to Michael Seidman, my editor, whose careful editing and suggestions for revisions greatly improved this novel.

and

To Pilot Robert Ruskay for keeping me straight on what can or cannot happen in the cockpit of a transatlantic airliner.

1

"SOME WOMAN PLAYING THE FOOL. SAYS THE WHITE HOUSE IS calling *person-to-person* for Professor Jonathan Michaelis." Alice Whitney had half-swiveled around in her chair, her palm covering the mouthpiece, her lips puckered. She looked like an annoyed carp.

Michaelis hurriedly put down the dissertation he had been reading and reached for the phone. "Don't hang up, I'll take it," he said. It probably *was* the White House, but there was no need to give old Alice palpitations.

"Michaelis."

"Jon? This is Ken Watson."

"Oh, yes, how are you, Ken?"

The voice in Washington was subdued. "Not too good, Jon. I'm afraid the whole thing's off. This juror-bribing business."

Michaelis settled back in his chair, light-headed. "Hell, I had nothing to do with that! Good God, surely—"

Watson interrupted. "Bless you, Jon, everyone knows you wouldn't take a crooked nickel. But you know how it is. As long as there is any hint of suspicion, as long as it can never be proved that you had nothing to do with it—"

"But—"

"The people around the President must be immaculate, pristine. You know what the press is today."

Michaelis stared out the window at the green, tree-shaded campus, fighting an urge to argue, yell, demand. Finally he said quietly, "I've been through a most rigid financial investigation. I've been checked by the FBI, the CIA, and God knows what other government agencies. What the hell, my whole life has gone into the computers."

Watson said, "I know, I know. Unfortunately it was before this bribery thing hit the media. And, to play devil's advocate, no one could be absolutely sure you don't have a hundred thousand dollars stashed away in a Swiss bank account."

Michaelis's forehead was wet, perspiration creeping down to his eyebrows. He moved his hand across his forehead slowly. "Suppose I can produce proof that I was not involved?"

Watson cleared his throat. "An impossible job, I would think. Anyway, you know how these appointments are. Once a name is wiped off and another substituted—"

Michaelis was silent for a few seconds. "Then the whole thing is hopeless?"

"I'm afraid so."

"Well"—Michaelis struggled to keep his voice even —"I want you to know that I appreciate everything you've done. I hope I haven't embarrassed you."

"You haven't. Not at all. You're by far the best man for the job. I'm just sorry as hell—"

The two men mumbled restrained good wishes and the call was terminated.

Michaelis sat, his shoulders hunched, despair and panic settling on him like a condemned man's hood. The chance of a lifetime, the opportunity to be one of the President's top aides, had been destroyed by a purely fortuitous brush with corruption. Probably there would never again be the special combination of circumstances which had almost sent him to Washington. He had counted on the appointment. Watson had said it was a certainty.

It was a minor consideration, but the appointment would have been a satisfying put-down for Diane. Smart, lovely, witchy Diane who had left her professor husband for a more exciting life, presumably with a more exciting man. He had never met "B.B.," Butler Baines. He hoped they would have an exciting life together, sharing shingles, chronic sinus drip, and the heartbreak of psoriasis.

The appointment was probably a fluke anyway. Michaelis had never been noticeably active in politics. His sponsor, if that was the proper word, was a powerful figure in the liberal wing of the President's party. Intrigued with Michaelis's book, *Realpolitik in an Unreal World,* he had set up a luncheon date. The two men found that they had much in common and became friends. Michaelis rationalized that he could play devil's advocate and sway the President on certain issues. Actually, the opportunity to work closely with the most powerful man in the world was irresistible.

Washington was to be his escape from academic life. He did not have the temperament of a scholar, though he managed to function creditably in this role. But it was a dead end. Sooner or later, they would find out.

He could go back to the big metropolitan daily where he had spent seven years, but that, too, had soured. He had been a top investigative reporter. He found corruption in startlingly unexpected places. His stories made headlines frequently.

He found, unfortunately, that when an honest investigator exposed corruption, he shot down the good guys with the bad guys, the good guys being those whose politics and philosophies matched his own. Dedicated, honest men were sometimes sucked almost unwittingly into ethical chaos by the very nature of politics. Demands, commitments, obligations, debts, television advertising time, the unbelievable cost of running a successful campaign. Following an investigative series written by Michaelis, one of the congressmen involved had bowed out with an overdose of sleeping pills. Michaelis had admired this man's ability and statesmanship.

If he had strong guilt feelings about the congressman, he felt even more guilt about the situation that had terminated his career as an investigative reporter. Cowardice or simple common sense? He had received a hot lead on one of the nation's richest men.

Brewster Fernwald was one of the world's powerful entrepreneurs. Newsmen who knew more than they could print marveled that he managed to remain outside the walls of a maximum-security prison. His reputed crimes were many. They ranged from the contracted murders of his father and brother to a strong connection with organized crime. He owned oil wells, shipping lines, banks, and worldwide manufacturing operations. He was so feared by his closest associates that the inner circle could never be broken. Evidence was nonexistent.

Michaelis's lead was small, but it could be the wedge that opened a coffin or two. He had hardly begun when he received a telephone call. The quiet voice at the other end of the wire said, "You will immediately cease any inquiries into the affairs of Brewster Fernwald. If you persist, you will be dead within a week. Do you understand?"

"Yes," said Michaelis. The connection was broken.

There is no escape from a high-priced hit man of the caliber Fernwald could afford. And no retribution either, regardless of the clamor the press would make for one of its own. The topflight hit man is never caught. He operates briefly in a given city, guided by cold logic, great care in the choice of time and place, and the knowledge that only an actual witness to the crime can bring him down. Witnesses do not survive. The hit man has no recognizable motive or connection with the victim. He's a businessman who does his job efficiently, leaves no trace, and departs the area with unhurried calm.

Common sense told Michaelis to drop the matter. A dead journalist is of no use to anyone, including himself. His emotions told him he was being cowardly. He squelched them angrily, telling himself that the only way to deal with Brewster Fernwald was to give him a dose of his own medicine. Perhaps he, Michaelis, would someday kill Brewster Fernwald.

In the meantime, he could hardly continue to devote his life to exposing judges who channeled their bribes through close relatives, and befuddled congressmen who dipped into campaign funds illegally. Not while Brewster Fernwald remained at large.

He had crept back to the university, half-convinced of his cowardice.

It was still there, outside the window. The green grass of the campus, youths slouching past awkwardly, pretty girls striding along, hair bouncing, unbrassiered breasts jiggling, skintight pants revealing every movement of rounded buttocks. Naive, lovely kids.

Alice Whitney's voice interrupted his reverie. She said, "I'll be damned. It *was* the White House."

Michaelis turned to her, forcing a smile. In her late sixties, Alice had been a secretary in the Political Science Department for thirty-eight years. She had been there two years before Michaelis was born. She was crabby, shrewd, efficient, and a valuable adviser when it came to faculty infighting.

"Yep. They thought they wanted me to come to Washington and work for the President. Now they've changed their minds."

"That effing von Dietrich thing?" Alice tried to keep her speech young, but couldn't quite bring herself to say some of the words the students used.

Michaelis nodded.

She made small chirping noises of disgust. "Idiots! Everyone knows you're too pure to take a bribe."

"Thank you." Michaelis rubbed his chin, not sure he had been complimented. "Nevertheless, I was one of the twelve jurors. Apparently seven of them got one hundred thousand dollars each."

Tall and slim, Michaelis took good care of his body. He worked out in the gym every day and could run ten miles without strain. At thirty-six he feared middle age. He had a lean, longish face with a strong chin. His cheeks sometimes looked dimpled. When he was weary, they appeared slightly sunken. In repose his mouth was a half-smile. Gray eyes stared directly into yours. His light brown hair managed some careless intrusions onto his high forehead. This, and the combination of bold eyes and constant half-smile, gave him a "know-it-all" look that some resented, particularly his male students. His apparent confidence in his own superiority was appealing to many women.

Alice was drumming her nails on the desk with exasperating monotony. Finally she said, "If I were you, I'd ferret out those bribe-takers and put them in jail."

He had been toying with the thought. "Pretty tough assignment. Nothing but hearsay evidence available. Impossible job."

Alice swiveled around to face her own desk. "Ha," she

said to the wall. "What happened to the intrepid investigative reporter you were before you crept back to the halls of academe?"

The intrepid reporter had turned as yellow as a pack of Kodacolor. "Ummm. That's how I know it would be an impossible job," he said.

On the other hand, why not? He could shake loose from his light summer schedule easily enough. Not that it would make any difference. The Washington appointment was lost. Whatever he did would not affect his academic career. He had tenure, and he was respected. The people who counted would know that a hundred-thousand-dollar bribe meant nothing to Michaelis. He already had more money than he could use.

So what was he after, revenge? Partly, he supposed. There was enough anger inside. But stronger was the nagging feeling that the situation was intolerable. Whatever his friends and the public might believe, he would always be conscious of unfinished business, an unfair blot on his integrity. At the very least, he had to make an effort.

He thought about Athena von Dietrich. In his mind there was still a dramatic, full-color image of her and her somewhat flamboyant beauty. She had long black hair that sometimes shifted to conceal part of her face, green eyes of the finest emerald, eyebrows that arched slightly upward from the center of her face, a perfect nose, a short, royal upper lip, and a mouth that was also in a perpetual half-smile. Her full red lips curved in a confident look of superiority, staring down each juror in turn. Even Michaelis had shifted his eyes first, embarrassed that he was being called upon to judge this beautiful woman.

Now he found that he had helped her get away with murder.

2

THE FIRST VOTE TAKEN IN THE JURY ROOM SURPRISED MICHAElis. Six to convict, six to acquit. Athena's guilt was obvious, Michaelis thought. She had shot her husband in the chest. The bullet had penetrated his heart, and death had been almost instantaneous. Two witnesses, the housekeeper and her husband, had heard most of the quarrel leading up to the shot that ended Karl von Dietrich's life.

The two witnesses were dead.

According to the housekeeper's dying statement, her husband had answered the door and found a masked man waiting. The gunman had shot him, then stepped past him into the house and shot her.

"The shooting of the witnesses, it did not have to be what you think," said Theodopolus. "It could have been a simple robbery. The man's money was taken."

"Strange coincidence," said Michaelis. "Particularly since they gave him no reason to shoot if he was there merely to rob. The noise might have alerted someone upstairs to call the police."

"Today these crazy people kill for the pleasure of it."

The argument had been going on for hours. The vote had changed to seven for acquittal and five for conviction. Michaelis was weary. "What about the maid's testimony?" he asked.

Huey Fan, the proprietor of a busy Chinese restaurant, said, "That woman!" He tapped his round, pasty forehead. "She is not one hundred percent. Then, too, what she say defendant say is not, ah—"

"Not inconsistent with the defendant's testimony," said Marsha Hallowell, one of the seven in favor of acquittal.

"Yes, not inconsistent," said Huey Fan. "She say defendant yell, 'Put that gun down!' and then she say, 'Give it to me, you fool.'"

The maid, Carlita, had testified to hearing the sound of a quarrel, but she had been too far away to hear more than the two sentences Athena had shrieked shortly before the reverberating crash of the gun.

Athena had claimed the shooting was an accident. The noise that resembled a quarrel was laughing, shouting horseplay. Her husband had been clowning with the revolver. She had taken it from him, and it had gone off accidentally.

"They were playing the fool. I have seen Occidentals play the fool many times in my restaurant," said Huey Fan.

"The Chinese never do?" asked Michaelis.

"Only when something loose up here," said Huey, tapping his forehead again.

Michaelis said, "I find the whole idea very hard to accept. The murder of the witnesses was more likely a hit job rather than a robbery."

The argument continued into the night. One by one the jurors in favor of conviction changed to the other side. Finally Michaelis rationalized that perhaps there was a reasonable doubt. With the score eleven to one, he shifted his vote.

As chairman, it was his duty to stand up in court and say, "We, the jury, find the defendant not guilty."

3

CRENDON, THE SEAT OF THE UNIVERSITY, HAD THE USUAL PROBlems of ambivalence. The townspeople both respected and distrusted the university. During the Vietnam conflict the university had been a center of antiwar activity, a sanctuary for traitors in the opinion of most of the inhabitants of the conservative little city. The humiliating end of the undeclared war and the scandals of Watergate continued the strain on the uneasy truce for several years. Now, however, attitudes were friendlier, though still tinged with suspicion, and the campus was regarded as a hotbed of drugs and sexual activity.

Michaelis parked his aged gray Volvo in the municipal lot, levered himself out into the hot June sunshine, and headed across the street to keep his appointment with the district attorney. Crendon's courthouse was a modern structure. A nine-storied glass block, it covered approximately a half-acre. Some twenty feet of grass formed a band around its perimeter. The building's stark design was broken only by a tall flagpole standing in the center of the concrete apron leading to the revolving doors. Pushing through one of them, Michaelis entered the building and rode the elevator to the fourth floor.

Curtis Loughney, the district attorney, offered his hand, smiling. "Now I place you, Professor," he said. "Have a seat." In his mid-fifties, Loughney had gray hair, crew-cut, a red face, and a nervous tic in his right eyelid. He was wearing a gray summer-weight suit, a white shirt, and a red tie. He stared at Michaelis's open-neck plaid shirt and his flared whipcord slacks. "Most men put on a tie and a jacket when they come to see the district attorney," he said.

Already bucking for a judgeship, thought Michaelis. "That's too bad. They must be very uncomfortable in this weather."

"Respect for the office, Professor," said Loughney.

"I see. Well, when you visit my office, you can wear a T-shirt."

Shaking his head, Loughney made his way to the big padded swivel chair behind his desk and sat down. Michaelis pulled a chair closer to the spacious, carved desk and eased into it quickly. The large office resembled a courtroom. On one side behind Loughney was an upright pole bearing the American flag; on the other side another supported a white flag with the City of Crendon's insignia embroidered in dark blue.

"Well, now, let me guess, Professor," said Loughney,

winking. "You've come here to confess all and turn in the hundred thousand dollars."

The winking, of course, was not intentional, but Loughney's flippancy annoyed Michaelis. "It's no joke. This idiotic mess has caused me to lose an important assignment in Washington."

Loughney winked. "Now, is that so? Well, maybe there's a silver lining. One less ivory tower voice in Washington confusing things."

"Thanks. Why don't you apply? They can always use another stuffed shirt to make the bright guys look good."

Loughney's mouth dropped open. "If you're going to be insulting, you can get the hell out of my office."

"What would you call the remark you just made to me?"

There was a silence while Loughney sat winking. Finally he asked, "What do you want here, Professor?"

"It's important to me that the seven jurors who were bribed be identified. And prosecuted, if possible. I'd like to know what, if anything, you are doing about the matter."

Loughney smiled, his big, square teeth clenched. Then he relaxed. "Since you are one of the suspects, Professor, it would hardly be proper for me to reveal the steps we are taking."

Michaelis leaned forward. "I'll match my full disclosure against your full disclosure any day. Has the FBI ever checked you out?"

Loughney was momentarily disconcerted. "No doubt. Nevertheless you are a suspect; I am not."

Michaelis stood up. "In that case, I suppose I'll have to work it out on my own. I've had a certain amount of investigative experience."

Loughney said, "Sit down. Don't rush off mad." He took a cigarette from a box on his desk and then pushed it in Michaelis's direction.

Michaelis sat down, shaking his head. "No thanks."

"I remember now. You're the muckraker who put two judges and a governor in jail."

"Juries put them in jail."

Loughney lit the cigarette. "Be reasonable, man. We have hardly any case here at all. Catherine Leeds states that her father *told* her he paid out seven hundred thousand dollars to bribe seven jurors to acquit Athena von Dietrich. Phillip Leeds is dead. The IRS wants to tax the estate for that seven hundred thousand as income. Naturally Miss Leeds would like to convince them her father was only acting as agent in handling the money."

"It's not the kind of story she would have dreamed up at the hairdresser's."

"Granted. The IRS is investigating all twelve jurors. They may catch some of them on tax evasion. If they succeed with any of these cases and give us some reasonable evidence, then we may prosecute on bribery charges. We can't prosecute on mere hearsay testimony. Even if we can prove, for instance, that you've salted away a sizable sum, and have even evaded taxes, you're still innocent of bribery until proved guilty. It is not your obligation to prove where you got the money; it is our obligation to prove that you got it illegally."

Michaelis leaned back in the comfortable leather chair and stared past Loughney at Old Glory. "In other words, you can't do anything until you see what the IRS comes up with?"

Loughney shrugged. "Oh, we've been checking on whereabouts and backgrounds. But the IRS can find hidden assets a lot more efficiently than we can."

He stubbed out his cigarette. "However, we do have a line on some possible bribees. Three of the buggers have left the country. Theodopolus sold his shoe repair store and went back to Greece. Keith Orcutt quit his job with the power company and emigrated to Australia. Huey Fan sold his restaurant and moved to Taiwan. It looks like these guys came into some unexpected fortunes. But if the IRS succeeds in extraditing any one of the three, I'll eat my hat for you on the stage of the Crendon Playhouse."

Michaelis nodded, sighing. He straightened up wearily. "I hear the money was laundered in Mexico before it got to Leeds. If you could trace it back to Athena von Dietrich, you could get her for bribery or perjury or something. Assuming that the double-jeopardy thing might protect her from another trial for murder."

Loughney flipped some nonexistent lint from his jacket.

"The IRS is trying to do that, of course. They have the resources. We don't. But so far I gather they've hit a stone wall down there."

Michaelis stood up again. "I need the names and addresses of the jurors and others involved in the case. Catherine Leeds, the Von Dietrich woman, Carlita, and the other witnesses. Will you give them to me?"

Loughney thought this over for a few seconds. "Why not? Quid pro quo, of course. You keep us informed."

"Who else would I want to keep informed?"

Reaching for his phone, Loughney paused. "Tell me, Professor, are you married?"

"Not recently. Why?"

"You're divorced?"

Michaelis said, "Yes, but what has that to do with it?"

"No children?"

Irritated, Michaelis said, "I have no children."

Loughney replaced the phone in its cradle without dialing. He stood up, a smug, unfriendly smile on his face, his right eye shuttering rapidly. "I mentioned that we checked the background data we could dig up on the jurors? You'd be amazed at the people who can get on juries. Of course, anyone on the voter registration is liable to be drawn. If they look okay, look respectable, well, that's all there is to it."

Michaelis asked, "So who was on the jury, Count Dracula in drag? I don't remember seeing him."

Loughney came around his desk, snatching another cigarette from the box as he did so. "There were some real weirdos. Do you remember a woman named Marsha Hallowell? Respectable librarian?"

Michaelis nodded. She had led the forces fighting for acquittal. A bit eccentric and a rabid conservative about a mile right of Ronald Reagan.

"When Hallowell was thirteen, she took her brother's twenty-two-caliber rifle from his room, marched downstairs, and killed her mother, her two sisters, and her brother while they sat at the table eating dinner. Luckily, Father wasn't home."

Loughney half-sat on the edge of his desk and lit his cigarette. "That was out in Chicago."

Michaelis stared at him. "If I remember correctly, she is a woman in her fifties, perhaps even sixty. Fifties is a long way from thirteen. Presumably she has long been cured of whatever childhood psychosis set her off."

Loughney exhaled smoke. "Fifties or thirteen, I wouldn't want to mess around with a woman capable of killing four people in one evening."

Michaelis said nothing. Loughney was obviously trying to make him feel uncomfortable.

"Then you'll probably remember Horace Strang, a *respectable* retired army colonel. He has a nice two-million-dollar house out on Maple Drive. Actually he's a high-priced killer. A mercenary."

Michaelis grinned. "Wish I had known. I didn't pay much attention to him. He sounds like an interesting guy."

Loughney frowned. "Well, here's a couple of other interesting ones for you. Thomas J. Swift, the *writer?* He happens to be a CIA agent. Maybe he'll terminate you with prejudice."

Michaelis laughed.

"Then there's Anthony Tedienzi. He happens to be the son-in-law of Carlo Grammatini. You know Grammatini?"

Michaelis nodded. "Boss of all bosses. Head of organized crime throughout the country."

Loughney said, "Let me say I don't want to be unfair about Tedienzi. As far as we know he has very little contact with his wife's old man. He's a CPA, and seems to handle perfectly respectable business." Loughney took Michaelis's arm. "Come on downstairs. I'll have Len Cates put the information together for you."

4

MICHAELIS CROSSED THE STREET TO THE PARKING LOT. HE WAS weary and mildly depressed. The situation was preposterous. Futile. The three men who had emigrated, for instance. Taiwan, Australia, and Greece. Nothing to it. Just take a trip around the world to investigate them. A modern Don Quixote. The windmills would offer something more solid to attack.

On the other hand, would it be better to sit around his empty apartment and brood?

He opened the door of the Volvo, then closed it quickly. Something was on the seat, on the passenger side. He wouldn't be the first investigative reporter to leave a car with his jawbone separated from his hipbone. He circled the car cautiously, examining it in minute detail.

In the rear there was the smell of gasoline, stronger than usual. There was no leak, no wetness on the ground. Then he remembered that he had had it filled on the way to the courthouse. The attendant had topped the tank off sloppily, spilling some down the side and on the ground.

He continued his careful examination. Dust on the right rear fender had been displaced in one spot, as though by a hand pressed against it for support. Michaelis got down on his knees and felt the underside of the fender. His fingers brushed against something. He levered the magnetized metal loose and brought it into the sunlight. A small black box of a kind he had seen before. A tiny transmitter. A tailing device. Why would Loughney want him tailed?

He slipped the transmitter in his pocket and continued his slow inspection of the outside of the car. When he came to the window on the passenger side, he stuck his head in cautiously and looked at the brown object lying on the seat.

It appeared to be a child's toy. A plush monkey about eighteen inches long. He pulled his head away, reached in with his hand, and felt around and under the monkey carefully. No wires. He lifted it out slowly.

The monkey's button eyes had been ripped from their sockets and hung by frayed threads. Part of each ear had been hacked away. Slashes across the mouth formed a deep X. Michaelis smiled, puzzled. What a cornball message. Like some kid playing gangster. He should have painted a skull and crossbones on the windshield.

He dropped the monkey back on the seat, then walked around to the driver's side. Opening the door, he felt under the instrument panel and released the catch that locked the hood.

With the hood open, the smell of gasoline was very strong again. He stared. Taped to the top of the air filter was a shallow pan filled with liquid. Nearby, taped to the engine block was a cluster of five sticks of dynamite.

Michaelis stepped back hurriedly. He had never heard of a car being rigged this way. It seemed incredibly amateurish. But then, it might just work. The movement of the car would cause the gasoline to slosh onto the hot engine block; the gasoline would ignite on the block, probably explode in the pan, which would provide the percussion to explode the dynamite.

This was one homemade bomb Michaelis could deactivate himself. From the appearance of its casing the dynamite looked fresh, and would not be dangerous to handle.

Let the police do it. Don't touch the evidence. It was possible that they could trace the materials to the idiot who had rigged the contraption.

He walked to the sidewalk and stopped a smiling youth with a mouthful of orthodontia. A dollar bill persuaded the boy to go across to the courthouse to fetch Loughney.

As he waited for Loughney in the hot sun, he searched for explanations. Who knew about his project other than Loughney? It had taken Michaelis three days to get the appointment. Loughney had been in the midst of a heavy trial schedule. Michaelis had, of course, discussed it with Hal Johnson, the dean of his college. A reason for abandoning his summer classes. But Hal was a close friend and completely trustworthy, and Michaelis had cautioned him about mentioning it. Alice Whitney might have guessed when she heard he was giving up his summer schedule. Loughney knew the purpose of the appointment, that it concerned the Athena von Dietrich case. He might have told some of his staff. Could it have gotten back to Athena von Dietrich? Were her people responsible for this childish warning? Who else would do it?

Loughney finally crossed the wide street, another man trailing a couple of steps behind him. He walked briskly up to Michaelis. "What's this about someone tampering with your car?"

Before Michaelis could answer, Loughney introduced the second man. "This is Detective Stein."

Michaelis and Stein shook hands. Stein had a good tan, straight black hair, and a thin beak of a nose.

Michaelis led them through the parked cars to the Volvo's slot.

Loughney and Stein stared under the opened hood. Loughney backed away a couple of feet. "Jesus, what a crapped-up arrangement."

Stein asked, "What made you look under the hood?"

Michaelis reached through the window and lifted out the monkey. "This."

Loughney and Stein examined the monkey, Stein silent and Loughney muttering.

Loughney placed the monkey on the roof of the Volvo. "I think we've got a retarded maniac at large."

Stein said, "The bomb arrangement could have worked, especially in this weather."

Loughney stuck a cigarette in his mouth and reached for his matches. Stein said sharply, *"Don't* light that."

Loughney put the cigarette back in his jacket pocket. "Sorry. Forgot about the pan of gasoline."

Michaelis reached in his own pocket. Holding the small transmitter by its corners, he brought it out. He offered it to Loughney. "Found this under the right rear fender. What's the point of tailing me if you're going to blow me up? I couldn't have gotten far."

Loughney took the transmitter, his winking lid now fluttering wildly. "Son of a bitch, that's not one of ours."

Michaelis smiled. "If it's not one of yours, why are you smudging up possible fingerprints?"

Loughney dropped the transmitter into his jacket pocket. "Nothing's smudged. It'll be checked out." He turned quickly to Stein. "There's only one idiot who could be behind a crazy mess like this."

"Who?" asked Michaelis.

Still looking at Stein, Loughney said, "The Hallowell woman. She's called me four times since the news broke. Absolutely hysterical about clearing her good name."

Michaelis shook his head. Hallowell had no reason to threaten him.

5

CATHERINE LEEDS LOOKED, MICHAELIS DECIDED, LIKE THE REGISTRAR in a concentration camp. Her yellow hair was pulled back tight from her forehead, and she wore glasses the size of pancakes. They magnified cold, gunmetal-gray eyes. Her angular face, naked of cosmetics, had the dry shine of plastic. Above her pointed chin a thick lower lip and a thin upper lip parted just enough in repose to reveal portions of two squarish teeth.

The apartment, located in a luxury high-rise in New York City, was obviously expensive. She led Michaelis down a short hall to a moderately large living room with floor-to-ceiling windows at one end. They offered a dramatic view of a long sweep of the East River. Directly across the choppy black water was Roosevelt Island.

She motioned to a cream-colored sofa and said, "Please sit down. Would you care for coffee or a drink?" The offer was noncommittal, bored, and said, "I hope you really won't bother me with it."

"Thanks, no." Michaelis stared at the thick Oriental carpet underfoot. I do not like thee, Catherine Leeds.

She sank into a cream-colored chair which matched the sofa, pulled her skirt down over her bony knees, and said, "The government is trying to ruin me. When you telephoned, I had a wild thought that you might be able to help me."

Michaelis smiled. "I hope I can help us both. It's very important to me, too." He glanced out the windows at one of the aerial tram cars swaying its way across to Roosevelt Island. "One thing I'm curious about. How did your father get tangled up with the IRS? He brought the money out of Mexico in cash, and he most certainly must have made his payments in cash."

"It was stupid bad luck. The night he came through customs they were having a crackdown. They were searching all luggage very thoroughly. They had a tip that a big heroin shipment was coming in."

Michaelis shivered, perspiration cold on his spine. The cab ride from Grand Central had been like a sauna; now the air-conditioned apartment felt arctic. Customs would, of course, report the money to the IRS. He wondered what sort of cultured crook Phillip Leeds had been? Ordinary crooks rarely live in tastefully furnished apartments on the thirtieth floor overlooking the East River, or have well-educated daughters who speak with *upper-clahss* accents.

"Just what did your father do? Aside from bribing jurors?"

The plastic face turned to glare at Michaelis. "You're being very rude. I didn't invite you here to slander my father."

"Sorry."

"My father hated that assignment. He refused to handle it, but he was forced to. My father was an expert on jewelry and paintings. Late in life he drifted into being a go-between for insurance companies. You know the sort of thing. A thief steals a painting insured for a million dollars and sells it back to the insurance company for a half-million."

"Who forced him?"

"I wish I knew. He wouldn't tell me. Only that it was

someone very important who could ruin him if he didn't agree. He said it was safer for me not to know."

"Too bad."

Catherine's lips curved downward, closing her toothy aperture. "Why don't you ask Athena von Dietrich?"

"Yeah."

"My father was very secretive about his clients. I don't even know the insurance companies he dealt with. But I *do* know that he was meticulous about reporting his income. He picked up eight hundred thousand dollars in Mexico. One hundred thousand was his fee, and he would have reported that as income. Maybe the IRS knows who gave him the hundred thousand he reported."

With bribery involved, no one would be named as paying that particular "consultant's fee," Michaelis was certain. Leeds had probably reported it as winnings from gambling. In any event, neither he nor Catherine had much chance of getting information from the IRS without taking them to court.

Michaelis said, "I've been wondering why whoever paid the money to your father felt it necessary to pay so much to the jurors? My guess is that most of them could have been bribed for a half or a quarter of the amount spent."

Catherine cocked her head slightly to one side. "It was extremely important to them that Athena von Dietrich not go to prison. They didn't want to take even the slightest chance."

"Who are *they?"*

"I don't know. But my father said it would be a disaster of great magnitude if von Dietrich went to prison."

"Hmmm." Michaelis stared at Catherine's hands. They had the same plastic sheen of her face. They were clasped tightly together on her lap, wrestling unobtrusively. He wondered if the woman was plastic all over.

"Will you help me?" she asked.

Michaelis said, "Well, yes, of course. Or do you mean in some way other than what we've discussed?"

Her mouth twisted. "You'll give up. You'll never get all seven. If you could get me just one, with positive proof. I mean, I'm going to be absolutely destitute if they tax that money as income."

Michaelis stared at her, uncertain as to what she wanted him to say.

"Get me just one, and I'll give you ten thousand dollars."

He shook his head. "That's not necessary. You're welcome to any proof I'm able to dig up."

"My lawyer says one solid bit of proof would kill the IRS claim. Get it for me and I'll give you ten thousand."

He stood up, smiling. He hadn't expected to get any information of value from Catherine Leeds, but he had long ago learned that a good investigator passes up no opportunities, however slight. "I'll do my best. We'll keep in touch." He glanced at his watch. "I must be going. I want to catch the four-twenty back to Crendon. Otherwise I'll be tied up in the commuter crush." Crendon was an hour and twenty minutes from New York, and had not until recently been attractive to commuters. More and more were moving there, however, and suffering the long round trip daily.

She got up quickly. "I'll drive you to Grand Central. I've got to go to midtown anyway."

Michaelis would have preferred to go alone by cab, but could think of no polite reason to refuse her offer.

They took the elevator to the building's basement garage, and waited silently for the attendant to bring around her car. Catherine seemed to have no capacity for small talk. Eventually a black Mercedes convertible rumbled softly alongside. The top was down. Catherine replaced the attendant at the wheel with an unsmiling nod, and Michaelis slid in on the passenger side. They accelerated up the long ramp.

She paused at the sidewalk, then moved slowly across and into the street. Three rapid explosions ripped the air.

The Mercedes veered to the left until it nudged a telephone pole and stalled. Catherine's dry plastic face was now a smashed pomegranate; pulp and shattered bone wet with blood.

Michaelis instinctively switched off the ignition, his hand trembling. A flood of contradictory signals besieged his brain, forcing a second or two of paralysis. Find the killer, hide from the killer, help Catherine. Catherine was beyond the help of anyone but a skilled surgeon, and probably beyond that. He thought wildly of giving her mouth-to-mouth resuscitation. She had no mouth. Or nose, or eyes either. Where had the shots come from? No one was in sight. He remembered a car approaching, but his attention had been more directed at possible pedestrians on the sidewalk as they eased out of the garage. He wrenched open the car door, sprinted down the ramp to the garage's cubbyhole office, snatched the phone, and dialed 911.

6

THE 1:13 A.M. TRAIN TO CRENDON STANK. THE AIR-CONditioning was not working, and the stifling sealed car's air was so thick and humid that it seemed to cling to the skin. Many of the passengers were asleep; some were drunk and restless. Snores were drowned out by occasional bursts of raucous laughter or noisy hostility. The car smelled of sweaty clothes, stale beer, and at one end of the coach near the toilet, a regurgitated mess had been left by a passenger who had failed in his or her rush to the toilet.

Michaelis sat alone at the other end, as far from the smell as possible. He had told his story to the police a number of times. First as a suspect: Catherine Leeds knew he was one of the bribees, and was going to reveal the same. When this was proved unlikely by the circumstances and the garage attendant's statement, Michaelis became a witness who should probably be held in protective custody. The third time around he was recognized as the Michaelis whose investigations for the *New York Graphic* had sent nineteen cops to Sing Sing. At this point the consensus switched to a quick, forced-friendly good-bye. The less they saw of Michaelis the better.

He sat hunched in a corner next to a window, physically and mentally exhausted. He had not eaten since lunch. Two double scotches had been gulped down quickly to avoid missing the last train to Crendon. He was sleepy and slightly befuddled. With the befuddlement was a feeling of guilt. His assessment of the situation had been woefully naive. Three people had now been murdered to protect Athena von Dietrich. Beginning with the housekeeper and her husband. Three people killed with cool professionalism. To further complicate the situation, the idiotic amateurism of the attempt to assassinate him did not fit in.

The Crendon police had probably finished examining his car, but he doubted he would be able to get it at this hour. Would there be a cab at the station? Probably not. A five-mile walk to his apartment near the campus? He groaned almost audibly. Maybe they had an empty cell at the police station?

What was so important about Athena von Dietrich? She was very rich, of course. But other than that?

Karl von Dietrich's father had been a multimillionaire Prussian industrialist. Wary of Hitler at an early stage of the demagogue's reign, Otto von Dietrich had moved his person and more than a billion deutsche marks to Switzerland. Otto's maternal grandmother had been Jewish. For this disloyalty, his manufacturing plants were confiscated.

During the allied occupation, the plants were returned to the family, but by this time old Otto had died, and Karl, who had become accustomed to living in the United States, had no desire to go back. He was content to let his older brother supervise the von Dietrich empire. However, Karl's share of the estate was substantial. Presumably Athena now controlled it. So she was jet-set rich, but what else?

Michaelis glanced at the large patch of dried blood on the left sleeve of his jacket. Catherine's blood. He would throw the jacket away.

Why kill Catherine Leeds? Had he been merely lucky? Were they trying to kill them both? Obviously they thought Catherine's father had told her more than he had. They might logically assume that she had told Michaelis. If they hadn't been trying to kill him this afternoon, they would be soon. He had started out to be the hunter; now he was to be hunted. The irony of it was that he still knew nothing.

The train was a local, and poked its way wearily eastward, stopping at every station. Crendon was near the end of the run.

They. Athena's army. Or was she merely a subsidiary figure in some large operation? Who, where, when, what, why, and how? The newspaperman's formula. Who was behind Athena? Why was she so important to them? Where were they, and how many were involved? When and where would they surface next? What the hell was it all about?

The train slowed for its stop in Crendon. Michaelis stood at the center doors watching the few remaining passengers in his car. None, apparently, were making any moves to get off at Crendon.

The doors slid open and Michaelis stepped out onto the long, raised platform. He looked forward and backward along the length of the train. Two men emerged several cars ahead and hurried off toward the steps to the parking lot. Another got off the car behind Michaelis. Michaelis stepped across the platform to the rail next to a telephone booth and pretended to be searching his pockets for a coin. Under the circumstances he would not walk the length of the platform with someone behind him.

The passenger walked past Michaelis with barely a glance.

If there was a cab, he had probably lost it to the men who got off at the head of the train. Michaelis hurried down the platform, arriving at the steps just in time to see the one taxi speeding away. The man who had passed him was walking toward one of the cars in the parking lot.

The police department, headquartered in City Hall, was on the other side of the tracks. To get across, Michaelis had to walk down a flight of steps to a dimly lit concrete tunnel. As he turned at the bottom of the steps to enter the tunnel, he saw a figure leaving it at the other end.

He paused, undecided. An ideal place for an ambush. His assailant could be waiting just around the corner on the steps leading up to ground level. Thirty feet underground, no one would see or hear anything. Not that there was anyone around to hear or see anything anyway.

He felt in his pockets. The nearest thing to a weapon he had was a pipe knife with a puny two-and-a-half-inch blade. Might as well rush into battle with his ballpoint pen.

Was he becoming paranoid? The blood on his jacket was very real. If he was not careful, he would be joining Catherine in the morgue. A different morgue, but similar in its chilling facilities.

He waited ten minutes. If there was an assassin at the other end, he would eventually become curious and come back into the tunnel to see what was keeping his quarry.

No one appeared.

Michaelis finally walked briskly through the empty tunnel and climbed the steps at the other end. The station, located near the exit, was dark, but moonlight brightening the small plaza reassured him.

He felt ashamed of himself for being afraid. Yet anyone who failed to be cautious in this situation was a fool. Too much fear could, as Thucydides said, "take away presence of mind." Locke, he remembered, had said something about fear being given to us to keep us on guard against the approaches of evil. He smiled at himself and his professorial nattering. A fragment of the Psalms posed the big question: ". . . of whom shall I be afraid?"

The streets were deserted. He crossed Main Street and headed in the direction of police headquarters some three blocks away. He walked near the curb, keeping a wary eye on darkened doorways.

In the army he had frequently thought about the nature of fear, especially in terms of his own fear of cowardice. Under fire, with his buddies falling around him, dead or horribly mutilated, would he crack? He decided it would be easier to lead a platoon into combat than to follow. His pride would keep him moving. He applied for Officer Candidate School and was accepted. Three months later he was a ninety-day wonder with a single gold bar on each shoulder.

In Vietnam he found that it *was* easier to lead. For some reason, being in control, having a certain responsibility, left no time to think about fear. As a first lieutenant in the Infantry, the performance and safety of the men in his platoon dominated his attention completely.

A black car gunned up behind and stopped alongside, brakes squealing.

A dim figure behind the wheel asked, "Give you a lift out to the university, Professor?"

Startled, Michaelis backed away, half-turning to run.

"It's me, Detective Stein," said the figure.

Michaelis couldn't see clearly enough to be sure that it was Stein. "I'm going to headquarters to pick up my car," he said. "I'll walk it."

"You can't get it tonight. The garage is closed. The property clerk won't be on duty until 8:00 A.M." Stein flipped open the door and slid out. In a second he was facing Michaelis. "Don't blame you for being careful. Get in, I've been waiting for you."

Michaelis got in the passenger side while Stein went around the car and resumed his place at the wheel.

"Why were you waiting for me?"

Stein lit a cigarette, shifting the car into drive. "Lot of flack from the New York P.D. tonight. They got a bit worried after you left. Seem to think you are in mortal danger, or something. Which you may well be."

"Yeah."

"Pretty shocking afternoon, I guess?"

"It shook me, all right."

"Maybe you should consider a nice little vacation in Sri Lanka or Lhasa?"

Michaelis laughed. "Not sure I could take rancid yak butter on my English muffin."

"Maybe the Gobi Desert?"

Michaelis asked, "Just who in hell *is* Athena von Dietrich?"

Stein drove in silence for a while. "I never discuss the lady."

"You're afraid to discuss her?"

Stein slowed to look at a street sign. "Don't know anything about her. Your apartment is down there to the right, isn't it?"

"Yes. Thanks."

Stein pulled up in front of the low red brick building and cut the motor. "Would you like a little helpful advice that could get me into trouble?"

Michaelis nodded.

"Loughney is an asshole. He talks a pretty smooth game. Good front, charming when he works at it. A first-class politician. But essentially he's small-town and naive about anything bigger than Crendon politics. He doesn't know what a tiger he has by the tail when it comes to messing with Athena von Dietrich."

"But you do."

"Don't know anything about her." He reached over and opened the door for Michaelis. "Good night and good luck."

Michaelis got out. "Thanks for the ride. I'll keep your cryptic words of wisdom in mind." Not that they had told him a damned thing, except that he was in big trouble, which he already knew.

Stein dismissed him with a brief wave and drove off.

Michaelis wearily climbed the stairs to his second-floor apartment. He'd open a can of soup, eat some toast, take a shower, a pill, and then to bed. Figure it all out tomorrow.

He unlocked his door, opened it, and flipped the light switch.

"Don't you ever go to bed, Professor?"

The voice came from Michaelis's favorite easy chair. In it sat Horace Strang. Michaelis remembered him well from the long hours in the jury room. He had a Walther machine pistol propped on his lap, the barrel pointing directly at Michaelis's midsection.

7

"SHUT THE DOOR."

Flat-nosed and pasty-faced, with shreds of thinning yellow hair curling on his high forehead, Strang looked like rejected work from a student mortician.

Michaelis eased the door shut with his heel, keeping an eye on the Walther.

"On your desk over there, you'll find a piece of paper I want you to sign. If you don't sign it, I'll blow your balls off. Then I'll cut you right in two at the middle."

Michaelis walked slowly to his desk and picked up a typewritten statement resting squarely in the center of an area cleared of books and papers. He was so tired the type blurred as he tried to read it. He skimmed the half-page statement. It was a formal confession. He was to sign a document telling the world that he had received $100,000 from Phillip Leeds as a bribe to vote for Athena's acquittal.

"What a ridiculous bunch of horseshit."

"Sign it."

"What good will that do you? A confession signed under duress is worthless."

Strang motioned with the Walther. "Sign it. You won't recant."

"Why won't I?"

"Because you'll have my word that I'll be back to kill you if you do."

Michaelis wondered whether Strang was psychotic. His first thought had been that Athena had sent Strang to kill him, but if he was collecting confessions, he certainly wasn't working for Athena. Who in hell was he working for?

"Why do you think I got one of the bribes? I was the last one on the jury to give in for acquittal."

Strang smirked. "Clever of you."

"Give me one good reason." Anything to stall for time.

"Teachers make peanuts. They're always broke. Even *professors.*" The last word was underlined in sarcastic falsetto. "Look for the guy who's broke; that's the guy you can bribe."

Michaelis laughed. *"That's* what you base your opinion on? You know something? You're a fucking idiot."

Strang raised the Walther slowly.

"Go ahead, shoot. I won't sign your goddamned paper because it isn't true." Michaelis heard his own words with horror. Had exhaustion sent him around the bend? It wasn't the kind of bluff a man in his right mind gambled on.

Strang lowered the barrel, grinning. "Death before admitting dishonor, huh? A man after my own heart. It makes me sort of sad to have to kill you."

Michaelis asked, "Are you serious about my being broke, needing money? If you are, you can open that top desk drawer and take a look at the copy of my last year's income tax form."

"Tell me what's in it, son. And make it accurate, because I'm going to check it later."

Michaelis moved away from the desk and sat down. "Okay, here's what's in it. Salary from university, forty-thousand. Income from writing articles for magazines and newspaper syndication, thirty-one thousand plus. Income from the Michaelis Trust, ninety-three thousand plus; income from tax-free municipals, eighty-two thousand plus; income from speaking engagements, four thousand plus. Quite a hunk of income for a starving professor."

Strang listened intently. He appeared to be silently adding up Michaelis's figures. "Get that form and toss it to me. Then go stand over there, facing the books." He motioned to the side of the room lined with bookshelves.

Michaelis found the tax form, folded the pages to hold them together, and tossed it to Strang. Then he took his position in front of the books, his back to Strang, his eyes staring at titles he could not, for some reason, read. If a blast hit him in the back of his head, what would be the last thing he would see? He forced his eyes to focus on the titles. *Gravity's Rainbow,* Pynchon. Now, that was a hell of a confusing book to die with. It was flanked by volumes of Kafka and Joyce. Not a comforting title in the lot. Ah, Saul Bellow—there was a fellow who had given him hours of entertainment as well as intellectual stimulation. Bless you, Saul Bellow, good-bye earth.

"Okay, Rockefeller, you can turn around," said Strang finally.

When Michaelis turned, he found Strang smiling. He had very white and very regular false teeth.

"Okay, buster, so you called my bluff."

A surge of relief was quickly overtaken by anger. Curiosity overtook the anger. What the hell was Strang up to?

"If you're so fucking rich, how come you live in a dump like this, and drive a ten-year-old car?" asked Strang.

Michaelis glanced around at his large, high-ceilinged living room. Dump? It had everything he needed to be comfortable. And why didn't he drive a Mercedes? He could afford one. How could he explain that wealth was not a status symbol within the faculty of a great university? And not offend the Walther?

"Maybe it's because I've never been interested in putting on a show with money my grandfather earned. Different kind of ego trip, I guess. I'd rather be measured for what I am as an individual, for whatever talents I have as a writer or a teacher."

The statement sounded pompous, Michaelis thought, but it was essentially true. Even as a reporter he had never flaunted his inherited wealth.

Strang stared at him, puzzled, then smiled. "Yeah, I can see what you mean. I earned every penny I've got the hard way, risking my ass. I got a right to drive that Lincoln Continental parked around the corner."

Michaelis curbed the smile that was forming. Careful not to be patronizing. Strang was as dangerous as a sandwich laced with *C. botulinum*. He said, "I could use a drink. How about you?"

"You got any good bourbon?"

"Wild Turkey."

"That's good enough."

Michaelis went to the kitchen to break out a tray of

ice cubes. He said through the open door, "You're obviously trying to track down the seven who took bribes. Why? No one's accused you, have they? I mean, you're rich. Why would you sell out for a lousy hundred thousand?"

He brought the Wild Turkey, ice cubes, and a couple of glasses out to the living room.

"For the same reason you refused to sign. I got my honor to think about, too. You think I want people to think I might be a lousy crook who would accept money to perpetrate a miscarriage of justice in a murder trial?"

Michaelis turned his face away and struggled to keep a guffaw from breaking loose. His voice under control, he asked, "Have you gotten any confessions?"

"You're damned right I have." Strang poured a liberal dollop of whiskey over ice cubes. "I caught up with that creep Orcutt in Melbourne. He signed. Latched onto Theodopolus in Piraeus." He tasted the whiskey and sighed with satisfaction. "Went to Taiwan, but couldn't locate that slant-eyed bastard Huey Fan. Got an affidavit from his brother, Fong, though. He came home with a lot of money even though his restaurant was practically bankrupt. Went downhill after the immigration authorities grabbed his three best cooks."

Michaelis shook his head, silently amazed. In a little over a week since the news had broken, Strang had flown around the world, tracked down two of the jurors and the brother of a third.

"Only seven more to go. I'm counting you out."

"Thanks."

Michaelis lifted his own glass, savoring the taste of the rich bourbon. "I guess we're both working in the same direction." He described his visit with Loughney, his trip to New York, and the murder of Catherine Leeds.

Strang listened, unbelieving. "This happened this afternoon?"

The hundred-proof bourbon on his still empty stomach had Michaelis feeling expansive. "You're damned right it did. You see this big brown stain on my jacket? That's Catherine Leeds."

"No shit!"

Michaelis nodded solemnly. "Do you know, uh—do you mind if I call you Horace?"

Strang frowned. "My friends call me Sting. You can call me Sting."

He had friends? "I'm Jon. Short for Jonathan."

Strang grunted. "One of them fancy names."

"Well, you tend to work with what your parents give you."

"Yeah."

His sting was ten times as deadly as a scorpion's. "Well, uh, Sting, I've been sort of wondering if your method is going to be all that effective. I mean, who are you going to present all those forced confessions to? The law isn't going to act on them."

Strang rattled his ice cubes around. "I'm doing it for my own satisfaction."

"But some guy who is innocent, and scared out of his wits, will probably sign."

Strang slurped the last of his whiskey, ice cubes bumping his lips. "I got good intuition. I knew you was scared shitless, but when you said, 'Go ahead, shoot me,' I knew right away you weren't one of them."

Michaelis poured them both another drink. "Okay, so what are you going to do when you get to Anthony Tedienzi?"

"So what's with Anthony Tedenz-what's-his-name?"

"He happens to be the son-in-law of Carlo Grammatini."

"No shit!" Strang picked up his drink and took a long swallow. "That baby could cause some complications."

They sat drinking in silence for a while. Michaelis mulled over his own situation. They'd be coming after him, thinking he knew what they thought Catherine knew. It would be comforting to have his own killer on hand for protection.

Strang said, "So what's the answer, buster? How do we pin these yo-yos to the mat?"

"I think the only way you're going to get the truth is from the people who hired Leeds to dole out the money. He must have told them who he paid. If von Dietrich was convicted, they'd want to take care of the double-crossers."

Strang thought about it.

"You might have an idea there. But how do I find these buggers?"

"Stick with me. I'm bait." He reminded Strang that he, Michaelis, seemed destined to share Catherine's fate.

Strang played with his drink, sloshed it around, drank some of it, then set it down and thought some more.

"You mean we grab some of these guys and lean on them?"

Michaelis nodded.

Strang leered at him. "I wouldn't mind leaning on that von Dietrich dame."

Sting might well find the lady tougher than he was, thought Michaelis. A lady with an even deadlier sting. "I imagine she's pretty well protected," he said.

Strang muttered to himself for a while. Michaelis could catch only a word here and there, but Strang was obviously enumerating a few things he would like to do to Athena von Dietrich. Finally he said, "No reason we can't do both. We can check out the rest of these monkeys. That won't stop the others from coming after you. You own any kind of weapons?"

"A thirty-eight S&W revolver." A holdover from the days when hate mail and threatening phone calls made a license possible.

Strang frowned. "Better than nothing, huh?" He stood up. "One thing, you gotta move in with me. This fucking place is about as safe as a tent. We won't find out anything by being massacred. I got good security at my place."

8

STRANG'S AIR-CONDITIONED CONTINENTAL HAD TINTED, BULLET-resistant glass windows. Nothing was *-proof* anymore. Fire-resistant, water-resistant, wrinkle-resistant. The forces of evil were always undoing proof, Michaelis decided. Maybe the word could be revived with something certain, such as a sun-proof cave.

They turned off the road into a dirt driveway which wound up a steep hill. The sign that had marked the turnoff read, *PET HOSPITAL, C. Harrison, DVM.* At the top was a graveled parking area and a barrackslike two-story frame building with a new coat of white paint.

Strang parked quickly with a sudden spewing of gravel. "You go in and talk to her. I'll stand guard. Then *I'll* talk to her if I'm not satisfied with your report," he said.

Michaelis remembered Cindy Harrison well. A fragile blonde with a mischievous look in her eyes. Hardly the type to threaten with a Walther machine pistol. He walked up three steps to the screen door and opened it, stepping directly into the large reception area. It was furnished simply to cope with the uncertain behavior of sick animals. Other than the clean linoleum floor, there were only plastic bucket chairs and two metal coffee tables. All could be washed down quickly to deodorize and antisepticize. The room was empty.

Voices, however, could be heard in the adjoining office. Michaelis took a seat near the partially opened door.

"—really very sorry, but this simply can't go on," said a male voice. "While it's true that you have valid accounts receivable that should make your business liquid, the fact is that you are not collecting the money owed you. Some of these bills are almost a year old!"

"I know I'm lousy at collecting bills. But when do I have the time?" The female voice, Michaelis was certain, was Cindy's.

There was an audible sigh. "Well, you must agree that we've given you adequate warning and have extended you far past our regular foreclosure date. I could be *censured* by the bank examiners." A chair squealed softly as it was pushed back. "Miss Harrison, obviously you're not businesswoman enough to make a go of this thing. Go work for another doctor who knows how to collect bills!"

"No."

There was a short silence. "Well, I can only say I'm sorry, but I'm going to have to close you down."

"Give me ten more days. I may be able to get some help from my uncle."

There was a short laugh. "The last time it was your rich aunt."

"I have a rich aunt *and* a rich uncle. My aunt wouldn't help me. She's never forgiven me."

"For what?"

"She thought she was putting me through *regular* medical school."

The man laughed.

"Give me ten more days?"

There was a soft groan. "All right, young lady, it appears you've conned me again. But I'm warning you, I'm coming back with a padlock in exactly ten days."

Cindy followed an elderly man from the office and escorted him to the screen door. He was wearing thick-lensed glasses and had a bemused smile on his face.

She turned and gave Michaelis a quick scrutiny. "If you have a sick animal in your car, bring him in. But be prepared to pay cash in advance."

He smiled. She was prettier than he remembered. Long blond hair tied carelessly to fall down her back, merry eyes of warm blue, delicate but regular features, and a mouth a little larger than necessary but quick to laugh, he was sure. A trim figure with soft curves in the right places. She was wearing blue jeans and a man's shirt open at the neck.

"You look familiar. Do you owe me money by any chance? I know, you're the man with the collie that had pneumonia. The collie's name was Chivas, but I can't remember yours. I'm so glad you came in to pay the bill."

Michaelis shook his head.

"No?"

"We were jurors together. The Athena von Dietrich trial."

"Oh." Her voice fell in disappointment, but recognition perked interest. "You're, uh, Michaelis? Professor Michaelis."

"'Michaelis,' or even 'Jon' will do."

She smiled. "If you got any of that loot, I could sure use about twenty G's of it."

Michaelis shook his head sadly. He didn't even care to joke about it.

A car roared up into the parking area, machine-gunning gravel against the windows. A car door opened and slammed, then a towheaded teenager awkwardly opened the screen door and staggered in carrying a bloody bundle.

"That fucking Doberman's killed my dog!"

Cindy hurried to him, and glancing at the bloody little male beagle, motioned for the boy to follow her.

Michaelis drifted back with them.

The beagle lay on her examining table, panting and whimpering, his coat torn open in a half-dozen places. Cindy made comforting noises, giving the dog a shot to ease the pain. She began cleaning and antisepticizing his wounds, then sewing them up with neat efficiency.

"Will he live?" asked the boy, tears still wet on his cheeks.

Cindy gave him a smile. "No vital organs damaged. He should be okay if he doesn't get an infection." The beagle licked her hand.

The boy sobbed loudly, then turned his head, embarrassed.

Cindy reached in the pocket of her jeans and brought up two quarters. She handed them to the boy. "Grab yourself a Coke from the machine in the hall and get yourself together. Your dog's going to be *okay.*"

His head bowed, the boy went to the hall. They could hear the clank of the Coke machine dispensing a can, and smiled at each other.

Michaelis said, "You know, you're a very nice person."

"That and a dollar will get me a ride on the subway, as they say down in New York." She expertly moved the wounded dog to a small plastic-covered pad and carried him to an adjoining room. "He'll sleep for several hours now."

She came back to Michaelis. "So you don't have a sick animal in your car, and you don't owe me any money, and we served on a screwy jury together. What do you want from me, Jon?"

He was mildly embarrassed. "Talk, I guess. One of the other jurors, Horace Strang, and I sort of have the quixotic notion that we should visit all the jurors and find out which seven got the bribes."

He told her about losing the Washington appointment.

She listened, alternately smiling and becoming sober-faced with sympathy.

"Do you think I got one of the bribes?"

"We're checking everyone."

"So is the IRS."

"Where did you get the money for the down payment on this place?"

"From my Uncle Josh. Months before the trial. You can check with the bank. I'll give old Blonker permission to reveal all the sordid details of my financial condition."

He smiled. "It's nice of you not to get angry."

"Why should I? I wouldn't mind knowing who besmirched my own reputation, such as it is."

The boy came back into the room holding an empty Coke can.

Cindy turned to him. "I think we'd better keep your dog here for two or three days to be sure he's all right. What's his name?"

"Boggling."

"Boggling?"

"For mind-boggling. My father says the things he does are mind-boggling."

"Such as?"

"Like chewing up a whole closet full of shoes, some of which cost a hundred dollars."

She made a face. "Well, tell your dad I've got to send

him a bill, but it won't be mind-boggling." She wrote down the boy's name, address, and phone number. He took one last look at the dog and left, whistling softly.

She came back to Michaelis. "I don't remember this Strang. Which one was he?"

"He has stringy yellow hair and looks like a warmed-over corpse."

"Oh, yeah, gottcha." She smiled. "Well, tell him to check with old Blonker at Crendon Trust."

"Was that Blonker who left?"

"Yep."

"I couldn't help overhearing your conversation." He had been deliberately eavesdropping, but never mind.

"Yes, well—"

"Will your uncle bail you out?"

She laughed. "No. He's furious. He says, 'I've kissed that forty-five thousand dollars good-bye, good-bye, *good-bye!*'"

"So why did you ask for ten days?"

Her lower lip trembled and Michaelis thought she was going to cry. "I just need time to, to adjust to it. I've put so much hard work into this place, and I love it."

"You actually have enough business to make the place profitable?"

"Sure. If I could collect say, ninety percent of what's owed me, I'd clear about ten thousand a year. Not much, but since I live on the premises it's adequate."

He rubbed his chin. "Collecting shouldn't be all that big a problem. Ever try getting out a series of nice letters and then following them up with telephone calls?"

"No." She stared at him blankly. "Is that what you're supposed to do?"

"Of course. Most people aren't dishonest, but many are slow in paying. After a month or two, they can't even remember whether they've paid the bill or not."

"Oh."

"I'll get one of the bright assistants in the Business School to work up a series of collection letters for you. He'll probably even make the follow-up calls for a small percentage of what he's able to collect."

Her shoulders slumped. "What's the use? We'd never get enough together in ten days. Banker Blonker is absolutely serious this time, I can tell."

"How much would you need to see you through a couple of months?"

She bit her lip. "Well, I would have to give the bank ten thousand. I owe utility and other bills. I have a couple of high school kids who help out cleaning the place and feeding the boarders and patients. I guess fifteen thousand would tide me over until we collected the bills. If we collected the bills."

"I'll lend it to you."

She stared at him, startled. "You aren't one of those loan sharks, are you? I mean, like fifty percent interest per week?" She smiled. "No, the university wouldn't hire a professor like that, would they?"

He smiled. "No interest."

She lowered her eyes, elation suddenly gone. "I'd love to accept, but, well—"

"No strings," he said. "Absolutely no strings. I'd just like to see you make a go of the place. I have a feeling you're an awfully good doctor. And the amount of money is no great sacrifice to me."

She looked up at him. "You're a rich professor?"

"Reasonably rich."

"Well, I do appreciate it and everything, but I'm afraid I just, well—"

He took his pipe out and filled it. "I know what you're thinking, but believe me, you're wrong. I've just gone through a very traumatic divorce. It has left me shaken and unsure of myself, and the last thing in the world I want is to become emotionally involved with another woman. I'd like to be your friend and help you out, but that's absolutely all there is to it. I like the way you took care of that little dog. Okay?"

She stared at him. "This is really weird."

His mouth turned down slightly. "Do I look like a man who has to pay out fifteen thousand dollars to find himself a girlfriend?"

She shook her head. "No, you look like the kind of stud who would find it very easy."

"Hey, wait a minute."

"Okay, that was uncalled for."

He took out his checkbook, scribbled in it briefly, tore out the check, and handed it to her. "Deposit this and tell Banker Blonker you have a new silent partner."

She looked at the check. "I can't do this. We hardly know each other."

"How well did you know Blonker when you borrowed money from him?"

"That was business. He makes money lending money."

Michaelis glanced around impatiently. "So if you want to make it strictly business, pay me whatever interest you think is reasonable." He stuck his freshly packed but unlit pipe in his jacket pocket.

"Okay, I will."

He turned to go, smiling. "Stay in there slugging. I'll send a fellow over to help you with the bill collecting."

She was still holding the check, staring at him when he opened the screen door.

He strolled out to the parking area. The gray-blue Continental was gone. Near where Strang had parked was a black Mercedes.

Michaelis reached for his .38, which nestled in a hip holster under his lightweight jacket, then relaxed when he saw that the driver and sole occupant of the Mercedes was a woman. She touched the horn to produce a soft, short toot, then motioned for him to come over.

He walked to the car.

"Michaelis?"

He nodded. She was attractive, with rather coarse, blunt features. The blond hair was obviously a wig.

"Sting asked me to pick you up. He had some urgent business to take care of."

"How—" Then he remembered that Strang had a telephone in his car.

"He said to bring you to his place. He has a couple of guys waiting to go with you to your apartment. To pick up whatever you need."

Michaelis walked to the passenger side and opened the door.

"I'm Angelica," said the driver. She was a busty woman

in her thirties. Michaelis wondered if she was Strang's girlfriend.

"Nice to know you," said Michaelis, sliding in and slamming the door.

She put the Mercedes into gear and expertly wheeled it down the curving driveway to the road.

"Sting is my fiancé," she said.

He wondered what to say to that. Best of luck? "That's nice. Hope you'll be very happy together."

"We're already very happy together."

"Great. A lot of couples wish they could say the same."

She glanced quickly at Michaelis. "You can say that again. What is it, seven divorces out of every ten marriages today?"

"Something like that, I guess."

They drove in silence for a few minutes. Then she said, "You shouldn't look down on Sting. He talks rough, but he's an educated man."

Who worried about his education? He was a creepy free-lance killer. "Does he think I look down on him?"

"Yeah."

"Well, tell him I don't."

Up ahead, two men were standing beside the road. Dressed in business suits, they definitely were not joggers. In fact, as far as Michaelis was concerned, they did not belong by the side of the road.

Angelica began to slow down.

Michaelis whipped out his .38 and pressed the barrel end against Angelica's side. "Speed up, don't stop!"

She slammed on the brakes hard.

Michaelis was thrown forward, cracking his head against the sloping windshield. The .38 exploded, the bullet traveling harmlessly out the window on the driver's side.

The Mercedes screeched to a skidding halt about fifty feet short of the men. Both started running toward it.

Michaelis pushed himself back in the seat. What the hell was she up to? He turned his revolver toward the open window on the passenger side.

The men were carrying small black automatics, but they hung like appendages to the right arm, pointing at the ground.

Michaelis took aim. "Stop!" he yelled. "Stop where you are or I'll shoot!"

Out of the corner of his eye he saw an old-fashioned straight-edged razor moving toward him, then felt the cold of its flat side against his throat.

"Shoot and I'll slice open your jugular," said Angelica.

— 9 —

ATHENA VON DIETRICH LAY BESIDE HER POOL SUNNING HERSELF. With her bathing cap off, her straight black hair gleamed in the sun, spreading over her shoulders and down her back almost to her waist. She reached behind her neck and, bunching the hair together, pulled it to one side to feel the sun on her back.

The pool was very large. In free-form shape it sprawled like a lake some two hundred feet in length. Colored concrete with a shiny glaze gave the sparkling water a deep blue tint. Grass of the healthiest green, manicured to perfection, provided a wide border around the small lake. Both the pool and the great Tudor-style castle were surrounded by eighty acres of estate-owned forest. The castle was located on a hill that rose high above the wooded areas, and the view was almost entirely of treetops.

Athena wore a minimal bikini, brilliantly white against her tanned body. She turned on her back and lifted one shapely leg to study the perfection of her red toenails.

Wolfgang Brillhagen sat watching her with an amused smile on his lean, overlong face. Straightening slightly in the canvas chair, he crossed one white-flannel-trouser leg over the other, then ran his fingers through his curly, honey-colored hair.

"Time to quit loafing in the sun, Thena. Everything is closing in."

She lowered her leg, removed her sunglasses, and focused her large brown eyes on Brillhagen. "It can only close in so far," she said.

"Until it stops with you?"

"Yes."

"The Leeds woman opened a Pandora's box."

Athena sat up, hugging her knees. "You haven't deposited the seven hundred thousand? Or won't she cooperate? All she needs to do is say she discovered this Swiss account, so her father obviously bribed no one."

Wolfgang shook his head. "Leeds is dead."

Athena stared at him silently for a few seconds. "Who?"

Wolfgang shrugged. "Not one of ours. Of course, it's possible that her father told her something."

Athena yawned, covering her mouth daintily.

"This is no matter to be yawned over, Thena."

"I'm sleepy."

"You realize that something unexpected could happen to you?"

"Or something expected."

His face contorted, as though he had felt a knife blade in his stomach, he said, "The loss to the world will be enormous if this matter is not resolved."

Athena yawned again. "I have taken precautions."

"Things do not always work out as we have planned when we are not there to see to it."

"My plans will."

Agitated, but rock still, Brillhagen asked, "Thena, what are your plans? Are you going to sit back and wait until they lose patience and kill you? And me?"

She got to her feet. "Wolf, sometimes you become so boring." She drew a large white towel about her shoulders and stalked away.

She followed a tree-shaded path of flagstones to the bottom of a steep hill. Metal stairs led to the top. She stepped on the bottom tread, pressed a button encased in an iron pole on her right, and stood motionless as the escalator came to life and bore her slowly to the summit.

Stepping off, she pressed the button on another post to

stop the machinery, then strolled along another flagstone path to a side entrance of the mansion.

Of stone and brick, and more castle than mansion, the building was a massive square, four stories in height, with corner hexagonal towers which rose another story above the roof. The original owner had been an Anglophile, and had obviously tried to copy one of the great halls of sixteenth-century England. Karl von Dietrich, having spent his childhood in a baronial castle in Prussia, had decided that this ugly Tudor edifice was large enough and impressive enough to suit his station in life.

Athena, born Anna Goldstein, had chosen in her teens to become a goddess. Daughter of Sir Yirmi Goldstein, knighted for his outstanding contributions to science, Anna had been pampered and spoiled by her doting but eccentric scientist father. She had been beautiful from birth, and became even more beautiful with every year of growth. It was her whim to change her first name to Athena. Being a goddess of wisdom had appealed to her at the time. She had genius I.Q. and felt qualified. "Anna" suggested a simple woman, and she, Athena, was so complex.

She shivered as she stepped into the chill of a lower hall. The walls were so thick that the building remained cold all summer. It was even colder in the winter, except for the living quarters, which were, in German fashion, overheated. Some fifty feet down the oak-paneled corridor a small elevator waited with its door locked open. She stepped in, released the catch, and pushed the "3" button.

Athena's suite on the third floor was enormous. With extra rooms partitioned off, a family of four could have lived there comfortably. The lounge, or living room, was fifty feet by thirty, with a huge stone fireplace at one end, and windows providing a panoramic view of the forest and countryside at the other. Athena's bedroom was almost as large. Eighteen-foot ceilings dwarfed her huge canopied bed with its roof and red velvet curtains. A bath as large as most master bedrooms had a sunken green marble bathing pool. A kitchen and dining area also served the suite.

Unlike the rest of the castle, furnished with heavy oak antiques, giant tables with Elizabethan carved melon bulb legs, intricately carved Gothic panels, linenfold doors, buffets, coffers, and portrait medallion paneling, Athena's suite contained comfortable modern furniture, boxy and lushly upholstered in white, with carpeting of buttery yellow in the lounge and white in the bedroom.

Hilda, Athena's maid, had flaxen hair and the pale face of fragile health. Her arms and legs had the bulging muscles of a male athlete, however, and she rarely had as much as a headache or a cold. She had been waiting for Athena.

"Your bath now, madam?" asked Hilda.

Athena shook her head. "Exercise first."

Athena exercised forty minutes a day, ten minutes on the Exercycle to warm up, then thirty minutes of vigorous, fast-paced calisthenics. What confused Hilda was the fact that Athena did not exercise at the same time every day, which was definitely not acceptable in the Teutonic scheme of things.

Picking up a book, Athena strolled to her huge bathroom and mounted the Exercycle. Propping the book on the handlebars, she began to read while pedaling briskly. She turned the pages so quickly anyone watching would have the impression that she was looking for some particular passage. Actually she was reading every word and retaining everything she read with amazing accuracy. Today she was rereading Darwin's *Origin of the Species,* certain that she would find somewhere that the evolutionary process skipped some humans, leaving them with the intelligence of shellfish. In ten minutes she breezed through the first hundred pages. She closed the book without marking her place. She would remember exactly where she left off when she picked up the book again.

Thirty minutes of calisthenics routine had her perspiring freely, but not breathing hard.

The sunken pool needed only hot water to bring it to the right temperature. Hilda dumped in a scattering of perfumed globules, turning it into a sea of white foam.

Athena unfastened her bikini, handed the brassiere and bottom to Hilda, and slid into the tingling, warm water. For an instant she sat completely relaxed, her mind blank. But the length of time Athena's mind could be blank was measured in milliseconds.

Poor Wolf, the only man she could really trust. Well, not trust completely, for Wolf had a tiny crack of weakness in his core. When the pressure became too great, he might break. She should try to send him away. Not that he would go.

She recalled the visit of her late husband's brother, Heinrich. A brief good-bye visit. Heinrich and his doctor knew that Heinrich had only a few months left.

It was a time of tragedy. Her father, Sir Yirmi, had been shot by West German terrorists only six weeks earlier. Executed, they had announced, as a warning to the Establishment that the rich and the great would be taken one by one. The fact that Sir Yirmi was a British citizen made no difference. He was part of the International Establishment. And he was connected by family with the von Dietrichs, billionaire capitalists.

Dying Heinrich von Dietrich then became the sole custodian of Sir Yirmi's secret. The secret had been developed in Sir Yirmi's laboratory in London under a grant furnished by Gesellschaft Dietrich. By the time a working prototype had been constructed in the company's Munich plant, the project had cost the von Dietrichs more than 20 million deutsche marks. The end result was so successful no one would ever be able to set a price on it.

Working alone, Heinrich destroyed the prototype. The three technicians who had helped construct it knew less than a tenth of the story. They knew how part of the prototype was constructed, and they had a glimpse of its tremendous power. But for all practical purposes, the secret was safe in the data sealed in a fat manila envelope.

It was this envelope that Heinrich had entrusted to Karl von Dietrich. He could then go back to Munich and die in peace, or perhaps the terrorists would get him first, and he would spit in their faces with impunity.

Possession of the envelope shattered Karl's easygoing way of life. He locked it in his safe and was unable to sleep for three nights. After he said a tearful farewell to Heinrich at the airport, he returned to the castle and thrust the secret upon Athena. Her genius father had developed it; secondly, she, Athena, was far brighter than Karl and would thus be better able to plan for its protection and its disposition.

Disgustedly she had snatched the envelope from Karl and gone to her suite. The next morning she ordered their two-engined jet readied for a long trip. With Wolfgang Brillhagen as copilot she roamed the earth for three weeks. Crendon airport to Gander, Gander to Shannon, Shannon to Dublin, then to London, Paris, Copenhagen, Stockholm, Munich, Athens, and Rome. In each city she made Brillhagen remain in the hotel while she walked the streets, the envelope taped to her stomach. She then left Brillhagen in Rome and visited three other cities, piloting the jet alone. When she returned to Crendon, she was the only person in the world who knew where the envelope was hidden.

Word of the discovery gradually leaked, of course, from the technicians. This led to discreet visits from Britain's M-6, from the CIA, from the Pentagon, the West Germans, the Japanese, the Chinese, from Israeli intelligence, and from a number of other organizations not readily identified. Aware that Karl von Dietrich had firmly disassociated himself from the problem, all sent their most charming men, each selected for his wit, appearance, and appeal to women.

Athena was equally charming in receiving them. She would not admit that the secret existed, but assured them that should she discover that it did, she would give their proposals serious consideration.

On the day of Karl's murder, the maid Carlita had admitted three spurious FBI agents to the house. One reopened the door to admit ten more intruders. Athena suspected they were KGB, though the two who did most of the talking spoke American English. The hours that followed crept by as Athena suffered relentless interrogation. While three agents questioned her with the aid of a PSE lie detector, the other ten searched the castle.

They could search, Athena thought wryly, for forty years and still not uncover all the possible hiding places in this gigantic labyrinth of a building. Even if the envelope was hidden in the castle, which it was not.

The blond, pink-skinned young man working the lie detector pointed out Athena's lies one by one as they appeared on his graph tape. Athena laughed and told him to take his silly machine away. The ten searchers returned, admitting defeat.

The scene, which had been acted with firm but courteous pressure, became ugly. The leader of the group was a middle-aged man who slightly resembled Charlton Heston. He regretted that he would be forced to apply some disfiguring, perhaps even lethal, torture if she did not talk.

Athena thought about that for a few seconds, then told him she would swallow her tongue and die if they did.

Charlton didn't believe her. A lighted cigarette was ground out on her bare right arm. She gritted her teeth and bore it without as much as a whimper, but the muscles in her throat began to work.

One of the agents, who had medical training, and long, thin fingers, went to work frantically. With the aid of a pencil he managed to reverse the process, but Athena had begun to turn blue. Another minute and the secret might have disappeared forever, as far as her inquisitors were concerned.

She now felt relatively torture-proof.

But she was no more than half-conscious when the agent explained that though she might hold her own life cheap, she might at least prize the life of a loved one. Had she understood that he meant to kill Karl, she might have wavered in her determination. She did not love Karl, but she felt a strong sisterly, if not wifely, affection for him. The shot was fired before she understood. The killer calmly broke the revolver and emptied the remaining bullets, wiped the butt, and folded it firmly into her right hand. Someone else jabbed her left arm with a needle.

They left, promising to return. Perhaps she had a mother, or a favorite niece somewhere?

She drifted off, trying fuzzily to remember whether she had any close relatives anywhere.

When Athena regained consciousness she was propped against a chair, still holding the revolver, which was resting on the floor. The police were there, surveying the scene.

She stood trial for the murder. Other than the housekeeper, her butler-handyman husband, and the maid Carlita, none of the other servants were aware of the visitors.

The cook was shopping in Crendon, and had been driven there by the chauffeur. Two other maids were taking their days off. Heavy cleaning in the house, and gardening service for the grounds, were provided by companies specializing in this work. Crews visited the estate three times a week. This was not one of their days.

The afterthought return of the intruders to eliminate the housekeeper and her husband destroyed two witnesses who would have testified for Athena. Carlita's testimony opened the door for the defense strategy planned by Athena. She had no memory of shouting at the man pointing the revolver at Karl, or having grappled with him, but she realized that in her panic she might well have done so.

There was no proof of the visit by the thirteen marauders, and without fixing public attention on Sir Yirmi's secret, the true story would seem fanciful. The police would present a clear-cut picture of a murderess with a smoking gun in her hand.

Let it be a tragic accident, and depend upon Athena's beauty and confidence to create sympathetic belief. Brillhagen disagreed. He wanted to stand on the truth. To hell with the widespread publicity. Every intelligence agency in the world seemed to already be aware that Athena was concealing a world-shaking development. What difference did it make if the general public knew about it?

Athena insisted upon doing it her way. Making a public circus of the situation would be intolerable. Her stubbornness prevailed, as always.

But who, Athena wondered for the thousandth time, bribed the jurors? Perhaps the KGB? If she was in prison, it would be difficult to extort information from her, or follow her to the secret's hidey-hole. She might appoint a trusted courier unknown to everyone to retrieve it and turn it over to the wrong government. Free, she would trust no one but herself. But then why set her up with the smoking gun? Perhaps the CIA? On the other hand, they could get to her in prison easier than the KGB. Perhaps it was a demonstration. We can put you behind bars for many years, a fate certainly worse than death for one of Athena's temperament, and we can save you from that fate. She shook her head disgustedly. She had thought her superb acting and her beauty had saved her, not sordid bribery.

"Hilda, turn on the Jacuzzi jet, please," she said, raising her voice slightly. Hilda came from the bedroom and switched on the Jacuzzi.

The bath became a whirlpool almost as turbulent as Athena's mind. She remembered the humiliating trial with anger. The juror with the half-smile, the supercilious air of superiority. A professor! She knew instantly that he would lead the opposition. And now he had lost his Washington appointment. Good! The self-satisfied prig.

She was weary of the curse her father and the von Dietrichs had put upon her. Holding 50 percent of the stock of Gesellschaft Dietrich, she was worth over a billion dollars. Her secret, protected with patents, would bring untold billions. She would be the richest woman, perhaps the richest person, in the world, if that meant anything. Used properly, her father's awesome creation could be a tremendous boon to mankind. Used improperly, which would certainly parallel its proper use, it would add another devastating weapon to the world's arsenal of oblivion.

She pulled herself out of the whirlpool and stalked to the bathroom's glass-enclosed shower to wash away the soapy oil. Standing under the warm rain, she gradually turned it colder.

Now she was truly a prisoner of her father's monster. Following the invasion and Karl's murder, Brillhagen had assembled a private army. Sixty security men patrolled the house and grounds in shifts twenty-four hours a day. Eight intelligence operatives, former agents, scouted the enemy. The most modern electronic devices continually scanned and swept the house and forest areas. A Berlin wall surrounded the property.

Outside the wall, surveillance by the enemy was equally scientific. The surrounding roads and farmlands were dotted with agents in almost every form of disguise, from fake telephone repair crews to pseudo hayseeds chewing stalks of real grass.

Athena dried herself, staring at her body in one of the bathroom's mirrored walls. At thirty-one she was still showing no signs of wear, flab, or any other physical deterioration. She could objectively admit to a beautiful body sadly underutilized. Not that sex was all that intriguing at the moment. An army under siege has other things to worry about.

Sex. She had done her duty as a wife. An unsatisfying duty. Karl made love with Prussian precision. First he would take a lengthy shower, shave, brush his teeth, spray himself with cologne, then enter the bedroom to mount for a very quick gallop. The sessions left Athena completely unmoved. They were necessary, though, because Karl wanted heirs, and she wanted to give them to him. None had appeared. She wondered whether it was her fault or Karl's. The question was now academic. If she married again, she would have her own capabilities checked.

Bodies! People were turned inward, too preoccupied with themselves and their bodies, living behind barriers of emotional reserve. What was a body? In a few years it would be all flab. She doubted that she would be one of those women who went to the surgeons every other year to be restructured.

The warm blower dried her shampooed hair. Brillhagen, Karl's cousin, was in love with her. He was content to be big brother for the time being. Eventually that problem would have to be faced. As a husband he would be safe, but would she be sorry? Brillhagen had his own fortune. Not as large as hers, but sufficiently impressive to rule out his marrying her for her money.

In the meantime, nothing could be decided until she unraveled the problem of the beneficent monster. Obviously it had to be developed under the protection of a powerful government, probably the United States. But the pressure of one-upmanship with the USSR would almost guarantee all-out weapon emphasis, with civilian use relegated to committees who would dawdle for years with feasibility studies, coupled with quiet sabotage subtly backed by the world's powerful energy brokers. Sir Yirmi's creation could generate unlimited energy at a fraction of today's cost.

She preferred Britain, but feared the feeble Lion would not be able to control the weapons aspect. West Germany should rightfully have it, for Gesellschaft Dietrich had paid for its development. But here again the risk was too great. West Germany was too close to East Germany.

The simple fact was that there was no powerful country in the whole damned world that would harness her father's monster for the public good. Rather than contribute another doomsday weapon, it might be better to let the secret moulder in its hiding place for eternity.

Brillhagen did not agree. Patent it in the United States and throughout the free world. Use his and the von Dietrichs' financial reserves to develop its civil use. Athena found this approach naive. Their resources, though vast, were puny compared to those of the international cartels who would slow its development. Brillhagen pointed out that some other scientist could at this very moment be traveling a similar path of research to a similar answer.

Furthermore, he argued, she wanted a commitment she could never get. What democratic government could guarantee protection to a service sold to the general public? The laws against monopoly were frequently enforced in the United States.

He was looking at it in black and white, thought Athena. If the stakes were high enough, even a democratic government might find a suitable compromise. She was asking for nothing corrupt, only that the public welfare be first priority.

Hilda came into the bathroom. "Frau von Dietrich, from the guards in the gatehouse is telephone. Seeking admittance is a man who says he is your nephew, Hans Kassenbach."

Athena grimaced. Hans Kassenbach, husband of Gretchen, Heinrich von Dietrich's daughter. Another man she detested. Gretchen, however, now controlled the remaining 50 percent of Gesellschaft Dietrich.

Athena lifted the phone in the bathroom and spoke in rapid German to Kassenbach. After establishing that he was truly Hans Kassenbach, she spoke to the guard. She would receive Kassenbach in the main lounge in half an hour.

Hilda brushed Athena's black hair until it gleamed like wet coal, then helped her into a butter-yellow sheath that fell a few inches below her knees. It was slit up the side, however, to reveal one shapely leg when she moved about.

Hans Kassenbach stood up as she walked into the chill of the gigantic, high-ceilinged room. Dressed in navy blue blazer, gray slacks, tattersall vest, white shirt, and red tie, Kassenbach was tall and square-faced. His brown hair made a straight line across his forehead; below this line his eyebrows met to form another rule. His mouth was a mournful, turned-down bow.

He opened his arms wide, approaching Athena. "Ah, Tante Thena, how beautiful you are!"

She submitted to a hug, but turned her cheek to be kissed. Aunt indeed! She was only three years older than Kassenbach.

"You will stay with us?" she asked reluctantly.

Holding her, he shook his head. "*Nein.* Alas, I am booked into the Pierre. I have much business in New York, and you are too far away, *nicht wahr?"*

She smiled, relieved. "True, it is a boring trip, and time-consuming when one is busy." She gently disengaged herself and led him to the end of the room where a small fire crackled in the huge Elizabethan fireplace.

Kassenbach shivered. "This place is a mausoleum, a, a railway station."

She nodded. "It was Karl's wish to live here."

Kassenbach's face drooped into greater mourning. "Ah, poor Karl!" He shook his head sadly.

They sat on a large sofa facing the fireplace, Athena moving about five feet away from Kassenbach. She turned to face him, tucking her feet up on the sofa. "May I offer you a drink, or perhaps coffee?"

He glanced at his watch. *"Nein, danke,* it is too early. In forty minutes you may give me a vodka martini and lunch."

"Jawohl," said Athena, wondering how she could stand the boredom of the next two hours.

"The little ones are well?"

"Ah, yes. Jolly little pumpkins! Such dear *kinder!"*

"And Gretchen?"

"Blooming!" He reached into an inner jacket pocket and brought out a silver cigarette case. Flipping it open, he offered it to Athena, then withdrew it. "You do not smoke, I remember." He lifted out a cigarette, pocketed the case, then brought out a long, slender cigarette holder. Fitting the cigarette into it with meticulous care, he lit the cigarette and puffed thoughtfully. "Ah, yes, Gretchen. I must tell you that I have finally persuaded her that she has no patience for business. She has given me full power of attorney to represent her interests in Gesellschaft Dietrich. From now on it is I who will make all decisions."

Athena smiled. "How interesting for you." Kassenbach was an ass, but fortunately Gesellschaft Dietrich's real management functioned with brilliant precision. She must make sure Kassenbach was not allowed to interfere.

He nodded. "And this, dear Thena, is the reason I have come here to see you today."

She stared at him, waiting.

"You have for many months had in your possession documents which are the property of Gesellschaft Dietrich. Twenty million marks have been invested in this project, and we shall not tolerate any further delay."

The ass was pawing the ground and snorting. She frowned. "Indeed!"

"You must turn this data over to me immediately." Kassenbach tapped the ashes from his cigarette daintily.

Athena said, "The project was my father's creation. Heinrich entrusted the data to us because he did not have confidence in Gretchen's or your judgment. I and I alone will decide when to release this material. There are vast problems of international importance involved. In the meantime, if you wish, I will reimburse Gesellschaft Dietrich the twenty million from my own personal funds."

Kassenbach's bowed lips turned slightly upward in what passed for a smile. "My dear Thena, should you refuse my request, you will have no personal funds available. I am prepared to go to court both here and in Germany and tie up your financial assets so that not a penny can be spent."

With an effort Athena controlled her mounting fury. "Kassenbach, you are an idiot. This data is so dangerous to the world that every major intelligence agency is prepared to go to any lengths to obtain it. I need only to spread the word that I have given these documents to you and you will not leave the United States alive."

Kassenbach removed his cigarette from the holder, crushed it out in a large onyx ashtray, then tucked the holder into his jacket pocket. Athena could see that his hand was trembling slightly.

"I do not frighten easily, Thena, and I do not tolerate insults."

He stood up, brushing at his jacket.

"In view of your contemptuous attitude, I cannot accept your hospitality for lunch. I see that I must put our attorneys to work."

Athena swung her feet to the floor and stood up to face him. "You have seen this fortress we live in? They have killed Karl and tortured me. Brillhagen and I are literally besieged. Go to court and I will involve you!"

He turned his palms upward. *"Ach!* What could one expect from an emotional woman!" He executed a quick military about-face and strode away.

10

MICHAELIS SAT IMMOBILE IN THE DARK. HIS ARMS WERE HANDcuffed behind him, and his ankles seemed to be tied to the legs of the chair. The tight black blindfold cut into his throbbing temples like a tourniquet.

What a stupid, bumbling jerk he was to be taken so easily! During his days as an investigative reporter he had been threatened many times with anonymous letters and phone calls. Other than wearing his revolver when he expected to be out alone at night, he paid little attention to these threats. He had never been attacked or confronted. He had never been *hunted.* He was an amateur sucked into a game with some very efficient pros.

Cindy Harrison. Another wave of embarrassment swept over him. She probably still thought he was trying to buy her friendship or more. He had never before let an impulse like this take over. Not that the fifteen thousand dollars made any difference. He rarely spent even half his income, and the surplus continued to pile up year after year. But what was he trying to play? Lord Bountiful? Cindy Harrison probably thought that, at the very least, he was a crackpot. Well, to hell with her. The impulse had been thoroughly altruistic. He wanted her to succeed with her little animal hospital.

He could hear the thump of footsteps coming down stairs. The footsteps crossed the room, passing close to him. In a few seconds he heard the clatter of ice cubes falling into a plastic bucket, followed by the clink of several being dropped into a glass. A faint aroma of whiskey was suddenly present, followed by the gurgling sound of bottle filling glass.

The footsteps approached him and stopped. The cold rim of a glass was held against his lower lip.

A gruff voice said, "Drink this, you'll feel better."

Michaelis kept his lips tightly clamped, moving his head back. Cyanide laced with bourbon?

There was a grunt, then a deep-voiced laugh. He felt movement against his hands, then heard the click of the handcuffs being removed. The blindfold was unfastened.

Strang stood before him grinning. "Welcome to Chez Strang." He tried to hand the glass of bourbon to Michaelis.

Michaelis slapped the glass out of Strang's hand. It hit the vinyl floor and shattered. Rising, Michaelis launched a wild upper cut in the direction of Strang's jaw, but still fastened to the chair legs, he tripped and sprawled on the floor only inches from the broken glass and splattered bourbon.

"Hey, calm down!" Strang yelled. He lifted Michaelis and the chair upright. "Be still and I'll unfasten your legs." He looked at Michaelis's contorted face. "But then maybe I'd better not. You might try to kick me."

"And I damned well ought to!" Michaelis yelled. "What the hell is the big idea, anyway?"

Strang glared at him. "The big idea was to teach you a lesson, you fucking amateur. You got to wise up. You'll not only get yourself killed, but me, too."

"Yeah? Well, you could have gotten Angelica killed with that crazy stunt."

Strang laughed. "Don't you worry about Angelica. If you ever learn to handle yourself as well as Angie, you'll be okay. Angie knows what she's doing." He slapped Michaelis's shoulder playfully. "The point is, you got to remember, never trust a woman!" He threw back his head and guffawed loudly.

Michaelis decided it was probably time to stop acting like a child in a tantrum, even though he was dealing with a case of arrested development. "Untie me and I'll take that drink," he said quietly.

Giggling softly, Strang bent over and untied Michaelis.

Michaelis stood up and stretched, looking around. They were in a basement recreation room fitted out with typical light wood paneling, leather chairs, sofas and tables, a stereo system, a video tape machine and a library of cassettes, probably pornographic, Michaelis thought, and a handsome bar in one corner. Michaelis walked stiffly to the bar, working the cramp from his legs. Bright overhead lights came from long, office-type fluorescent tubes. He put ice cubes in a fresh glass and poured himself a stiff jolt of Wild Turkey.

He turned back to Strang. "All right, how would you have handled the situation?"

Strang smiled. "Simple. You shouldn't have gotten in the car at all. You didn't know her, you never saw her before in your life. You didn't even know I had a girlfriend, right?"

Michaelis sipped his drink. "Okay, you wouldn't have gotten in the car. Then what?"

"Pretend to believe her. Otherwise you might have found yourself looking at a forty-five and *have* to get in the car. So you smile and say, 'Okay,' then snap your fingers and say, 'Excuse me just a second, I left my briefcase back there.' Then you head for the hospital. She's not ready to shoot you in the back, yet. Get a grip on your thirty-eight as you walk. Once inside, telephone for a cab, keeping your eye on the door."

"Suppose when I walk up to talk to her I find myself looking at a forty-five?"

Strang strolled to the bar and made himself a short

drink. "Well, then you got trouble. But figure it this way. She wanted to kidnap you, not kill you. At least, not kill you there. Otherwise she would have shot you as you came out the door and then gunned the hell out of the lot. So she wants to kidnap you, temporarily, anyway. Now, she can't drive and hold a gun on you safely. This means she's got to make you drive. She's got to move to the passenger side. Whether she gets out and walks around, trying to keep you covered, or slides over, or makes you slide over, trying to keep you covered, her movement offers you a chance for evasive action, a chance to bring your own weapon into play. The odds are against you, but you still got a chance. With Angie on the other side, I would say you would have got plugged."

"Yeah." Michaelis felt both foolish and incompetent. "I've got to be suspicious of everybody."

Strang lifted his drink, tasted it, and put it down. "Not so. You got to develop a gut feeling about *when* to be suspicious. You got no right to go around killing off innocent mailmen and delivery boys."

Michaelis laughed.

Strang grinned. "Okay, let's go over and sit down. We got things to talk about."

His drink in hand, Strang led Michaelis to a round oak card table with four leather chairs grouped around it. Strang set his drink on the table, then went back to the bar to collect the bottle of Wild Turkey and a bucket of ice cubes. Michaelis sat down across from the chair Strang had chosen.

"First on the agenda, this dame Cindy Harrison. Did she or didn't she?"

Michaelis said, "Definitely not." He described the conversation he had overheard. "The banker was definitely going to foreclose."

"Was?"

"I lent her fifteen thousand."

Strang jerked his head back. "For what?"

"So she could keep the animal hospital going."

Strang nodded, smiling. "Oh, yeah. Good-looking chick, huh? You moving in on her, huh?" He rubbed his chin. "That could cause some complications."

"I'm not moving in on her."

Strang swirled the ice around in his glass. "You got no agreement?"

Michaelis shook his head. "It's not the kind of thing you're thinking about."

Strang thumped his glass down. "Look, man, when you give a dame a lot of money like that, you got to have a clear understanding with her. Dames got no sense of honor. She's just as liable to take that dough and buy her boyfriend a spiffy new car."

Michaelis smiled. Strang had obviously had some bad experiences with women.

Strang said, "I'm serious, man. If you're going to be trotting down there seeing her all the time, we got to cover you. If you're going to be bait, we set the scene, not you. Otherwise you get killed and we haven't accomplished a damned thing."

Michaelis reached into his jacket pocket and brought out the pipe which was already packed with tobacco. No point in trying to convince Strang that he had no plans for Cindy Harrison. "I'll stay away from her until we're out of the woods on this thing," he said.

"Okay. Now, if you want her to move in here, that's okay, too."

Michaelis shook his head. "Keeping that animal hospital going is the most important thing in the world to her." He lit his pipe and puffed on it until it was burning evenly.

"Okay, so we understand each other. But before you cross her off the list, you got to call that banker, what's his name?"

"Blonker."

"You're kidding."

A telephone, white speckled with multicolor polka dots, occupied a corner of the bar. Michaelis put his pipe in an ashtray and shoved back his chair.

The phone had a set of intercom numbers for various rooms in the house as well as four outside lines. Michaelis got Crendon Trust's number from the operator, and after a slight delay, got through to Blonker. Blonker had heard from Cindy Harrison. He confirmed that old Joshua Harrison had indeed given Cindy the $45,000 down payment. The date of the sale of the animal hospital preceded the murder of Karl von Dietrich by five days, and the actual selection of the jury by two months. Cindy had managed to pay off only $11,000 of the $65,000 owed.

Michaelis thanked Blonker, then called the head of the university's Business Administration School. After exchanging amenities, Michaelis arranged for a student to help Cindy with her bill collecting.

Strang, who had been listening, said, "Okay, so your bird is clean."

"Clean as the dew on a spring morning," said Michaelis.

Strang stared at him, beaming. "Now, that's a *nice* thing to say. I wish I could think of nice things like that to say to Angie." He fished a notebook from his shirt pocket and thumbed the pages. "Okay, let's knock off an easy one. How about this guy Thomas Swift? A writer. Ever heard of him?"

"Yep. He's a CIA agent."

Strang scratched his scalp where it showed through his thinning hair. "He's a spook? How do you know that?"

"The Crendon D.A. told me."

"Son of a bitch!"

Michaelis smiled. "That doesn't mean he wouldn't take a bribe."

Strang nodded. "But maybe we got to handle him with kid gloves."

Michaelis picked up his glass and tossed down the remaining Wild Turkey.

Strang said suddenly, "Hey, I forgot you came in here blind. You got to see my establishment and meet my entourage." He swaggered over to the bar, picked up the phone, and punched out a two-digit number. "Tarboys to Zero 1," he said, then banged the handset back into its cradle.

Within seconds rapid thumps sounded on the carpeted stairs. The two men who had been waiting on the roadside entered the room quickly. During the confusion and stress of his kidnaping Michaelis had noted subconsciously that they were identical twins. In their mid-twenties, both had curly black hair, big, bland brown eyes, long chins, and blue-shadowed jowls. Both were very thin and about six feet tall. They wore identical blue jeans and plaid shirts.

"Donald and Ronald Tarboy, meet Professor Jonathan Michaelis."

They came forward to shake hands. The one on the left said, "I'm Donald. My brother's Richard, not Ronald. Sting's just joking with that Donald-Ronald thing." He had a slow drawl from somewhere in the South.

The other one said, "Ole Sting calls me Ronald, I just don't hear him."

Strang said, "You better hear me, son."

"No, *sir,* you got no right to poke fun at a man's name."

Strang muttered something about getting himself a new set of Tarboys.

Angelica made an entrance. She was wearing a floor-length side-wrap skirt of hand-painted white, yellow, red, and green print crepe de chine with a loose-fitting top striped in matching colors—and pulled over to expose one shapely shoulder. Michaelis decided that her thick blond hair was not a wig, merely an unusual dye job. She came toward him to shake hands, one long, slender leg alternately exposed and covered as she walked.

Strang said, "My God, will you just look at this gorgeous dame!"

"Oscar de la Renta," she said.

She shook hands with Michaelis. "Sorry I cracked your head."

Michaelis smiled. "My fault. Should have shot you while I had the chance."

"Wrong move!" said Strang quickly. "She was probably traveling about sixty miles an hour. You could have gone smack into a tree, or head-on into another car."

Angelica said, "If you'd had your seat belt buckled, I couldn't have bounced you off the windshield."

Michaelis nodded. "So what would you have done if I had been buckled in?"

"Stopped anyway. You wouldn't have shot me."

She was right. He'd have a very hard time shooting a woman unless she was coming at him with a butcher knife.

Strang said, "I'm going to show Jon around the joint,

then the Tarboys will go back to his apartment with him to get his clothes.

Angelica drifted to the bar. "I'll stay here and bloody up a Mary."

Michaelis found that the recreation room was labeled Zero 1 because there were three other large rooms in the basement area, Zero 2, 3, and 4. Zero 2 was a fully equipped shooting gallery, automated with moving targets at various depths of field.

Strang hefted a long-barreled .22 target revolver and quickly picked off ten dime-sized bull's-eyes mounted on a slowly turning wheel.

Michaelis whistled softly.

"You gotta come down here and sharpen up your marksmanship with that thirty-eight," said Strang.

"Yep, I suppose I'd better," said Michaelis. He had started out with the idea of finding a few sniveling bribees, and now he was in a damned war.

Zero 3 was an armory with weapons enough to equip a platoon for almost any type of operation. Metal gleamed everywhere, oiled and in mint condition.

Zero 4 was an indoor swimming pool and mini health spa with whirlpool bath, sauna, and body-conditioning equipment. Off this area was all the machinery necessary to provide central air-conditioning, heat, and hot water. There was even a diesel generator to produce electricity in a blackout.

"I see you even have complete Nautilus equipment," said Michaelis.

Strang thumped Michaelis's arm. "The best of everything, man. You want to work out and take a swim?"

"I'll wait until I get moved in."

They went upstairs to look over the rest of the house, wandering through large rooms tastefully furnished and all indicating the professionalism of a decorator.

"You must have quite a staff to maintain a place this big," said Michaelis.

Strang shrugged. "Not so many. Angie runs a tight ship. We got Mrs. Culp, our cook; Fanny and Nancy Culp, her nieces, as sort of maids; and Jed Jarvis, an old top sergeant of mine who's sort of butler and general handyman. That's about it."

"The Tarboys live in?"

Strang smiled. "Yeah, my live-in bodyguards. Part of my army."

"Where's the rest of your army?"

Strang took his arm and led him into the library. "Oh, I got a dozen or so old buddies who live in the New York area I can call on for reinforcements."

The library was floor-to-ceiling books except for one wall that was floor-to-ceiling glass, offering a view of grass and a well-tended garden.

"Beautiful library," said Michaelis. "You have time to read all these books?"

Strang gazed around at the walls of books. "Oh, sure. I only work once in a while on a consultant basis. What I don't read, Angie reads."

"What sort of consulting work do you do?" Michaelis asked, immediately sure that he shouldn't have brought the matter up.

Strang looked away. "Well, usually it's pretty confidential. Like, maybe somebody has a little war going on and wants to hire some real professionals. One of my men is worth fifty of the amateurs they slap in armies."

Michaelis nodded. A hired killer. Mercenaries killed for money, motivated by no moral or patriotic convictions. The element of risk, of course, was great, and probably in some cases the mercenaries identified with the aims of the side that hired them.

Strang said, "Well, that's the two-dollar tour; you can see the upstairs later. Let's get you moved in. I'm sort of anxious to check out that writer."

Thomas Swift lived in a run-down gatehouse which had once been part of an estate. The estate had been divided into two-acre plots, and the small stone cottage now rested on the periphery of expensive homes, a poor relative wearing crumbling stucco and weeds.

For backup, Strang posted the black Mercedes driven by Angie two hundred yards south of the house. Richard

Tarboy, driving a BMW, waited two hundred yards to the north. Donald Tarboy remained outside in the Continental.

Writers come in all shapes, sizes, and colors, but Thomas Swift was unique. Even the BIG MEN'S store would have trouble fitting him. Almost seven feet tall, he was barrel-chested and long-armed, with thick biceps straining the material of his summer-weight shirt. He had a big head to go with his massive body. It was topped by a pile of black curly hair that fell over his ears like a wig and framed a huge ruddy face, a large triangle of red nose that jutted angrily, big tombstone teeth, and inquisitive, unblinking brown eyes.

Strang stared at him, stunned. This was a writer?

"Are you Thomas Swift?" he asked.

Swift sneered. "That's right. If you're fans and want to find out where I get my ideas and what I eat for breakfast, I'll tell you right now that I get all my ideas from the Holy Bible, and I eat sauerkraut and pigs' knuckles for breakfast. And if you have any books you want autographed, bring them out and we'll get that out of the way. I'd invite you in, but I'm working, and I can only see people for extended visits by appointment." He paused and stared at them, waiting.

Michaelis asked, "Don't you remember us? We were on the Athena von Dietrich jury together." How could he have forgotten this monster? He remembered now that Swift had sat quietly, saying little during most of the deliberations.

"The what?"

"The Athena von Dietrich trial. We were on the jury together."

"Oh, that." Swift gave the matter careful consideration. "Yeah, I seem to remember you."

"We'd like to come in and talk about it," said Michaelis. Swift filled the door frame like a second door.

"What's to talk about?"

Strang said, "Seven of the jurors were bribed. We're sort of curious about who got the money."

"Oh, that." Swift moved back to close the door.

Strang stuck his foot and leg against it, holding it partially open. In the same motion he had his Walther out and pointed at the portion of Swift's midsection still showing. "Step aside, Kong, we're coming in. This thing will drop an elephant."

Swift opened the door. "You're aware that this is an illegal display of firearms? An entry by threat of violence? There must be some law against it. A man's home is his castle."

Strang stuck the Walther back in its holster. "Our honor is at stake. We got a right to know who got bribed, since we didn't."

Swift stepped aside. Strang and Michaelis walked in, keeping a wary eye on the giant.

Swift's cottage was one large room. The ceiling had been removed to expose knotty old oak beams, and stainless-steel-framed skylights had been installed in the roof, providing an incongruous mixture of the modern and the old. A large stone fireplace dominated one end; at the other a small kitchen had been partitioned off with a counter. A double bed occupied the corner opposite the kitchen. It was neatly covered with a heavy maroon bedspread. In the corners flanking the fireplace were bookshelves, tables, desk, and typewriter. The center of the room was the obvious social zone. It contained two long sofas upholstered in beige Naugahyde, with matching upholstered chairs forming a rectangle.

Thomas Swift collapsed on one of the sofas, stretching out and occupying its full length. He closed his eyes. "Go away, you bother me," he said.

Strang said, "If I shoot him, he won't hurt himself falling down."

Michaelis lowered himself onto the opposite sofa. "Easier for the undertaker's men, too. They can roll him right into the basket."

Swift's lips fluttered in a soft raspberry. "Mercy me! What despicable human beings!"

Strang said, "He doesn't believe I'll shoot him."

"I know all about you, Strang," said Swift, opening his eyes. "You, too, Michaelis."

"So what?" asked Strang.

"Michaelis wouldn't let you shoot me without a fair trial."

Michaelis laughed.

"You think we're kidding around?" asked Strang. He eased the Walther out of its holster again and checked the cartridge clip.

"I think you both ought to grow up."

Michaelis asked, "You don't think we should be concerned about who got bribed and who did not?"

Swift levered himself to a sitting position. "Who cares?"

"I do. I'd like to set the record straight, publicly."

"You're both naive."

"In what way?" asked Michaelis.

"The trial was a farce. Athena von Dietrich didn't kill her husband. He was killed either by the KGB or the East Germans, the SSD."

"Bullshit," said Strang.

"On what do you base that statement?" Michaelis asked.

"Everybody in the international intelligence community knows it. Ask your friendly neighborhood CIA man."

Strang lowered himself into a chair, crossed his legs, and rested the barrel of the Walther on his knee, pointing it directly at Swift. "Even if that bullshit is true, which I doubt, what in hell has it got to do with your taking a hundred-thousand-dollar bribe and causing us to be tarred with the same brush?"

Swift smiled. "Extenuating circumstances, Strang. I knew she was innocent before the trial began. There was nothing morally wrong in accepting money for voting the way I intended to vote anyway."

Michaelis pulled out his pipe and tobacco pouch. "You could spend a long time in prison explaining that principle of morality."

"Nobody's going to put me in prison."

Strang carefully reached into his jacket pocket and pulled out a typewritten statement. He sailed it over to Swift. "Sign that and we'll get out of here."

Michaelis filled his pipe, glancing at Swift while he tamped the tobacco down.

Swift read the statement, then looked up and grinned.

Strang tossed him a ballpoint pen.

Swift caught it and scribbled a signature on the statement. He moved to the end of the sofa nearest Strang and handed him the paper, then stuck the pen in his own shirt pocket.

Strang said, "Okay, so you can keep the pen." He looked down at the statement, then raised the Walther. "You son of a bitch, you wise-ass, you—"

Michaelis leaned over and grabbed the paper. Swift had signed it "Arbolt Free."

Swift held up his hand. "*Wait* a minute. Arbolt Free happens to be my real name. Thomas Swift is a pseudonym. I use others, too. Carruthers Pasternak, Harvey Jerome, Pamela Archibald, you name it."

"Horseshit," said Strang. "You got any proof? Lemmie see your Social Security card."

"My accountant has it. I'm always losing it, so he keeps it for me."

"Yeah!"

"Arbolt Jefferson Free, that's my name. My father, Jefferson Free, was a direct descendant of Thomas Jefferson. My mother's family name was Arbolt. That's how I got stuck with it."

Strang sighted along the barrel of his Walther. "I've about had it with you, Swift. Which pseudonym do you want on your tombstone?"

Swift's voice was suddenly harder and more hostile. "Put that damned thing down, Strang. You're over your head."

The cottage door opened with a crash. Two men stepped in quickly, both holding big blue .45 automatics. One said, "Don't move, stupid, or I'll blow your fucking head off. Now drop that pistol fast."

Strang half-turned. The fraction of a second he needed to swivel the Walther around was too little time. He dropped it reluctantly. It thumped loudly as it hit the carpet, then softer as it bounced and came to rest.

The intruder who had spoken was a tall man wearing a navy-blue raincoat and a blue rain hat pulled down over his forehead. He had a button nose and a mustache so large and stiff it looked pasted on. His partner wore a loose-fitting beige raincoat with a matching rain hat. Face chalky white, a slash of tightly pressed red lips, and violet-tinted wraparounds gave him the appearance of an actor overdressed for a gangster role.

Blue raincoat motioned to Strang and Michaelis with his automatic. "You two go over by the bed and stand facing the wall, hands over head, and lean against it."

Strang disgustedly moved around the sofa in the direction the gunman had indicated.

"You, Swift, get your hands up and move your ass over here fast."

Swift got up slowly, raising his hands, and moved toward them. Suddenly he dived to the floor and rolled like a massive log spinning wildly down a flume. The two men toppled, bowling pins with thrashing arms and legs. Swift was on his feet with the speed of a cougar and leaped out the door in almost the same instant, bouncing beige raincoat behind him. The second intruder had grabbed Swift's ankle and was now being dragged away like a doll that had somehow attached itself to Swift's leg.

Blue raincoat scrambled to his feet and ran after them.

Strang hurried over and picked up his Walther. Michaelis drew his .38 and started for the door.

Strang said, "Wait!"

Michaelis stopped. "What do you mean, wait! These are the guys we're supposed to lean on, remember?"

Strang held up his hand. "All in good time, pal. I've found it very hard to get information from a corpse. You want to go have a shoot-out?"

"They'll probably kill Swift."

"Naw, that baby can take care of himself but *good.*"

Michaelis stared at Strang.

"I got a gut feeling that Swift was telling the truth about the von Dietrich dame," said Strang.

"Uh-*huh.* Russian spies."

Strang half-sat on the arm of the nearest sofa. "Like I been telling you, I got an almost infallible instinct for spotting a lie when it's told to me personally. Write me a letter and I wouldn't know from zilch. Talk to me face-to-face and I'm a living polygraph. He was telling the truth about what he believed about the KGB killing von Dietrich's husband. The other crap, well, he was just trying to make an ass out of me."

Michaelis lowered his .38. Strang's attitude made sense. Dead men couldn't give you much information.

Michaelis walked to the door and peeked out cautiously.

"How's the weather out there?" Strang asked.

"Quiet. Don't see anything."

Strang eased himself up. "Well, let us proceed with caution. Check out the troops."

The front yard, covered with high grass almost going to seed, was empty. Some hundred feet away, behind overgrown rhododendrons, they could see the roof of the Continental.

They walked slowly down what was left of the path to the gate, keeping an eye on the bushes to the right and left.

Donald Tarboy was sitting calmly in the Continental. He reached over and flipped open the door.

"They went that-a-way," he said, pointing south. "Talked to Angie on the CB and warned her."

"Good," said Strang, sliding in.

Michaelis holstered his .38 and got in the back.

"See if you can raise Angie," said Strang.

Donald switched on the CB and spoke softly into the microphone. He waited a couple of minutes and then turned to Strang. "If she's receiving, she's not answering."

Strang said, "Pull in her tracking transmitter and get moving! Tell Ronald to follow."

Donald slipped the big car into gear and plunged forward, rubber burning. Keeping his eyes on the road, he blindly fiddled with one of the dials on the instrument panel. Michaelis could hear a faint beeping.

"I said tell Ronald—" Strang yelled, then grabbed the microphone and said, "Ronald Tarboy, come in. Tune in Angie's tracking transmitter and follow. Ten four."

Richard's voice came back on the speaker. "Ain't no Ronald here. Would you want to be speaking to Richard?"

Strang said loudly, "Get going, you Britchard! You're going to aggravate me once too often."

Expertly driven by Donald, the Continental sped along

curving suburban roads and managed to keep Angie's signal strong. They were soon on the turnpike heading for New York.

Richard whipped past them in the BMW going about ninety. He waved, grinning. Donald floored the gas pedal, and the Continental moved alongside.

"Cut out that crap! No goddamned racing!" yelled Strang. He motioned for the BMW to go ahead. Donald slowed and dropped behind.

"Let Richard get close to her. If she has any of those scumbags in the car, they won't recognize the BMW," said Strang.

They were soon crossing the Whitestone Bridge, heading for Long Island.

"At least the fuckups aren't going into the city," said Strang. They could not only lose Angie in Manhattan traffic, but she could lose the quarry.

Donald Tarboy said, "How about a pool? La Guardia, JFK International, or one of the airport hotels?"

Strang pulled out his wallet. "I've got five on JFK."

They finally found the BMW parked near the United Airlines building at JFK International. Strang collected five dollars from Donald, who muttered disgustedly and said, "I wanted JFK and you made me take La Guardia by jumping in with your old five dollars before I had a chance to open my mouth."

Strang said, "Well, be faster putting your goddamned money where your mouth is."

Michaelis sat tight, having ignored the game.

Richard Tarboy left the BMW and slid into the back seat of the Continental. He lit a cigarette and settled back. "The two hard cases pulled up here with the big guy. You won't believe this, but the big guy looked sort of happy. Spaced-out happy. Just a quiet, gentle zombie. They were in a maroon-colored Oldsmobile. One of them stayed in the car with the big guy and the other one went in to the Finnair ticket counter. I got behind him in line. Three tourist-class tickets for Helsinki leaving at eight tonight."

"Finnair? In the United Airlines building?" asked Michaelis.

Strang said, "Yep, they're in there." He turned to look at Richard. "Angie followed them away from the airport?"

"Yeah. What took you guys?"

"Accident. Took us ten minutes to get around it," said Donald.

Strang scratched his head. "Helsinki. Practically in walking distance of Leningrad. Could those scumbags be Russians?"

Michaelis asked, "If they were Russians, wouldn't they use Aeroflot?"

"You got a point there," said Strang. He moved his arm off the seat back and faced forward, sticking a cigarette in his mouth. "Anyway that flight stops at Amsterdam and Copenhagen. They might have plans for him in one of those two places. Also, maybe they don't want anybody to see him taken aboard Aeroflot. He stands out like six sore thumbs."

"That's true," said Michaelis. He wondered why Strang was so familiar with flights to Helsinki.

Strang glanced at his wristwatch: 4:30 P.M. He lit the cigarette and turned back to them. "We can't let those KGB turds get away with this! Ronald—er, Richard—I want you to trot in and get us some tickets to Helsinki." He pulled out his wallet and thumbed through the bills, muttering. "Hell, I don't have *that* much cash. I'll have to go in and put it on American Express."

Michaelis accompanied Strang into the building and stood by while he signed for two tourist-class tickets and three first-class seats to Helsinki and return. The Tarboys, who would not be recognized, were to keep an eye on Swift and his captors. Strang explained that he, Angie, and Michaelis would hide out in the first-class lounge and board the big DC-10 without being seen by the passengers in the tourist section. With luck the whole party could get to Helsinki without making waves.

As they walked away from the Finnair counter, Michaelis asked, "How do you plan to get weapons through airport security? It gets tighter every day."

"Don't worry," said Strang.

"Okay. They give us trouble, we kick them to death."

Strang stopped and took Michaelis's arm. "Look, we travel clean, but wherever we stop, Amsterdam, Copenhagen, or Helsinki, I got contacts, see. Weapons are no problem."

Michaelis nodded. Strang apparently knew his way around every major city in the world.

They strolled on back to the Continental.

Strang said, "But we got another problem. I just remembered, you have to get off the damned plane in both Amsterdam and Copenhagen and wait for a while. We'll be in with all the in-transit passengers."

As they approached the curb, Richard Tarboy got out of the Continental and returned to the BMW.

Michaelis said, "Well, they don't know Angie. All we need is wigs, sunglasses, and maybe mustaches."

Strang belched softly. "Yeah, I've got that crap, but I sure hate like hell wearing it. It's uncomfortable, and I'm such a handsome guy it's a shame to disguise it." He turned and leaned over the BMW. "Ronald, you in there? You in that little fart bucket?"

Richard moved over to the window and looked up. "You're insulting me and a mighty fine car. The car's going to bite you in the ass while I go out looking for some jerk named Ronald."

Strang scratched his head. "Well, when you get back, take the little fart bucket home."

As they climbed into the Continental, Strang in front with Donald and Michaelis in the back, Strang said, "Angie will be in touch with us. If they went into Manhattan, she probably lost them."

Donald started the engine and snaked the big car through JFK's complex exit roads.

Michaelis said, "I've never been to Helsinki. How big is it, about a half-million people?"

"Yeah, about," said Strang. "Interesting. Lousy with Russian *tourists.* We'll need those damned disguises for more than the trip."

11

FINNAIR'S FIRST-CLASS SECTION WAS STAFFED, AS MIGHT BE EXpected, by willowy blue-eyed blond stewardesses offering gourmet delights. Dom Pérignon, vodka, scotches, bourbons, vintage wines, cognac, Lapland beer, and Finnish smorgasbord.

Angie, who had checked the tourist section on boarding, again walked back to look around after takeoff. Returning, she reported that the quarry was wedged between his captors in a three-seat section, making it a very tight squeeze. He seemed to be sleeping.

Strang held out his glass for more Dom Pérignon. "Well, nothing much can happen until Amsterdam. Might as well enjoy." He twirled the corner of his big fake Guardsman's mustache and winked at Angie.

She lifted her glass. "Here's to Helsinki. Thank God it's summer."

Strang slapped his head. "This shitty wig is not only hot, it's itchy. And the lousiest part is you can't scratch." He was wearing gray curly hair to match his gray-brown mustache.

Angie looked around to see if any of the other first-class passengers had heard him. The section was sparsely filled, and the nine other passengers were some distance from their group.

Michaelis sipped Chivas Regal on the rocks. His wig of red hair was hot, too. A few more scotches and it would be even hotter. He had decided against a mustache. With red hair and wraparound sunglasses to wear when they left the compartment it was unlikely that he would be recognized from the brief meeting in Swift's cottage. He finished the scotch and decided to switch to Lapland beer. The smorgasbord items were many and thirst-producing.

Later they dined on *filets de veau strasbourgeoise, coeurs d'artichaut, pommes boulangères,* salads, Finnish cheeses, fruit, *bavaroise au rhum* with *sauce au chocolat,* all accompanied by Dom Pérignon. Coffee with cognac followed. Michaelis lit his pipe, but propped it in the ashtray after a few puffs, feeling drowsy. He looked at Strang and Angie, who were seated across the aisle. They were both asleep.

Bowing to Strang's superior knowledge of tactics, Michaelis had followed his lead without questioning. He now had some second thoughts. With the writer and his captors virtually prisoners aboard the giant jet, it would be easy to obtain Swift's release.

He leaned across the aisle and nudged Strang.

Strang was immediately awake and alert without moving a muscle. "Yeah?"

"I'm wondering if we shouldn't tell the captain what's up and ask him to have the Dutch police waiting at Schiphol."

"What would that get us?"

"Well, at least the guy wouldn't get killed or tortured."

Strang raised his eyebrows. "Wouldn't get killed or tortured in the *near future."*

"We're in a position to help him now. The future is not our responsibility."

Strang shook his head slowly. "Then we don't find out anything. Look, they got papers proving they're taking an emotionally disturbed guy home to Amsterdam, Copenhagen, Helsinki, you name it. They couldn't have gotten him on the plane otherwise. They got a valid passport with his picture on it. They got everything they need. All that happens is we get bogged down for days in Amsterdam while the police try to check out who's telling the truth."

"Well, for God's sake, what's the alternative?"

Strang shook out a cigarette and lit it. "We wait until the time is right and take Swift back. We also find out more about what the hell is going on."

"He could still get killed as a result of our waiting."

Strang grunted. "In his line he's going to get killed sooner or later anyway."

Michaelis pried his pipe from the small ashtray and lit it. "The Dutch police could get him detoxified in a couple of days and see that he was completely rational."

Strang turned to face him. "Look, Professor, if you want to run your own show, alone, hop to it. If you're going to work with me, we do it my way."

A slow flush of anger spread through Michaelis, then gradually dissolved. He had gotten himself into something bigger than he knew how to handle. His survival depended on Strang and his army. Whom else could he turn to? Inexperienced kids in his classes? His friends on the faculty? He had to work with Strang or find a completely new identity fast.

He said, "Okay, Sting, we'll do it your way."

Strang smiled, settled back in his seat, and closed his eyes.

At Schiphol, Swift and his kidnapers stayed with the in-transit group. Swift walked slowly, his eyes blank and lifeless. His captors settled him in a chair between them and sat, each holding one of Swift's arms. They stared straight ahead.

Michaelis strolled away, glancing idly at the duty-free shops. Big wheels of Dutch cheese. One shop featured a giant, put-it-together-yourself cookie house. *Knusperhous. Maison de pain d'épice. Peperfroekhuisse. Casa de dulce. Papparkakshus.* Was there a child in the world who wouldn't be fascinated by this monstrous collection of cookies? The box was as big as an orange crate, with the finished product depicted in full color. Michaelis wondered how one stuck them together to make the house, but could not read the directions in Dutch. It would take a large birthday party of kids to demolish it. Maybe if he and Diane had had children. He dismissed the thought. Sentimental nostalgia. Hard to picture Diane as a mother anyway. He'd like to marry and have a family someday. He had the resources to give them a good start in life, and maybe they'd get a better handle on it than he had. He recognized that here again he was thinking of himself as a failure. All his friends looked upon him as highly successful.

He returned to the departure gate and waited with Strang and Angie, mildly depressed.

The stop at Copenhagen had been brief. They had barely left the plane before it was time to return.

Michaelis yawned, glancing at his watch: 6:45 A.M. New York time. They were on the approach to Helsinki, scheduled to land in fifteen minutes, 2:00 P.M. Helsinki time. A night without much real sleep, though he had dozed intermittently.

Michaelis yawned again and then said, "Hope we don't lose them. Half-million people isn't much by New York standards, but it's still a pretty good-sized city. Plenty of places to get lost in."

Strang, watching Michaelis, had to yawn himself. "If they could shrink that guy about twenty percent, he'd be easier to hide. Anyhow, the Tarboys will try to grab separate cabs and tail them."

Angie asked, "We're all booked into the Intercontinental?"

"Yeah. But I told the Tarboys if these creeps land in a hotel to try to get themselves a room there."

"I like the Intercontinental," said Angie.

Strang shrugged.

"I like that dining room and nightclub on the top floor with the big glass windows overlooking the Baltic Sea. And the dancing!"

"Dancing, schmancing," said Strang.

Angie glanced at Michaelis. "Sting dances like a bear that just woke up from hibernating all winter."

Michaelis laughed.

Sting said, "This disco stuff makes me feel silly. Everybody's prancing and preening and performing by themselves. A man's got to be a fucking exhibitionist to want to dance that way."

"Go back and crawl into your cave," said Angie, smiling. "There are plenty of Finns around who'll dance with me. Or maybe even a real live professor."

• • •

Coming from New York's wet heat, Helsinki's summer was delightfully cool. The cab worked its way along crowded streets, past buildings that looked vaguely Russian, many painted dark mustard yellow, a few faded green; the rest were weary graystone. There were frequent glimpses of the sparkling black waters of the Baltic.

Angie said to Michaelis, "While you're here you should see the Sibelius monument and the cave church. They're both fantastic."

Strang made a sucking click of disgust. "This ain't exactly a sight-seeing tour we're on, sweetie."

"So what. There are always a lot of hours when there's nothing to do. He should go to Hvittrask and see Eliel Saarinen's houses. Or even to the famous health spa, Haikko. Haikko Manor is beautiful."

"Haikko won't do him much good, honey. He goes farting around like a tourist his health's going to be beyond repair." Strang slapped his knee and guffawed.

"Plenty of museums, too?" asked Michaelis tongue in cheek.

"Yes," said Angie, miffed. "But if Sting's going to be crude, I'm going to shut up."

"Aw, honey, I didn't mean to—"

"Yes, you did."

Strang yelled, "I did not, and that's an order!"

They rode the rest of the way to the hotel in silence.

Michaelis sat in his room at the Intercontinental familiarizing himself with the Heckler & Koch P9 pistol Strang had produced within an hour of their arrival. He loaded the magazine with 9mm Parabellum cartridges, shoved it home, and then sighted on an imaginary enemy. It felt comfortable in his hand. He fastened the detachable shoulder stock and aimed it rifle-fashion. More accuracy, undoubtedly, but awkward to carry around.

Strang had reserved a three-room suite consisting of two bedrooms with a lounge in between. Michaelis's bedroom overlooked the front entrance of the Hesperia, another luxury hotel almost next door. He stared out for a moment, watching an airport bus unload.

Strang gave a short knock and entered. He glanced at the pistol lying on the sofa. "That's a damned good little weapon. Better than the thirty-eight you left home."

Michaelis said, "I'll take your word for it. Shoulder stock! It must be powerful."

"Yeah, well—"

"What's next on the agenda?"

Strang slouched into one of the easy chairs. "Just heard from Donald. Our man and his friends are holed up in the Kalastajatorppa Hotel."

"The *what?*"

"Well, you pronounce it, goddammit."

"I'm sure I couldn't even spell it."

Strang smiled. "Anyhow, Donald and Richard got a room on the same floor, right down the hall. They're taking turns keeping an eye on the situation. So far no one has entered or left the room."

Michaelis yawned, not from boredom but from fatigue. "So what's the next step?"

"I think we go over very late in the night and take our friend back. Five of us should be able to handle two of those schmucks."

Michaelis looked at the Heckler & Koch. "I should have a silencer for that thing."

"You have. I just didn't get around to unwrapping it."

Michaelis glanced at his watch. It was now 9:15 A.M. New York time, 4:15 P.M. Helsinki. He yawned again.

"I didn't get any sleep last night. So what do we do with Swift after we get him?"

Strang paced up and down, his hands locked behind him. "Well, let me explain something. The Kalastajatorppa is a very big hotel. Three large buildings connected by tunnels bored through solid rock. I sent Angie over to try to book a room in Building A, which is across the road from Building B, where Swift is being held."

He paused to scratch his head. "So we go over and discombobulate the two scumbags, zip Swift down the steps to the tunnel and across to the other building. We hole him up there until the drugs wear off."

Michaelis smiled. "Hope he doesn't have withdrawal

symptoms." He had a mental image of Swift thrashing around, demanding a fix, and trying to throw all five of them out the window. He yawned again.

Strang asked, "Why don't you sack out for a few hours? I slept pretty well on the plane, but you look like you could use some."

Michaelis nodded, heading gratefully for his bed. He drifted off thinking that Strang's ploy was pretty good. If it worked, the opposition would be searching the whole city, overlooking Strang's audacity in hiding Swift practically on the premises.

At 8:00 P.M. Strang woke Michaelis. A waiter was in the next room taking their orders for dinner. Michaelis put on his shoes, splashed water on his face, and joined the group in the living room. A frosty bottle of vodka rested in an ice bucket. The waiter, a short, stocky Finn with sand-colored hair, was waiting patiently.

"What are you two having?" Michaelis asked.

Angie said, "Veal, french fries, string beans, salad."

"And Chablis," said Strang.

"Sounds good to me," said Michaelis.

After the waiter left, Michaelis helped himself to vodka. Russian caviar, shrimp that had to be shelled, stuffed hard-boiled eggs, and small hot pastries filled with meat and cheese accompanied the vodka.

"You live well while you're working, Sting," said Michaelis.

"Why not?" asked Strang, cracking another shrimp.

"Sting is a gourmet *and* a gourmand," said Angie.

"Oh, yeah? Well, you don't do so bad packing it away, sweetie."

"I can't compete with a guy who puts away three dozen oysters as an appetizer."

Strang tossed down a small glass of vodka. "Oysters keep lead in the old pencil."

Angie blushed.

"That's an old wives' tale," said Michaelis.

Strang coughed. "Don't disillusion me. If you believe in something, it works."

Dinner arrived with two bottles of Chablis in a large ice

bucket. They ate, drank, and laughed more than necessary. Michaelis decided that the other two were as nervous as he was about the approaching confrontation. Tangling with the KGB was no trivial matter.

When they finished eating, Michaelis said, "I need to get out and jog about five miles."

Angie said, "Sting's planning to hit the Kalastajatorppa about three A.M. So there's loads of time. You can dance it off upstairs."

Sting said, "Oh, God," drawing it out like a groan.

Angie stood up. "Proper shirts, ties, and jackets, men," she said, then went into their bedroom and shut the door.

"Women can be a real pain in the ass at times," said Strang. "I hate these damned discos."

Michaelis went to his room to bathe and dress. He had missed his morning shave and shower and it was now afternoon in New York. He put on a lightweight gray summer suit, a blue shirt, and a black knit tie. He buckled the new holster Sting had supplied to his belt and slipped the P9 into it, sliding the holster far enough back so that it wouldn't show with his jacket unbuttoned. He tucked the silencer in his jacket pocket.

Stepping out of the elevator on the hotel's top floor, they edged into a crowded corridor. The large bar lounge was packed, wall to wall, with every table occupied and standees four deep at the bar. The ballroom-sized nightclub was equally crowded. Dancers were jiving to "Singing in the Rain" played at disco tempo, which amused Michaelis. Surely the song went back to the thirties, if not the twenties. Old movies on TV. Jimmy Durante?

The music finished and the band immediately shifted to fox-trot music. Something for everybody. Strang grudgingly allowed Angie to pull him out to the dance floor.

Michaelis worked his way through the crowd at the bar and ordered a vodka. Ten marks. With the mark three and a half to the dollar, the drink was $2.85, about on a par with a top-quality place in the United States. But this was native vodka. Imported scotch would probably have to be paid for in gold.

A girl squeezed in next to him.

"You are American, yes?"

"Yes."

"I am Russian princess."

He turned to look at her more closely. In her twenties, she was shapely and attractive, with coal-black hair and milky complexion.

"Really?"

"No. My great-grandmother was lady-in-waiting to the czarina. We are old White Russian family."

More likely old KGB family, Michaelis thought.

"What you do back in America?"

"I'm a journalist. I specialize in politics."

She looked alarmed. "I am not political."

He shrugged.

She took his arm and guided him to a less crowded spot. "Later you come to my room, five sixteen. We have a drink and talk, no?"

Seeing the look on his face, she added quickly, "We drink and talk only. I am not bad woman."

He smiled. "Some other time, perhaps. Tonight I am engaged."

She lowered her eyes. "Before you leave Helsinki, yes? There is something important to discuss." She held out her hand. "I am Olga Kazamanov."

He held her hand briefly. "I'm Daniel McGuffey." He had to spell it for her.

She turned with a smile and slipped into the crowd, leaving Michaelis bemused. She had to be KGB or a high-class prostitute. And if he had learned anything at all about women in his thirty-six years, she was no prostitute.

Angie came to claim him for some disco numbers. Sharing Strang's feeling, Michaelis did not care too much for this type of dancing. Too stylized and coyly sexual. When a couple danced cheek to cheek, body to body, moving as one body, it was honestly sexual. Disco was good exercise, however, and the overstuffed feeling left him.

Later he drifted into the roulette room. This type of gambling was legal only as a charitable operation, the proceeds going to hospitals and other worthy organizations. Bets were limited to one-mark chips, with no more than one chip allowed on any one position.

The croupier was Olga. She smiled but said nothing as he gave her fifty marks and received a deck of chips.

So that was her cover. But was she necessarily KGB? Maybe she was CIA. He put a chip on 9 and one on black. Nine would come up soon, it always did. Nine was his lucky number. And playing black stretched the number of chips he needed to lure 9 into action. KGB, CIA? Let Strang figure that one out.

The ball stopped on 9 three times, and when Strang came to fetch him, Michaelis was a hundred marks ahead.

"I don't get any kick out of this penny-ante stuff," said Strang.

Michaelis cashed in his chips, winked at Olga, and strolled out.

It was now 2:30 A.M. They sat in the suite going over final plans. Angie had been a busy woman. Her rented car was waiting down in the parking area. All locks on doors that needed to be opened had been checked for pickability. All were relatively simple. She had even rented a collapsible wheelchair in case Swift was incapable of walking.

Strang jerked and pulled the wheelchair into operating condition and stood staring at it. "I hope the sonofabitch can fit into this thing. He must weigh at least three hundred."

"It was the biggest I could get," said Angie.

"He'll fit," said Michaelis.

Strang said, "He better. Otherwise we got to get us four native bearers and two very strong poles."

The silence in the hotel at 3:00 A.M. was absolute. If there was even a mouse stirring, he was being as quiet as a burglar who has inadvertently broken into a funeral home.

They crept down the fire stairs on rubber-soled shoes, and made it to the parking area without meeting any Intercontinental personnel. With Angie at the wheel, Strang and Michaelis pushed the rented Ford until the engine caught softly, avoiding the clatter of the starter.

Donald and Richard Tarboy were waiting for them at the fire exit door of Kalastajatorppa's Building A, and led them up to the third floor to take a brief look at the room Angie had rented for Swift's recovery. It was adequate. A real problem would be to keep Swift quiet until he made the trip back to reality. The man who supplied Strang with weapons had agreed to try to locate a discreet doctor who might be able to help speed up the process.

They left the room and headed for the basement entrance to the tunnel. This door was locked, but Angie managed to pick it in less than two minutes. She flipped on the lights and they entered the long white tube. Rough-hewn, blasted out of rock, the curved sides and ceiling gleamed starkly with fresh white paint, so shiny that Michaelis wondered if it was enamel.

"Weird," whispered Angie.

They moved quickly and silently into the white cone. It seemed to go on forever, a snow tunnel headed right for the North Pole.

Angie picked the lock at the other end and they headed up the fire stairs to Swift's room. The lock on his door was more difficult. After about ten minutes she managed to release both bolts. She pushed the door very slowly and quietly until it was open about an inch.

Strang wadded up a section of newspaper and set fire to it, dropping it on the hall tiles. When it finished burning, he ground out the glowing ashes with his foot. Little was left but a strong smell of smoke in the air.

Angie rapped loudly on the door, pushing it open and flipping the light switch. Trying her best to imitate a Finn speaking English, she called, "Please do not panic, sir. There is a small fire on this floor, nothing serious I assure you! However, we must evacuate the rooms until we are certain it is under control."

The agent with the button nose and large mustache hurried out into the hall, sniffing. He was wearing striped pajamas. Strang enveloped him in a bear hug and shoved a handkerchief into his mouth. Michaelis grabbed his arms, pulled them back, and snapped on handcuffs. Angie taped the gag in place, then bent and taped his ankles together.

At the same time, the agent's chalky-faced partner was sitting up in bed, his hands groping blindly on the night table for the small box containing his contact lenses. The Tarboys sauntered over and quickly made him as immobile as his partner.

Swift was snoring away in a big easy chair, his ankles cuffed to the chair legs, his arms bound snugly to his chest.

Swift's kidnapers were deposited on the twin beds in which they had been sleeping so peacefully only minutes earlier. Now they were twisting and turning and making muffled sounds behind their gags.

Angie bent to pick the locks on Swift's ankle cuffs. The others worked to untie the elaborate system of ropes holding his upper body. They then fitted him into a much more efficient method of restraint, an oversize straitjacket Angie had obtained from a local hospital supply company. The jacket secured behind, the four men lifted Swift into the wheelchair and strapped him securely to it.

Before leaving, Strang's army divided the room and bath into five sectors. Each participant made a microscopic search of an assigned area, gathering up any documents, letters, books, magazines, or other materials which might shed light on the situation.

The operation had taken fifteen minutes from the time they had grouped in front of Swift's door. It coincided exactly with the timetable Strang had prepared.

Bumping Swift's more than three hundred pounds of body and wheelchair down four flights of not overly wide fire stairs was not easy. Strang, Michaelis, and the Tarboys were perspiring.

Donald Tarboy said, "We should have just dropped this fucker down the elevator shaft."

"Watch your language, there's a lady present," said Strang.

Richard Tarboy said, "Think about the fun we gonna have pushing him *up* to the third floor in the other building."

"We're going to need a block and tackle," said Donald.

"Stop bitching and concentrate on the task at hand," said Strang.

The basement corridor was finally reached. They rolled Swift quickly to the tunnel entrance and started back through the white tube.

The group was within forty feet of the end of the tunnel when a trim, obviously feminine figure suddenly appeared at the exit. Resting against her shoulder was the stock of a

Walther machine pistol. A wicked-looking magazine extending downward promised a surplus of firepower.

She dropped to the floor with the speed of a trained soldier and lay confronting the group in the prone position, offering a difficult target.

"Drop your weapons!" she said loudly. "One burst of this and you'll be the biggest lump of Swiss cheese in Finland!"

Michaelis stared, amazed. It was his croupier friend, Olga Kazamanov. And she didn't have a trace of an accent. At the moment he was walking behind the wheelchair. He whipped out his Heckler & Koch P9 and held the muzzle to Swift's head.

He yelled, "Put your gun down or I'll blow his brains out!"

Out of the corner of his mouth Strang said, "Now you're getting the hang of this business, Professor."

12

OLGA CONTINUED TO LIE THERE, HER MACHINE PISTOL READY TO print out her initials on each of them. Finally she said, "You sound like real Americans, not KGB Americans."

Strang yelled, "You got it, sister, we're sons of the red, white, and blue."

"And daughters," added Angie.

Olga smiled. "I heard you were here. But just what the hell do you think you're going to do with my helpless boyfriend?"

Michaelis said, "We're going to take him to another hotel room, get a doctor, try to get him detoxified. He's drugged to the eyeballs. We *stole* him from the KGB."

Olga thought for a few seconds, then asked, "Who was known as the Sultan of Swat?"

"Babe Ruth," said Michaelis.

She nodded slightly. "Who was the Manassa Mauler?"

"Jack Dempsey," said Sting.

She tucked her feet back and levered herself to a standing position with both hands still cradling the machine pistol. It continued to point directly at them.

"I think we're probably on the same side," she said.

"Truce?" asked Michaelis.

She nodded, lowering the machine pistol and walking toward them.

"Let's get him to that room you mentioned. He looks in awful shape."

It took a team effort to get Swift up the steps from the basement in the Kalastajatorppa's Building A. With the Tarboys above pulling, and Sting and Michaelis below pushing, they made it with many muffled grunts and groans. Once in the back area of the first floor and into the self-service freight elevator, they were able to get him into the room and onto one of the twin beds quickly.

Angie left with the Tarboys to return the wheelchair to their suite in the Intercontinental.

Olga, whose name turned out to be Leslie Greenhaven, slumped into one of the chairs. She asked, "What are you jerkos doing messing into a situation like this? Tomorrow every KGB lurking in Helsinki will be on your tail."

Sting nodded. "Should have killed the bastards. Angie's tough, but that kind of thing turns her stomach. Then the professor here would probably have got all upset about it, too."

She stared at Michaelis. "Professor?"

Michaelis smiled. "I'm Jonathan Michaelis, currently serving time in the Political Science Department of Crendon University."

She nodded, still puzzled. "Not Dan McGuffey, eh?" With an absentminded look she added, "Jonathan. That's my man's middle name."

"Who?" asked Michaelis.

She pointed to Swift. "That big lug. Thomas Jonathan Swift."

Michaelis glanced at Sting. "See, your document is okay."

Sting shrugged.

Leslie asked, "What's with the document?"

Michaelis explained their mission, mentioning Strang's trips to Greece, Australia, and Taiwan to get signed confessions.

She stared wide-eyed at Michaelis, then at Sting, and then back to Michaelis. In a few seconds she began to giggle. The quixotic nature of their undertaking was too much for her.

"I can't believe this," she muttered.

Sting was annoyed. "You can't believe a man would want to protect his honor? The bribery scandal caused Michaelis here to lose an appointment in Washington. He would have been one of the top advisers to the *President of the United States.*"

Her gaze was more interested when she shifted her eyes to Michaelis.

She turned back to Sting. "We've got a quid pro quo thing here. I want one of you guys to stay here with me until Tom comes out of it. As soon as he's functioning I'll make arrangements to get you out of Helsinki. It's that or the KGB will ship you over to Leningrad for a fate worse than death. *If* you're both still alive."

Michaelis swallowed hard. Sting laughed. He said, "Okay, sister, you got a deal." He stood up. "I gotta call a friend who can put me on to a doctor who'll keep his trap shut."

Leslie shook her head. "I'll take care of the doctor."

She went to the unoccupied bed and perched on the edge to telephone. She managed her call in a way that not even a portion of a word could be heard.

She stood up and turned to Michaelis. "Now I remember you. You're the investigative reporter who had half of Congress and all of the lobbyists in Washington suffering dire states of constipation."

Sting said, "That's the corniest euphemism for *scared shitless* I have ever heard."

Leslie turned to Michaelis. "How come this peasant uses words like *euphemism*?"

Michaelis said, "He's an enigma within an enigma."

Sting turned to stare at Michaelis. "Sonofabitch! Now I remember you. You put the whammy on my ex-wife's brother, a no-good sergeant in the NYPD. He was so crooked he could only see around corners, not straight ahead. Shake, pal." He held out his hand and Michaelis reluctantly shook it.

Sting scratched his scalp, disturbing a few of the yellow strands of hair which didn't quite cover it. He said, "Well, I guess you're elected to stay here with this beautiful but deadly dame. Angie's good, but I'm not sure she's a match for the KGB, even with the Tarboys around. I got to get the hell out and stay with her."

Michaelis nodded. "You better had. But keep in touch. I gather our deadly dame is going to use her organization, whatever it may be, to get us out of Helsinki."

He turned to Leslie. "Right, deadly dame?"

Leslie had a grim smile. "Call me that once more and I'll trade you to the KGB for a psychotic cryptographer they're holding."

Sting left the room with a quick wave of his hand.

Michaelis asked, "What if I prefaced it with *beautiful?"*

She continued to smile. "If you have any thoughts of a quickie while papa sleeps, forget it."

"He's your father?"

"My husband. And quite capable of tearing you limb from limb, slowly. That is, when he gets his wits back."

Michaelis laughed. "You could tell him I'm gay, and that it couldn't possibly have happened." He mentally kicked himself, wondering why he was talking this way. He really had no thought of trying to seduce Leslie Greenhaven. Maybe danger had provoked it.

The doctor arrived. He was short and slender, a typical Finn who looked vital and refreshed, as though he had just come from a sauna where he had been thoroughly flailed with wet leaves. He chatted for a minute in Finnish with Leslie, then went to the bed to examine Thomas Swift.

Michaelis had to help him turn Swift over so that he could loosen the straps of the straitjacket. He examined Swift carefully, listening to his heart with a stethoscope, taking his temperature with a rectal thermometer, taking his blood pressure, bending over to smell his breath, and pulling back his eyelids to stare with a small flashlight. He took a hypodermic needle from his case, filled it, and gave Swift a shot. He then turned to Leslie and spoke again in rapid Finnish.

Leslie said to Michaelis, "He needs you to help him turn Tom over and fasten the straps. He thinks we had better keep him in restraint until he's fully recovered. He may get a bit wild when he's coming out of it."

Michaelis helped the doctor turn Swift over and fasten the straps, then turn him again so that he would lie on his back. It wasn't easy. They really needed a derrick.

After the doctor left, Michaelis asked, "How long before he's going to be rational?"

Leslie shook her head. "No more than two days, he hopes."

Seeing the look of consternation on Michaelis's face, she said, "Cheer up. You get to spend two whole nights with me, and there's only one bed for the two of us."

Michaelis grinned.

She said, "I think you'll find the lounge chair quite comfortable."

He continued smiling. "I knew you were going to say something like that. But I thought you'd be fair enough to share the bed in shifts."

She shrugged. "Whatever. Anyway, it will take me at least that long to arrange to get five of you on a plane safely. We're a bit shorthanded. Economy measures all around these days. Even some of my best friends in the KGB have been laid off."

13

KENT CARBIN, MASTER OF THE GATE OF THE VON DIETRICH CASTLE and boss of some sixty security guards, waited patiently for Wolfgang Brillhagen to appear for a conference. They met daily in one of the castle's small reception rooms.

Carbin was six foot two with wide shoulders and a slender, muscular body. He had curly gray-white hair clipped short, prematurely this color as he was only forty-five, and bushy eyebrows over eyes the color of glazed plums. His big mouth was set in a permanent frown. He had a thin, rather long and pointed triangle of a nose and a high forehead. Wearing army chinos and an officer's shirt with a shoulder patch of blue with white lettering reading "Chief of Security," he stood perpetually at attention, and even sat at attention, his back as straight as a rule.

Brillhagen entered the room and said, "Please sit down, Mr. Carbin."

Carbin sat without relaxing any muscles.

Brillhagen sprawled in a chair. "Any new problems?" he asked.

Carbin shook his head so slightly that it was hardly noticeable. "Herr Kassenbach's lawyers continue to come daily demanding to see Mrs. von Dietrich. I continue to tell them that she is not in residence at this time."

Brillhagen nodded. "And they continue to ask when she will be in residence," he said.

"Yes, sir."

Brillhagen said, "We have no real problem with them. Let them sue and be damned."

"Yes, sir."

Brillhagen rubbed his chin. "I'm sure I don't need to

tell you again to have your men always prepared for any group trying to force entry. Shoot to wound, and if necessary, to kill. The law is on our side."

"Yes, sir."

Brillhagen leaned forward. "I don't anticipate any violence from Mr. Kassenbach, but there are others who will stop at nothing. If an attack occurs, you will probably have prior warning from our outside patrol, but your preparedness should not be dependent upon this. Be constantly alert."

"Yes, sir."

About every third day Brillhagen repeated his warnings, but Carbin was a patient man and he pretended to listen carefully each time.

Brillhagen stood up. "If you have nothing further to report—"

"No, sir."

"Then back to your post."

"Yes, sir." Carbin stood up, did an about-face, and marched off.

Brillhagen smiled. In spite of his sophistication, his Teutonic soul responded to this rigid military brevity.

He strode back to one of the castle's elevators and rode it up to Athena's suite.

She was standing by one of the huge windows staring at the forest below. She turned as he knocked briefly and entered the room.

She said, "Wolf, I am so sick of being a prisoner here. What am I to do? I want to go to Paris, Rome, Cannes. I want to see my friends."

He strolled over and faced her. She put her hands on his chest. He cupped her elbows. "Marry me. We will leave whenever you wish, and I will protect you."

She sighed. "And I will get you killed and I will be held prisoner or worse."

He smiled. "Well, marry me anyway. It will provide a diversion for you."

She laughed.

He said, "No, I am quite serious. You know that I have always been in love with you."

She pushed slightly, moving away an inch. "We are like brother and sister. We have been close and affectionate friends since childhood."

He laughed. "If that's the case, my thoughts of you have frequently been incestuous."

She stood silently staring into his eyes. Finally she said, "Wolf, for family reasons I married a man I did not love. I'm not sure it made either of us very happy. I know that for me it was a barren relationship."

He shrugged, looking down.

She put her hand under his chin and raised it gently. She said, "Wolf, if it will make you feel any better, I'll go to bed with you. After all, I am no shrinking virgin."

He grimaced. "You'd lend your body in payment for my being your protector? I could as well go to a prostitute."

She grasped his shoulders and shook them gently. "Wolf, if I did this, it would be because of my great affection for you. I do not need to buy your protection."

She wiped a tear from the corner of her eye. "I wish with all my heart that I could say I love you."

He hugged her, muttering, "This ridiculous situation has us both crazy."

He guided her over to a sofa and sat down, pulling her down beside him.

"Thena, we must get rid of this monster. Arrange to sell it to the United States government. It is the only country you can depend upon to use it with restraint and protect it as well. Whatever they promise, they will of course develop it for military purposes, but there will be powerful *restraint*. Just as they have proved with nuclear weapons. Remember, it has been more than forty years since Hiroshima."

Athena stared straight ahead. "I would rather destroy the plans than have them used for killing. Don't you realize the weapon they could create would be exactly *a hundred times* more destructive than any nuclear weapon?"

Brillhagen shook his head. "Thena, numbers are meaningless if the weapon is never used. In spite of what you say about the international power brokers, your father's great discovery *would* be used for power produced at hundreds of times less than the cost of oil. No group would be powerful enough to keep it from public use. No sane person wants to be dependent upon fanatical Moslem theocracies. I assure you—"

Athena put her hand over Brillhagen's mouth. "Wolf, your logic is unassailable. But my emotions do not respond to logic. I see millions of children mutilated and dead."

Gently removing her hand, Wolf said, "Remember, not only has it been more than forty years since nuclear weapons were used, it has been sixty-eight years since poison gas has been used in a major war. The mere threat of awesome destructive power is sufficient."

Athena snuggled closer to him, touching his cheek and tucking her face into the angle of his neck and jaw. "Wolf, I feel that I am floating in some unreal existence, that I am myself becoming unreal, a being disconnected from life."

He sighed loudly. "It's this damnable isolation."

She kissed him, barely touching his lips, then pressed hard against his mouth, her lips parted.

After a moment she pushed away and said softly, "Wolf, come to bed with me tonight. I'm lonely and numb. I want to have some feelings again. At least I will know that I am still a woman."

Brillhagen continued to hold her tightly but did not reply. She was sure he would be there.

During their adult friendship Brillhagen had always had a mistress, a series of beautiful young women because he never stayed with one more than a year. He had never married, probably because he had always wanted to marry Athena and would settle for no less, even after she married Karl von Dietrich.

Had she made a mistake in suggesting it? Brillhagen's months of forced celibacy were caused by her situation, and she may have subconsciously rationalized that she should make it up to him. Or was it because she was bored? To face the truth of the matter, she wanted him, wanted the intimacy of an affair. Marriage was too serious. She did not want to marry him. She wasn't sure she wanted to marry anyone again. Men, especially German men, were too possessive, too demanding. They had to be in charge, to make the decisions. One had to be so sly, actually making the decisions but working them around so that the male egoist thought *he* made the decision. It was tiresome. On the other hand, she certainly did not want a wimp who looked to her for all the decisions.

She stood up, holding on to his hand. "Come, let's go for a swim."

"All right," said Brillhagen, not particularly enthusiastic.

They changed and went down to the two-hundred-foot-long pool that looked more like a lake. Athena dived in and swam several laps. Brillhagen merely collapsed on the grass and lay in the sun, his right forearm covering his eyes.

Athena finally climbed out and toweled herself dry. She pulled off her swimming cap and let her hair fall down her back. She was wearing her minimal bikini. If that didn't perk Wolf's interest, nothing would. She sprawled on the grass next to him.

Wolf sat up and stared at her, smiling.

Carbin marched up to them. He looked at Athena, his eyes moving from her breasts to her thighs with the stare of a man viewing a porn movie.

He said, "Sorry to disturb you, Mrs. von Dietrich. Lieutenant Goudenough is at the gate and would like to speak to you."

Lieutenant Goudenough was the officer who had arrested her for the murder of her husband.

Athena shrugged. "Let him come up here if he wishes to."

After Carbin left she slipped on a terry-cloth robe. "I hate these creeps who rape you with their eyes."

Brillhagen said lazily, "When you wear a swimsuit that revealing, what man could resist?"

Athena stared at him. She said, "I'm *so* sorry. It happens to be today's fashion. I'm sure you know that we silly women like to be wearing the current styles. Shall I get golf knickers for my swimming?"

Brillhagen said, "Thena, don't be angry. I am just jealous when other men see so much of you."

She sat down and tweaked his nose.

"Ouch!" said Brillhagen.

Lieutenant Goudenough approached. He was a heavy-set, large man with a red face and small, sunken gray eyes. His brown hair had a short, military cut.

Athena pulled a canvas chair over. "Please sit down, Lieutenant."

Goudenough eased himself into the chair, sighing. His shirt collar was dark with perspiration.

Athena pulled another chair close to him and sat down.

Brillhagen decided that he should pay attention and sat up, facing them.

Athena asked, "Well, Lieutenant, what can I do for you?"

Goudenough fanned his face with one huge hand. "Little matter has come to my attention. Your security men roughed up a newspaper reporter who managed to get over your wall. Think he used a utilities company cherry picker and shinnied down a rope. They broke his arm in the struggle."

Athena said, "He was lucky they didn't shoot him."

Goudenough wiped his mouth with his big hand. "Yeah, well, he has filed assault charges against the two men who roughed him up. You can prefer trespass charges against the reporter. Of course, assault is much more serious. I'm gonna have to arrest those two men."

He ran his tongue over his fat lower lip. "Thought I'd let you know so's you can have your lawyers down to bail them out."

Athena said, "Thank you. I appreciate it."

He nodded. "Welcome."

Then, wiping the perspiration from his forehead with a large red-and-black-checked handkerchief, he said, "Mainly I wanted to talk to you about your security here. Know more about your problems than you think. My son is a big shot in the FBI." He paused to smile shyly. "I owe you one for the bad time I gave you after your husband's death."

Athena smiled. "You were doing your job with the only evidence you had. I've never blamed you for it."

He nodded. "Most women would. Too emotional. Don't see things clearly."

Athena thought, male chauvinist too old to change, no point in discussing it. She merely smiled.

Goudenough said, "This cherry picker thing opens a nasty can of worms."

Athena asked, "What's a cherry picker?"

He looked surprised. "You never seen linesmen working on high electricity wires? This kind of truck they use has a long boom with a bucket on the end. Can raise a man sitting in the bucket maybe fifty feet high and swing him right over your wall."

Brillhagen said, "Our road patrol saw the cherry picker, and even though the man in the bucket seemed to be working on telephone lines, they took the precaution of stationing men opposite it on our side of the wall. They nabbed the guy before he could even let go of the rope."

Goudenough nodded. "You were lucky. Your road patrol covers the perimeter of the estate every twenty minutes. A cherry picker hidden in a side road could wait until the patrol passed, move in quickly, put two or three men over the wall, and move out of sight before the road patrol returned."

Brillhagen levered himself to his feet and got himself a chair. "You're right. Carbin should have thought of that, especially after we caught the guy. I should have thought of it."

Goudenough said, "Yeah, well, hindsight. I would guess no area of that wall should be unobserved for more than five minutes."

Brillhagen nodded. "We must have more patrols traveling the perimeter faster. I'll arrange it with Carbin."

Goudenough untangled himself from the canvas chair and stood up. "Well, nice talking to you people."

Athena said, "Thanks again for your advice."

"Welcome."

Brillhagen stood up. "I'll go down to the gatehouse and talk to Carbin. He's going to be two men short as it is, unless we can bail them out fast."

Athena said, "While you're there, call Mr. Brophy and ask him to send one of his young men to the Crendon police station immediately and make arrangements for someone to come here to pick up a check for whatever the bail amounts to."

Brillhagen nodded and strolled off with Goudenough.

Athena watched him until he was out of sight. She wondered what would happen tonight. If he doesn't come, she thought, I am a woman scorned. And hell hath no fury like a woman scorned. She giggled.

She threw off her robe and dived into the pool. After the heat of the sun the water seemed icy, but it was stimulating and somehow reassuring. She swam laps vigorously, her mind repeating a silly mantra, "I'm Athena von Dietrich and no one can harm me."

14

IN PREPARING FOR BED SHE IGNORED THE FRESH NIGHTGOWN Hilda had laid out for her and slid between the sheets naked. She giggled silently. Brillhagen would arrive wearing his pajamas, and there would be enough confusion getting him unclad.

He was so long in arriving she had dozed off and was awakened by him sliding in next to her, his hand gently caressing her breasts. She turned on her side, put her arms around him, and pressed her body tightly against his, feeling his hardness hinged against her stomach. Brillhagen had at least left off his pajama pants but was still wearing the jacket. She unbuttoned it and ran her fingers through the curly hair on his chest.

Brillhagen was a much more skillful lover than Karl had been. She managed to reach a shuddering, vibrating climax, something that had never happened with Karl. Later, Brillhagen pounded away inside her for two more climaxes before they nestled together and went to sleep.

The sky was still black outside when the bedroom lights suddenly flooded the room.

Athena sat up suddenly, the sheet falling away from her.

Carbin stood just inside the door, a machine pistol cradled under his arm. He stared at her breasts, a trace of saliva showing on the corner of his mouth.

Athena pulled the sheet up quickly, covering herself. Wolf struggled awake.

Carbin said, "Sorry to disturb you. Intruders have gotten into the grounds. Wanted to be sure they hadn't made it up to Mrs. von Dietrich's suite."

Wolf nodded. "You think they may have gotten into the castle?"

Carbin shook his head. "Working only with flashlights, it's hard to tell exactly where they are. There are a million dark hiding places around the castle grounds and in the woods. They're probably hiding in the woods, but it's better to be safe than sorry."

Brillhagen said, "Yes, of course."

"As soon as daylight comes we'll be able to find them," said Carbin.

"How in the hell did they get in?" asked Wolf.

Carbin stared blankly. "Don't know. Not with a cherry picker, that's for sure. If they scaled the wall, no alarms sounded in the gatehouse. I don't know how they could have avoided tripping them off."

Brillhagen asked, "Could they have parachuted in?"

Carbin smiled. "There's been no sound of a plane."

Athena said, "It's fanciful but how about a balloon? It could glide over if the wind was right."

Carbin shrugged, smiling. He said, "Well, that would at least limit them to one or two men at the most. I've never seen a very large basket under one of those balloons."

He turned to Wolf. "Mr. Brillhagen, can we leave Mrs. von Dietrich in your protection? You have adequate weapons, I know, and I think if you lock yourself in the suite she will be safe. I want a large detail to search the castle, and adequate men searching outside, too."

Wolf nodded. "I'll protect Mrs. von Dietrich. Deploy your men where you need them. Be sure every entrance to the castle is well guarded."

Carbin gave a half-salute and left, closing the door silently.

Brillhagen slid out of bed and said to Athena, "Put on some comfortable clothes quickly. I must get my Uzi and find us a place to hide. Or it might be better just to stay in my suite."

Athena hurriedly put on underwear, jeans, and a white sweater as he watched. "Put your pants on, dammit," she said.

He laughed and reached for his pajama bottom.

She snatched a drawer of her bedside table open and lifted out a .38-caliber Smith & Wesson revolver. She handed it to Wolf, then glanced at her watch. Ten minutes after four. Dawn would be coming soon.

They started down the long, wide corridor leading to Brillhagen's suite. The hall was dimly lit by plastic-shaded ceiling lights.

A figure stepped out of a doorway near the end of the corridor. Dressed completely in black, he had a mask with eye holes and a slit for his mouth. He carried a machine pistol.

He said, "Drop that gun. You can keel me, but this theeng spray you with fifty slugs while I go down."

Before the intruder had finished speaking, Wolf fired, and with almost the same motion slammed Athena and himself to the carpeted floor.

Wolf's shot struck the masked man squarely in the face. He crumpled, his machine pistol clattering wildly. Bullets gouged the wall and ceiling, raining bits of plaster down on Athena and Wolf.

Athena started to get up.

Wolf held her down. "Wait. There may be others. He may not even be dead."

Holding the .38 in his right hand, Wolf crawled slowly toward the man in black. When he reached him, he took the machine pistol and thumbed on the safety. The would-be killer was obviously dead, his mask bubbling blood. Wolf motioned for Athena to come on.

He handed her the .38 and picked up the dead man's machine pistol. It was a 9mm Parabellum Walther MPL submachine gun. What was this trash doing with a good German weapon? Scum!

They made it to his three-room suite. He locked and double-bolted the door, then searched the three rooms, living room, bedroom, study; the bathroom. He looked in the closets and under the bed. "Well," he said, "unless they batter the door down we won't have any further problems."

He went to a closet and lifted his Uzi submachine gun down from the top shelf. He fitted a forty-round magazine into it and placed it on a table.

He laughed. "We could hold off an army briefly with all these weapons."

Athena said, "Are you going back to sleep?"

He shook his head.

"Well, then, I am," she said, heading for his bedroom. At the door she turned. "Don't doze off."

Wolf smiled. "I'm sure it would wake me if they battered down the door."

Athena said, "I think they would blow it open. You might be dead before you woke up."

His face became a trifle pink. "I will stay awake and on the other side of the room from the door."

Yawning, Athena said, "Good." She went into the bedroom and closed the door.

Wolf sat down facing the door. Athena was too damned smart. It was stupid of him not to think of their blowing the door open. They were obviously terrorists hired by the KGB—Cubans, probably. The man he had killed had the small build of a Cuban. Why bother battering the door down when one could simply stick a small plastic explosive in the door, the edge wedged into the small crack between the bottom of the door and the floor?

But the real problem was, how were they getting in? The wall was twenty feet high and five feet thick. The top was matted with electrified barbed wire and embedded with sharp triangular pieces of glass and metal. The current in the barbed wire was strong enough to provide a painful shock, but not strong enough to kill. Sensors scanned the wall five feet above the top and were sensitive enough to differentiate between a sparrow flying over and a human trying to climb over.

If a parachutist tried, even from something as unlikely

as a balloon, he would stand a good chance of being trapped in the treetops of the thick forest surrounding the comparatively small area of building and grounds.

He would have to have a serious talk with Carbin. There was no excuse for intruders making it over the wall. Had they been asleep in the gatehouse when the alarms flashed and sounded?

The sun was up now, bringing in another bright summer morning. He went to the window and stared at the forest below.

He was about to turn away when he heard faint sounds of shooting. Carbin and his men had located the bastards.

He dressed, putting on gray slacks and a red plaid shirt, then woke Athena. After she was fully awake he said, "Come, double-bolt the door after me and keep the Walther handy. I think Carbin and his men have found them. I want to go out and see what's going on. Carbin may need help."

She was lying on top of the bedspread, still dressed in her jeans and sweater. She swung her feet to the floor, picked up the Walther, and followed Wolf into the living room. She wanted to tell him to stay, but that would be cowardly.

Wolf cradled his Uzi and bent to give her a quick kiss.

She said, "Be careful. If anything happens to you—"

He touched her cheek. "Don't worry, nothing will happen to me."

He went through the door and closed it. Athena leaned against it for a few seconds, then double-bolted it. She went to the chair across the room that Wolf had used and sat, the heavy Walther resting on her lap.

If anything happened to Brillhagen, whom would she be able to depend upon? That drooling creep Carbin? He would be sniffing around her, trying to get into her bed. She could ask Lieutenant Goudenough to help her find another tough ex-mercenary.

Since the earliest seeping of daylight, Carbin and his men had been searching the forest. When Brillhagen finally found them, he saw that they had killed two more of the black-clad invaders.

Carbin said to him, "We fanned out and covered the

woods pretty thoroughly. I think there were only three. The one you offed in the castle and these two."

Wolf said, "What I want to know is how did they get over the wall?"

Carbin shook his head. "You got me. The alarm systems are all working perfectly."

"Maybe the men monitoring them were asleep?"

Carbin's big mouth twisted into an ugly frown. "I check these guys out continuously. They know that anyone caught sleeping, or even not paying attention, will be fired immediately."

"Maybe the road patrol missed a cherry picker?" asked Wolf.

Carbin glared at Wolf. "The road patrols cover the perimeter every five minutes. I don't believe you can maneuver a piece of equipment that large and noisy into position and put three men over in five minutes. Anyway, the road patrols check the side roads as they go by."

"Yet they got in."

"Yes, they got in."

Wolf glanced at the two black-clad corpses. "I don't see any wings on those bastards. They sure didn't fly over."

Carbin said, "They weren't dropped in either. No parachutes. We know no plane flew over. Mrs. von Dietrich mentioned a balloon?"

Wolf nodded.

"It's possible that a balloon could descend quietly to a treetop. It's damned unlikely, but I suppose a good athlete might get out of the basket and climb down a tree," said Carbin.

Wolf shook his head. "I would think the branches at the treetop would not be sturdy enough to support a man's weight."

Carbin thought for a few seconds. "With luck it might bend and break but put him within reaching distance of a stronger limb."

Wolf shrugged. "Check with Lieutenant Goudenough and any other sources you may have. See if anyone in the area has a balloon."

Carbin said, "The kind of people we are dealing with

would not advertise the fact. Collapsed, a balloon could be hidden in any garage."

Wolf said, "You're probably right."

Carbin nodded, then turned away.

Wolf said, "Just a minute. There's another possibility. The KGB and other major intelligence organizations have millions at their disposal. Most men would be tempted if offered, say, a hundred thousand each."

Carbin whirled around, his face red. "My men are loyal. We've fought together, died together. Not *one* would take money to betray his buddies by letting these bastards in."

Wolf nodded. "I hope you're right. But remember, even Christ had his Judas. Think about it. Someone who's unhappy and has serious personal problems. A sick wife or child."

Carbin stared at Wolf, his face grim. "The whole idea is an insult to me and my men." He turned away. "I've got to call Lieutenant Goudenough and have these corpses removed."

He strode away.

Wolf stared after him. Should he replace Carbin and his whole group? There were always at least five men around the gatehouse, and at night the day shift was also there, sleeping in dormitory bunks. Shifts changed. It would be difficult to single out a small group for bribery. They would all, including Carbin, have to be into it. Carbin ran a tight ship. Better stick with him. But *how* did the three men get in?

He made his way back to the suite and rapped on the door.

Athena's voice was faint. The heavy door was an effective sound barrier. "Who's there?" she asked.

"Wolf."

"How do I know it's Wolf?"

"Don't you recognize my voice?"

"How many times did you make love to me last night?"

Wolf said, "Eighteen."

Athena said, "Brillhagen wouldn't be such a liar. What's your middle name, Wolfgang?"

"Must I?"

"Yes."

"Gustav."

She opened the door. "Okay, Gus, come in."

He walked in, put the Uzi down, and gave Athena a slap on the rear. "Call me Gus and I'll call you Anna."

She gave him a harder slap on the rear.

He said, "Sit down. We must have a serious talk."

She sat.

"I am worried. I don't know how these three men got into the grounds, got into the castle. The alarm systems are working perfectly." He rubbed his cheek, feeling a bristly stubble. He had not even shaved or showered. Disgusting to start the day off without showering and shaving. "It's possible that Carbin and his men have sold out and are betraying us. But since they killed the other two, this doesn't seem likely."

Athena bit her lower lip. "Maybe they were sacrificed. For a larger group that got into the castle and are hiding, waiting to take me hostage."

Wolf thought about it. "If they got a large group safely into the castle, why would it be necessary to kill the other two?"

"Perhaps they were afraid you would be along shortly. Then they would have to turn the prisoners over to the police and they might talk."

Wolf nodded. "Possible. Maybe they are not ready to make their move. *However,* they could have hidden those men in the woods easily. I could not search the whole eighty acres of forest myself, and they would be sure that I wouldn't even try. I would have to depend on a large group to do that."

He sighed and picked up the Uzi. "Bolt up. The only way we can be sure is for me to search the castle."

Athena looked forlorn. "Now I am going to worry about you for hours."

He bent over and kissed her. "Don't worry. Old Gus will do a cautious, careful job. And my faithful Uzi will take care of any troublemakers."

Wolf started with the attic, which was largely open space. There were no boxes large enough for a man to hide in. He pried open two large trunks, even though they were locked and not likely to contain a live body. Both were filled with old clothes. In the second he found a large leather portfolio with *Anna Goldstein* lettered in gold on the flap. It was stuffed with dusty old letters which he, of course, would not read. A snapshot of Athena at about age eleven fell out as he held it up to see whether there was anything other than envelopes in it. Pigtails and a mouthful of orthodontia. She was adorable, even with all the metal in her mouth. They had played together that far back. Checkers, hide-and-seek, later chess. Brillhagen's father and Sir Yirmi Goldstein were close friends, with homes in adjoining properties in London.

He slipped the snapshot in his pocket and went down to the fourth floor, which was unoccupied and not cleaned by the service that came in three times a week. Cobwebs sealed all the doors. All he had to do was walk down the corridors. Any door opened would have webs damaged at side, top, or bottom.

The back section of the third floor was reserved for the servants. These doors were all unlocked, and he checked each room carefully, including one in which Hilda was taking a nap. He apologized and explained the situation to her. He hurried off when she started wailing.

Of the six large suites in the front portion of the third floor only two were occupied, his and Athena's. He searched five of them, and spoke to Athena through the door of the sixth.

The second floor had a multitude of smaller suites for guests. He searched each one wearily, muttering to himself that Karl von Dietrich must have planned on conventions being held there.

The first floor, with its huge rooms, was easy. Wolf hurried through the gigantic living room with fireplaces at each end, the huge formal dining room, the smaller family dining room, the large library with a smaller adjoining study that Karl had obviously used as an office, the spacious kitchens, one sufficiently equipped for a banquet of a hundred or so, a smaller one in general use for the family in residence, pantries and storage rooms, a walk-in refrigerator, restaurant-size dishwashers, a large laundry room with commercial-size washers and dryers, a smaller room for dry-cleaning equipment, and a lounge for kitchen workers to relax in between frantic meal preparations. His search took only ten minutes.

He went to the basement muttering. Karl von Dietrich was an idiot. A modern estate would have been much more sensible.

The basement had large open areas that also let Wolf's search move rapidly. At the front of the building was a modern area with clean tiles on the walls and floors. It contained an indoor swimming pool, a whirlpool bath, and a fitness gym with Nautilus equipment. Wolf worked out every morning on the Nautilus equipment and soothed his muscles by soaking in the hot whirlpool bath. The area needed only a cursory glance.

He moved into the dusty areas containing the huge furnace, utility gauges, a diesel-operated power generator in case of power failures, metal boxes filled with wiring, and a row of wooden doors apparently for storage rooms, which were all nicely sealed with cobwebs.

He put the Uzi down and dusted off his hands, wiping them on his trousers. Thank God the boring job was done. He picked up the Uzi and went back to his suite.

He had to rap loudly on the door. Finally Athena asked, "Who's there?"

"Gustav von Dummkopf."

She opened the door. "Welcome home, Herr Dummkopf."

He laid the Uzi on a chair. "This place is what Americans would call a white elephant."

"So?" she asked.

"So there are no villains in residence."

She smiled. "Well done, Sir Galahad."

He brought out the snapshot. "Remember this?"

She looked at it and laughed.

"Remember the fun we had?"

She threw her arms around him and hugged him. "My Wolf. I had the handsomest boyfriend any little girl could dream of."

"May I keep it?"

She nuzzled his neck. "Of course."

He said, "Well, now I must take a shower and shave and ponder some more."

"About what?"

"How the three men got in."

"So I'll double-bolt the door and sit across the room with the Walther?"

"Please," he said, and headed for his bedroom.

In the shower he thought about the night before. Athena's participation had been so obviously enjoyable to her, perhaps she would find that she loved him in a way she couldn't love Karl. Karl had always impressed him as a cold fish, a man without passion.

She opened the bathroom door and stood watching him shave.

"You are not guarding the door?"

She said, "The three men who got in are dead. I thought of a way they might have gotten in."

"How?"

"A tunnel under the wall."

Wolf gave her a skeptical look.

"No, listen. Think of this. These people have unlimited resources. They buy or rent a piece of property somewhere around the perimeter of the estate, as far away as two hundred yards. They build a barn or something over the hole they are going to make, dig down about twenty feet, get their surveying instruments properly lined up, and head right for the castle grounds."

He scraped off the last bit of lather. "And they come up where?"

"Somewhere in the forest, of course, where they can camouflage the opening."

"How?"

She said, "Very easily. On the top of their trapdoor, cut turf with weeds, moss, and whatever else you find growing in the woods."

He splashed hot water on his face to wash the remnants of lather off.

He said, "I suppose it's possible. Pretty big project, though. Very rocky soil in this area. Be a very long time building."

Athena said, "They can buy unlimited manpower. And they have had what, over a year since they killed Karl?"

He dried his face and splashed witch hazel on it.

"We definitely should check it out. I'll speak to Carbin about it," he said.

There was a loud rapping on the hall door.

Athena hurried back to the living room. She picked up the Walther and asked, "Who's there?"

Carbin said, "Lieutenant Goudenough to see you, Mrs. von Dietrich."

She unbolted the door, still cradling the Walther.

Goudenough entered, staring at her curiously. She handed him the Walther. "This is what the creep was carrying when Wolf shot him with my thirty-eight."

Carbin half-saluted and left.

Goudenough smiled. "I noticed he went down spraying the wall and ceiling. Are you telling me that crazy Brillhagen shot it out with him armed with only a thirty-eight?"

Wolf came in the living room pulling a T-shirt over his head. He said, "I'm very good with a thirty-eight, Lieutenant. I can shoot the fuzz off a bee with a thirty-eight. Now, with a forty-five, I wouldn't have tried it."

Goudenough nodded. He said, "Lucky he fell backward. If he had fallen forward, you two would look like Swiss cheese."

Wolf shrugged. "When a man is hit squarely in the face, he usually falls backward. The impact is in that direction."

Goudenough put the Walther down and slumped into a chair. "You sound like you been in a war."

Brillhagen nodded. "Vietnam."

"I thought you were a Dutchman."

"A German. I am of German descent. However, Mrs. von Dietrich and I grew up in London, and we both have British citizenship. I am also a citizen of the United States. I have dual citizenship, which the British recognize but the United States doesn't. So please don't report me to the State Department. I did my bit for Uncle Sam in Nam."

Goudenough grinned. "I sure won't. Do you have dual citizenship, Mrs. von Dietrich?"

"I'm not telling."

Goudenough laughed. He stood up. "Just thought I'd let you know that the FBI is looking into the origin of these three bodies we've hauled away. Won't find out anything much, probably. Then we've got to have a coroner's inquest.

We'll need Carbin and Mr. Brillhagen, probably, but no need to take Mrs. von Dietrich away from the safety of this enclave."

Athena said, "It's beginning to look less and less safe. The alarm systems were working perfectly and no one knows *how* those three men got in."

Goudenough nodded. "I heard."

"Mrs. von Dietrich thinks they may have dug a tunnel under the wall." Brillhagen explained Athena's idea.

Goudenough stood for a while thinking it over. "It's possible, I suppose. We could check out the properties surrounding the estate."

Wolf said, "Why not let our private investigators do it? If they find anything suspicious, they can call you in."

Goudenough smiled. "Really appreciate that. You know we have a pretty small department." He picked up the Walther and headed for the door. "Well, got to go now. No rest for the wicked."

After he left, Wolf asked Athena, "Do you think we could have some breakfast, lunch, or something or other?"

Athena patted his cheek. "Yes, we certainly may. And even if cook is having hysterics in her room, I personally will cook bacon and eggs and toast for my man."

Wolf smiled happily. He liked the sound of *my man.*

Kent Carbin had designated military ranks for all his men. He was captain. He had a first lieutenant, four sergeants, and four corporals. The rest were privates.

His second-in-command was First Lieutenant Wayne Betz, a solid, chunky man with the strength of a sumo wrestler. He had short black hair combed down over a portion of his forehead, brown eyes with eyeballs that bulged slightly, a small nose, small mouth, and cheeks a bit sunken.

They sat in Carbin's office discussing the latest developments.

Carbin said, "Her Majesty thinks the enemy may have tunneled under the wall."

Betz smiled. "Not an impossibility. Be easy to camouflage an opening in the forest."

Carbin nodded. "I suppose you'd better organize a search."

Betz leaned back and lit a cigarette. "I wonder if low-level aerial photography might help. We might see something from above that we might not notice at ground level. Would be expensive, though."

Carbin picked up his own pack of cigarettes. "Expensive! Don't you realize that bitch has assets worth more than a billion dollars. Think of it, one thousand million dollars!"

Betz looked a little uncomfortable. "I'll arrange the aerial photos," he said.

Carbin said, "And I hear this Brillhagen kraut is worth about half that much." He paused and then continued. "At times I sort of wonder if we shouldn't be making a hell of a lot more out of this than we are."

Betz said, "We're getting paid more than three times what security jobs usually pay."

Carbin waved his hand. "I know. It just seems like we ought to be able to parlay this situation into something really big."

15

THOMAS JONATHAN SWIFT WAS COMING OUT OF IT BUCKING AND rearing, a look of frantic terror in his eyes, angry grunts and cries coming from his twisted mouth.

Leslie stood as close as she dared. She repeated over and over, "Tom, look at me! Tom, it's Leslie! Everything is all right!"

His feet kicking wildly, Swift tumbled off the bed, falling in between the twin beds.

Leslie screamed, "My God, he's going to hurt himself! He'll break something!"

Michaelis pulled one of the beds over to make more room. Swift was lying facedown in the triangle, kicking his heels up like an enraged mule.

Michaelis asked, "Why don't you call that doctor? Maybe he can calm him, give him a sedative."

Leslie grabbed the phone and punched out a number. After a few words with the doctor, she replaced the phone wearily.

"He says no more drugs. His system must be purged of drugs. He says we should wrap a blanket around his legs. Fold it and loop it around several times so it provides padding."

There was a noisy rapping on the door.

Michaelis hurried over to it. "Who's there?"

"Sting."

It sounded like Sting but Michaelis couldn't be absolutely sure. He asked, "Who was the Manassa Mauler?"

Sting said, "Jack Dempseykov. Let me in you jerk."

Michaelis opened the door.

Sting strode in, slamming it behind him. He stared at Swift.

Michaelis said, "He's in a manic withdrawal rage."

"I don't blame him. I'd be fucking mad myself." Sting glanced hurriedly at Leslie. "Excuse my language, miss."

Leslie said, "Yeah, cut out the fucking obscenity and help us tie a blanket around his legs so he won't hurt himself."

Grinning, Sting helped them. They managed to bundle Swift's flailing legs together with a blanket and turned him on his back. He lay there staring blankly at them, growling like a wounded lion.

Sting said to Michaelis, "I got seats booked on Finnair to get us out of here tomorrow. We've done our bit for the Company, right, Miss Leslie?"

Leslie hurried to Sting. Clutching his jacket, she stared up into his eyes soulfully. "Help me get Tom back to the States. He's in greater danger than any of us."

"Why?" asked Sting.

She looked down. "He's a double agent. The KGB just caught on."

Sting whistled softly between his teeth. "He's a brave

man. I got to respect a man that'll take that kind of risk for his country."

One small tear rolled down Leslie's cheek.

Sting patted her shoulder. "Okay, little lady, I guess we're hooked."

She brushed away the tear. "He'll be okay by tomorrow. The doctor told me he'd have all his wits about him no later than tomorrow night, maybe sooner."

Sting was silent for a few seconds, then said, "I'm sending Angie and the Tarboys back on a separate flight."

Leslie said, "Right. You should."

"I think we'll be okay once we get aboard Finnair," Michaelis said. "The worst public relations the Russians have ever had was during their war with brave little Finland."

Leslie nodded. "Yeah, they have a pretty tight, smooth relationship now. And the Finns don't want us messing around here any more than they want the KGB."

Michaelis stifled a yawn. He hadn't slept very well in the lounge chair. "I want to go back to the Intercontinental. Take a shower and put on some clean clothes."

He looked at Leslie. She shrugged.

"You'll be okay for a while?"

Sting said, "I'll stay. Tell Angie I want to put her and the Tarboys on a flight today, so get packed."

Michaelis stifled another yawn, nodded, and headed for the door.

Sting said, "Look both ways before you cross the street, son."

"Also watch your ass, Professor," Leslie added.

Michaelis laughed. He opened the door and looked up and down the corridor. It was empty. He stepped out and closed the door.

He made it to the lobby without any problems and asked the doorman to call for a cab. Cabs do not cruise in Helsinki.

The cab whisked him to the Intercontinental quickly, without any threatening vehicles following. Michaelis relaxed.

As he strolled into the Intercontinental lobby, an excited voice cried, "Professor Michaelis!"

He turned to see a very blond, very fair-complexioned young woman hurrying over to him. Slender, she had lustrous green eyes and prominent breasts. He recognized Ingrid Hugel from Crendon University's German Department.

She embraced him and gave him a faculty kiss on the cheek.

"How are you, Ingrid?" he asked, smiling.

She continued to hold her hands on his shoulders, staring up at him. She said, "You may now address me as Dr. Hugel."

Michaelis presented a dutiful beaming smile. "Congratulations! So now you have your doctorate!" he said.

"Ja," she said. "And what are you doing in this distant land?"

He shrugged. "Just knocking around the world a bit."

"Are you staying here?" she asked.

He nodded.

"Will you have dinner with me and my friends to celebrate?"

He shook his head. "Wish I could, but unfortunately I have other commitments."

She squeezed his arm. "Well, then, just one drink with me now to celebrate? Please?"

Michaelis glanced at his watch and smiled. "No more than five minutes, I'm afraid. I have an appointment."

Giggling, she tugged him into the small bar off the lobby. At one end two Finns were surrounding a bottle of Finnish vodka, toasting each other with quick swallows from small shot glasses. At the other end were two tall blond men, in their early twenties, Michaelis estimated. One wore jeans and a black leather jacket; the other was wearing gray flannels and a gray tweed jacket.

Ingrid led Michaelis to the tall blond men.

She said, "Meet my colleague, Professor Michaelis. We are both on the faculty of Crendon University, one of the finest private universities in the United States."

She turned to Michaelis. "This is my friend Adolf, and this one is Konrad."

Adolf raised his palm and said, *"Heil."*

Konrad laughingly offered his hand to be shaken.

The men were sharing a bottle of cognac. Adolf pushed a clean glass to Michaelis and started to pour. Ingrid stopped him. "I know my friend's favorite drink, a Perfect Rob Roy, and I will tell the bartender exactly how to prepare it."

Michaelis said, "The cognac will be fine. I really must leave in a minute or so."

Ingrid said, "No! You must have your favorite drink." She began instructing the bartender. "Two ounces of scotch, one-half ounce of sweet vermouth, one-half ounce of dry vermouth, and a twist of lemon."

It wasn't his favorite drink, but he remembered having ordered one when he happened to be with Ingrid. Why spoil her fun? She had obviously had a few and was well into her celebrating.

Making sure that the bartender had everything exactly right, Ingrid inspected the drink and then handed it to Michaelis.

She said, "Now the three of you drink a toast to Dr. Ingrid Hugel."

Adolf grinned and lifted his glass. Michaelis and Konrad raised theirs. Michaelis said, "To our dear friend, Dr. Hugel, we offer our heartiest congratulations on her newly acquired doctorate."

The three men drained their glasses while Ingrid smirked, stepping back from the bar to bow.

Michaelis set his glass down on the bar with a thump. Enough of this nonsense, time to go. He edged off the barstool to stand up. His knees buckled and he found himself sprawling on the floor.

He put his hands down and tried to raise himself. His elbows had somehow acquired greased joints.

Adolf and Konrad lifted him to his lifeless feet. Adolf said to the bartender, "This poor fellow has had too much. We must get him home where he can sleep it off."

The bartender nodded.

They walked Michaelis's useless legs into the lobby, Ingrid following, wringing her hands like a distraught wife whose husband has disgraced her.

Michaelis was conscious, but his limbs simply did not function. As they made their slow way through the lobby,

Michaelis caught a glimpse of Angie out of the corner of his eye. She looked horrified.

The last thing he remembered was being shoved and hoisted into a waiting limousine.

When he regained consciousness, he found himself in complete darkness sitting comfortably in an upholstered lounge chair. His wrists were handcuffed together, and his left ankle seemed to be handcuffed to something on or near the floor. He bent over, moving both hands down to his left foot. The ankle cuff was fastened to a pipe running horizontally near the floor, and probably near a wall. It felt warm. Hot water pipe?

He moved his head from side to side staring into total blackness. He sniffed. The smell was that of a damp, musty basement.

Ingrid Hugel! A respectable member of the faculty at Crendon University! Slipped him a mickey! She probably had East German connections along with her two friends who "walked" him to the limousine. Who would anticipate this sort of thing? Probably he should have, but dammit he knew the woman well. She'd never be able to go back to Crendon after pulling something like this. Of course, maybe she was sure *he* would never be going back to Crendon. She was probably a sleeper who had been in the United States for years. What a story for the faculty club. If he lived to tell it.

At least Angie had seen him being hustled out of the lobby. There wouldn't be much delay in Sting starting to look for him.

His mouth and throat were parched, and quick, regular stabs of pain attacked his head. They obviously wanted information from him. And the horrible realization of his true situation came to him. He didn't have any information to give.

Of course, he had helped steal Swift from them, and they would find it hard to believe that it was an act of altruism. They would assume he was a CIA agent. Maybe Leslie would trade somebody for him. In spite of the pain in his head, he smiled at the idea.

Something was moving toward him in the darkness.

Even though he could see nothing, he could sense it. Involuntary panic sent his hands up to protect his face.

A strong light was beamed directly into his eyes. He blinked, then squinted. He could see nothing but light.

A voice behind the light said, "Professor Michaelis, so you are now awake."

Michaelis lowered his hands. Guessing, he would say that the voice was that of a Russian who had been educated in England.

"Are you comfortable?" the voice asked.

"No," said Michaelis.

The voice said, "This I do not understand. We have given you a most comfortable chair. You could spend a lifetime in that chair. Admit the chair is comfortable."

Michaelis said, "The chair is comfortable. I am not."

The voice said, "We merely wish to have a confidential talk with you, Professor, after which we will release you to go your own way. We know that you are an amateur treading where even professionals fear to tread, stumbling into matters which are none of your concern."

Michaelis said, "That's true."

The voice laughed softly. "You're a good actor, Professor, with your stumbling and bumbling."

Michaelis's fleeting feeling of relief disappeared. He was now back in the position of a man who would *know* things they wanted to know.

He said, "I am not a professional in intelligence and I am not an actor. My involvement is a personal matter."

There was a long silence. How close to him was his interrogator standing? The glare in his eyes was so intense that he had to keep his eyelids almost shut, squinting. He couldn't even estimate the distance of the light from his eyes.

The odor he thought was mustiness was now stronger and more resembled spent gunpowder. And another odor was present. The man speaking to him smelled of hospitals. Formaldehyde? Doctor? Undertaker?

Maybe the basement served as an execution chamber.

The voice said, "You have direct access to the President of the United States."

Michaelis shook his head. He carefully explained the

situation. His book, *Realpolitik in an Unreal World,* the congressman who was impressed, the contact with Ken Watson, the lost position as a presidential aide because of the jury-bribing scandal.

He concluded by saying, "I know now, of course, that the trial was a farce, that Athena von Dietrich's husband was killed by hostile intelligence operatives trying to obtain information."

The voice said, "Ah-ha. You are acting for the President of the United States to obtain this information."

Michaelis laughed, just one short *ha.* "I'm sure the President has much more experienced people than me working on that."

The voice was becoming irritated. "You have met with Catherine Leeds, you have met and negotiated with Athena von Dietrich and made a deal for your government. You are here because von Dietrich in her flight to dozens of cities throughout the world chose to hide her father's secret here in Helsinki. She has sent you here to obtain it."

Perspiration popped out on Michaelis's forehead. The situation was really becoming thick.

He said, "I have never met or spoken to Athena von Dietrich. The only time I ever saw her was when she was on trial. I have had no dealings whatsoever with her."

The silence that followed was extended. Finally, Michaelis asked, "Why would she hide the plans here in Helsinki, only a stone's throw from Leningrad?"

The voice said, "Because she is a brilliant woman, and Helsinki is the last place in the world anyone would think of looking."

Michaelis shook his head. "I can't help you. I know nothing about the situation."

A big hand blurred through the blinding light carrying a hard, open-handed slap. The blow was hard enough to send shock waves through Michaelis's head, and knocked it at least four inches to the right.

"You will tell me where von Dietrich's plans are hidden, and we'll let you live," said the voice.

Michaelis raised his hands to feel his head, which was still buzzing. He was sure that if he could see anything it would be blurred.

"What a waste," he said.

"Waste? What do you mean, waste?" the voice asked.

Michaelis cleared his throat. "If I knew anything, I still wouldn't tell you, and I would at least have the satisfaction of knowing that I was dying to protect my country's interest. Since I do not know anything, I will be dying because of your stupidity. It's damned depressing."

This brought a whiplike crack on the other side of his head.

A couple more of those and he wouldn't be conscious. Or maybe he would continue to be conscious for a long time. In the end he would still be babbling, "I don't know."

Suddenly rage flooded his mind and body. His interrogator was close enough to slap him. It was now or never.

He tensed his calf muscles, moving his feet back to lunge up and outward. He bent his head, raised his hands, and leaped up.

The top of his head crashed into a face, his handcuffed hands were clutching garments covering a chest, and his right knee was delivering a cruel blow to a crotch.

His opponent crumpled, groaning. The light bounced on the floor and went out.

Michaelis fell on top of his tormentor, the foot handcuff tearing painfully at his left ankle. He grabbed the bloody face under him and banged it against the concrete repeatedly. His opponent was soon unconscious if not dead.

It was difficult searching the man's pockets with his hands cuffed together. One hand could go only so far into a pocket, and two hands wouldn't fit. He managed finally to fish out a key ring. Feeling the keys carefully in the dark, he separated two small ones. One opened the cuff on his ankle, and the other freed his hands.

He quickly ran his hands over the unconscious man's torso. He expected to find a gun and was not disappointed. A holster was attached to the man's belt and had been pushed around to the small of his back. Michaelis pulled the pistol out and ran his hands over it. It was an automatic, and by its shape, probably a Luger. He was now armed, which might help in getting out of the place. How much would depend on how many were upstairs. He shoved the Luger in his belt.

He felt around on the floor for the light. His fingers finally touched it and he was able to pick it up. It was a large, powerful flashlight, but useless. The bulb had probably cracked when it dropped to the floor. He shoved the grip end into his back pocket; it was heavy enough and long enough to serve as a weapon.

Then he kneeled and groped along the concrete floor searching for the handcuffs he had discarded. He remembered his pipe lighter. He flicked it on just long enough to find the handcuffs. He quickly cuffed the ankles of his unconscious interrogator who was still breathing, now loud, almost snoring. Should he handcuff his hands, or save the second pair for immobilizing someone else on the way out? He decided to keep them. The man on the floor couldn't get around very effectively with his feet bound together, even if he regained consciousness.

Taking slow steps, one arm outstretched, and flicking on his lighter briefly, he explored the cellar.

It was a large room, at least half of it filled with packing cases. There were no windows. A flight of steep wooden stairs led to the first floor.

He climbed them slowly, testing each tread for squeaks. The door at the top appeared to be heavy and solid. He tried the knob, turning it slowly and silently, pushing and pulling. The door was locked tightly without the slightest give. The keyhole was large and made to accommodate an old-fashioned key. He returned quietly to the bottom of the steps and flicking on his lighter, examined the key ring he had appropriated. The keys were all flat and modern.

He went back and searched the pockets of the man on the floor. He found a handkerchief, a wallet, change, a cigarette case filled with Marlboros, an extra clip of ammunition for the Luger, and a lighter. No long, old-fashioned key. Had his cohorts locked him in just in case a situation such as this developed? Not likely. The key probably bounced away somewhere in the darkness during their struggle.

Michaelis put the ammunition clip, the extra lighter, and the wallet into his jacket pockets. If he got out alive, Leslie Greenhaven would undoubtedly be interested in the contents of the wallet.

Someone would eventually be coming down to investigate the delay in Mr. X's return. Probably soon. How long would they expect him to stay?

The ideal would be to take out the next visitor as silently as possible. A shot would alert everyone upstairs. If he could only stand by the door and bang him on the head with the flashlight. No room for that at the top of the stairs. There were no handrails flanking the steps. Any kind of scuffle would send one or both of them into a bad fall.

He crept up to the top of the steps again. Placing his right hand over the keyhole, he felt along the wall next to the door frame. No light switch. He flicked on his lighter just to be sure.

Descending, he again used the lighter to survey the low ceiling. No overhead light fixture that he could see. Probably an old farmhouse dating from the time when farmers carried oil lanterns to the basement.

Whoever came to look would probably have another flashlight. He couldn't see any alternative to the obvious. It was going to be a shoot-out between him and an unknown number upstairs. Better build himself a fort with the packing cases. He hoped they were well filled with something that resisted bullets.

He shoved four of them out to face the steps. They were very heavy. He barely managed to hoist four more on top to provide a wall about five feet high by three feet in width, with a length of about twelve feet. He left a two-inch crack between two of the top cases to fire through.

His fort was completed not a minute too soon. The click of the heavy old lock was loud in the silence of the basement. The door opened, light in the background vaguely silhouetting a figure.

"*Konrad, was ist los?*" the voice asked.

Konrad, eh? *That* sonofabitch, thought Michaelis. He aimed carefully and squeezed the trigger.

The ear-splitting explosion was accompanied by a short scream and an agonizing grunt. The figure fell onto the stairs, then tumbled over the edge to crash on the hard concrete below.

A woman screamed.

Ingrid? That bitch! If those three were all he had to contend with, his problems were almost over.

Michaelis peeked through his shooting crack. All he could see was a shiny barrel suspended near floor level at the top of the steps.

Ingrid said, "Michaelis, come out of there with your hands up. I have a machine gun and I'll cut you to pieces if you fire a single shot."

He aimed six inches above the barrel and fired.

A burst from an Uzi ripped across his packing cases.

She was obviously lying on the floor. His chances of hitting her, shooting uphill, were very small. He groaned loudly and made gargling sounds in his throat. Sooner or later she would have to investigate.

She called, "Michaelis, are you hurt? There's still time to get a doctor, you know. We don't want you to die. Throw the gun out and we'll help you."

He crawled to the left edge of his fort and lay there silently, peeking around to keep an eye on the top of the steps.

The light at the top of the steps was dim, and probably only daylight in the house. Had he been unconscious all night? The barrel of the Uzi continued in the same position.

He would wait her out.

Minutes that could have been hours passed.

His whole body began to ache from lying motionless on the cold concrete. Curiosity would get the better of her sooner or later, he told himself.

Suppose, however, that she left to get reinforcements? No way would she leave the Uzi lying there. As long as the Uzi was there, Ingrid would be there.

Finally she said, "Michaelis, you don't understand. We don't want to hurt you. Throw the gun out and let me get help for you."

Oh, God! He felt a sneeze coming. He took a deep breath and squeezed his nose. He managed to suppress it.

Another hour seemed to pass.

She said, "Michaelis, I'm coming down. If you're playing tricks, we'll just kill each other."

Something white seemed to be moving down the steps.

He withheld his fire. The thing seemed to collapse, then slid off the steps to one side, white cloth fluttering. It hit the concrete with a small, dull thud. She had shoved something covered with a sheet down the steps.

He had *almost* fired.

Okay, Ingrid, so much for your decoy. He steadied the Luger, concentrating on the barrel at the top of the steps.

It began to move as she edged over the threshold, crawling. It's pretty hard to crawl down steps. She seemed to be edging herself down sideways, step by step.

He waited until he had a clear view of her right shoulder. He fired. She screamed and the Uzi sprayed holes in the ceiling, then bounced down the steps and over one side to clatter as it hit the concrete below.

Michaelis scrambled to his feet and ran to the steps in a crouch. If she had any backup, he would probably be lurking behind her. Michaelis ran up the steps.

Ingrid had pulled herself to her feet painfully and was clutching her shoulder. Michaelis caught her, pulled her hands behind her, and snapped on the handcuffs he had saved. His shot had cut a bloody swath across her shoulder and back. A flesh wound, it was in no way lethal.

She spit in his face.

He wiped it off with his sleeve and gave her face a hard slap.

Her head jerked to the side. Her lips curled. "Big brave man. Slap a woman who has her hands cuffed behind her."

He asked, "Would you rather I spit in your face?"

She turned away hurriedly.

He grabbed the handcuffs holding her arms behind her and said, "Come on. We're leaving here with you in front of me."

He shifted his left hand to hold Ingrid's handcuffed wrists and held the Luger, which he had stuck in his belt, in his right hand.

He shoved her. "Move it," he said.

They marched through a farmhouse that had no furniture and was apparently abandoned.

Outside, on the rickety old steps, she asked, "What do you think you're doing with me anyway? When the police find out what you've done to my friends, you'll be freezing your ass off in Lapland shoveling reindeer shit."

Michaelis laughed. "You'll be up there to help me, and I won't even try to help you keep your ass warm."

She tried to jerk away. He held on tightly. They went down the porch steps to a dirt pathway that led to a road about a hundred feet away.

She said, "I wouldn't let you touch me if you were the last man left on earth."

He said, "I would have definite reservations about having intercourse with a rattlesnake anyway."

She kicked backward, grazing his right shin. He raised her hands up until her arms were painfully bent.

He said, "I'm not turning you over to the police. I'm going to give you to a young woman who will enjoy talking to you immensely."

She thought about that, silently.

When they reached the road, he asked, "Which way is Helsinki?"

She turned and started to walk to the right. He turned her around and walked her in the other direction.

She said, "This is not the way to Helsinki."

He nodded. "I know. I'm looking for a deserted wooded area where I can put a bullet through that stupid brain of yours and leave you there to rot."

Her sharp intake of breath was audible.

She finally stammered, "Why, why do you want to do that to me? I'm only doing my job, just like you're doing your job."

He said, "We're really headed toward Helsinki, aren't we?"

Her "yes" was in a very small, almost little girl's voice.

He said, "So I told you that because you're a lying bitch."

In the distance there was the sound of a car approaching. Michaelis hustled Ingrid off the road and into some bushes, pushed her down on her face, and collapsed beside her.

There were two limousines, and both stopped.

Sting came stomping through the bushes. He stood over

them. "Here we been combing this damned city for twenty hours looking for you and you're out here making out with a dame."

Michaelis got slowly to his feet. Keeping an eye on Ingrid, he said, "I was kidnaped by some SSD jerks. This is one of them. I think Leslie will be glad to talk to her."

Sting nodded, smiling.

"The other two, either dead or in various states of disrepair, are back in the farmhouse."

Michaelis bent over and grabbed Ingrid by the waist, then lifted her to her feet.

Sting took charge. He hustled Ingrid into the back seat of the second limousine with Angie. Richard Tarboy was in front in the driver's seat.

Sting said to Michaelis, "Get in with Ronald-Richard and take the dame to Leslie. She's in the same room, and Swift's okay. Donald and I will check out the farmhouse."

Michaelis said, "Be damned careful. There are at least two submachine guns lying around and I don't know how badly those guys are hurt. If Konrad is conscious, he's hopping around with his feet cuffed together. The other one is Adolf, and it's pretty hard to kill an Adolf."

Sting asked, "How come this woman has blood all over her back?"

"Flesh wound. I shot her while she was spraying me with an Uzi."

Sting's eyebrows rose. "I got to recruit you for my army," he said.

Michaelis shook his head. "I had all the army a man could want in Vietnam."

Sting snickered and gave Michaelis a friendly slap on the back. He turned and followed Donald Tarboy up to the lead limousine.

Ingrid was silent during the trip back to the hotel. She shifted occasionally to position her handcuffed wrists more comfortably, and stared past Michaelis to look out the side window.

Walking with Ingrid between them, Michaelis and Angie slipped into one of the back entrances of the Kalastajatorppa and went up the fire stairs. Angie had thrown a raincoat over Ingrid's shoulders to conceal the dried blood on her clothes and the handcuffs.

Leslie was happy to see them. Even Swift was happy to see them. He was sitting in a comfortable chair wearing jeans and a plaid shirt and no straitjacket.

Leslie said, "Well, Ingrid, imagine meeting you again."

Ingrid said something in German which sounded like a grave insult, but Michaelis's German was not extensive enough to include vernacular insults.

Angie retrieved her raincoat. Leslie stared at Ingrid's back. "We'll have to get my friendly doctor. We wouldn't want that wound to become infected, would we?"

"Go fuck your brother, you bitch," Ingrid said, still speaking German. This Michaelis could translate.

"Crendon University would not care for that kind of language, Ingrid."

Ingrid glared at him. She said, "Fuck you, too, you pompous asshole."

Michaelis nodded. He said to Leslie, "I think Ingrid was whelped in the gutters of Hamburg."

Leslie asked, "Are rats whelped? Or is it only dogs?"

"Dogs only, I believe, but I'm not sure." He shook his head sadly. "Did you know that Ingrid is a respected member of the German Department at Crendon? Who would have thought having a drink with her would get me a mickey?"

Swift laughed. "Women can be treacherous all right," Leslie said.

"Said she was celebrating getting her doctorate. Was it a DM or a DT, Ingrid?" Michaelis asked.

Ingrid stared at him, lips curled.

"Come on, was it Doctor of Murder or Doctor of Torture, Ingrid?"

"With regard to you, either would be fine."

"Let's get the hell out of here," Angie said. "This place is giving me claustrophobia."

With five of them in the bedroom it was a bit crowded, especially when one of them was the massive Tom Swift.

As they left, Leslie said to Michaelis, "Thanks for Ingrid. I'll do something nice for you one day." At the door she clutched Angie and in a low voice said, "I owe you all a big one. You saved Tom's life. If there is anything, I mean *anything* I can ever do for you, let me know and I'll come running."

Angie patted Leslie's cheek gently. "Don't worry about it, you're an okay person right from the top of the barrel."

16

THE AERIAL PHOTOGRAPHER LOOKED DOUBTFUL. "BE A COMPLETE waste of your money," he told Brillhagen. "I flew over the property this morning. At least eighty percent of the ground is shielded by leaves. If you want me to take a helicopter and photograph the twenty percent where the trees are not so close together, I can do it."

Brillhagen shook his head. "No thanks. I was afraid this wouldn't work."

"If you want me to come back in the fall when the leaves are gone—"

Brillhagen smiled. "Too late. I'm afraid our only alternative is to conduct a search on foot."

Carbin nodded. "I agree. I'd like your permission to hire twenty temporaries. I'll lay out a grid and we'll check every inch of the estate."

The photographer stood up. "Well, nice meeting you," he said, shaking hands with Brillhagen and Carbin. "I'm glad you're pleased with the photographs of the periphery of the estate."

Brillhagen said, "Yes, they're quite sharp and have been useful."

As the photographer walked away, Brillhagen said to Carbin, "Okay, get on with organizing the foot search."

He went back to his study to review the photographs

already taken of a two-hundred-yard-wide sweep around the periphery of the estate.

There were three barns and two rather large sheds which might have provided cover for the digging of a tunnel. There were eight houses in the area. It had not begun in one of their basements: Unofficial meter readers had inspected the basements of all eight houses. Spurious fire inspectors had checked the barns and sheds, but could not offer a conclusive opinion. Two of the barns had dirt floors partially covered with farm equipment and straw. The excavated dirt would easily have been tucked away and the entrance trapdoor concealed.

Even Lieutenant Goudenough couldn't help them there. Making a farmer empty his barn of equipment was not, he said, "in the cards." There was no way he could get that kind of search warrant on such flimsy evidence of possible criminal activity.

Athena strolled into Brillhagen's study and peered over his shoulder.

He looked up and said, "I'm still trying to figure this out. We've got to search the grounds on foot for the exit, but it would be a big help to know where the entrance is."

Athena had already heard a discussion of the barns and houses, and their inability to go any further in that investigation.

She asked, "How about someone digging a fake well?"

Brillhagen slapped the table. "Perfect! They wouldn't even have to conceal the entrance."

Athena tousled his curly hair. "Find the exit. That way we can capture them one by one. Otherwise they may dig another tunnel."

Athena was only partially right this time, Brillhagen thought. They might catch a few of them, but the others would soon realize that another tunnel was required. Still, it would take them months to dig a new tunnel.

He said, "Carbin is organizing a search. When he is ready, I'll go with them and see that it is done thoroughly."

He picked up his phone and dialed the gatehouse.

"Captain Carbin," came over crisply.

"Brillhagen here. I want you to have your people outside the wall check for recently dug wells."

There was a silence, then Carbin said, "That's a good suggestion. Will do."

Wolf said, "Mrs. von Dietrich's idea. When are you beginning your search of the grounds?"

"Tomorrow at six A.M.," said Carbin. "I have twenty temporaries arriving tonight. I'll throw in twenty of our regulars. We'll have forty men checking every inch of the estate."

Wolf said, "Good. I'll join you."

He replaced the phone, shoved his chair back from the desk, and pulled Athena down onto his lap. They were now sleeping together every night, partially for her protection but mainly because their isolation had suddenly become wonderful. Brillhagen was crazily in love with Athena. While she couldn't admit to herself that she loved Wolf, she found their intimate relationship both exciting and reassuringly comfortable. Wolf was an exceptional lover. Athena had never experienced this type of lovemaking, had never been fully aroused. She had been a virgin when she married Karl. Karl could hardly believe it. As rich as he was, Karl had no understanding of how little privacy a very rich girl had. In addition to two security guards, Athena had a companion, Aloysia, a former policewoman, who was with her constantly, even sleeping in the same room with her. In her late teens Athena was allowed privacy during her dates with suitable young men, but the security force was always close at hand, and the boys never went beyond adolescent kissing and pawing. Some of the boys had the impression that if Athena so much as whimpered someone would rush into the room and shoot them. Her father's assassination proved that the family had not been overly cautious.

Wolf unbuttoned her shirt and slipped his hand in to cup one of her breasts. "Let's go to bed," he said.

She kissed him. She said, "Bed is for nighttime. This is midmorning. You will wear your poor thing out, using it so much."

"Never!" he said. "It is a durable instrument."

Athena patted his cheek. "It is a beautiful morning. I want to swim, loll in the sun, do my exercises, read a worthwhile book, sit in the whirlpool bath, and have Hilda give me a nice massage."

"I will give you a massage," said Wolf.

She laughed. "Your technique does not exactly relax my muscles. I want a Hilda massage."

Wolf sighed deeply. "Why must you be so Teutonic in your fixed regimen? Relax and enjoy yourself."

Athena said, "I will enjoy you tonight. In the daytime I will enjoy other things."

Wolf lay on his back staring at the white ceiling, now gray in the moonlight. Athena was cuddled in a fetal position, sound asleep, with her back to him. He glanced at his watch. The fluorescent hands pointed to 1:45 A.M. How long could this impossible situation continue? How could he convince Athena to free herself, and him, from her father's monster? As Americans would put it, he was in a *no-win* situation. Athena's stubbornness had little logic. Of course the United States would produce a superweapon from Sir Yirmi's discovery, but what difference did it make? Nuclear weapons already provided the threat of wiping out human existence on most of the earth. As a weapon, Sir Yirmi's discovery would provide an explosive capacity about a hundred times greater than nuclear weapons, but there would be no residue to sicken and gradually destroy those who survived, no radiation contamination, no plutonium seeping into the lungs. Actually the earth would be better off if Sir Yirmi's big bang replaced the nuclear big bang.

Shots sounded outside the castle. Brillhagen sat up hastily and nudged Athena awake. The fast, almost continuous clatter of machine pistols seemed to come from several directions.

"Get dressed," he said.

They dressed hurriedly: Athena in jeans and a white sweater, Wolf in gray slacks and a blue shirt. Athena rushed into the bathroom but came out in seconds.

Wolf cradled his Uzi in his arms and headed for the living room. Athena followed, carrying her .38.

As they entered the room, a blast blew the hall door off its hinges. Splintered into three large pieces, it fell to the floor.

Wolf peppered the opening with a clatter from the Uzi.
A voice from the hall said, "Throw your weapons out or we throw in a grenade."

Perspiration wet on his forehead, Wolf grabbed Athena and hurried her into the bedroom, locking and bolting the door.

The grenade exploded in the living room. The blast brought a frightening shriek of metal tearing, along with the deeper pitch of ripping walls and ceiling. Two small pieces of shrapnel pierced the bedroom door.

The bedroom door blew off its hinges.

Wolf sprayed the opening with the Uzi.

The voice said, "Throw your weapons out or we give you another grenade."

Wolf hastily pushed Athena into his study, bolting the door. He muttered, "Where in the hell are Carbin's men?"

The next crash resounding in the bedroom was like a truck hitting a brick wall at seventy miles per hour. Pieces of shrapnel came through the study door.

Wolf pushed Athena down behind his large desk and crouched next to her. There was nowhere else to retreat to.

The study door collapsed with another crash.

Wolf again opened fire.

The voice said, "Throw your weapons out or you get another grenade. You have no place to go now."

Wolf looked at Athena.

"We must give in," she said. She tucked her revolver into the band of her jeans and adjusted her sweater over it.

Wolf said, "Hold your fire."

He put the safety on the Uzi and hurled it across the floor into the open doorway.

The voice said, "Come out with your hands high over your head."

Wolf stood up and pulled Athena to her feet. They walked together into the shattered bedroom, hands high.

Two black-clad, black-hooded invaders stood waiting, both holding machine pistols.

One put his weapon down and proceeded to frisk the two prisoners, starting with Athena and fondling her breasts in passing. She stared at him wide-eyed as he did this.

He found the revolver and removed it, a snickering sound coming from the mouth slit in his mask. He stuck the revolver in his pocket.

He found nothing when he frisked Brillhagen.

He picked up his weapon and turned to his companion. "Take Herr Brillhagen to the library. If he escapes, you will wish you were dead. The princess and I will go to her suite and have a conference."

A gun barrel poking his spine, Brillhagen was marched away.

The other man grasped Athena's arm. He said, "Come on, Your Majesty, we'll have a talk about your secret."

He hustled her through the two bombed-out rooms and into the corridor. They were quickly inside her suite. He double-bolted the hall door.

Shoving her further into the room, he gave her a hard push that sent her stumbling backward. She landed seated on one of the large sofas.

Looming over her, he lifted his mask and pulled it up over his face and head, letting it hang down his back. Butter-yellow hair and bright blue eyes took some of the curse off a flat face and small, piglike nose.

"Remember me?" he asked.

"Kurt Wessel!" said Athena. "You've become a criminal again!"

"I'm working for a good cause."

"What cause?"

He grinned. "The extermination of rich bitches and bastards who think they own the world."

She asked, "What have I ever done to you, Kurt?"

"You treated me like dirt."

"I did not!" Athena rubbed her forehead. "In fact, I saved you from going back to prison."

Kurt said, "That was your fault, too, wriggling your ass around in front of me all the time."

Athena's face became pink. "I did no such thing. My father would never even let me wear tight clothes."

He sat down beside her, resting his machine pistol on the sofa on the side away from her.

Putting his arm around her shoulders, he said, "I have always had fantasies of stripping you naked and—"

She tried to pull away, but he held her tightly. "You don't have to tell me the rest," she said.

He bent over and kissed her hard.

When he released her, she said, "Kurt, be gentle with me and you can have what you want. Otherwise you will have to rape me, and I will claw your eyes out."

Nodding, he bent over and unzipped her jeans, then began tugging them down over her hips. So engrossed did he become in trying to pull her panties down with the jeans that he did not notice her reaching into the neck of her sweater and bringing out a long thin knife with a flat handle. She had taped the sheath for it between her breasts when she rushed into the bathroom earlier.

She plunged it swiftly upward into his chest, slightly nicking a rib but continuing right between them and into his heart.

He gave a small yelp, tried to stand up, and then collapsed on the floor.

She bent over him and twisted the knife around to be sure his heart was properly stopped, then withdrew the blade and wiped it on his black costume. She carried it to the bathroom, washed it with warm soap and water, dried it with toilet paper, and returned it to its sheath.

She glanced at the body before picking up Kurt's Walther machine pistol. One totally undesirable citizen removed from this world. He had served five years in prison for manslaughter, having brutally killed his wife in a quarrel. Prior to that he had been arrested a number of times for assault and robbery, convicted, and served surprisingly short, lenient sentences.

Sir Yirmi had been interested in a prisoner rehabilitation society. On the recommendation of the society's secretary, he had employed Kurt as a chauffeur and mechanic to help drive and service the family cars.

During one of the few times her companion was not with her Kurt had lured her into one of the pantries off the kitchen and began a rough attempt to make love to her. Athena was nineteen at the time and embarrassed by the situation. She carried on a completely silent struggle to free herself. Footsteps were heard. Kurt released her and hurried away.

Bruised and disheveled, she straightened and smoothed her rumpled clothes and crept to her room. As soon as her father came home she would tell him about Kurt. Her mother was away, in Cannes or Nice, she couldn't remember which.

Kurt had called her on the house telephone. He had cried, begged, pleaded, sobbed. If she told, he would go back to prison. He didn't mean what he had done. It was a moment of craziness. If she would forgive him, he promised he would never, never do anything like it again. She had finally relented and agreed not to tell her father.

And now the pig thought he could rape her!

She examined the Walther, turning the safety off. Wolf had been taken to the library. She walked slowly into the corridor looking for any other black-clad invaders, then went quietly down the steps and edged along the wall to the library door. She turned the knob very slowly and silently, then pushed gently. The door opened a crack. She could see nothing of the interior. She pushed more, opening it wider, hoping for no squeaks.

Wolf and the enemy were seated at a table, facing each other across it. The black-clad man's machine pistol lay on the table pointed at Wolf. Her view was partially of the man's back and somewhat less of his side. It appeared that his finger was curled around the trigger of his weapon.

If she could depend upon her aim, she could shoot him, but these pistols fired so rapidly and jerked a bit. She might easily kill Wolf, or cause the man to fire and kill Wolf. Even if she could find the adjustment that allowed only a single shot, if the Walther had such an adjustment, she might only wound him, and his first reaction might be to shoot Wolf.

They were too close together.

Wolf saw her and grinned.

The black-clad man said, "I'm not falling for any of theese *look behind you* sheet, krauthead."

Athena took a chance and said, "You'd better because I'm about to blast you straight to hell."

The man half turned. It was all Wolf needed. In a swift plunge forward he had the barrel of the gun twisting it to one side. It clattered away, bullets tearing into the bindings of books across the large room. Wolf, half-lying on the table, finally managed to wrench away the gun from the man's grasp.

Athena rushed in and faced him with the Walther.

He raised his hands. "Don't shoot!" he squawked.

Kent Carbin came running in, skidding to a stop when he saw that Brillhagen and Athena were unharmed.

Brillhagen asked, "How is it that these men were allowed to get into the castle *again.*"

Carbin bared his teeth. "Because they killed three of my men guarding the entrances."

Brillhagen was embarrassed. He nodded. "I'm sorry."

Carbin said, "We have state troopers, the FBI, and Lieutenant Goudenough's men all milling around outside. It's a fu—goddamned circus."

Brillhagen motioned toward their prisoner. "Well, you can take this crud along. Have they all been rounded up?"

"Are you kidding? In the dark, in the woods?"

Brillhagen covered his embarrassment by asking quickly, "How many do you have?"

"Two dead, two alive. How many have you found in the building?" asked Carbin.

Brillhagen said, "One alive down here, and upstairs—" He looked at Athena.

"One dead upstairs," said Athena.

Brillhagen gave her a look of awe. "And you have his weapon."

She nodded.

"How in the world—"

"Tell you later," she said quickly.

Two state troopers came in and took the prisoner away.

Lieutenant Goudenough strolled in. "What a donnybrook! You still haven't found out how these bastards are getting in?"

Brillhagen shook his head. "We planned to search the woods tomorrow with a crew of about forty men. Try to find a camouflaged tunnel opening." He glanced at Carbin. "Don't know whether tonight's fracas—" He hesitated. "Three of Captain Carbin's men were killed."

"The search will go on," said Carbin. "We'll find any men we lost in the dark that way, too."

Athena said to Carbin, "It's small consolation, but

you may tell the families of these men that I will set up trust funds for them so that they will be well provided for."

Carbin nodded. For the first time he looked almost friendly. He said, "That's decent of you. But I suppose with all your wealth it will be no hardship."

Athena turned away without answering.

Brillhagen said to Carbin, "You have a very snotty manner which should be curbed. I wouldn't blame Mrs. von Dietrich if she decided to forget all about the trust funds."

"Sorry," said Carbin. He turned and strode off.

Lieutenant Goudenough said, "I wouldn't trust that man as far as I could throw my aunt Elvira, and she tips the scales at two sixty-two."

Brillhagen smiled. "Carbin's very efficient, but arrogant. But aside from his personality he does his job well. Replacing him would mean bringing in a whole new crew of sixty men, plus twenty temporaries here to help search tomorrow."

Goudenough glanced at his watch. "You mean this morning. It's quarter of four." He turned, and with a wave of his hand, strolled off.

Athena and Wolf went back to the castle and inspected the bombed-out rubble of Wolf's suite. Most of the furniture and all of the walls were badly damaged, but his clothes, in closets, and other personal possessions were undamaged. There were plenty of empty suites on the floor and he could move to another one as soon as convenient.

They went to Athena's suite, deciding to nap, if possible, until it was time for Wolf to join Carbin in the search of the grounds.

In spite of the problems of the night before, Carbin had the search organized by the appointed time. With a draftsman's skill, he had drawn an accurate map of the estate. Lines numbered one to forty indicated each man's search path. Placed at intervals of five feet, each searcher would scrutinize the ground area to his right and left, providing a double check. Starting at the lower right hand corner of the estate, the forty men would move off abreast. At the upper right hand corner of the estate they would move over another two hundred feet and start back. With the multitude of trees to go around and cause some confusion, it was still the best possible plan, Brillhagen decided, but wondered whether the job could be finished in one day. The eighty-acre estate would require many back-and-forth marches of the group. One sweep would cover less than an acre's width.

For a while Brillhagen walked with the men, watching them move fallen branches and carefully inspect any turf or weeds that might conceal an opening to the tunnel. Fortunately the trees were so thick that there was little growth on the ground. The fallen leaves from last winter had been cleaned away, removing what could have provided effective camouflage and would have necessitated a raking of the whole area.

He left the search group and went back to the castle. He was satisfied that they were doing a conscientious job.

He thought of going to one of the empty suites to sleep but realized that from now on he would have to stay with Athena constantly. Suppose she had been alone when the enemy started hand grenade blasting the suite room by room? Actually she had done pretty well on her own after they were captured and separated. He smiled at the irony of it. Perhaps he needed her more than she needed him. He shrugged. Whatever, two guns were better than one.

He banged on the door of her suite and finally woke her. After she heard his voice she unlocked the door and let him in.

After she relocked and double-bolted he went to the house phone and ordered breakfast sent up from the kitchen.

Athena was looking drawn and wan. He took her in his arms. "It's the man you killed, isn't it?" Undoubtedly her first.

She nodded. "I don't know why. These are subhumans ready to torture and kill me."

Brillhagen held her tighter. It was exactly what they would do. Torture her to find out, and kill her to be sure no one else got to the treasure first. He would like to kill them all rather slowly.

She decided that it was disgust with the way she had been forced to trick Kurt Wessel, using the promise of her body to distract him. The humiliation of having to let him unzip her jeans and paw around trying to pull her panties down. She raged over the fact that women were subjected to this kind of violation by men. She was almost angry with Wolf for being a man.

He shook her gently after she told him about it, her voice verging on hysteria. He said, "You mustn't feel that way about men in general. Ninety-eight percent of men, probably ninety-nine percent, would never rape a woman."

She asked, "But how many of them would have that fantasy lurking in their minds? A real sex thrill, taking a woman by force, right?"

He smiled weakly. He said, "I suppose that atavistic urge might lurk in more men than the small percentage that act on it. But—"

She laughed. "You, of course, have never had that fantasy."

Wolf shook his head. "In my adolescent fantasies the girl was always ecstatic, driven, panting to have me make love to her."

Athena smiled. "How about your grown-up fantasies?"

He released her and flopped down on a sofa. "With regard to sex, there are no fantasies, only reminiscences."

She bent over and slapped his face gently. "I'm just part of the crowd, am I not?"

He looked down. "Never. I love you. I never asked anyone else to marry me."

There was a gentle rap on the door.

Brillhagen got up quickly and stood near it, cradling his Uzi. "Who's there?" he asked.

A timid young woman's voice answered. "Rowena, sir, with your breakfasts."

He opened the door, still holding the Uzi at the ready.

A redheaded young woman in a maid's uniform rolled a cart into the room, glancing at the submachine gun with casual interest.

Wolf closed and bolted the door.

The maid said, "I hope everything will be all right, sir. Cook is in bed, all broken out from the shooting. A right mess she looks. Spots, spots, spots everywhere." She took a deep breath. "So I had to cook your breakfast."

Athena said, "I'm sorry to hear that. I will look in on her. Perhaps we can find some kind of lotion for her."

Wolf said, "I don't blame her for being allergic to gunfire. It's amazing that we all don't break out."

Athena laughed, then turned to Rowena. She said, "I'm sure the breakfast will be fine, Rowena. Thank you for being so brave."

Rowena beamed. "Never been so excited in my entire life. Wow!"

Wolf laughed, but sobered quickly. Rowena wouldn't have found it so exciting staring into the muzzle of a submachine gun held by a black-clad executioner. But then, they should be thankful that the younger members of the staff were not demoralized.

As the sky was darkening about 8:00 P.M. a bedraggled, weary Carbin came to the suite to report that the search had been completed. No tunnel opening had been found.

Brillhagen said, "There *must* be a tunnel. There's no other way they can be getting in."

Carbin shook his head. "I would stake my life on this search. There is no tunnel opening on the grounds. I'd bet everything I possess that no tunnel opening exists. I checked my men constantly during the search."

After he left, Wolf and Athena sat staring at each other silently.

17

MICHAELIS WAS STILL A BIT SHAKEN FROM HIS EXPERIENCE IN THE basement of the old farmhouse. Vietnam had been bad, but not, somehow, as bad as the farmhouse basement. A sort of numb resignation had kept him going in Nam. That and his buddies, being part of a team effort, a very big team, and falling back on childhood conditioning, *my country, right or wrong,* when he had doubts about why they were there. The farmhouse left a particularly bad taste. Sting had found both Adolf and Konrad dead. Had it been necessary for him to repeatedly bash Konrad's brains on the concrete? Well, kill or be killed. Just as well. Otherwise Sting probably would have finished them off.

Now, in the comfort of the suite at the Intercontinental and sipping a scotch on the rocks, he felt a big surge of relief. Back in Crendon in a day or so for good old familiar places and faces. He could forget Konrad's bloody head.

Sting said, "Angie, I got reservations for you and the Tarboys to head back to the States tomorrow. I know I'm a soft-headed jerk, but I promised that Leslie dame I'd get the hulk out of Finland. You know who I mean, Tom Swift."

Angie set her drink down with a thump. "You *what?*"

Sting turned up his palms. "I promised. He's a double agent and the Russkies have caught on to him."

Michaelis drained his glass and got up for a refill. He had forgotten about Sting's promise to Leslie. The world suddenly became bleak again.

Sting said, "Michaelis and I can handle it. To look at him you wouldn't believe it, but this guy is a one-man army."

Angie said, "I'm staying."

"You're going," said Sting.

"I'm staying," said Angie.

The argument continued for some time.

Angie finally agreed, but insisted that the Tarboys stay.

They compromised. One Tarboy would go with her, the other would stay with Sting and Michaelis.

Sting turned to Michaelis. "We also got some unfinished business in the States. We got four confessed bribees. We need three more."

Michaelis nodded dully. Marsha Hallowell would probably revert to her childhood psychosis and shoot them. Or Anthony Tedienzi would arrange concrete overcoats and give them a refreshing swim in the Hudson River.

The presidential appointment. He didn't really want to work with the guy in the White House. Sheer ego trip. He disagreed with him on almost all of his policies.

There was a knock on the door. Sting opened it and ushered Leslie Greenhaven in.

She smiled and said, "Hi, everybody."

Angie and Michaelis nodded glumly.

"I just dropped by to talk about arrangements for Tom," said Leslie.

Angie said, "He seems to be fully recovered. Why can't your own people shepherd him back?"

Leslie sat down. "May I have some of that scotch?"

Sting poured scotch over some ice cubes and handed the glass to her.

She said, "My problem is that I don't have anyone I can trust with something this tough." She sipped her drink. "We're very shorthanded here."

Sting said, "Michaelis and I will manage."

Leslie smiled and turned to Michaelis. "Ingrid told me all about the shoot-out at the OK Corral. You wouldn't by any chance be interested in my recruiting you, would you?"

Michaelis shook his head sadly. "It would be fun, I know, but Sting and I have other commitments."

Sting said, "Well, now, if you want to serve Uncle Sam, I'll take care of the other matter."

Michaelis hastily downed some more scotch. "Actually, I have other commitments. My contract with Crendon University, for one thing."

Leslie said to Michaelis, "It's not true that you tried to rape Ingrid, is it? I know she's an awful liar."

Michaelis laughed. "I'd rather tackle a giant tarantula. I shoved her down in the bushes because I didn't know whether the approaching cars were unfriendly, friendly, or neutral."

His cheeks were burning. The lousy little wretch. "So what have you done with Ingrid?" he asked.

Leslie said, "I traded her for two of our people."

Michaelis's eyebrows rose. "She's that good?"

"She certainly is, and she shouldn't be running around loose. I let sentiment get the best of me," said Leslie.

Michaelis shook his head. "I hope our paths don't cross," he said.

Sting said to Leslie, "You must be the station chief here."

She said quickly, "I don't know what you're talking about." She turned back to Michaelis. "Ingrid is *very* angry with you. She's out to get you. It's a personal vendetta." She took a big swallow of her drink. "She's a sleeper in the States and not active, but while you're here, *watch out.*"

Michaelis said, "Her cover is blown as far as Crendon University is concerned. Maybe she'll become active."

Leslie lit a cigarette, then blew some smoke in Michaelis's direction. "It's possible. Keep it in mind when you're on a dark street." She laughed. "Ingrid says when she catches up with you, she's going to cut off your thing. So be doubly cautious."

Michaelis's face became an even darker shade of red. "What a crude person," he said.

Angie, who had been trying to stifle a laugh, broke into a loud guffaw.

Sting controlled his, but his voice trembled slightly when he said, "That woman is really mad at you, Michaelis. We got to protect you from a fate worse than death."

Angie's laughter became hysterical. She couldn't stop. When she finally quieted she got the hiccoughs. She decided to go to their bedroom and lie down.

Leslie turned to Sting. "So when are you going to take over Tom?"

Sting rubbed his forehead. "First I'm getting Angie off to New York tomorrow. One of the Tarboys will accompany her. I'll book us for the following day. Michaelis, Swift, the other Tarboy, and myself in first class. We could get new disguises, but it wouldn't help. There's no way you could disguise Tom Swift."

Leslie asked, "What is this *Tarboy* stuff? You racist or something?"

Michaelis laughed. "They're brothers, twins. Tarboy is their last name."

Leslie said, "You just gave me an idea. We have a delegation of Ethiopian politicians here on a junket. Apparently they want to visit Leningrad, but not officially."

Sting smiled. "Convert Swift into a big black politician."

Leslie nodded. "However, if he's with your party, they

will make the connection immediately. You'll *all* have to be black."

Sting laughed. "Maybe I'll meet a good-looking black chick."

Leslie frowned. "We can do an expert makeup job, one that will get you by as a black, but don't try any conversation with a real black person. I think you'll blow it."

Sting's mouth turned down. "I don't know about that."

Michaelis poured himself another drink. "As I see it, Swift is in danger here, and will be when he gets to the States. I don't think the KGB would want to bloody up a Finnair ship."

Leslie said, "If they're desperate they would. And in this case they *are* going to be desperate."

Michaelis sipped his drink. This was definitely his last one. No allowing himself to get drunk. Not with Ingrid after him. He said, "Then they are going to have to get close enough to him to use a knife or a blunt instrument."

"Why?" asked Sting.

"A shoot-out on a plane would probably kill everybody. Bullets ripping holes in the fuselage, destroying the air pressure in the cabin, bullets hitting wing gas tanks and blowing up the plane—I'm sure the KGB is aware of that."

Sting said, "All they need is one bullet in his head."

Leslie shuddered. "Don't talk about it."

"One bullet would draw fire from us," said Michaelis. "At least they would expect that."

Leslie stood up. "I'm beginning to like the idea of making Tom a black man. He has brown eyes and curly black hair. We make the curls tighter and we have an Afro hairstyle. Stain his face, hands, and arms dark brown. Pinstripe suit, white shirt, and red tie. Not a prizefighter but a big-shot politician from one of the African countries. Get him an Ethiopian or Zambian passport."

Sting slapped the coffee table. "Now you're talking!"

She said, "You black men escorting him will also be expensively dressed."

She headed for the door. "Okay. I've got a lot of work to do in a very short time. I'll need to know the flight time as soon as you have the reservation."

"Where can I reach you?" asked Sting.

She said, "You can't. I'll call you tomorrow afternoon." She opened the door and slipped out.

After the door closed, Sting said, "I'm feeling better about this deal."

Michaelis had a frightening thought. "What if this suite is bugged? The Russians are very good at that."

Sting clutched his jaw as though a toothache had struck. He picked up the phone and made a call.

Tight-lipped, he said to Michaelis, "Got a man coming to check it out. If we are, Leslie's black man goes right out the window."

Michaelis settled into a state of somnolent awareness. The three drinks had made him sleepy, but the specter of Ingrid coming at him with a knife was not easy to doze with. Unbelievable. No one at Crendon would believe it. A sadistic, crazy woman. Not really crazy; a fanatic, say.

Sting's electronics expert arrived. He was a sandy-haired Finn with little command of English.

He took the phone apart, then put it together again. He said, "So, is not there."

He scanned the room for likely places, took two lamps apart, then put them back together again. "So, is not there," he said.

Watching the man work, Michaelis said to Sting, "I thought they just brought in one of those electronic devices that beep you right to the bug."

Sting said, "I think they do. But not here."

The expert went to the windows and began to examine the drapes. "So, is here," he said in a monotone.

The bug was hidden in the lining of the drapes. In front, a tiny triangle, unnoticeable in the pattern, had been cut to provide better reception of the sound waves.

Sting thanked the expert, tucked a bill in his hand, and sent him on his way with a pat on the back.

After the door closed, he turned to Michaelis and yelled, "Oh, shit! Why didn't you think of it earlier?" He snatched the small device from the drapes, threw it on the floor, and stamped on it with his heel.

Michaelis glared back. "You're the expert. *You* should have thought of it." He poured himself some plain soda.

"Anyway, it wasn't there earlier. If it had been we would never have gotten Swift out of that room. In fact, we'd probably all be dead."

Sting rubbed his chin. "You got a point there."

He began to pace the room, muttering to himself. He paused in front of Michaelis and said, "That damned woman wouldn't tell me where I could get in touch with *her.* Now that poor sonofabitch is gonna get dyed dark brown and then they're gonna have to bleach him out. Not to mention the same thing for his two escorts."

Michaelis closed his eyes. Good-bye to a great plan that might have assured them an uneventful trip home.

The phone rang. Michaelis picked it up.

"Strang?" asked a female voice which sounded like Leslie.

"No, Michaelis."

The voice said, "Tell Strang to stop destroying government property. The instrument is ours and it was there for your protection."

"How do I know it's Leslie?" he asked. "What state is Little Rock in?"

"Arkansas." She pronounced it correctly as *Arkansaw.*

"Okay, I'll tell him," said Michaelis.

She disconnected.

He turned to Sting. "That was Leslie. The bug is theirs. She says it was for our protection."

Sting stopped pacing and smiled. "I'll be damned. They probably have a room nearby. Somebody comes here to cause problems, reinforcements suddenly arrive."

"You didn't know they *cared.*"

Sting gave him the finger.

Michaelis sipped his soda water. What a boring drink. "We're going to need some new disguises," he said. "Ingrid might even be on the flight."

If Ingrid was on the plane— He didn't even want to think about it. Not only that, they would be unarmed unless Sting—

"You'd better figure out some way to get some weapons aboard, even knives if nothing else. I'm damned sure Ingrid or whoever they send will be armed."

Sting shook his head. "No way. She won't be able to

bring anything aboard. Security is too tight these days. Damned terrorists."

Michaelis said, "How about poison? How would you like for her to drop a tiny cyanide tablet in your scotch?"

Sting laughed. "Tell you what. We'll arm ourselves with good old-fashioned straight-edge barber's razors. Almost as good as a knife," he said.

Michaelis shrugged. "I suppose they would get past the monitors in a shaving kit. Better than nothing, I guess."

He tried to imagine defending himself with a straight-edge razor. His opponent's only vulnerable spot would be his or her neck. Literally go for the jugular. Blood spurting all over him.

Ingrid could dust them with that lethal invisible powder they had. Usually it was used, he had read, by someone shaking hands with an enemy. The agent who uses it has five minutes to apply an antidote. In seven or eight days the recipient dies of cardiac arrest. If shaking hands could do it, certainly someone dusting a bit on the back of your neck would probably work equally well. Or would it? Maybe the hand shaking worked the powder into the pores.

Why assume they would have Ingrid on the flight? It was logical. She was obviously one of their best and most ruthless operatives. She would recognize them. And killing Swift was a number one priority. She would undoubtedly be cleverly disguised. A kindly old lady wearing thick-lensed glasses and carrying a knitting bag?

He turned to Sting. "Ingrid will probably be on the plane disguised as god knows what."

Sting threw himself down on a sofa and closed his eyes.

Michaelis picked up a day-late copy of the *New York Times* and read it. He wondered vaguely where AIDS had originated. Had it always been around, with the virus simply unidentified? The eventual diagnosis at death being the failure of the first vital function to give way completely? Heart, lungs, liver, kidneys, blood corpuscles? There were worse situations than he was in, but not many.

The phone rang. Michaelis answered it.

"Tell Sting that we'll begin work on the problem as soon as he gets Angelica and her escort on the plane and returns to the suite. You, Michaelis, remain in the suite after breakfast and we'll get to you first."

Michaelis said, "Okay. Thanks."

He woke Sting up and gave him the message.

Michaelis examined his new face in the bathroom mirror. He decided that apart from his close-cut Afro wig he looked more like a Sikh or a dark brown Hindu. No worry, Leslie had explained. Black Africans and Caucasians had been mixing for hundreds of years. Many Africans did not look like typical blacks today. No one would be suspicious because of the color of his eyes, gray, or the shape of his nose or mouth.

The logic of converting Sting, Donald Tarboy, and himself to blacks was unassailable. They could not only escort Swift to the plane, but cluster around him on board to provide additional protection.

Donald Tarboy had gone ahead to the airport with all their luggage. Michaelis picked up his flight bag and waited for Sting to finish contemplating his own brown face. Sting looked like an angry black cop trying to direct traffic in a Manhattan gridlock with the temperature at 100 degrees. Perspiration stood out on his forehead.

Sting asked, "Do you think sweat will make this color run?"

"No," said Michaelis. "Probably nothing less than a nitric acid rinse will get it off."

He glanced at his watch. The limousine bearing Swift was due in two minutes.

"Let's go," he said.

They rode the elevator to the first floor, walked with an unhurried pace through the lobby and out the main entrance.

The limousine pulled up right on schedule. The chauffeur jumped out and hurried around to open the door for them. Michaelis let Sting have the seat next to Swift, pulling down one of the folding seats for himself. Three men couldn't sit in the back seat when one of them was Swift.

Facing them, Michaelis studied Swift. He decided that Swift looked more like the King of Siam in chinos than an

African. Impressive, however. He could pass easily as a powerful, light-brown black man.

For the chauffeur's benefit the three men chatted in Amharic, using some hastily learned and practiced sentences. "I do not speak any English." "The food is good." "Thank you, yes, I will have another drink." "Do you think the weather will be good?" "I am cold." "I am too warm."

Since the stewardesses would not speak Amharic, they would depend upon Michaelis's French to get that additional drink. No English would be spoken.

Donald Tarboy was waiting for them in the airport's departure area.

They were hustled through customs and on to the plane ahead of all the other passengers. Offered their choice of seats in the first-class section, Sting chose the front two on the left, and the two seats behind. He placed Swift at the window, slender Donald Tarboy next to him on the aisle. He gave Michaelis the window seat behind Swift and settled himself into the aisle seat.

Michaelis opened his flight bag, found his toiletries kit, unzipped it, found the straight-edge razor, and slipped it into his jacket pocket.

Watching him, Sting grunted and did the same thing.

The other passengers began to file in. Some surprised looks were directed at the black men already seated.

Michaelis turned and studied faces. None were familiar. There was a black-haired young woman seated at the rear of the section, but he couldn't get a clear view of her face.

Sting and Michaelis passed some sentences in Amharic back and forth for the benefit of the two American businessmen sitting behind them. One had already opened his portable computer and was busy tapping the keys. The other man was speaking softly into a tape recorder. From the words Michaelis could hear, this passenger was an American salesman dictating a report of a meeting he had had with a customer interested in buying a thousand second-hand Chevrolets.

Across the aisle were four Japanese businessmen conversing vociferously in Japanese.

Further behind him he could hear various other languages. Finnish, German, Italian, and Spanish words drifted by.

Michaelis wondered if he dared relax.

The dark-haired young woman came slowly down the aisle glancing sideways at faces. At the front she turned and surveyed the group, as though looking for a friend. Ingrid's blond hair was now black, and pulled into a tight ponytail, making her forehead higher, her face taut. She was pale, looking both hard and annoyed. She walked slowly to the back of the section, hardly glancing at the four black men.

In French Michaelis asked Sting, "Did you see what I saw?"

Sting said, *"Oui."*

Why was she on the plane? Probably she had found out that their group was no longer at the Intercontinental, Michaelis decided. Would she get off the plane at Copenhagen, having satisfied herself that they were not aboard, or would she go all the way to Amsterdam or New York? If she stayed on beyond Copenhagen, it could become a very bad scene. Some of her colleagues were probably scrutinizing the passengers in the big cabin.

It was going to be a lovely trip with Ingrid aboard.

Michaelis wondered whether he could bring himself to slash at that white throat if she came at him with something lethal. He hoped Sting was right about the tough security. At least she wouldn't be packing a Walther. Of course, even without a metal weapon, she could easily garrote one or two of them while they slept. Obviously no one should sleep. Or she could dust them up with some of that deadly powder. In a low voice Michaelis asked Sting if he had heard about the KGB's deadly handshake.

Sting said, "You don't mean this tracking powder they're using? I've heard it's either harmless or mildly carcinogenic."

Michaelis shook his head. "No, the two are entirely different. I read about the deadly handshake several years ago in a definitive book on KGB operations."

Sting nudged with his elbow, smiling. "Don't worry, I ain't shaking hands with anybody."

Michaelis asked, "Suppose Ingrid sprinkled some on the back of your neck when she went by?"

Sting said, "I wouldn't like that, old son. But you don't have to remind me that we got to be alert every second during this goddamned flight."

Michaelis lit a cigarette. Pipes and cigars were verboten.

He said to Sting, "Maybe I worry too much, but I'm baffled by Ingrid. She dyed her hair black, but has made no effort to really disguise herself. What is she up to?"

Sting said, "She's up to throwing you off balance by creating questions like that."

Properly put down, Michaelis was silent for a while, listening to the muted rumble of the engines and wondering when the stewardess would bring drinks.

"Do you think Ingrid is on to us?"

Sting shrugged. "She gave no indication of it whatsoever. But then, would she?"

Michaelis crushed out his cigarette. "I wonder how many of her people are on board?"

"Good question," said Sting.

The speaker system came alive to announce that they were on the approach to Copenhagen airport and would be descending shortly.

Leaving the plane at Copenhagen, Ingrid sauntered into the holding area with the rest of the passengers. She was not getting off there. Michaelis watched her closely but unobtrusively. When she was facing in his direction, he was looking past her, or to one side. She spoke to no one. But then it was a very short wait until they were asked to return to their seats.

As they boarded the plane, Michaelis said to Sting, "I think she's spotted us."

Sting slapped his back. "Maybe she has business in Amsterdam."

If she had business in Amsterdam, Michaelis decided, it was probably to slip a grenade into Swift's pants.

The stewardess offered champagne, which was customary in first class. Michaelis asked for scotch; Sting wanted bourbon. Swift and Donald Tarboy asked for Cokes. Swift wasn't taking any chances, and the Tarboy brothers came from a teetotaling South Carolina family. In the small towns there, if you're a church member, being a drinker is about on a par with walking naked down Main Street.

Sting and Michaelis took turns dozing during the long flight to Amsterdam. Michaelis wished his head had come equipped with a rearview mirror. Any kind of attack had to come from the rear. When he was on duty, he half-sat sideways in his seat so that he could glance to the rear frequently. An element of safety was provided by the stewardesses. There were three on duty in the first-class cabin, and all three seemed to be moving around constantly fetching drinks, pillows, blankets, snacks, and magazines.

Sting should have picked seats in the last row, with all the passengers sitting in front of them instead of behind them. He pointed this out to Sting.

Sting explained that the doorway between the first-class section and the large cabin was covered by only heavy fabric curtains. No door to click, squeak, or groan. The curtains offered an ideal opportunity for sneaking up on people just inside the first-class cabin. In their present position the enemy would have to walk all the way to the front of the plane and would thus be much easier to spot.

"If you had eyes in the back of your head," said Michaelis.

Sting said, "I have. My hearing is very acute."

Michaelis laughed.

Sting said, "Listen, sonny, these people have some weird and wonderful weapons. One that might be used here is about the size of a fountain pen, but thicker. It is activated by a heavy spring mechanism. Pointed within five feet of you, it can drive a small metal dart right into your heart. Someone ducking around the curtain could do the job in a split second and be back at his seat in the big cabin before anyone realized what had happened. With our man seated down here, the assailant would have to come within five feet of Swift, and having done the job, walk or run back up the aisle."

Michaelis said, "Okay, Pop, I got the message."

The loudspeaker finally mentioned the approach to Amsterdam.

Would the black widow leave the plane at Amsterdam? Michaelis hoped so.

Ingrid followed them into the holding area of Schiphol Airport. She was going to accompany them to New York. Good. He could have her picked up there and incarcerated. Ingrid Hugel, SSD agent and murderess. But how could he prove it? His word against hers. Sting, Angie, and the Tarboys could testify. But he suspected that they would not want to do so. Sting would want to have as little to do with the law as possible. Though he had served on the jury that acquitted Athena von Dietrich, civic duty offered no real threat of detailed investigation. Of course the CIA would be very interested in latching onto Ingrid, but then again they might prefer to have her free. Better a known enemy than an unknown killer.

Keeping a protective eye on the group, Michaelis noticed that they were clustered near the store selling the giant cookie house, *Knusperhous.* He thought again of Diane, and if they had had children. What if Diane could see him now? Foreign agent deluxe followed by the murderous Ingrid, who had sworn to deprive him of his manhood.

He smiled, almost laughed.

Ingrid strolled up to the group. She offered her hand to Swift. "I understand you are an Ethiopian cabinet minister. You must know my good friend, Salu Absoma?"

Michaelis glanced quickly at his watch.

Swift put his hand behind his back and said in Amharic, "I do not speak English."

Michaelis got behind Ingrid. If she had the poison on her hand, all they had to do was keep her there for five minutes. Sting and Donald Tarboy moved to surround her.

Michaelis said in French, "He speaks only Amharic. He will not shake hands with you because it is against his religion to touch any woman not of his immediate family."

She turned to stare at him. She held out her hand. "Perhaps you will shake hands with me and ask him how my friend Salu Absoma is."

Michaelis put his hand in his jacket pocket and fingered the straight-edge razor. He said, "I cannot shake hands with you for I, too, would be defiled. It is not our policy to discuss our cabinet ministers with strangers." He glanced at his watch. Only a minute and a half had passed.

She turned to Sting. "Are you as unfriendly as your companions?" she asked.

Sticking his hand quickly into his pocket, Sting said in Amharic, "Would you please direct me to the toilet?"

Michaelis said in French, "He, too, would be defiled."

Ingrid glanced at her wristwatch.

She turned to Swift and reached up suddenly to pat his cheek, saying, "Big man, you know you're really very cute."

Michaelis grabbed her wrist in a tight grip.

"You must not touch any of us," he said.

He glanced at his watch. Two minutes and ten seconds.

She tried to twist away. Michaelis held on hard enough to stop her circulation.

Donald Tarboy grabbed her other wrist.

Michaelis said in French, "She is a pickpocket trying to rob us. We must turn her over to the police." He glanced at his watch. Two minutes and forty seconds.

Perspiration was beginning to dot Ingrid's forehead.

"If you don't let me go, I'll scream *rape!*" she said loudly.

Three minutes.

Michaelis said, "It will take some time for the police to sort this all out. Will it be worth missing our plane to put this pickpocket in jail?"

Three minutes and twenty seconds.

Ingrid twisted toward Swift, tears in her eyes. She said, "Swift, let me go and I'll owe you a big one!"

Swift said to Michaelis, "Let her go. I can't stomach killing a woman this way."

Michaelis felt a big surge of relief. He could shoot Ingrid in self-defense, but this nauseated him, too.

He let go of her wrist. Tarboy released the other wrist. She ran off, probably in the direction of the women's lavatory. She had one minute and ten seconds left to either swallow or apply the antidote. He wouldn't be particularly unhappy if she didn't make it.

Back on the plane Donald Tarboy prowled the tourist cabin searching for Ingrid. He reported back that she was not on board unless she was hiding in one of the lavatories.

Michaelis asked Swift, "Do you believe her when she says she owes you a big one?"

Swift nodded. "Yes. Ingrid will keep her word."

Michaelis asked, "For example, how will she pay off this debt?"

Swift shrugged. "Help me out of a tight spot sometime. A real tight spot."

Michaelis said, "If she doesn't kill you first, right?"

Swift grinned. "That, too."

Michaelis stared out the window. Nothing but clouds below. He turned back to Swift. "I'm still baffled. I wouldn't trust her anywhere at any time for anything."

Swift laughed. He said, "It's not a matter of honor among thieves, or some kind of code we have. It's a matter of the individual. Some people who make promises are obsessive in their determination to keep them. Ingrid is one of those people. She may be one of the trickiest, dirtiest, most murderous bitches you have ever encountered, but when she says she will do something, she does it. Some kind of crapped-up childhood conditioning, I guess."

Obsessively honest or not, Michaelis hoped he would never again have to deal with Ingrid Hugel. He wondered if she had really received her doctorate. It wouldn't be beyond her arrogance to show up at Crendon to try for tenure in the German Department.

Leslie Greenhaven had evidently notified colleagues in New York. A young man with close-cropped yellow hair and an air of innocence hurried them through customs. His name was Jack Plumb. He explained that they had a limousine waiting for Swift and that they would be glad to take Michaelis, Sting, and Donald to Manhattan. That the service was deeply grateful for their efforts in saving Swift's life, and if they could give out medals, which unfortunately they were not allowed to do, the three heroes would certainly receive them. They would, of course, be reimbursed for all expenses of the trip to Finland and return. Having made his speech, he watched as their baggage was wheeled out to the limousine.

Sting said they would settle for a letter from the President commending their actions.

This set the young agent back on his heels, but he said he would see what he could do.

They walked out through the large JFK Airport lobby toward the exit, Swift striding between Plumb and Sting.

Suddenly Ingrid stepped out from behind a very fat woman. She was holding a wicked-looking pistol with a silencer attached. It was pointed right at Swift.

She said, "Here's the big one I promised you, Swift," then pulled the trigger. There was a small pop. Swift clutched his chest and collapsed slowly onto the floor. Plumb was still trying to get his revolver out of its holster.

Ingrid ran, disappearing quickly into the crowd.

Michaelis bent over Swift, who was grimly clutching his bloody shirt front. "Obsessive in her honesty, all right," he muttered.

Swift said softly, "Pretend I'm mortally wounded. Look distraught, get an ambulance."

Astonished, Michaelis asked, "Aren't you?"

Swift shook his head. "It hardly broke the skin. I can feel half the bullet is still outside."

Michaelis said, "I don't understand. She got you at point-blank range."

Swift winked. "She accomplished her mission and gave me the big one she promised, too."

"But how in hell—?"

Swift said, "She probably removed half the powder in that shell."

Plumb was bending over Swift yelling, "Get an ambulance!"

Swift said to Plumb, "You get one. I'm wounded, and I want to talk to Michaelis."

Plumb straightened up, red-faced. He turned and ran to the nearest phone.

Sting and Donald Tarboy were lost in the crowd chasing Ingrid.

Swift said to Michaelis, "Tell the ambulance people not to talk to the press, make this very clear to Plumb. The story is I'm critically wounded, on the brink of death."

Michaelis nodded, his expression puzzled.

"If the truth gets out, Ingrid will have to come after me again. She couldn't tolerate failure on her record."

Michaelis smiled. "You need a few months of recuperation, right?"

Swift said, "That and a better disguise."

18

ATHENA'S DAILY ROUTINE ONLY BARELY KEPT HER AT PEACE WITH the world and her existence in a luxurious prison. Brillhagen was bored. Lying on the grass bordering the swimming pool, he sat up suddenly and idly contemplated his tanned, well-muscled body. Aside from managing his investments, which he could do by telephone from the castle, there was little of his old, active life left. Amateur tennis tournaments, golf, the theater in New York and London, driving his Ferrari, socializing with his many friends among the international jet set, the company of other men, close friends, dinner parties at fine restaurants, and even a new conquest here and there, which he put out of his mind, telling himself that he truly loved Athena and that she was worth all of the things he missed. But he was still depressed.

Athena was aware of his state. He tried to hide it by smiling a lot and joking about their situation. She wondered, too, how long she could stand this isolation without becoming a dull zombie.

The poolside telephone rang. Brillhagen opened the weatherproof box, answered it and turned to Athena. "Carbin says a Mr. MacVeagh Pratt from the State Department would like to see you."

Athena said, "Let him come up." She got to her feet and put on her white terry-cloth robe. Her bikini was somewhat informal for a visit from the State Department.

MacVeagh Pratt was a tall, distinguished-looking man with dark hair graying at the temples, blue eyes, a large mouth revealing very white teeth, and a prominent but straight nose. He was wearing an expensive white summer-weight suit, with a blue shirt and black knit tie.

Athena stood up to shake hands with him, and introduced Wolf.

Brillhagen pulled up one of the canvas chairs for him, then sat down in one close by.

Pratt stared around at the forest, the castle, and the huge swimming pool. "Lovely place you have here, Mrs. von Dietrich," he said.

Athena nodded, smiling. That out of the way, she hoped he would get down to business. "It will do. Rather dismal in the winter, I'm afraid."

Pratt said, "Right."

"Why are you here, Mr. Pratt?" She had no patience for social clichés when important matters to be discussed were waiting in the wings. His next remark would be a comment about the weather.

He smiled. "I see you like to get right down to business. I appreciate that."

Athena nodded.

Pratt took a deep breath and distended his cheeks a bit expelling it. He said, "Well, as you can understand, we have a rather unusual situation here. We, as you must know, have used our influence with the local police to allow a great many illegal things to go on here. You have your own army, equipped with weapons that are clearly illegal, and the corpse count is becoming a bit difficult to explain. Murderous scoundrels all, of course, but still bodies that need to be legally explained and put to rest. Lieutenant Goudenough is in a delicate spot with his constituents who hear about these bodies and question the situation."

Athena said, "I should think the CIA would have adequate experience in disposing of bodies."

Pratt gave her an embarrassed smile. "Well, when they start turning up by the dozen—" he said.

"There have not been that many," said Athena quickly.

"Perhaps not, but—" said Pratt.

Athena said to Brillhagen, "Perhaps we should relocate. London would be fun, wouldn't it? The Queen has offered me a twenty-room suite in Buckingham Palace, and will provide security forces from the British army. We wouldn't have to deal with people like Carbin and his security guards."

Pratt's face paled and his mouth turned down. He said, "Well, I hope that nothing I have said would indicate that you are not *very* welcome here, in spite of the legal problems we have to cover up."

Wolf said, "If we were in England there would be no problem about bodies. Any intruder shot by the British army would be killed quite legally."

Pratt held up his hand. "Now, please, do not jump to conclusions. I am not here to complain about your security measures. Heavens, if necessary we'll provide a detachment of the army to help protect you."

Athena said, "Actually we are becoming very bored here. We can't even leave the place without fear that we will be attacked by murderers with guns. You make it so easy for people to have guns in this country."

Whether it was the warm sun, or nerves, Pratt's forehead was wet with perspiration.

He said, "Please do not concern yourself about security measures here. If necessary we will get a company of Marines to guard your property and escort you to any place you might wish to go."

He mopped his forehead with an immaculate white handkerchief. "Let me tell you why I am here," he said. "Our government is exceedingly anxious to know whether you will consider any further negotiations with regard to your father's invention."

Athena asked, "Is the government prepared to guarantee that it will be used for nothing but the production of very inexpensive power?"

Pratt took another deep breath, expelling it from puffed cheeks. "No nation could guarantee that absolutely. After all, it's a matter of public record that we are working in this direction at Fermilab. Other scientists are doing the same abroad."

Athena laughed. "And it costs them billions to produce something less than the size of a fly's eye. In a hundred years you may have your monstrous weapon and cheap power, too, but I won't be around and it will not be on my conscience."

Pratt stared at her stony-faced, but after a moment, relaxed. "Look at it this way. We're the only nation in the world that you could really trust to protect this discovery. Even if we made a weapon from it, we wouldn't use it. We haven't used our nuclear capacity in forty years, and we've never used poison gas in combat. Both are readily available. And as a side note, we are certain that the Russians used poison gas in Afghanistan. Our primary interest is the development of cheap power. This would remove our country from dependence upon unstable, volatile countries such as Iran."

Athena said, "I've had that lecture from Wolf."

Pratt glanced at Brillhagen, smiling, hopeful that he had an ally.

Brillhagen shrugged. "Athena is not one to change her mind easily, once it is made up."

Pratt turned to her. "Mrs. von Dietrich, if you should change your mind, will you promise to give first consideration to the United States?"

Athena thought about it. After a moment she said, "Yes, I can promise that. Unless, of course, we should have to go to England. Then I would feel more or less indebted—"

Pratt said hurriedly, "We'll provide your entire security force if you wish. All soldiers or Marines."

Brillhagen sat up straighter. "Say, that would be—" he started.

Athena held up her hand. "I'd want to think about it."

Brillhagen realized that she did not want to be indebted for this protection. She preferred, as always, to be in control.

Pratt got to his feet slowly. Reaching into his jacket pocket, he brought out two business cards. He handed one to Athena and the other to Brillhagen. "You can reach me at this number twenty-four hours a day. If you have another attack here, I would appreciate your getting in touch with me immediately."

Brillhagen assured him that they would.

Pratt shook hands with Athena and Wolf, then sauntered off in the direction of the gatehouse.

When Pratt was out of earshot, Brillhagen said to Athena, "I can understand your reluctance to become indebted to the U.S. government for security, but we have some real problems here. There is no tunnel. Carbin's men have searched every square foot of the estate. Yet these bastards are still getting in. How? I suspect the U.S. Army could do a hell of a lot better job of protecting you."

Athena shed her terry-cloth robe and lay down beside Brillhagen. She said, "Wolf, use your brain. It is not indebtedness to the government that worries me. Picture this estate under the control of the army. Power corrupts. If I decided to leave this country, the government might decide that it is in the best interest of the nation to detain me. The telephone switchboard is in the gatehouse. We could become prisoners unable to even contact anyone outside."

Wolf smiled. "This is not the Soviet Union. We are both citizens. They could not hold us incommunicado for very long."

She patted his cheek. "When the stakes are high, one cannot predict how badly good people may act."

Wolf sat up. "You're right, I suppose. And, as poker players would put it, you have a strong ace in the hole."

Athena was puzzled. "What is the hole the ace is in?" she asked.

Wolf laughed. "It is the card that is turned facedown. The other cards are faceup, and the other players can see what you have, except for the possible *ace in the hole.*"

Athena nodded. "I see. My card that is turned down is the location of my father's papers."

Wolf said, "I'm surprised that you have never played poker." He moved the palm of his hand along her thigh.

She pushed his hand away. "I have led a very sheltered life," she said.

The sky suddenly darkened, streaks of lightning flashed and were followed by the rumble of thunder in the distance. The air seemed to be thick with moisture; you could almost drink it, Wolf thought, and coupled with the continuing roar of thunderclaps it reminded him of Vietnam. He shivered.

Athena asked, "Are you ill?"

He smiled. "No, just the storm and the humidity."

Rain started to fall in torrents.

Athena clutched her robe and ran for the escalator. Wolf followed, laughing. He climbed the moving steps to catch up with her.

"Why are you laughing?" she asked.

He wiped water from his eyes. "We are dressed for swimming, and we run to keep from getting wet in the rain."

"I do not like the lightning," said Athena.

He said, "Even if there were no lightning, you would run from the rain."

Athena turned to look at him over her shoulder. "Swimming is swimming. Taking a shower is for the bathroom," she said.

After they reached the castle, Wolf went to his rooms, took a shower, then put on gray slacks and a blue open-neck shirt. He had to have it out with Carbin. There was carelessness somewhere, and unless they could locate it, there would be another break-in, and they might not be as lucky next time. As it was, three of Carbin's men had been killed. Those of the enemy invaders who survived provided no useful information. The government agencies were cautious in dealing with local lawmen such as Goudenough, but they did inform him that most of the perpetrators captured were probably employees of the KGB or the SSD, the East German intelligence agency. Several were identified as Cubans.

He glanced out the window and noted that the rain was slackening. He pulled a lightweight vinyl poncho over his head, rode the elevator to the first floor, and left the castle to walk down to the gatehouse.

Carbin was not happy to see him. Seated in his office with his feet on his desk, smoke curling upward from a cigarette that seemed to be stuck to his lower lip, he gave Wolf a hostile stare, removed his feet from the desk, and pulled his swivel chair closer.

"When you want to see me, telephone and I will come up to the castle," he said.

"I want to talk to you here. I want to familiarize myself with the way you are operating."

"Why?" asked Carbin.

Wolf resented his brusque bark. "Why? Because these

people are still breaking in, and you have not found out how they are doing it. This situation cannot be allowed to continue."

Carbin shrugged. "There is no tunnel, they can't get over the wall, so they must be dropped from the sky."

"Impossible," said Wolf. "First, no parachutes have been found. Secondly, the only safe target large enough for a parachute jump would be the swimming pool. Certainly no one has landed there."

Carbin pulled the cigarette from his lip, taking a little dried skin with it. "Maybe they jump into the trees and climb down."

Wolf said, "They do not come down through the trees, either from a jump or easing out of a balloon basket."

Carbin shoved his chair back and put his feet on the desk again. "How can you say that?" he asked.

Wolf said, "The black coveralls they have been wearing have been analyzed by forensic specialists. If they had come down through the trees, there would be a great deal of evidence left on the cloth. Leaf dust, bark dust, bark abrasions, possibly sap from broken limbs, and various other indications that would be impossible to avoid. Also the skin of their hands would provide other indications of the climb down."

Carbin stared at him, contempt barely concealed. He wet his lip and put the cigarette back and puffed on it. Finally he shrugged and said, "Then they must be flying in on their own little birdie wings."

Wolf's face was grim. "This is no time for joking. You've lost three men. The next time they may get through to Mrs. von Dietrich."

Carbin produced a phony smile, showing a lot of teeth. "Things are rough all over, I guess," he said.

"You can give no explanation, and I can find no explanation but one which you have refused to accept. I'm afraid you'll have to face up to the fact that the only possible answer is that some of your men are betraying you."

Carbin brought his feet down to the floor with a loud thump, then stood up quickly, his face red.

He said, "If you weren't my employer, I'd knock the living crap out of you."

Wolf said, "Try it and you'll lose most of your teeth."

Carbin lowered himself back into his chair slowly. "Our quarreling isn't going to settle anything. If you want to replace me and my group, that's your privilege. But even if I had a bad apple or two, there's *no way* they could compromise the operation. I have twice the number of men on duty at night as during the day. There are a number of men constantly around the gatehouse, both inside and out. There's no way one or two men could open the gate for a vehicle, or let unidentified men on foot come through the gatehouse."

Wolf leaned back and closed his eyes, thinking. Finally he said, "Suppose by prearrangement just *one* of your men shut off the wall alarms for just fifteen minutes, say from three to three-fifteen A.M.?"

Carbin got up, and motioning for Wolf to follow him, walked out to the dayroom where the off-duty men congregated. He pointed to a large metal panel on one wall.

He said, "That box houses the master switches for electricity throughout the estate." He took a small key from his pocket and held it up for Wolf to see. "This is the only key, and I keep it on my person at all times. It would take a crowbar to bust open that box, and as you can see, there isn't a scratch on it."

Wolf asked, "What happens on your days off? Surely you must leave the key with someone? If a circuit breaker flips one of the switches off, the box has to be opened."

Carbin looked startled. "Oh, sorry. When I'm not here, I leave the key with Lieutenant Betz."

Wolf nodded. "And if he has to leave the gatehouse for any length of time, who does he leave the key with?"

Carbin crushed out his cigarette and lit a fresh one. He said, "I don't think either Wayne or I ever get so far from the gatehouse that it would be a problem. At least it has never been with me."

Wolf stared at him. "Then when you were on duty you have never turned the key over to anyone other than Wayne Betz?"

Carbin squirmed uncomfortably. "Well, actually, I suppose I may have. Wayne and I have to take different shifts. Say, if I had to go into Crendon for a meeting with

Lieutenant Goudenough, I would leave the key with one of the men." He continued hurriedly, "It's always been in the daytime, so it couldn't have any bearing on the attacks. It never occurred to me that the switch box was a security risk. I was only concerned with the circuit breaker flipping one of the switches off."

Wolf asked, "Do you remember the names of the men you left the key with?"

Embarrassed, Carbin shook his head. "Not offhand. Maybe if I sit down and think about it. Anyway, what could he do with it? He couldn't go into Crendon and have a dupe made."

Wolf said, "He could take a wax impression and have a key made later."

Carbin clicked his tongue disgustedly. "You been reading spy books. Look, even with a key, what's he going to do? The dayroom has men in it all the time. So what's the guy going to do, say, *Excuse me, fellows, I've got to shut off the wall alarms so my friends can get over it?"*

Wolf looked away, impatient. "There's quite a bit of talking going on in the dayroom, right?"

Carbin nodded.

"So he could pick up the phone, pretending it rang, put it down and say, *Hell, the circuit breaker's flipped the lights in the garage area,* and then proceed to open the box and shut off the wall alarms," said Wolf.

Carbin got up and stared out the window behind his desk. He collapsed back into his desk chair, turned his palms up, and stared at Brillhagen. "You want me to put a twenty-four-hour guard on the box?"

Wolf shook his head. "I don't appreciate your sarcasm. You can set up more rigid security with the key. Whenever it is out of your hands, or Wayne Betz's hands, the person signs for it, noting the time taken and the time returned. You can also alert your men to challenge anyone opening the box. If the lights have gone out somewhere, have it checked."

Carbin stared at him silently for a few seconds, then asked, "Anything else?"

Brillhagen stood up. "Keep thinking about it. You may come up with some other way that could be used to get in.

The switch box didn't occur to you; maybe you'll think of some method that hasn't occurred to me."

Carbin's dour expression lightened. "You've decided I have a brain or two?" he asked.

Brillhagen smiled grimly. "You came to us highly recommended. This is a very difficult situation we're in."

Carbin sighed deeply and tilted his chair back. "You can say that again," he said.

Brillhagen strolled back to the castle, wondering if he should recheck Carbin's references.

19

AFTER BRILLHAGEN LEFT, CARBIN SAT FOR A LONG TIME STARING into space. His days here were numbered. Especially if there was another break-in. And there would be another break-in, because he didn't know how in the hell the bastards were getting in.

Now, if Brillhagen were out of the way, he would be in control. Athena von Dietrich wouldn't know where to turn. She would have to depend on him for protection.

He might even end up in her bed. He licked his dry lower lip at the thought, then lit a cigarette. If Brillhagen had a fatal accident. If . . .

What kind of fatal accident could be arranged? Suppose he hit his head and drowned in the pool? Unfortunately he never came to the pool without Athena von Dietrich. She was the one who liked to swim.

Suppose he shot himself cleaning his revolver? Or took a dive from the roof? Or drank a little cyanide in his brandy?

Poison would be tough to pass off as an accident.

Brillhagen jogged around the shady paths meandering through the forest. Some of the areas were fairly dark. Camouflage a strong wire in one of the very dark areas? If he didn't break his neck when tripping over it, Carbin would be on hand to complete the job.

Brillhagen worked out regularly in the fitness gym. He soaked in the whirlpool bath after his exercises. A radio toppled into the whirlpool bath?

The last idea was the safest. Tripping in the path while jogging, Brillhagen might well fall without injuring himself too severely, and then put up a hell of a fight with anyone trying to break his neck. And even if he, Carbin, won, both he and Brillhagen would be badly marked up from the fight. Lieutenant Goudenough's medical examiner would spot bruises and abrasions on Brillhagen that did not come from the fall, and Goudenough would certainly notice Carbin's own suspicious bruises.

The radio would have to be an old one they would assume might have belonged to Karl von Dietrich. In the suites used by Brillhagen and Athena the radios were large stereo models with record and tape players. There were also television sets with VCRs, but no small bedside radios.

A new radio might create suspicion. Athena might say, "I have never seen this," and ask, "When can Wolf have bought it?" Neither of them had left the estate in months, and if Brillhagen had had someone buy it for him recently, he probably would have shown it to Athena. She was certainly liable to question where a new radio came from, and to ask the servants.

This might cause Goudenough to act, to send his men around checking stores. There were thousands of stores in the New York area, and it was unlikely that they would hit on the one from which he had bought the radio. On the other hand, the brand and type of radio could narrow their search considerably. The worst problem was that it would establish suspicion that Brillhagen's death was not accidental. And who would have any motive to kill him? He, Carbin, would be singled out for close scrutiny. But why not a KGB operative? There would need to be strong evidence of a break-in, and the KGB agent would hardly be sneaking around in the morning.

He should have thought of it during one of the break-ins. Not easy, though, because Brillhagen stuck close to Athena during any fracas.

No alternative. He would have to find a small, well-worn old radio. Maybe the Salvation Army had a store in New York. Goudenough might have the secondhand stores checked. He would have to disguise himself. Probably a black wig to cover his prematurely gray-white curls and a large black mustache would be enough.

He was the kind of man people remembered. Unusually tall, with very wide shoulders, and a distinctively shaped nose. He would need to be very careful when buying the radio.

In prowling the castle, ostensibly for security checks, but mainly for snooping, he had heard classical music played loudly in Brillhagen's suite. He smiled. Brillhagen would die happy. Then a sudden uneasy question skittered through his mind. Why do I hate this man? I'm going to enjoy killing him.

As a mercenary, Carbin had killed a number of men. Black men, Hispanic men, Oriental men, Caucasian men. Anywhere there was a little war going on, Carbin was there drawing a fat paycheck. But he didn't enjoy the killing. It was just a job with a high risk factor.

Brillhagen sat in the whirlpool bath humming as the hot water lashed at his leg and arm muscles.

Carbin approached with the radio. He said, "I found this down here. I remembered that Mr. von Dietrich liked music with his bath."

Brillhagen shrugged, smiling.

With the dial set for a classical music station, Carbin suddenly turned the volume up high. Beethoven's Ninth Symphony came to life, filling the air with its majesty. Brillhagen smiled again. What German could resist Beethoven's Ninth?

Carbin came closer, apparently to set the radio on the wide shelf on one side of the bath. Brillhagen was mesmerized, listening to the music. He had only a fraction of a second of unbelieving horror when he saw Carbin toss the radio into the swirling water.

Carbin did not wait to see or hear Brillhagen's death throes, the gasp, the wild, agonized thrashing which sent gallons of water splashing over the side.

He left quickly, and within less than a minute was at the entrance of the castle checking the man on guard duty there. As he talked to the guard he kept his fists clenched. He watched over the guard's shoulder as he entered the exact time of the inspection in his book.

Glancing around, Carbin hurried away without returning the guard's salute. He went into a large first-floor rest room reserved for gala occasions and crowds. He entered a booth and locked the door, then carefully peeled off the ovals of adhesive tape that had covered his fingerprints. Flushing them down the toilet, he left the booth and went to a washbasin where he removed the sticky residue from his fingers.

20

LYING IN BED, SAFE IN STRANG'S HOUSE, MICHAELIS LAZILY TOYED with the idea of joining up with Leslie Greenhaven. It would be an exciting life, full of danger. Kill or be killed. With Ingrid after him anyway, what did he have to lose? She was obsessive in her determination to carry out any threats or promises she made. If he let Leslie recruit him, he would at least have a certain amount of organizational protection in dodging Ingrid. He would have to kill Ingrid or spend the rest of his life looking over his shoulder. If he killed Ingrid on his own, he might be caught, tried, and put in prison. Under Leslie's aegis he could kill Ingrid and everything would be taken care of efficiently. Then there was the matter of Brewster Fernwald and his own cowardice (or was it just plain common sense?) in giving up his career as an investigative reporter. In his new role he might be able to continue his investigation of Fernwald. He might even get away with terminating Fernwald with prejudice, or whatever they called it.

The idea of becoming a paid intelligence operative working for the government became more appealing the more he thought about it. The killer part was vaguely repugnant. Still, he had killed two men in Helsinki, an unknown number in Vietnam, all in self-defense. Although in the cellar when he had bounced Konrad's head repeatedly on the concrete, much more than necessary to protect himself, he could not be certain that he meant to kill him or merely to assure that he was unconscious and no longer a threat. He suspected that he had meant to kill him. Justifiable rage at the way he had been treated, he decided.

The big question: Did he wish to give up his tenure at Crendon University? Maybe he could wangle a year's sabbatical. It would give him time to decide whether he really wanted to make a career of intelligence work.

Academic life had much to offer. Comfort, intellectual stimulation, the company of interesting friends, staying young with bright young people. There were always a few gorgeous undergraduates in his classes. He would probably end up marrying one of them. She would be at least fifteen years younger than he was, and that might be a problem.

The faint smell of bacon broiling drifted up from downstairs. He rolled out of bed and headed for the shower.

Sting was in the breakfast room morosely eating a half a cantaloupe. Angie was in the kitchen cooking. She saw Michaelis and asked, "How many eggs?"

"Two over easy."

She brought him a chilled half cantaloupe.

Sting said, "Time to find three more reprehensible scalawags who besmirched our honor."

"Must we?" asked Michaelis, digging into his cantaloupe.

Sting put down his spoon. "What do you mean, *must we?* Of course we must."

Michaelis ate some of his melon. He said, "It seems to fade in importance now that Ingrid is prowling around somewhere nearby hoping to kill me. Maybe my priority should be to kill her first."

Sting laughed. "Professor, you're getting all sweaty with bloodlust," he said.

Michaelis laughed.

Sting said, "Come on, there are only five of these monkeys left to talk to, and three of them took the dough. All five live in this area. We can take care of this little matter in a day or two."

Angie, who had come to the archway separating the kitchen from the breakfast room, guffawed. She said, "You sure polished off Swift in a hurry."

Sting said, "That turned out to be a very special case."

Michaelis finished eating the cantaloupe. "Swift told me the hundred thousand was sitting in a Swiss bank account. If we could get the name of the bank from him, we could get the other names from the bank. Swiss banks will cooperate if a crime is involved."

Sting asked, "Where are those damned eggs, Angie?"

"Coming up," she yelled.

He turned to Michaelis. "That could take a month. Why bother?"

As Angie brought them platters of eggs, bacon, and toast, Sting said, "Speaking of Ingrid, we could stake you out naked in the back garden and put the word out. Then when she comes charging in with her knife ready to deprive you of your family jewels, we pounce on her. Meanwhile, Angie has been videotaping the whole thing."

Michaelis shook his head. "That scenario is pornographic."

Sting waved his fork at Michaelis. "We could make a fortune selling it in the snuff market, that is, if we didn't pounce. You could be immortal."

"Thanks a lot," said Michaelis. "Speak to my agent."

Strang, who was wearing an old-fashioned silk smoking jacket, reached in his pocket and brought out a small notebook. He flipped the pages until he found his list.

He said, "Lemmie see now. We got George Hobble, advertising executive, Peggy Warren, boutique owner, Olivia Perkins, housewife, Marsha Hallowell, librarian, and Anthony Tedienzi, CPA, whose father-in-law is Carlo Grammatini, boss of all bosses in the United States. I'm not anxious to meet that monkey, but if necessary, by God, I'll do it."

• • •

The offices of Hobble, Penitent & Grossfire occupied the top four floors of a brand-new skyscraper in mid-Manhattan. Staring at the board listing in the ornate lobby, Michaelis said, "Looks like our man has no need to sell out for a hundred thousand. Apparently he's a partner in a very successful advertising agency." He whistled softly. "Four floors including the penthouse."

Strang said, "Maybe he has very expensive hobbies, like a dame or two on the side."

They rode the elevator up to the penthouse floor, which was the fortieth.

The receptionist, a metallic-blond robot, gave them a cold stare. "George Hobble? You'll find him on the thirty-seventh floor. Speak to the receptionist there."

Michaelis muttered, "Strange."

Strang said, "Maybe he's scared of heights."

On the thirty-seventh floor the receptionist was a fat, graying woman. She had her nose buried in a copy of *Vogue* and hardly bothered to look up when Michaelis asked to see George Hobble.

She said, "Corridor on your left, seventh office down on the right."

As they walked down the hall counting offices, Michaelis said, "We're in peasant country. This Hobble must be a poor relation of the Hobble in Hobble, Penitent & Grossfire."

Strang said, "Yeah. No announcing us, we just walk right in."

George Hobble was a disheveled-looking young man with stringy blond hair, protruding upper front teeth, and a spotty complexion. He wore a slight air of desperation. His phone tucked against his shoulder, he was yelling into it.

"Listen, shitface," he screamed, "you have that five G's over to me before five this afternoon unless you want a pair of pulverized kneecaps. Get it, five G's before five!"

Out of the corner of his mouth Strang said, "He sounds like a fucking loan shark."

Hobble slammed the handset down with a plastic thudjangle.

He looked at them and asked, "What do you jerks want? If it's money, that's Tuesdays and Thursdays only."

Strang strolled in, letting his jacket swing open casually to show his .45 automatic tucked in its holster.

"We want to have a few words with you, hotshot," he said, yanking a straight chair over to Hobble's desk.

Michaelis took another chair and pulled it close, letting his jacket fall back to reveal his holstered .38 S&W.

Hobble made a fast swipe at his desk drawer, but he was too slow for Strang. Strang had his wrist in a grip that made Hobble's face whiter and his pimples redder.

Strang said, "Relax, son, we're not here to do business with you. We want to have a chat about the jury we served on together."

"Jury?" asked Hobble.

"The Athena von Dietrich murder trial."

Hobble leaned back, relaxed. "Oh, yeah, that. I remember you." He looked at Michaelis. "Yeah, I remember you, too, Professor."

Michaelis said, "I remember you also." Only vaguely, he mentally amended. Hobble hadn't had much to say during the long discussions.

Hobble dug into one ear with the eraser end of a pencil. He brought it out and examined the smidgen of wax carefully. "So what's with the trial?" he asked. "And why are you carrying all that firepower?"

Strang said, "It's duly licensed firepower. Sometimes we deal with nasty people."

"So?"

"So seven people on that jury got one hundred thousand dollars each. Michaelis and I got nothing," said Strang.

Hobble brought his overbite down onto his lower lip. "So holy shit, is that my fault?" he asked.

Michaelis asked, "You related to one of the owners of this agency?"

Hobble nodded. "Yeah, my shitfaced uncle. I'm starting at the bottom of the ladder, with the fucking ladder sitting in a well. I mean, man, I am really at the bottom of the ladder."

Strang said, "So the hundred thousand you got gave you a start in the loan-sharking business."

Hobble said, "I didn't get any hundred thousand, and I'm not in the loan-sharking business. You become a cop or something? They wouldn't have had you on the jury if you were a cop."

Strang leaned forward. "No, I'm not a cop. I just want the record kept straight." He pulled out his Xeroxed document and slapped it on Hobble's desk. "I want you to read this paper and sign it."

Hobble read his confession carefully, his lips moving part of the time.

He tossed it back to Strang. He said, "I didn't get any hundred thousand, and I'm not signing nothing."

Strang said, "Sign it or you won't live to collect the five G's before five."

Hobble became still paler. "Suppose I sign it. What are you going to do with it, turn it over to the cops?"

Strang shook his head. "It's for my personal file. If anyone questions my integrity, I show him these documents. In my work, integrity is very important."

Hobble chewed on the pencil he had used to dig into his ear.

Strang said, "I don't intend to turn these documents over to *any* law enforcement people." He handed Hobble a ballpoint pen.

Hobble took it and chewed on the end of it. "Wouldn't do you any good if you did. You come in, put a gun to my head, and say sign. You're forcing me to sign a lie with the threat of death. It won't hold up."

Strang said, "So sign. Maybe we'll forget about your loan-sharking business."

Hobble shrugged and signed.

Strang folded the document and put it into his inside jacket pocket. He stood up.

Michaelis pushed his chair back and also stood up.

Strang said, "Keep your nose clean, hotshot."

"Get lost," said Hobble.

As they walked out the door, Strang grabbed Michaelis's arm and pulled him against the wall at one side of the door.

Hobble's voice came around the corner quite clearly. After a few seconds of punching out a phone number he said, "Gino, this is Hob. Couple of weird characters just left my office, both carrying but say they aren't law. They're on to my little bank, and I don't know whether they have any funny ideas in mind, like maybe trying to muscle in. One of them is named Strang. He's an ex-mercenary with a face that looks like dried dog vomit, and the other is Michaelis, a professor at Crendon U, only he used to be the top-shit investigative reporter who did a number on your family, if you remember."

There was a pause while Hobble listened. Strang had snapped to attention with Hobble's description of him, and Michaelis had had to hold his arm to keep him from going back into Hobble's office to take care of the matter.

Hobble finally said, "Thanks a million, old buddy. I don't have no muscle to take care of something like this."

There was a soft thud as he hung up.

Strang and Michaelis walked quietly back to the elevator.

Michaelis said, "It's not enough I have Ingrid out to kill me, whoever bribed the jurors out to kill me, and now you've got the mob on my tail."

Strang slapped his back. "Cheer up. You'll find that living dangerously is the only real spice of life. It makes you cherish every day you're still alive, and live it up to the hilt, man!" he said.

Michaelis said, "I can't wait to start all this cherishing. I don't even have a beautiful girl to cherish yet."

Strang asked, "What about the beautiful lady veterinarian you gave fifteen G's to?"

Michaelis said, "Lent to, not gave. Strictly business."

Strang stared at him unbelieving. After a few seconds he nudged Michaelis and asked, "You hear what that snotbag said about me looking like dried dog vomit? That pimple-faced, buck-toothed sleazebag?"

Michaelis nodded. He said, "I don't think your face looks *that* bad."

"Thanks for nothing," said Strang.

Michaelis said, "Actually you have a strong face that radiates wisdom, guile, and cunning."

"Now you're talking sense," said Strang. "Let's go have a drink."

Michaelis glanced at his watch. "At ten o'clock in the morning?"

"I got to steel myself. We got three women to talk to. Threaten them and they get all hysterical. We got to develop some other tactic."

Michaelis said, "Appeal to their better natures."

Strang laughed. "Women don't have better natures. They got only one thing in mind, *money*. Maybe I gotta offer them money."

Michaelis punched his arm lightly. "That's nonsense. The world is full of women who are honest, kind, generous, and intelligent."

"Honest! Man, you've got bubble gum in your brain. Lying is a way of life with them. They're con artists super deluxe." said Strang.

They strolled into a cheap bar, the kind that caters to the eight-o'clock-in-the-morning traffic.

Michaelis said, "A lot of women developed these traits because it was their only defense in a male-dominated world."

Strang shook his head wearily. "Grow up, will you?"

Michaelis ordered a Bloody Mary. He was convinced that bartenders put very little, if any, vodka in a Bloody Mary. With all that spicy stuff in the tomato juice who could tell the difference? Bloody Marys never gave him any kind of buzz that indicated alcoholic content. This early in the morning he did not want the buzz.

Strang ordered a double scotch on the rocks.

They drank in silence, Michaelis wondering whether he should get himself a flak jacket, or one of those vests some of the cops wore. He shrugged. Ingrid was probably a crack shot. Get him right between the eyes. Hobble's friend Gino would sprinkle him with a rain of rapid firepower, some of which was bound to hit him in the neck or face. His unknown enemy, the mysterious person or group who provided $700,000 to bribe the jury. They would strike as suddenly and unexpectedly as they did in killing Catherine Leeds.

One of these days he would have to have a visit with Madame Athena von Dietrich.

Peggy Warren's luxurious boutique on upper Madison Avenue obviously catered to very rich East Siders. While she waited on a customer, Michaelis examined the price tags on various items of feminine frippery. The least expensive item he found was marked $400.

While the store was a symphony in fluff, Peggy Warren herself was dressed in a no-nonsense gray suit and white shirt, with a bright red bow tie her only concession to frivolity. She was wearing very large mod glasses which could have provided vision for several eyes on each side. Her hair was black, but probably dyed in a special way that gave it the sheen of a brand-new Mercedes. Her face was ordinary, neither beautiful nor ugly. Michaelis's mother would have described her as *plain.* Her violet eyes added a touch of beauty to her nondescript nose, mouth, and chin. She was about five feet six inches tall and had a slender, attractive figure.

Her customer left without buying. She came over to them, staring at Michaelis. "I seem to remember you from somewhere. Now, where did we meet?" She turned to Strang. "I remember, on the jury."

Michaelis said, "The Athena von Dietrich murder trial."

She clasped her hands together. "Yes, of course! How nice to see you again," she said.

"We'd like, if possible, to talk to you privately about the situation," said Michaelis.

"Oh," she sighed. Neither of them was in the store to buy a gorgeous negligee, or maybe some cute lace panties, for wife or girlfriend.

She glanced around at the store, now empty of customers. "Well!" she said. "Let me think—"

Michaelis said, "If you're worried about customers coming in, perhaps we could take you to dinner?"

She giggled. "My husband's insanely jealous. If I went to dinner with two such handsome gentlemen, he would simply froth at the mouth," she said. She glanced at Strang and gave him a big smile.

Strang preened.

"Anyway," she said, "I'm a hardworking girl. I keep the store open until about ten at night."

Michaelis said, "I suppose we could come back at closing time. Could you spare us five or ten minutes after you lock up?"

She lifted her hand for a brief wave. "Oh, that won't be necessary. My assistant is about through eating her lunch. When she finishes she can cover the floor while we talk in my office."

Michaelis breathed a sigh of relief.

A customer came in. Peggy darted over to her.

Strang nudged Michaelis. "You take care of this one, will you?"

Michaelis asked, "How am I going to tell whether she's lying? You're the one with the built-in lie detector."

Strang shook his head. "Forgot to tell you, my infallible instinct only applies to men. Hell, women are lying all the time. No way to tell when they're lying."

Peggy's assistant, a stringy, tall girl with waist-length straw-colored hair, came out of the office at the rear of the store. Peggy spoke to her briefly, then motioned for Strang and Michaelis to come to the office.

It was a small, windowless room crowded with filing cabinets and a small desk almost covered with stacks of invoices and other papers. She slid into the armless swivel chair behind the desk. The only other furniture consisted of two straight chairs facing the desk, and there was barely enough room for them.

Strang and Michaelis sat down, knees almost touching the desk.

Peggy folded her hands on the desk and asked, "Now, what can I do for you gentlemen?"

Michaelis said, "We have a little problem here. You've probably read about the bribes paid to the jurors, one hundred thousand to each of seven jurors."

She nodded uneasily.

"General Strang here, and I, deeply resent this shadow that has been cast upon our integrity. We have been seeking out the bribees and obtaining signed statements from them. We have no intention of turning these statements over to any law enforcement agency. They are for personal use only. If, for instance, Crendon University questions my suitability for continued tenure, I will show them these statements in confidence."

Peggy continued to nod uneasily.

Michaelis continued, "We have obtained five statements from jurors who accepted bribes. We need two more, and we have reason to believe that *you* received one of these hundred-thousand-dollar deposits in a certain Swiss bank."

Strang unfolded one of the statements and handed it to her.

She stared at it, her mouth slightly open. Pulling herself together quickly, she said, "I certainly *did not* receive any bribe."

She read the statement quickly. "I'll sue you for slander, that's what. Or libel, or whatever," she said.

Michaelis smiled. He said, "Then it would appear that we must have our lawyers institute an *amici probantur rebus adversis* to uncover your financial records and transactions from the date of the jury trial to now. We have the name of the Swiss bank involved, so we shall be able to pin things down nicely. As you may know, Swiss banks do not maintain confidentiality in a criminal case."

Peggy became very pale and swayed slightly in her seat. Michaelis was afraid she was going to faint.

Finally she said in a tiny voice, "You promise to keep these statements confidential?"

Michaelis said, "Yes, in the way I mentioned."

She grabbed a ballpoint pen and signed the statement quickly, then handed it to Michaelis. *"Please* don't ruin my life," she said.

"We'll do everything possible not to," Michaelis said.

Out on the street Strang said, "Thanks for the promotion. I retired as a lieutenant colonel. Always wanted to be a general, though."

"You're welcome," said Michaelis. "Which would you prefer for your new uniform, one, two, three, or four stars?"

Strang said, "I'll have to think about it. By the way, what was that *amici probantur* stuff? You studied law or something? It sounded real impressive."

Michaelis laughed. "It was the only Latin phrase I could think of that sounded legal. Actually it's a quotation from Cicero. It translates 'Friends are proved by adversity.' "

Strang slapped Michaelis's back a little harder than he cared for. "Sonofabitch! You're one slick son of a gun!" he said loudly. He glanced at his wristwatch. "Time to take a break for lunch. We got to go out to Westchester County for the next two."

Michaelis would have preferred a quick hamburger and coffee, but Strang insisted on a "great little Italian restaurant" he and Angie frequented. Instead of the light lunch Michaelis preferred, he had to settle for a double martini, a big platter of cold antipasto followed by ravioli and veal marsala. The meal also required a bottle of red wine.

He went to sleep during the fifty-minute ride to Brickstow, New York, where Marsha Hallowell was the town librarian.

Strang woke him by poking his shoulder. "Rise and shine, soldier. We got only one more confession to go. I'm bettin' on Marsha the librarian."

Now that he knew Marsha Hallowell's background he felt a little queasy about harassing her. He shuddered to think of the adjustment she had had to make over the years following the massacre of her entire family at age thirteen. It probably still gave her nightmares.

He said, "I wouldn't if I were you. She impressed me as being a pretty straightlaced lady."

Brickstow's public library was a small building of red brick trimmed with white, with a two-story ceiling for the main area. The second floor was set back, providing more bookshelves and the librarian's office.

Marsha Hallowell had gray hair pulled into a tight bun at the back of her neck, a clean chiseled face, and very alert blue eyes. Michaelis decided he wouldn't pull any phony Latin phrases on *her*.

She recognized him immediately. Professors impressed librarians if no one else, Michaelis decided.

"Professor Michaelis," she said, smiling. "What brings you to my humble little library?" She turned to Strang. "And you are—" She held up her hand. "Don't tell me, it's, ah, Colonel Strang."

Michaelis said, "You have an excellent memory."

She smiled. "Well, one doesn't serve on a murder trial jury all that often." She motioned to the two chairs available. "Please sit down."

Michaelis explained their mission, mentioning that they now had six signed confessions.

She leaned back. "How fascinating!" she said. "I would be forever in your debt if you would give me Xerox copies of those statements, with the seventh, too. It would be such a relief to be able to show them to my Board of Directors. Of course they believe me when I assure them that *I* was not involved in getting any of that money, but it is the sort of thing that, well, I suppose in their minds they will never be a hundred percent sure."

Strang wasn't pleased with the way things were going. He unfolded another of the statements and thrust it at her. He said, "We think you received one of the payments. So sign this and we won't say anything to your Board of Directors."

She sat up straighter and began to glower. She said, "How dare you make such an accusation! I think I'll call my lawyer."

Strang held up his hand. "You'll need him. We'll have our lawyers initiate an *amici probantur,* uh—" He turned to Michaelis and asked, "What was the rest—?"

Michaelis said hastily, "Never mind *that.*"

Strang said to Marsha Hallowell, "Now, we know librarians don't make much money, and it would be a big temptation for you, and we ain't really blaming you. We just want to set the record straight. So if you force us, we'll just have to get a court order to uncover all your financial assets and transactions since the date of the jury trial."

Red-faced, Marsha Hallowell snatched up the statement and ripped it into several pieces.

Then she stood up and yelled, "You two utterly disgusting pigs dare to come into my office stinking of alcohol and garlic and presume to accuse *me* of accepting a bribe! Get out before I call my custodian and have you thrown out!"

They edged their way out and crept down the stairs to the main floor. Michaelis was afraid she might come out and throw something at them or start screaming, "Stop, thief!"

Strang breathed a sigh of relief when they got outside the building. He said, "You know that woman didn't take any hundred thousand dollars. I don't know why you insisted we come here and talk to her."

Michaelis laughed. "We'll have to see that she gets a Xerox copy of all seven statements when and if we get the last one."

Strang nodded. They strolled back to the Brickstow station to catch a train headed toward New York. The next candidate for a confession lived in Treadmore, which was down the line on the way.

Strang said, "Don't worry, old son. We'll get number seven."

Michaelis watched the southbound train approaching in the distance. He said, "The next one makes me uncomfortable because I have a feeling you're going to go racist on me, which bugs the hell out of me."

Strang asked, "You mean because this Olivia Perkins is a black woman?"

Michaelis nodded.

The train pulled in and they got on.

After they found seats Strang said, "Listen, I got nothing against black people. They'd probably have the same percentage of crooks and honest people as white people have, except for one important factor. One hell of a lot of them are poor as hell. And if you're real poor, you got big, big temptation."

Michaelis said, "Okay. But if you talk down to her, or act in a patronizing way, I'm walking out."

Strang's pasty face became a bit pink. He said, "Listen, I respect any person, black, yellow, white, or pistachio. I don't know where you get the idea I'm a racist."

Michaelis said, "Maybe I owe you an apology."

Many professional military types he had known tended to have rather bigoted views. In Vietnam they were not fighting Oriental human beings, they were trying to exterminate some very low species of deadly insect. On the other hand, he had heard that relations between South Korean troops and American soldiers had been good, with officers and soldiers exhibiting reasonable respect for each other.

"I accept your apology," said Strang.

Michaelis said, "I said *maybe.*"

Olivia Perkins lived in an old yellow brick building in what was obviously a black neighborhood. It was now late in the afternoon and the streets were busy with people, almost all black, coming home from work.

Michaelis was pushing the buzzer button under her name when Olivia herself appeared carrying a bag of groceries.

Fumbling for her key, she asked, "Why are you pushing my button?" Then she recognized Michaelis.

She said, "I remember you. We were on that jury together. You're Professor, uh, Professor—"

"Michaelis," said Michaelis.

She said, "That's right, Professor Michaelis." She grinned and asked, "To what do I owe the honor of this visit?"

She looked at Strang. "And you were on that jury, too."

Strang nodded.

Michaelis said, "If you can spare us a few minutes, we'd like to talk to you about a situation concerning the jury."

She said, "Sure, come on up. My apartment's a mess, but what can you do when you're working all day?"

They followed her up the steps to the fourth floor and waited while she unlocked the three locks on her door.

Slender, Olivia was wearing a new pair of designer jeans and a smart-looking white blouse. Her black hair was straight and cut short in the current style. Her face was light brown, with large dark eyes and a nose more Caucasian than African. She had a large mouth and very white teeth.

She ushered them into her living room.

"I'm going to make coffee. Would you care for a cup?" she asked.

Michaelis asked, "Sure it won't delay you in preparing your husband's dinner?"

She smiled. "My poor husband works the five-to-midnight shift. We don't see much of each other except on weekends."

She closed the door and double-locked it. "Please sit down. I'll make coffee," she said.

The living room was small and had only two windows, one overlooking the street and the other facing an air shaft.

It was neatly furnished with a large sofa and matching love seat upholstered in beige, and a lounge chair with matching upholstery. A long coffee table of polished walnut stood in front of the sofa. The white plaster walls were decorated with several large framed prints of Impressionists, including a Monet, a Renoir, and a Degas.

"Nice apartment," said Strang.

"Very pleasant," said Michaelis.

She returned with a tray bearing mugs of coffee, with a cream pitcher and sugar bowl. "Hope you don't mind instant," she said.

Michaelis and Strang, sitting on the sofa, agreed that they didn't.

She took her cup to the easy chair and put it on an end table next to the chair. She sat down and lit a cigarette.

Michaelis said, "You have a nice place here."

She shrugged. "We do the best we can with what we have. I work as a bookkeeper, my husband's a foreman at the Blatchklugel plant. Between us, we make out pretty well."

Michaelis again explained their mission.

She listened carefully, then when he finished said, "And because I'm black, I suppose you came to me first."

Michaelis held up his hand. "On the contrary, you are next to last. We have six signed statements, with only one more to go."

She crushed out her cigarette. "Mind if I see them?" she asked.

Michaelis shook his head. "As I mentioned to you, we promised each of these people strict confidentiality and promised that we would show them only if our integrity is questioned. In other words, if Crendon University decided that with this shadow on my reputation I might not be a suitable faculty member, I would show these statements to the president of the university."

"I see," she said. She lit another cigarette. Shaking the match out, she said, "Well, gentlemen, I know you think we black folks are desperate and poverty-stricken, and all that, and that it would be natural to grab that hundred thousand. However, let me point out that my husband makes thirty-one thousand per year, and I earn twenty-two thousand. We are not on poverty row. In fact, we have managed to save about twenty-five thousand toward that house we're going to build someday."

Michaelis said, "That's great."

Strang handed her a statement. "Sure you don't want to sign and get it off your conscience?"

Olivia folded the statement into a paper airplane and sent it sailing across the room.

Then she beamed at Strang, showing a lot of white teeth.

Michaelis sipped his coffee. He asked, "May I bum one of your cigarettes? I've given them up."

She got up and handed him her package of Carltons, then lit his cigarette for him.

She said, "I will admit I was tempted when that man called. Then I thought, Jesus, a secret Swiss bank account, the IRS, and what if I was the only juror holding out for acquittal? That would look really bad, and embarrassing, too."

Michaelis asked quickly, "The man who called. What did he sound like? I mean, a gangster, a foreigner, any particular kind of accent?"

She said, "He was definitely a foreigner. Maybe Russian. He sounded a little like Mr. Krassinoff, the butcher."

They thanked her for the coffee and left.

Strang mumbled a few obscenities. "Nothing left but Grammatini's son-in-law. Some fucking luck we have."

21

ATHENA WAS DISTRAUGHT AND UNCONSOLABLE. BRILLHAGEN HAD been her mainstay, her pillar of strength. She had no one to turn to. She had had intimate friends in London, but with time and distance they were no longer intimate. She had no close relatives other than the von Dietrich family, relatives only by marriage, and uncomfortable people to be with as well. Even with Brillhagen alive as her protector her situation had been menacing enough; without him it appeared to be unbearable.

The funeral had been held in the castle and attended only by Athena, Lieutenant Goudenough, the servants, Carbin, and six of his security guards as casket bearers. Kassenbach had offered to fly over for the funeral, but Athena had discouraged the trip. Brillhagen's only close relatives were old and fragile, and begged off the transatlantic flight.

Athena, frozen-faced with grief and some fear, saw Carbin for the first time as a human being. He was sad, kind, and avuncular, and during the service she saw him surreptitiously wipe away a tear. The hard-boiled martinet had suddenly become a tender, considerate, dignified middle-aged man.

By permission of the Crendon City Council, Wolf was buried in a beautiful small glade on the estate.

Goudenough had some reservations about calling Brillhagen's death an accident. It was possible, of course, that Brillhagen had carelessly put the radio on one of the narrow rims of the whirlpool and that, say, his elbow or some other movement might have dislodged it. But this script did not fit Brillhagen's character. He was a careful, precise man. Yet there was no evidence to point to anything other than an accident.

There were no fingerprints on the radio. It was possible, Goudenough decided, that the pebbly-textured plastic surface of the radio would probably only retain partial oily prints or smudges which might be washed away by the 100-degree swirling water. Brillhagen's body had been in the water two hours before being discovered. He and Athena had had their morning coffee before he left for his workout. If he had not appeared again until lunchtime, it would not have been unusual. Some mornings he went for long walks through the woods, bird watching with his binoculars, or merely strolling the inside perimeter of the wall to personally check the security of their fortress.

One of the servants who went in to clean the exercise area had found him.

Several hours after the funeral Carbin telephoned Athena and requested an appointment. She told him there was no need for an appointment, he could come to her suite immediately.

He appeared, carrying his military overseas cap in his hand, presenting a perfect picture of a respectful subexecutive.

"Please sit down, Captain Carbin," Athena said. Wolf had joked about Carbin's wish to be addressed as "Captain." Actually he had retired from the regular army in that rank.

Carbin sat down. He said, "I hate to disturb you at a time like this, but your safety is of paramount importance. Without Mr. Brillhagen to protect you, you may be in considerable danger alone in your suite. I would like your permission to station one of my best men in your living room every night."

He paused for a deep breath and then continued, "We still do not know how these people are getting in, and until we do there is always the possibility that they may be able to get into the castle again."

Athena was silent for a few seconds, reluctant to agree. Finally she said, "Well—"

Carbin said hastily, "There will be no invasion of your privacy. Should you wish to entertain friends in your suite, the guard will go to the suite next door and remain until you tell him to return."

Friends, thought Athena bitterly. Where were they? It was a mistake to give your life over to one person as she had done with Wolf. But then, not many people would enjoy living as a hostage, even in this luxury. Perhaps she should hire a woman companion.

She said, "I suppose you are right. Just be sure the man you choose is not only reliable but intelligent. I would not want one of your brash young men tapping on my bedroom door with the idea that the lonely widow might need consoling."

Carbin smiled. "I assure you I would have him before a firing squad at dawn if he dared," he said. After a short pause and a small smile from Athena he said, "Seriously, I will choose very carefully and try to provide a stable, middle-aged married man."

Athena stood up. "All right, that's settled," she said.

Carbin got up, gave her a half-salute, and left, walking jauntily.

She went into her bedroom, locked the door, and collapsed onto the large sofa. She had to pull her life together somehow, and perhaps that meant leaving this prison. Disguise herself somehow. A blond wig and dark glasses? Live in New York, say, a suite at the Waldorf. Do some useful work. Set up a charitable foundation and manage it. Perhaps try to do something constructive for the homeless men, women, and families in New York City. There were hundreds of thousands of them. Do more than provide shelter and food; try to find jobs for them.

She shook her head. Wishful thinking. There were no jobs for most of these people, and if the experienced social workers of the city couldn't solve it, who was she to think her money would make the difference?

Lethargy had invaded Athena's system like some benign drug. She stopped her exercises, stopped swimming, and ate almost nothing. She slept a great deal, and spent hours sitting at one of the windows staring down at the forest that surrounded her prison. A thousand thoughts skittered through her mind, but not one would pause to be examined carefully. She would disguise herself and go to New York. Where would she get a disguise, a wig, a different face? Some costume house that dealt with actors, perhaps. What would she do in New York? She would see people, lots of people. Interesting people? She could go to school. Learn to sculpt, or paint, or perhaps write professionally. She had finished Oxford with a first. She could write very well; at least the essays and other papers she had prepared were all graded excellent.

But if they caught her! The trauma of the dreadful day *they* invaded her home, tortured her and killed Karl in cold blood. Whom could she trust? How could she get the wig and disguise without it being known to others?

There was a light tapping on her living room door. She went to it and asked, "Who's there?"

"Captain Carbin, Mrs. von Dietrich," said Carbin.

She unlocked the door and opened it.

Carbin stood there with a large wicker box in his arms. "Cook tells me you are not eating enough to keep a bird alive. I hope that something here may tempt your appetite."

Athena stood aside while he brought the box in and set it on a table.

She said, "How kind of you."

The hamper looked terribly expensive, and she wouldn't dare try to reimburse him.

She opened the lid and stared at the large jar of caviar, the jars of pâté, a variety of cheeses, jellies, and jams, a loaf of French bread, English crackers and biscuits. There was even a box of Godiva chocolates.

"How nice!" she said.

Carbin stood there smiling. It occurred to her again that Carbin was important. He was the only one who stood between her and chaos. She should try to know him better, to understand him.

It was lunchtime. She said, "I won't accept this unless you share it with me."

He backed up a step, saying, "Well, now, I wouldn't want to impose my company on you."

She said, "Your company will be most welcome."

He said, "Well, then . . ."

She picked up the phone and called the kitchen. She asked them to have Rowena put a bottle of Moet in an ice bucket and bring it up to her suite.

She said to Carbin, "Please sit down, relax."

Carbin sat down, beaming. ". . . lift your tender eyelids, maid, and brood on hope and fear no more."

She stared at him astonished. "Yeats!"

Noting her surprise, Carbin said, "I am not an uneducated man. My years in the army have made me rough and crude, but I have a degree from a fairly impressive university."

Athena lifted some of the items from the hamper and placed them on the table. "And which university would that be?" she asked.

"Yale," he said.

She turned to look at him. "That is certainly an excellent university," she said.

He shrugged. "My family lived in New Haven, and twenty-five years ago it wasn't all that expensive, especially if you lived at home."

He paused, frowning, and then said, "Of course, I was a townie and wasn't really accepted by the rich kids. Not that I had any time for them. I had a job to help with the expenses, so about all I could do was go to classes, work, and study."

Athena nodded. She called the kitchen again and asked them to send up some plates, napkins, and silverware, explaining that no food was required, but they could send up a large pot of coffee later.

The champagne, plates, and silverware arrived.

For the first time in weeks Athena found that she had an appetite. They drank champagne, ate pâté de foie gras spread on French bread, caviar on biscuits, cheese on both bread and crackers, and even two or three chocolates.

Over coffee Athena told him about her depression and her feelings of isolation, and asked his advice about disguising herself and venturing into New York.

Carbin was somewhat dubious about her traveling. He

said, "I would certainly have to accompany you." He agreed to check into the matter of an adequate disguise.

She mentioned her thought about taking a course on writing professionally, possibly fiction, since she was not sure she was capable of dealing with the serious subjects that were required at Oxford fifteen years ago.

Carbin rubbed his chin. He said, "I can understand your feelings very well. You have suffered great tragedies. First your father's death, then your husband's, and now Mr. Brillhagen."

He sipped his coffee, staring at her sadly. "My life, too, has been marred by tragedy. My teenage daughter was killed in an automobile accident. It broke up our marriage," he said.

Athena nodded sympathetically. "How horrible," she said softly.

Carbin said, "Yes, my wife blamed me for her death, though I really had little to do with it. My wife did not want her to drive at all because she was a bit wild. Inherited some of her father's adventurous nature, I suppose. Anyway, on her own she learned to drive using her friends' cars, and got her license. Well, you simply cannot stop a youngster from driving in today's world. I bought her a car. All her friends had cars."

Athena poured them both some more coffee. She said, "I can understand that. My father would have done the same thing."

Carbin stared down at the table, ostensibly deeply moved.

"She was a careful driver. I lectured her, worked with her at it. She was killed by a drunk who drove into the rear of her car at ninety miles per hour. Fortunately he was killed also, or I'd be in jail now for killing him," he said.

Athena stared at Carbin, sharing some of his sorrow. How different this man was when you got to know him. He had lost his daughter and his wife and now lived in the barracks with his men, a lonely bachelor. No wonder he was bitter and sometimes rude.

She said, "You really should find yourself a wife. You are still young enough to have a family."

He shrugged. "I suppose I should, though somehow—" He smiled. "Well, to get to more cheerful subjects, I think your idea of trying your hand at writing would do wonders for your depression. Keeping very busy has saved me."

He glanced at his watch and stood up. "I'm afraid duty calls. This has been a most enjoyable lunch. Let me think about getting you safely to New York."

Athena stood up. "I've enjoyed it, too. We'll have to have lunch again one of these days, though I must insist upon providing the meal."

At the door Carbin paused and said, "You wouldn't consider having a professor from Crendon University come here and tutor you?"

Shaking her head, Athena smiled. "To keep me going, I think I would need one of those workshop courses, and association with others who are trying to write professionally."

He smiled, gave her a salute, and left.

She sat for a while finishing the bottle of champagne. Carbin had drunk very little. Obviously he was strict with himself as well as with his men about drinking on duty.

She got into her bikini feeling much more cheerful and slightly drunk, put on her terry-cloth robe, and went down to the pool to lie in the sun and swim. She decided that she would begin her exercise program again tomorrow.

Carbin smiled all the way back to the gatehouse. Maybe he should sign up to take that fiction writing course with her. His dead daughter and alienated wife were improvisations developed on the spur of the moment to gain Athena's sympathy. Carbin had been married twice. In each marriage the woman became a slovenly slut and cheated on him in his own bed. He beat up both of them and obtained uncontested divorces. He now had a relationship with a young woman in Crendon who worked as a checkout cashier in a supermarket. It cost him only a hundred dollars a week to provide her allowance. If she cheated on him, he would not have to pay lawyers for a divorce, and he would not beat her up. He doubted that she would. She had a small child with a father who had fled the city the day she announced that she was pregnant. The extra hundred dollars a week was desperately needed.

He had attended Yale, but only for two years. Yeats had been his favorite poet, and by consulting the *Oxford Book of English Verse* in the Crendon Public Library he had found the quotation that seemed to fit Athena's situation. Though he wasn't really sure. Professors seemed to find many meanings in poetry that Carbin missed. At least Athena had been pleased, perhaps because she was surprised that he even read Yeats. He agreed with himself that all in all, he was a very clever man.

Though Brillhagen's suggestion that one or more of his men might be disloyal had angered him, he accepted that it could be true. Very tight control was now placed on possession of the key to the switch box. Maybe there would be no more break-ins.

He decided that he would continue his campaign to ingratiate himself with Athena slowly and carefully. Remain the perfect gentleman, do not take liberties or assume anything. Wooing her could not be done overnight. His image must be that of an affectionate, caring uncle. But since he was only ten years older than Athena, marriage was not impossible if she gradually became completely dependent upon him.

He might one day be lord of the manor, a man with a legal attachment to a billion dollars. Of course her lawyers would see that he had no control of her assets, but if she died, he would have a legal claim worth millions. If she died.

The following day he approached Athena while she was sunning herself at the pool side. No rude stares at her breasts and thighs this time. He kept his eyes focused on her face, or to one side of her face.

She sat up, smiling, and slipped the terry-cloth robe around her shoulders.

He handed her a copy of Eudora Welty's *One Writer's Beginnings*.

He said, "I found this a most charming book, and thought you might enjoy it, especially since you are thinking of trying your hand at writing."

She accepted it, vaguely surprised. "How thoughtful of you," she said.

She turned the pages, glancing at some of the photographs. "I remember reading reviews of it a long time ago and thinking that I should order a copy."

He stood there, beaming.

She said, "Pull up a chair and sit down if your duties will permit."

He pulled over a canvas chair and sat down. If he sat on the grass it would be undignified, in uniform. Then, too, the grass might stain his trousers.

Athena asked, "Have you thought any more about getting me to New York?"

Carbin nodded. "I think I have a plan that might make it reasonably safe."

He straightened the crease of his trousers over his knees. "I'm thinking of Rowena McGrath. She's an honest Irish girl who takes her religion seriously. I believe she can be trusted."

Athena stared at him, puzzled.

"She's about your build, slender, and five foot nine, I would guess," said Carbin. "Say we got you a wig, red hair styled the same as Rowena's, put a few freckles on your face."

He paused and lit a cigarette.

"Say I picked you up in my car at the castle. When we drove through the gatehouse, my men would say, 'Captain Carbin is having a date with Rowena.'"

He held up his hand. "That's not to say my men are not to be trusted, but sometimes what appears to be harmless gossip can give the enemy a clue. Say one of my men tells his wife he saw you and I leaving together for the evening, and his wife tells some other wife. Well, these people who are trying to get to you are very clever, very thorough in their investigative skills."

Athena nodded, impressed.

"Rowena would be the only one who knew. She would stay in your suite during the entire evening while you were away. Before we left, you would leave word that you did not wish to be disturbed, whatever the circumstances," said Carbin.

Athena thought about it. It sounded safe, and would enable her to attend evening classes, or the theater and dinner. Limited, but better than the way she had been living.

She said, "It sounds good. If Rowena will cooperate."

He laughed. "Oh, she will. She'll love being part of our little conspiracy. She admires you greatly." He paused to rub his cheek for missed stubble in shaving.

"Then, too, I presume you will pay her well for this extra service, which she will earn by lazing around in your living room watching television or movies on your VCR, or sleeping," he said.

Athena ducked her head, smiling. "I expect she will. What do we do next?"

Carbin got to his feet. "Tomorrow is Rowena's day off. I'll take her to New York. We'll see a theatrical costumer. Our story will be that she has a role in a play featuring twins. Her twin needs a wig to match Rowena's hair exactly, and she also has to learn how to make up this girl's face so that her complexion and freckles match Rowena's. We may have to go to a cosmetologist for that."

Athena laughed. "I must say you are very inventive. You should take the fiction writing course, too."

Carbin said, "I'll have to. I could hardly just lurk around as your bodyguard. That *would* call attention to you."

Athena asked, "As Rowena McGrath, wouldn't I be safe enough if you just dropped me off at the class?"

Carbin shrugged, appearing to think about it. "Well, let's say you might be eighty percent safe alone, ninety-five percent safe with me keeping an eye on you." He hastily lit a cigarette. "I won't embarrass you. We can pretend we don't know each other any better than we know any of the other students."

Athena said quickly, "It wouldn't embarrass me if we were known to be together. I just thought—"

Carbin held up his hand. "It would be better if we pretended we were not together. I can keep an eye on the people around you, and on you, without appearing to be a jealous boyfriend."

She said, "Well—"

Carbin said, "As a matter of fact, I will enjoy taking the

course. My life has been rather colorful, what with combat service and all that. I might even become a fairly good writer."

Athena got to her feet. "I expect you have much more exciting things to write about than I do," she said.

Carbin shook his head. "With your Oxford background, I'm sure you'll be a much better writer than I will ever be. I wouldn't aim any higher than a slam-bang good adventure story."

With a wave of his hand, he hurried off to find Rowena.

Athena went back to the castle to do her exercises and enjoy a massage by Hilda. As she spent her half hour pedaling her Exercycle she read Eudora Welty's entire book, and agreed with Carbin that it was both charming and beautifully written. Carbin had good taste. How could she have earlier misjudged his character and personality so completely?

22

SMILING, MICHAELIS SAID TO STRANG, "WELL, THIS IS IT, AS WE used to say when we trotted off the landing barges."

Strang laughed. They were about to leave the house for their final visit, a call on Anthony Tedienzi, son-in-law of the boss of all bosses.

Strang said, "Don't be so fucking dramatic. As far as I'm concerned this guy is just another jerk. And it's got to be him, unless we're all wrong about Hallowell or Perkins."

Michaelis pulled his trench coat from the hall closet. It was raining outside. "He's probably our man, all right, but I doubt very much that he'll sign anything. He's got a lot of clout."

Strang was about to put on his raincoat. He laid it on a chair. "I've been thinking, and I think you're right. I think I better wear my little tape recorder. He may get stubborn about signing, but he may say something incriminating or even admit it."

"Good idea," said Michaelis. He stood by the door waiting while Strang went upstairs to tape his recorder to his stomach.

In rating enemies, Michaelis gave Ingrid several more points than Gino's boys, whoever they were. Ingrid was more dedicated. Tedienzi, though, was a complete unknown.

When he slid into the passenger side of Strang's Eldorado, he immediately lowered the sunshade. It contained a mirror, probably for cosmetics use, but it also made an excellent rearview mirror for the passenger.

Strang pulled out of his driveway. He was one of those who always back cars into driveways and leave front end first.

They headed down the Hutchinson River Parkway to the George Washington Bridge. Tedienzi's office was in Trembleton, New Jersey.

Michaelis said, "There's a white Mercedes following us."

Strang slowed a trifle. The Mercedes pulled out and went around them, speeding by without even a glance from its driver.

Strang said, "Keep watching. We got Gino to think about."

Michaelis said, "I'm thinking more about Ingrid. That woman is a fanatic. If she had been Japanese she would have been a kamikaze pilot."

Strang gave him a quick look. "A dame is a dame. Look how she almost peed in her panties when we were holding her with that five-minutes-to-death poison on her hand."

Michaelis said, "I expect you would have been pretty nervous yourself."

Strang grinned. "Look how she paid Swift back with that fake assassination. A cream puff! A dame with a heart."

Michaelis kept staring at the mirror. "I thought you believed dames had nothing in their hearts but a consuming desire for money."

Strang said, "I'm not arguing with you on that. But the two thoughts ain't necessarily incompatible. In order to keep getting money, you got to survive."

"There's a dark blue Volks Rabbit following us. In fact, she's almost tailgating us. An old white-haired lady," said Michaelis.

Laughing, Strang asked, "Has she got green eyes?"

"I can't see her face that clearly. Your rear wipers are moving pretty slow," said Michaelis.

Michaelis saw the Rabbit switching to the slow lane.

"Hey!" he yelled. "She's switched to the slow lane and is coming up on my side."

Strang stepped on the gas hard. The heavy Cadillac surged forward.

Strang said, "Well, if we can't leave a little old four-cylinder Volks in a cloud of dust, I'll eat my hat."

Strang's speedometer rolled up to ninety and the Volks was still there, gradually edging up.

"She's probably got an eight-cylinder engine in that damned thing," said Michaelis.

Strang said, "If she has, we're in big trouble. She's pushing less than half our weight."

"She's still moving up," said Michaelis.

Strang said, "You better bend over and put your head between your knees. The door will protect you."

Loosening his seat belt a little, Michaelis bent over.

Strang said, "Protect your head. When she gets almost even with us, I'm going to swerve and knock that piece of souped-up junk right off the road."

A shot ripped through the shatterproof window.

Michaelis wasn't sure exactly how he could protect his head. He rested his face in the crook of his right arm.

Michaelis peeked up. "You okay?" he asked.

Strang said, "Yep. Hold on, boy!"

He swerved hard to the right.

A cacophony of clanging and the shrieking of ripping metal sent a quick chill up Michaelis's spine. He tensed himself for a smashup of crushed metal and mangled bodies, then relaxed as the Cadillac disengaged and swerved slightly to the left.

He raised his head to look. No Rabbit alongside. He glanced back. The Rabbit was off the road, nose plunged into high weeds.

He said, "I hope she's mortally injured."

"Not a chance. A cat like that has eighteen lives. Nothing wrong with that dame but a wrecked Volkswagen," said Strang.

Michaelis asked, "Did you see her face?"

"Yep. Old green eyes herself with a white wig and fake wrinkles," said Strang.

Michaelis opened a pack of almost no tar or nicotine cigarettes and lit one. "I meant to tell you, I'm thinking of joining up with Leslie Greenhaven."

Strang snickered. "Why?"

Michaelis tapped his cigarette end into the ashtray. "So I can kill Ingrid before she gets me and not go to jail for it," he said.

Strang slapped the steering wheel and guffawed. "You tie yourself up for life in the Company to take care of a little thing like that?"

Michaelis said, "It doesn't seem a little thing to me. Murder can get you a life sentence."

Strang waved his right hand in the air. "Nothing to it. As far as the law is concerned, nobody knows you got any motive for killing her. Be sure there are no witnesses, and no cop is ever going to bother you."

He laughed. "Of course some of her associates may figure it out. You don't need to worry about a life sentence there. They're solid advocates of the death penalty, with some zingy torture beforehand."

Michaelis said, "Cheer me up some more."

They were entering Trembleton. Strang stopped in front of a drugstore. The banged-up door on the passenger side opened after a struggle. Michaelis got out to get directions.

Tedienzi's office was in a small building of cream-colored concrete and glass located on Dogget Avenue, the town's main street.

A young man with a bandit's large black mustache, his black hair slicked down close to his scalp, paused as he was about to enter the building to stare at the damage on the right side of the Cadillac. He was wearing bifocals.

He whistled softly. "You guys tangle with a rig?" he asked.

Michaelis said, "Believe it or not, a Volkswagen Rabbit."

The stranger gave another low whistle. "Bullet hole in the window, too," he said.

"Yeah," said Strang.

They followed the young man into the building. Pausing for a quick glance at the directory board, they hurried to the elevator. The stranger was holding the door for them.

All three got off at the fourth floor. Strang and Michaelis followed the stranger, looking at company names on the white glass doors.

The young man unlocked the door bearing the name "Anthony Tedienzi, CPA."

He was startled to see them following him into his tiny reception room. He scurried into his office and slammed the door. There was a click of a lock turning, then another scrape and thud of a bolt being slammed home.

"Go away, I had nothing to do with it!" Tedienzi yelled through the closed door. "I got nothing to do with Papa Gee. Ask any of the wise guys, they'll tell you that."

Michaelis moved close to the door. He said, "I'm Professor Michaelis, and General Strang is with me. We were on the Athena von Dietrich murder trial jury together, remember?"

There was silence on the other side of the door.

Michaelis asked, "Don't you remember us? On the jury at the Athena von Dietrich trial?"

"So what?" asked Tedienzi.

"So we want to talk to you about a situation that has developed," said Michaelis.

"I didn't have anything to do with it," said Tedienzi.

Strang yelled, "You were on the goddamned jury with us. Now, come on out and talk. We're not here to harm you."

Michaelis said, "Look, we're respectable citizens. If we were here to harm you, we'd just kick your damned door down."

Tedienzi asked, "If you're so respectable, why are people shooting at you?"

Michaelis laughed. "That's a good question. A crazy woman pulled up alongside and fired at me. General Strang swerved and knocked her car off the road. She was obviously an escaped mental case."

Tedienzi said, "Beat it, will you, or I'll call the cops."

Michaelis was becoming more annoyed by the second. "Oh, hell, go on and call the cops. We're here to see you on legitimate business, and if you want to discuss it in front of the cops, that's okay, too. If you want to make an ass out of yourself, go ahead. And once the cops get here, what in hell do you think you're going to charge us with?"

Strang said loudly, "We're here to talk about jury bribing and the hundred thousand bucks you got for voting to acquit Athena von Dietrich. Guess the cops will be pretty interested."

The bolt slammed back, the lock clicked open, and Tedienzi opened the door and stood with a small automatic in his hand.

Strang said, "Let's go in your office and talk where we can be comfortable. You don't need that popgun."

He shoved past him and flopped into a chair facing Tedienzi's desk. Michaelis followed and sat in the other visitor's chair.

Tedienzi went around the desk still pointing the automatic in their direction. He settled into his swivel chair and rested his elbow on the desk.

Strang said, "Put that damned gun away or I'll take it from you, and I guarantee your arm will be broken while I'm doing it."

Michaelis said, "General, the Pentagon wouldn't approve of that kind of activity."

"Fuck the Pentagon. I'm getting fed up with this wimp." He turned back to Tedienzi. "Now, for the *last* time, put that gun down."

Tedienzi laid the gun on his desk.

Strang pulled his jacket open. He said, "Now, Anthony, you can see my forty-five in its holster. I'm going to reach into my jacket pocket on the other side and bring out a document I want you to read. Okay?"

Tedienzi nodded.

Strang brought out his folded confessions. He said, "We've tracked down six of the jurors who got a hundred thousand dollars. We *know* you are number seven."

He carefully explained the confidentiality of the statements, then handed an unsigned one to Tedienzi.

Tedienzi read the statement, then tossed it on his desk. "You've really got rocks in your head. I'm not signing that crap," he said.

Michaelis said, "Maybe we should talk to Papa Gee about it."

Tedienzi laughed. "That old bastard. He's the one who got me into this mess."

"How so?" asked Michaelis.

Tedienzi said, "Well, see, I had a couple of good clients lined up and I wanted to get into my own business. I had saved up ten thousand, but I needed another ten to get started. My wife asked Papa Gee to arrange a loan for me. He sent a guy to see me." Tedienzi stopped to shake his head wearily. "I figured that being *family,* the interest rate would be reasonable. In a few weeks I found this shark was charging me twenty-five percent. A week! It was nine months before I even got in the black, and I still didn't have any real money to pay him off with. I owed the bastard ninety thousand dollars plus the original ten."

He rubbed his forehead. "I went to church and prayed all day for three days. Nothing happened. I went to Papa Gee. I said, 'You gonna let this pig put me, your daughter's husband, in a wheelchair for the rest of my life?' He says, 'Naw, that's dirty business, crippling a man. Vito will just shoot you in the back of the head and dump you in the river. No pain. Just *boom* and you feel nothing.' "

Tedienzi ducked his head and stared at the desktop for a moment. "My wife went to Papa and begged. He told her no, it would not be honorable for him to interfere, to stop crying, he would find her a better husband."

He looked up at them solemnly. "You see, Papa Gee doesn't like me."

Michaelis stifled a huge laugh with difficulty.

"So I went back to church and prayed some more. My prayers were answered!" said Tedienzi, smiling with a lot of white teeth. "The trial, a guy telephones and offers me a hundred thousand. I grab it and pay off Vito. Papa Gee can't figure it out. Nobody can figure it out."

Michaelis said, "You sure had a close call there."

"Brother! Did I!" said Tedienzi. "Let me tell you. Starve to death before you borrow from a loan shark."

Strang shifted in his chair. "So congratulations. Now, just sign this and we'll be on our way."

Tedienzi shook his head. "No way. Papa Gee wouldn't like it."

Michaelis nudged Strang. "To hell with it. Let's go," he said.

If Strang tried to threaten Tedienzi, it might start some unnecessary fireworks. Tedienzi's gun was lying within an inch of his hand. He hoped the tape recorder was working well.

Back in Strang's battered Cadillac they played the tape and found it perfect.

"Mission completed," said Strang. "Tonight we got to celebrate. Let's take Angie out to dinner and live it up. I'll tell her to get you a date."

Michaelis said, "Forget the date. I'm already living dangerously."

Strang slapped his back and roared.

Michaelis wasn't in much of a mood to celebrate. He sighed. Now all he had to worry about was Ingrid. Strang made it sound easy. Just knock her off with no witnesses around. It was one thing to knock off some unsuspecting victim, another to go after a tigress who lived with danger and had her antennae constantly tuned to suspicious or dangerous circumstances. In a duel with Ingrid, the odds were on Ingrid.

23

IN HER DISGUISE AS ROWENA MCGRATH, ATHENA FELT WONDERFUL. She looked twenty-three instead of thirty-one. What was it, the tiny sprinkle of freckles, the beautiful red wig, the skin cream that subtly changed her complexion? She had always been described as beautiful. Now she was cute. Being cute can be fun for a woman who has always been sedately beautiful. She felt like dancing a jig.

Kent Carbin was pleased, too. When he suggested it, he wasn't sure it would work. It would be a disaster for him if anything happened to Athena. Athena was his pot of gold at the end of the rainbow. Staring at the two women standing side by side, he could see a slight difference, of course, but one had to be looking for it. There would be no problem with their going to New York. The expeditions to New York were necessary, whether to the theater or to attend a writing class. It was the only way he could get to know her intimately. On the estate there would always be a gulf between them. Employer and employee. She lived in the castle, he lived in the barracks.

She turned to Carbin. "Well, when do we go? I can hardly wait."

Before he could reply she said to Rowena, "I love being Rowena McGrath. I do appreciate it so much, Rowena."

Smiling, Rowena made a slight curtsy. "You're *wel-come!* It's so exciting!"

Athena kissed her cheek. "You're a darling."

Carbin cleared his throat. "There's a course in novel writing at the New School. It starts next week, on Monday."

"Oh," said Athena, disappointed.

"Well, actually we could go in today, enroll in the

course, have dinner, and go to the theater. I mean, you're already in costume, why not take advantage of it?"

Athena brightened. "Lovely." She turned to Rowena. "If you don't have a date for this evening?"

Rowena shook her head. "I don't go out very often. The boys are all the same in what they're after, and I have yet to see *one* who looked like Mr. Right." She turned to go. "I'll have a grand time loafing and snacking with the TV."

Carbin said to Athena, "By the way, since you will be registering as Rowena McGrath, you'll need to pay for the course in cash. I think it's about two hundred and fifty, or something like that. Since I'm using my own name, I can give them a check."

Athena nodded. She said, "One thing I want to make clear. Since these trips are primarily for my benefit, I must insist upon taking care of all expenses."

Carbin was silent for a few seconds. It didn't fit into his scheme to be a gigolo. On the other hand, she would never consent to his spending a lot of money on her. Face it, he was an employee.

Athena could sense the male ego struggling against accepting the situation.

Carbin said, "At least let me pay for my own course, so that I can feel that whatever I get out of it belongs to me. If you want to make the entertainments your treat, that's okay."

Athena smiled. "Fair enough." Carbin's old bluntness was surfacing, but this time she did not find it offensive. After all, he was a macho male, and one had to make allowances for his pride.

Cash was no problem. Athena had a considerable amount of money and a fortune in diamonds on hand in case of an emergency. In her precarious situation she conceivably might have to flee for her life, but would, she hoped, have time for a quick trip to the hidden wall safe in her bedroom.

It was the first time Athena had seen Carbin out of uniform. He was wearing a well-tailored suit of dark gray, a white shirt, and a tie of thin maroon and black stripes. She approved of his taste.

He said, "You remind me of the first date I had in college."

She smiled, pleased in spite of her better judgment.

Carbin's car was a huge old Buick that dated from the years when they were big, heavy, and roomy. The black paintwork and chrome fittings had the luster of a brand-new car. The seats were upholstered in luxuriously soft tan leather.

As he opened the door for Athena, she said, "What a beautiful old car."

Carbin smiled. "It's a classic year. I restored it myself as sort of a hobby, including the eight-cylinder engine, which runs like a Rolls-Royce."

"How clever of you," said Athena.

He shrugged. "I like to keep busy doing something interesting in my spare time. Helps to endure the loneliness."

Athena nodded, sliding into the passenger side.

Carbin said, "That's one reason why I'm looking forward to the writing course."

The guards saluted as he drove through the gatehouse. He nodded but did not return the salutes.

Athena folded three one-hundred-dollar bills and slipped them into his jacket pocket. "For the entertainments," she said.

He grinned. "I know you must have me pegged as a male chauvinist," he said. "I'm not, really. I believe most of the things women's libbers want are justified."

Amused, Athena asked, "In what ways don't you agree with them?"

They entered the turnpike to New York, the big Buick's powerful engine hardly audible.

He said, "It's hard to pin down. It's just that I believe that certain male and female instincts are basic and not a matter of conditioning."

Athena nodded, agreeing with him, but not ready to sort out what might be basic and what might be acquired.

Registration at the New School took little time, even though they were careful to do it separately. Athena went in first while Carbin waited in the car. When she returned, he went in and was the last to be allowed to register. The class was full.

To Carbin it was a sign that his luck was holding out. From Brillhagen's death to now everything had moved along perfectly.

He had selected a small French restaurant that was both good and expensive, but not likely to be frequented by the glitterati. Not that wandering columnists would recognize Athena, but better play it safe. On the way down he had watched the rearview mirror carefully and was fairly certain that he had not been followed. In a smaller restaurant it would be easier to keep an eye on any approaching trouble.

Two tables away, Strang, Angie, and Michaelis were celebrating the successful conclusion of Operation Bribee.

Athena recognized Michaelis. The smug, self-satisfied professor on the jury that tried her for murder. The one who had stared at her so skeptically during her testimony. She was certain he was on the side to convict. Good-looking, with a charming smile, he obviously thought he was a devil with the women. And probably was, she admitted to herself.

Carbin recognized Strang. They had commanded separate companies in a sleazy little African war. He wasn't anxious to talk to Strang. Strang had retired from the regular army as a lieutenant colonel, Carbin had left as an overage-in-grade captain. Carbin had some unhelpful letters in his 201 file.

Athena was feeling mischievous. She was still saucy Rowena McGrath. She pushed her chair back and stood up. "Excuse me a minute," she said to Carbin.

She sauntered over to Michaelis's table and stood near him.

"Professor Michaelis!" she said. "Remember me, Rowena McGrath? I was in your Poly Sci III class."

Michaelis stood up. Hundreds of students paraded through his classes during a given year. How could he have forgotten this one?

He said, "Of course, Eileen—uh, I mean, Rowena. How are you?"

Her voice sounded familiar, and there was something familiar about her face, but how could he have forgotten that gorgeous hair?

Athena stared at the huge magnum of champagne sitting in an ice bucket next to Strang.

Strang, who had had a few ounces of scotch before beginning on the champagne, said, "We're celebrating a gigantic coup. Will you join us for a glass?"

Michaelis said quickly, "Rowena, uh, this is Angelica Strang, Colonel Strang's daughter, and Colonel Strang." Turning to Strang, who was frowning, and Angelica, who was giggling, he said, "This is Rowena, uh—"

"McGrath," said Athena.

Strang said, "He's kidding. Angelica is my fiancée." He pulled out a chair from the next table, which was vacant, and said, "Sit down and have a drink with us."

Athena said, "Thanks, but I must get back to my friend." She glanced in Carbin's direction.

Strang looked over. "For God's sake, Kent Carbin."

"You know him?" asked Athena.

"Yep," said Strang. He took a swallow of champagne. "If he's your friend, you'll never need an enemy."

"You don't like him?" Athena asked.

"No."

"Why not?" she asked.

Strang said, "Look, honey, he's your friend and I don't want to spoil your evening. Let's just say it's purely personal."

There was an awkward silence. Athena said, "Well, I guess I'd better get back. Nice meeting you all."

Michaelis, who was still standing, said, "It was nice to see you again, Rowena."

She nodded and went back to her table.

Michaelis sat down looking puzzled.

Strang asked Michaelis, "Could you get me a job on the faculty, maybe?"

Carbin stood up when Athena returned to the table.

"What's going on?" he asked. "You're breaching your security. Do you know those people? Do they know who you are?"

Athena shook her head and explained.

After they were seated, Carbin said, "You really should keep a low profile, not mix with strangers except where it is necessary. Strang is a weirdo bastard, but sharp as hell. Give him fifteen minutes with you and he'll know your hair is a wig, your freckles are phony, and your complexion has been altered by makeup."

Athena giggled. "He doesn't like you either."

Carbin asked quickly, "What did he say about me?"

"He said, 'If he's your friend, you'll never need an enemy.'"

Carbin laughed. "I've had my share of enemies, but I'll swear to you that there's not a beautiful woman among them," he said.

The Broadway hit show Carbin had selected was a romantic comedy. Athena laughed a lot, and had the feeling that it was the first time she had laughed in years. For some reason she also felt good about spoofing Michaelis. He really was an attractive man, and she wouldn't mind knowing him better.

When they returned to the castle, she said, "It really was a great evening, Kent. We'll have to do it again soon."

He briefly pondered kissing her, then decided against it.

"Haven't enjoyed myself so much in years," he said, grinning.

Michaelis and Strang were finishing up the magnum of champagne. Angie sat in a dazed but happy trance.

Michaelis said, "Well, we cornered all the bribees, but we still don't know who did the bribing."

Strang said, "I think we can let that one rest."

Michaelis, who was also feeling the effects of the champagne as well as the predinner cocktails, said, "I beg to disagree with you."

Strang stared at him slightly cockeyed. "Indeed, old chap, and may I ask why?"

"Why? Because they killed Catherine Leeds and almost killed me at the same time. Because they probably think Catherine Leeds told me something. Because I have enough problems with Ingrid without worrying about them." Michaelis paused, thinking that Ingrid sounded like a troublesome wife.

Strang tossed his head back. "My, my," he said, "my!"

Angie came to long enough to ask, "What are you two arguing about?"

Strang said, "Go back to sleep. We're not arguing."

Michaelis said, "Are you not aware that *they* will probably find out about the seven confessions we have obtained, and feel that our explorations could lead to *them?"*

Strang tilted his head back and looked down his nose. "I say, old chap, it's possible that you may have a point there."

Michaelis said, "I think we'd better go home and get some sleep." He waved his arm around in exaggerated circles and shouted, "Waiter!"

It was as black and stuffy as the inside of a closet when Michaelis woke, his head pounding. There was a faint sound of movement. He wasn't sure whether it was coming from somewhere in the room or it was the sound of his brain cells grinding each other to a pulp. He reached under his pillow, located the grip of his .38, brought it out, sat up, and switched on the bed lamp.

Ingrid was standing ten feet away, frozen. She was wearing a jumpsuit of dark purple and had her blond hair bound up tightly in the same material. In her right hand she was holding a hunting knife with a blade about six inches long. It had been honed so sharp that the gleam was gone from everything but the blunt edge.

Michaelis thought, this has got to be a nightmare.

He said, "Drop that knife or I'll shoot."

The knife fell silently to the carpet.

In one downward swoop she unzipped the jumpsuit and shrugged out of the sleeves until the whole garment fell down to her ankles. She was wearing nothing underneath but white bikini panties. She bent over, pulled off her black tennis shoes, stepped out of the crumpled jumpsuit and kicked it aside. With a smiling glance at Michaelis she tucked her thumbs into the top of the panties and pulled them down and off.

"Now you can see that I am completely naked and cannot harm you," she said to Michaelis.

He stared, unbelieving. He should have shot her while she was holding the knife and clothed. He said, "Move over to the window, away from the knife."

She moved back a few feet.

Michaelis, who slept in the buff, slid out of bed without embarrassment. Crouching, he groped blindly for the knife, keeping his eyes on her and the .38 aimed.

His hand finally located the knife. He rose out of his crouch and backed to the other side of the bed, putting more distance between them.

"Put on your clothes," he said.

She shook her head. "I came here to kill you, but I've decided to make love to you instead."

He stared at her, bewildered. A gorgeous, deadly naked female. Her breasts were perfect, and possibly from her own excitement her nipples stood out, hard. She had a flat stomach, a narrow waist, beautifully rounded hips, and long, shapely legs.

She started walking slowly toward him.

"Stop!" he said. "I'll shoot!"

She paused. "You'd shoot a defenseless naked woman?"

He began to back toward the door. Get help. Get Strang and Angie. Ingrid probably had a capsule of poison dust tucked in her ear. He couldn't shoot her, but he could crack her on the head with the butt of the .38. But with the knife in his left hand and the .38 in his right, he couldn't shift his grip to the barrel without dropping the knife. That would never do, not with Ingrid within leaping distance.

She managed to get between him and the door and continued her slow approach.

"Strang, Angie!" he yelled.

She shoved his revolver aside and pushed herself tight against him. "Shut *up,"* she said, plastering her open mouth on his.

He tried to break away, but her hands were locked behind him and an attempt to detach them would mean dropping either the revolver or the knife.

She was rubbing her body slightly up and down against him, her tongue sending tingles as it darted against his.

He was becoming aroused in spite of himself.

Stop it, you damned fool, stop it, he yelled to himself. Stop, stop, stop!

She pulled her mouth away and said softly in his ear, "You know what the lady spider does with her man after she lets him fuck her? She eats him." She licked the lobe of his ear. "In your case, I'm going to eat you first."

She slid down his body until she was kneeling and began to lick the underside of his engorged member.

He tossed the knife behind him, shifted the revolver barrel to his right hand, and brought the butt down on her head with a hard whack. Her hair, bunched up by the tight cloth, cushioned the blow somewhat. She yelled out in pain, but was not unconscious. He lifted his arm to hit her again.

Looking up, she screamed, "Don't hit me again, please!"

"Strang! Angie!" Michaelis yelled. "Tarboys!"

He yanked the purple cloth upward and off her head, then grabbed her by her long hair and began backing toward the door, pulling her across the floor.

She began screaming loud enough to wake neighbors a mile away.

The door popped open. Strang, Donald Tarboy, and Angie rushed in.

Strang said, "Holy God, how in the hell did she get in here?"

Michaelis explained, embarrassed at his nakedness, but thankful that his tumescence had receded.

Ingrid huddled on the floor, her face in her hands.

Angie said, "Get some clothes on, you shameless, green-eyed bitch." She was especially angry because Strang was obviously enjoying the show.

"I wasn't going to kill you," Ingrid sobbed.

"Ha," said Michaelis. Then, "What are we going to do with her?"

"Kill her, of course," said Strang.

Angie said, "There'll be no killing in this house. What you do outside is your own business, but you're not going to dirty up my house killing anybody."

Michaelis asked, "We have to take her somewhere else and kill her?"

Strang muttered, "Guess so. Wouldn't want her stinking up the basement anyway."

Michaelis grabbed Ingrid's hair and pulled her face up. "Ingrid, if I let you go, will you owe me a big one?"

She thought for a few seconds. "Yes," she finally said between clenched teeth.

"Truce? You swear it?"

"Yes, dammit!" she said.

Michaelis struggled into his bathrobe and watched while she pulled on her panties, got into the jumpsuit, zipped it up, tied her hair up in the purple cloth, put on her sneakers, and left the room.

Strang and Michaelis escorted her downstairs to the front door and watched as she walked along the driveway.

Strang said, "Sometimes I can't figure you out, Michaelis. You have this gorgeous naked dame in your room who's willing and you don't take advantage."

Michaelis smiled. "She was willing because she wanted to kill me while I was preoccupied."

Strang snorted. "You had the knife. How could she kill you?"

Michaelis was silent, thinking about it. Possessing a woman who had crept into your bedroom to kill you would have been a very memorable experience, very titillating. He wondered whether she would have responded or merely remained passive. He shook his head. Back to sordid reality.

He asked Strang, "Did you see that little agate ornament in her hair. Ball-shaped thing slightly smaller than a marble?"

"Yep, why?" asked Strang.

"That was a pin about five inches long, tapered from about an eighth of an inch thick to a needle point. Had I become absorbed in making love, it's highly possible that this pin might have entered my temple here"—he pointed to his left temple—"and ended up here." He put his finger on his forehead about five inches from his left temple.

Strang laughed and slapped Michaelis's shoulder. "That dame came prepared for almost anything but your blundering around doing everything wrong."

"What do you mean, wrong?" asked Michaelis, indignant. Considering the fact that he had been awakened from a deep, hung-over sleep, he thought he had done pretty well.

Strang said, "You should have shot her when she was fully clothed, threatening you with the knife." Shaking his head, he said, "Come on, let's go to the kitchen and make some coffee. We'll never get back to sleep after all this shit."

They watched in silence as the boiling water dripped through the coffee maker. Michaelis wondered when Ingrid's next attempt would be. He had beaten her down twice, and how much did the promise of a fanatic such as Ingrid mean?

Strang said, "I don't think it was very smart of you to let her go."

Michaelis said, "Swift told us she's obsessive about keeping her word. Certainly she faked the assassination attempt because she *owed* him."

Strang laughed. "Her interpretation of the big one she owes *you* might be entirely different. They're pros working against each other. In your case she is inspired by sheer hate."

Michaelis shrugged. "I guess I just can't kill a woman. If she had rushed at me with the knife, I could have shot her."

The dripping completed, Strang lifted the glass pot off and poured them each a cup. He said, "In that case you had better give up the idea of joining Leslie Greenhaven."

Michaelis yawned. "I have," he said. Then after a few seconds, added, "I think."

They drank black coffee in silence. Michaelis was weary and depressed. Get away from the whole business. Go back to Crendon University in the fall, possibly show the president the seven confessions, though it was not necessary, and let that be the end of it. Unfortunately the job was not finished. Last night he had egged Strang on about finding the source of the bribe money and the murderers of Catherine Leeds. And he was right. They might well decide that he and Strang alive were a big threat.

He said to Strang, "Last night we were talking about the people who paid out seven hundred thousand and killed Catherine Leeds."

Strang nodded, then sipped his coffee.

"I think probably the first person we should call on is Athena von Dietrich," said Michaelis.

24

ATHENA WAS BECOMING FOND OF CARBIN, ATTACHED TO HIM IN A way that she might have been to a lively uncle or an older brother who devoted his time to pleasing her and trying to make life interesting for her.

The writing course had opened the door. The assignment was to write a chapter of a novel. The instructor, a book editor, read a student's chapter at each session. The students criticized or approved and the instructor added professional comments.

Athena and Carbin read each other's work and made suggestions, then polished and rewrote. Since neither of them was close to being professional, they did a tremendous amount of rewriting and discussing, which Athena looked forward to daily. Their trips to New York for dinner and the theater also lifted her spirits. She enjoyed being Rowena McGrath. She became a different person, younger and carefree without the weight of her father's now monstrous secret on her shoulders. It was an act, of course, but she felt close to really living the role.

There was a worm of worry growing, however. The looks of adoration she noticed from time to time suggested that he was becoming enamored in a way that could cause difficulties. She had no interest in him as a lover, and it was not wise to encourage a possibility that might well be in his mind. He brought her fresh flowers every morning.

She would have to have a talk with him about it, but it seemed such an awkward cliché. Kent, I want you as a friend *but* . . . However, if she waited until he tried to kiss her or brought up his romantic intentions in some other way, it would be even more awkward.

Carbin was a volatile person with strong reactions. If he

got the idea that she was leading him along only to put him down, he might revert to the nasty, rude person he had been before. Then she would have to cut out the dinners in New York and the writing course and settle back into her lonely depression.

She invited him to lunch. Over coffee she steeled herself and began. "Kent, we're good friends and I enjoy your company very much, but I think—"

"You think I'm falling in love with you." He paused to light a cigarette.

"Well, you're a very beautiful woman and almost any man would be attracted to you. I can't say that I'm not. But the gap between our life-styles and backgrounds is too big."

He puffed on his cigarette, staring at her. "Believe me, I have no hopes beyond just being a good friend."

Relieved, Athena said, "Let me have one of your cigarettes."

He offered her the pack with one cigarette tapped partially out. She took it and waited while he lit it for her.

"The gap you mention doesn't make all that much difference if people truly love each other," she said. "I do feel that we have a warm friendship, which I really appreciate. But there's no spark that will carry it further."

He nodded. "I understand."

"I'd rather you knew how I feel now than to become hurt later," she said.

He ducked his head slowly. After a silence he said, "I'm glad you brought this out into the open so that we understand each other."

He crushed out his cigarette and stood up. With a warm, adoring smile, he said, "Well, I must get back to my duties."

She smiled. He was such a sweet, understanding man, and so quick in perception.

Carbin left the castle and strolled down to the gatehouse. Warm friend wasn't what he had had in mind, but he had at least moved up a notch in the world. Handled in the right way, warm friend could exert quite a bit of power. In thinking it over he had to concede that even if he became her lover she would never marry him. She was a shrewd woman, and smart enough not to marry anyone who might be a fortune hunter. Which would limit the field to only very rich men. She hadn't even married Brillhagen, who was her lover and said to be tremendously rich, but, of course, not nearly as rich as she was.

Using only two fingers, Athena pecked away at the portable electric typewriter she had had Carbin buy for her when they began the writing course. She was still revising her chapter.

The phone rang. Carbin said, "Mrs. von Dietrich, Professor Michaelis and Colonel Strang are here to see you. Do you wish to see them?"

He always called her Mrs. von Dietrich when anyone else was present. It had become "Athena" as they worked and dined together.

The haughty, skeptical political science professor, thought Athena, had seemed very nice when she had met him as Rowena McGrath.

She said, "Yes, have them come up."

After a brief delay Michaelis and Strang were ushered into her suite by Carbin. As he neared her he asked in an undertone, "Shall I stay?"

Athena shook her head. "Not necessary."

Carbin left reluctantly.

Michaelis introduced himself and Strang.

"Please sit down," said Athena. She glanced at her watch: 4:00 P.M. She said, "I was just about to order coffee. Would you care for some, or tea?"

Michaelis selected a comfortable chair next to a long glass-topped coffee table trimmed with gold alloy. He said, "Coffee would be fine."

Strang sat down near Michaelis, also facing the coffee table. He said, "Thanks, I'll pass. Been taking in too much caffeine lately."

"Perhaps you would like a beer or a glass of wine?"

Strang smiled. "Beer would be good. Molson's if you have it."

"We do," said Athena. She picked up the phone and ordered. Then she turned her typewritten pages facedown before returning to the sofa on the other side of the coffee table.

She sat down, folded her hands on her lap, and asked, "What are you gentlemen here to see me about?" She turned to Michaelis. "I remember you, Professor, you were on the jury at my trial."

Michaelis smiled. "Some trial. A fraud from beginning to end," he said.

"You mean because I was acquitted?" Athena asked.

Michaelis rubbed his chin. "Well, seven of the jurors were bribed. However, we know now through intelligence sources that it was probably the KGB who killed your husband and set you up."

Athena nodded. "That is true."

"Why didn't you use that defense?" Michaelis asked.

Athena bit her lower lip. "Because I was afraid that it might give some other countries an idea."

Michaelis said, "It was lucky for you that seven jurors were bribed. The story you concocted was full of holes."

Athena stared at him, indignant. "I thought it was rather good myself," she said.

Rowena knocked and entered the suite with a tray. She bent over placing the coffeepot, cups and saucers, a glass for Strang, and the bottle of Molson's on the table and then straightened up with a smile.

Michaelis said, "Well, hello, Rowena McGrath."

She stared at him blankly.

Athena said, "Rowena, don't you remember telling me that you met Professor Michaelis and Colonel Strang at La Courette?"

"Oh, of course! How are you, Professor? And, uh, Colonel?"

Poor girl, Michaelis thought, a college graduate forced to work as a maid. So many young people were having a difficult time getting a decent job. She is probably embarrassed at my seeing her.

He said, "I'm fine. How are you?"

She said, "Just great! I love my job here."

Athena smiled.

Spunky youngster, Michaelis thought, but then remembered that she had been on a date with the much older security chief. Not so good. Strang said he was a bad apple.

Rowena gave them all a big smile and sauntered out,

her buttocks moving seductively under her tight skirt. Strang watched with pleasure.

Michaelis said, "Rowena was one of my students at Crendon."

Athena stifled a giggle and poured coffee for Michaelis and herself.

"Was Rowena a good student?" she asked.

Michaelis studied the coffee table, then said, "Please don't tell her, but I don't remember. Hundreds of students go through my classes in a couple of years, and I suspect she was there perhaps three years ago."

Athena thought, at least he's honest.

Michaelis smiled. "Don't know how I could have forgotten anyone that pretty and vivacious."

Athena sipped her coffee. "Did you come here today to talk about the trial?"

"Indirectly," Michaelis said. "You probably remember that Colonel Strang was also on the jury. When the news leaked to the press that seven jurors were bribed, it put both of us in an unfortunate position. I lost a White House appointment because of it, and Colonel Strang was pretty angry at having his integrity tarnished."

He paused to sip some black coffee.

"To make a long story short, we decided to find the seven jurors who were bribed."

Athena asked, "And did you?"

Strang put his glass down and said, "You're damned right we did. And we have confessions from all seven."

Athena had a moment of panic. Were they going to turn the names into the district attorney? Would she have to stand another trial?

She drank some coffee, her hand trembling slightly.

"Are you going to have them prosecuted?" she asked.

Michaelis could sense her dismay, her thought that it would mean another trial. He said quickly, "Certainly not. Since we know you were innocent, it would not only be pointless but very unfair to you. Anyway, we got them on the basis of promising a degree of confidentiality."

Athena wondered if they had come seeking a big bribe. She couldn't believe Michaelis was that type.

Strang said, "They couldn't try her again. Double jeopardy."

Michaelis sipped some more coffee. "I know, but they might try her for something else. Cook up a perjury indictment, say."

Athena bit her lip nervously. She said, "Well, I'm very grateful that you are not going to dig up the whole mess again. If there is any way I can reciprocate—"

Michaelis frowned. "We didn't come here for any reciprocity."

She could see he was angry. "I didn't mean it that way. It's just that, that you frightened me with those confessions." Her eyes were becoming teary.

Michaelis said hastily, "I'm sorry if I upset you. We have no intention of showing the confessions to anyone except in confidence." He drank some more coffee. "Mainly we obtained them for our own satisfaction."

Regaining her composure, Athena said, "I would like to believe this is a social call, but since it obviously is not, perhaps you would tell me why you are here."

Michaelis had meant for the visit to be sternly investigative, with no holds barred. Athena was a likely suspect. She had a strong motive, and was rich enough to pay out the $700,000 a hundred times over. But now that he had met her he found himself waffling. He didn't believe in love at first sight, but what had struck him was certainly similar. He wanted to hold this woman in his arms and protect her.

Finally he said, "Well, we have one piece of unfinished business. Whoever paid out the money killed Catherine Leeds and almost killed me. We wonder if you have any ideas about who did this."

She nodded slowly. "I see. You think I may have done it."

Strang said, "You had a strong motive, and certainly the means."

She looked Strang squarely in the eyes. "I did not do it. No one associated with me did it."

Strang shrugged. "Well, obviously you wouldn't admit it if you had."

There was a strained silence, until Athena finally said,

"You have talked to the jurors who were bribed. Why didn't you ask *them* who paid them?"

Michaelis lit one of his no-tar cigarettes. "It was done through anonymous telephone calls and money placed in a Swiss bank or banks."

Athena poured more coffee in his cup and replenished her own. "If you can give me the name of the bank, or banks, I may be able to help you. I have influential banking connections abroad."

Michaelis was embarrassed. He said, "It was stupid of us, but getting the confessions was not easy, and neither of us thought of pressing for details."

"I suppose we could go back to them," Strang said, shaking his head. "But then they would be sure we were preparing a case against them."

Athena sipped her coffee. After a long silence she said, "My friend, Wolfgang Brillhagen, believed the KGB did it."

"Why?" asked Strang.

"If I were in prison, they could not keep track of me or get at me. This place is an armed fortress, but even so we have had two raids since the one in which my husband was killed. In those raids three of our security guards were killed and I was held captive briefly in the last. Several of the raiders were also killed and were identified as Cubans probably trained by the KGB."

Michaelis whistled softly.

Athena rubbed her forehead wearily. "And now that my dear friend Brillhagen is dead I am even more vulnerable."

"Was he killed in one of the raids?" Michaelis asked.

She shook her head. "A stupid accident. The radio he was listening to fell into the whirlpool bath." She bent her head, suddenly overcome with her old grief and loneliness.

Michaelis wanted to move to the sofa, put his arm around her shoulders, and say, "There, there, cheer up."

She looked up and stared at Michaelis with a tremulous smile. "I'm a lonely prisoner here. Will you stay and have dinner with me? We can have a swim first and lie in the late afternoon sun for a while."

Strang, who was not sure he was invited, said, "Angie will be expecting me home, but Jon—"

"I'll be delighted."

Athena politely suggested to Strang that he call Angie and have her join them. She was pleased, but didn't show it, when Strang said he had promised to take Angie to a friend's party.

Carbin stopped Strang's car at the gate and asked, "Where is the professor?"

"We were invited to stay for dinner, but I have another engagement."

Carbin nodded sullenly and motioned him through.

He went back to his office, put his feet on the desk, and lit a cigarette. He had noticed at the restaurant, when Athena was Rowena McGrath, that she was attracted to Michaelis. The professor could cause complications if he and Athena got too chummy. Someone would have to drive Michaelis home. He would take on that job. An accident? Wouldn't do. Too soon after Brillhagen. Even if Athena bought it, Goudenough wouldn't. He would have to think about it. Maybe he could discourage Michaelis in some more subtle way. Like breaking his leg? Athena would probably nurse him back to health.

Athena took Michaelis to Brillhagen's suite to look for a pair of swimming trunks. A battery of lawyers had taken over Brillhagen's financial estate, but so far no one had bothered to go through his personal effects. She found a brand-new pair, navy blue and white, still in its plastic wrapping.

"There," she said. "I think these will fit you. You can change in here and meet me down at the pool."

She turned to leave.

Michaelis said, "Wait just a second, please."

He pulled his jacket back to show her his holstered .38. "I hate to leave this lying around. Are there any children here?" he asked.

She held out her hand. "No, but I will lock it in my desk."

He handed it to her. "Be careful, it's loaded."

She smiled. "I am experienced with guns. I have even fired an Uzi."

Michaelis stared after her, eyebrows raised, as she left and closed the door. He changed to the swimming trunks, which fit well, and went down to the pool.

She was wearing a yellow bikini which covered very little of her perfectly proportioned body. Her breasts were neither too small nor too large, they were exactly right. The white cord that held the front and back triangles of her bikini left exposed a seductive expanse of smooth rounded hips and buttocks. Even her cute dimpled navel was beautiful, Michaelis decided, shifting his eyes from her and then back for another quick look several times.

They swam four laps of the huge, lakelike pool, then dried themselves and sat on the grass.

"Why are you carrying a gun?" Athena asked, smiling. "Are some of your disgruntled students homicidal?"

Michaelis laughed. "No, I would say they are all pretty gruntled."

"Seriously?" she asked.

"You mean why are they gruntled, or why am I carrying a revolver?"

She gave his cheek a gentle slap. He caught her hand and pretended to bite it. She squealed. He kissed her hand and gave it back to her. We're acting like a couple of preteenagers, he thought. Pretty soon they would be playing hide-and-seek, so that he would have an opportunity to grab her when he found her.

He said, "I'll tell you why I'm carrying a revolver."

He gave her a brief account of the Helsinki situation and Ingrid, who might still be looking for him. Or the master briber who had paid out $700,000 and knew he had talked to Catherine Leeds before she was killed.

After his story trailed off, she shook her head. "You seem to be in almost as much trouble as I am."

He smiled. "Not quite. Ingrid definitely promised not to kill me if I let her out of Strang's house alive."

"She'll settle for just crippling you up a bit."

Michaelis looked at her. "This is the sunny side of your nature coming out?"

She laughed, then got to her feet. "Time for preprandial cocktails."

Michaelis showered and dressed in Brillhagen's suite, idly wondering whether Brillhagen had been Athena's lover. And how could a man smart enough to be her friend or lover be careless enough to have a radio placed where it could topple into a whirlpool bath? Be a good way to kill someone, however. Could Athena the billionairess have become tired of her lover?

What a nasty thought. Athena would never do anything like that. The turn his own life had taken recently had made him paranoid. His ex-wife might do something like that, but Athena, never. Athena was lovely and beautiful and kind. Honest, too, he was sure. He had never encountered a billionairess before, and this worried him. He would have some qualms about marrying a *millionairess.* How could he allow himself to fall in love with a billionairess?

Over some potent martinis Athena said, "I have a confession to make. It was me who teased you at La Courette, pretending to be one of your former students."

Michaelis looked blank. "That was Rowena McGrath," he said.

Athena shook her head. "Me."

He said, "Impossible. I may have been a bit drunk, but I could never forget that red hair."

"Wig."

He laughed. "I'll be damned."

"I wanted to meet you," she said.

He took a healthy swallow of martini. "I'm delighted."

She said, "Don't be. I wanted to find out if you were the kind of prig I expected you to be."

He looked down. "And was I?"

"No, you were darling," she said. "The way you kindly pretended to remember me."

He looked up. He would never have thought of himself as *darling.* Women were strange.

"I'm glad." He lifted his drink. "I think you are exquisite, wonderful, and the loveliest woman I have ever met."

She said, "Don't overreact to these martinis, or where will it all end after you've had wine with dinner?"

"And a brandy afterward," he said.

Over dinner in Athena's suite they found they had much in common. Michaelis's wide-ranging knowledge of political philosophy and history, both national and international, fascinated Athena. Her life in England, her knowledge of international affairs, and her father's career as one of England's greatest scientists intrigued Michaelis.

Finishing his brandy, Michaelis said, "We could talk all night."

Athena smiled mischievously. "Not *all* night," she said.

After dinner they took a long walk through the grounds on winding paths that circled the castle and made occasional turns into landscaped plantings and wooded areas. The failing summer evening light sent them back to Athena's suite.

Athena asked, "How are you at chess?"

Michaelis shrugged. "Karpov I am not, but I can handle the better than average player."

She brought out a chess set that had probably cost more than Michaelis's Volvo. The white pieces were beautifully carved ivory, and the black pieces were a lustrous dark green and carved from jade.

They played two long games to a draw. Athena could have won the second game, but decided to forego her feminist ideals and pander to the male ego.

Michaelis glanced at his watch. Almost midnight.

He said, "This has been the most enjoyable evening of my life."

Athena glanced at her watch. "It's still early. How about another game?" she asked.

Michaelis shook his head. "I almost got beaten the last time. Better quit while I'm ahead . . . even," he said, smiling.

"It would be humiliating for you to be beaten by a woman?"

He held up both hands as though she were about to strike him. "Oh, no, never, not at all, that wasn't what I meant. Oh, God, no!" he said. Beware the wrath of angry feminists.

"Then why are you afraid to lose?" she asked.

He thought about it.

Finally he said, "I suppose when a man is trying to impress a beautiful woman he is attracted to, I suppose he wants to prove that he is at least her equal."

Athena grinned. "That's one of the best waffles I've

heard in a long time." She patted his cheek. "Let's have another drink and watch a movie. I have several of the newest ones for the VCR."

He was flattered that she wanted him to stay, but cautious. There was no future in their relationship, whatever it turned out to be on a temporary basis. On the other hand, maybe her wealth didn't mean all that much to her. Certainly it had not brought her happiness.

He smiled and said, "Fine."

She sent down for a bottle of Black Label. Michaelis made them mild, tall drinks, and they sat together on the sofa and watched a movie, a major hit, "R" rated. The heroine's bare breasts quivered and flattened against the chest of her muscular lover. Her mouth partially open, she panted with painful ecstasy in the throes of a climax that extended unbelievably. While the camera later focused on her alone, and never moved below the upper portions of her body, the bouncing of her shoulders and back gave the impression that she was being pounded unmercifully.

Athena snuggled closer to Michaelis. "Close your eyes," she said. "This is vulgar."

He closed his eyes and kissed her. It became a long, passionate kiss.

Then Athena pulled away from him, turned off the television set, and glanced at her watch. It was after two in the morning.

She said, "It's too late for you to go home. You can stay here tonight." She struggled to her feet. "In the morning we can have a swim and breakfast together."

Michaelis had keys to Strang's house and would not need to wake them, but getting a cab to come from Crendon at this time of the night would not be easy. Staying overnight was perfect, even if it resulted in nothing more than a swim with Athena and breakfast together.

She said, "You can have Wolf's suite. It has been cleaned and provided with fresh linens and everything else a guest would need."

He liked the thought that it was right next to hers. Who, if anyone, would visit another suite before the night was over? No one, probably.

She took his arm. "Come, I'll escort you," she said.

Just outside her door Carbin was seated, holding a Walther submachine gun on his lap.

He stood up and said to Athena, "No one I could really trust was available tonight, so I'm pulling guard duty myself. If the professor is ready to leave, I'll have one of the men drive him home."

Athena bit her lower lip, annoyed. "Professor Michaelis will not require any transportation tonight. He is going to stay the night and will be in Mr. Brillhagen's old suite."

Carbin nodded and then turned to watch them walk to Brillhagen's suite. He had noticed a slight smudge of lipstick on Michaelis's cheek. He couldn't, he decided, let this go on much longer. Michaelis would be moving in, taking Brillhagen's place in Athena's bed.

Athena opened the door to Brillhagen's suite and stood back for Michaelis to enter.

She said, "Lock up good, we never know what's going to happen here." She gave him a quick kiss and left.

When Michaelis took off his jacket, he noticed his empty holster. Oh, well, he would remember to get his .38 back from Athena tomorrow.

25

CARBIN DROVE MICHAELIS TO STRANG'S HOUSE AFTER LUNCH THE next day. Other than discussing directions, the whole trip was made in silence.

After Michaelis got out and went into the house, Carbin drove slowly around, surveying the area. Strang's house sat on a four-acre plot and was shielded on three sides by wooded areas. The road that ran past Strang's house curved around the wooded area on the right side.

The layout offered a simple solution. It was a very quiet, rich neighborhood with excellent distance between homes, and the likelihood of anyone stopping him would be minimal. Very early in the morning someday soon he would disguise himself, steal a car, park around the bend. When Michaelis came out, he would be in the woods with his rifle and a telescopic sight. He could put a bullet in Michaelis's head in one shot. Run back through the woods to the car and take off. Return it to a spot near where he had stolen it, then reclaim his own car.

He parked around the bend, made his way through the woods to a point where he could see Strang's front door.

His wristwatch had a stopwatch mechanism. He flicked it on, ran through the woods to his parked car, and flicked it off after he had climbed in and slammed the door. One minute and fifteen seconds. Of course if anyone was with Michaelis, and chased him through the woods, he might be in trouble. But anyone with Michaelis would surely stop to give aid, to see how seriously Michaelis was hurt.

He drove back to the castle whistling "Yankee Doodle Dandy."

Strang had something of a leer on his face while he discussed Michaelis's prolonged absence.

They were eating a late breakfast on the patio at the rear of the house. "Chess, eh," Strang said, smirking. "Did you make all the right moves?"

Michaelis ignored the innuendo. "You know, if she's right about the KGB paying out the bribe money, we might as well forget that project."

Strang nodded. "Been thinking along those lines myself. If *she* didn't do it, who else?"

"She didn't do it," said Michaelis.

Strang said, "I also have a gut feeling that she didn't."

"So we drop it."

Strang grinned. "All you can do, man, is keep your ass covered," he said.

Michaelis finished eating his bacon and eggs. "I'm not sure it's a problem if the KGB did the bribing. I don't see any way we could lay it on them. They're too big, too secret, too anonymous. So why should they worry about me?"

Strang asked, "Why would they worry about Catherine Leeds?"

Michaelis sipped his coffee. "Do you have any other cheerful comments to brighten my day?"

Strang laughed. "You'll just have to stay here, old buddy."

Michaelis lit a cigarette. "Hate to impose on you this way."

Strang shook his head. "No imposition. Angie and I enjoy your company. Fact is, we both enjoy a little excitement. I get bored as hell without it."

Michaelis gave a short laugh. This kind of excitement he could do without. All he wanted was Athena safe and happy in his arms. He went into the house and called her.

"When can I see you?" he asked.

Athena paused to think, then asked, "How would you like to take me out on the town tonight? A big date in the Big Apple?"

"As Rowena McGrath?" he asked.

"Yes," she said.

"You're prettier, but I'll put up with a redhead if necessary," he said.

For her date Athena selected a white summer dress that allowed a modest amount of cleavage to show. She had just finished adjusting her red wig when Carbin came to the suite to call for her. He was nattily dressed in his dark gray suit, white shirt, and navy blue tie. It was time to leave for the city and the writing class.

Athena clasped her hands together. "Oh, damn, I forgot all about the class!" she said. "I've made a dinner date with Professor Michaelis."

Carbin flared up inside but controlled it. He smiled benignly. "No harm done," he said. "Won't hurt to miss a class. Good for you to have something different to do."

She said, "Don't turn your chapter in. I want to be there when he reads it."

Carbin shook his head. "I won't go. I'd better trail along and keep an eye on you."

Athena said, "I don't think that will be necessary. I am well disguised."

"When it comes to your safety, you should let me be the judge," said Carbin.

She turned to him frowning. "Kent, I do not wish to be chaperoned. Professor Michaelis is quite capable of protecting me."

Carbin shrugged. He said, "Your wish is my command," a slight note of sarcasm in his voice.

He strolled back to the gatehouse fuming.

He watched as Michaelis was allowed through the gate driving his old Volvo. "Cheap bastard won't even buy a decent car to take his date out in," he said in an undertone.

Athena and Michaelis had a long dinner at La Courette, lingering over brandy and talk until it was too late to go to the theater. As they finished, Athena said, "I would like to go for a long walk where there are lots of people. I see the same faces every day."

They walked south to 42nd Street, then west toward Times Square. Athena stared like a child at the cosmopolitan mix of faces and oddities of dress. Whites, blacks, white Hispanics, dark Hispanics, Orientals, women wearing clothes that ran the gamut from worn jeans to ballroom dresses, drifters who shuffled past wafting odors of filthy clothes and street living, sassy street kids pushing and shoving, small crowds around black men running three-card monte, street vendors selling costume jewelry, watches, radios, tape recorders, hot dogs, egg rolls, shish kebab, meatball wedges, telephones, panty hose, and socks.

The princess leaves her castle to mingle with the masses, Michaelis thought.

Athena said, "I feel as though I have been let out of prison for good behavior."

His hand on her waist, Michaelis hugged her closer as they walked.

After they had strolled a mile or two of city blocks, Michaelis asked, "Seen enough faces for one evening?"

Athena nodded.

He hailed a cab to take them to the garage where the Volvo was parked.

Athena was subdued and silent during the drive back to Crendon. As they neared the city she said, "I don't want to go back to Sing Sing yet. Take me to your place."

Michaelis started to tell her that he was staying with Strang, then had second thoughts. He went to his apartment every second or third day to pick up his mail, but always in daylight. *They* had probably given up looking for him there. If he was very careful, it would probably be all right. He automatically felt inside his jacket to touch the butt of his .38, which he had reclaimed from Athena.

He said, "There are some people who seem to want to kill me. I'm not sure I should put you in this kind of danger."

She said, "If they were after you very strenuously, they could have killed you a dozen times tonight."

He laughed. "You're right. But we must be very careful entering and leaving the building. They may be watching it."

When they reached his apartment, he parked on the other side of the street. "Lock the door on your side. I had better go in and search the place first."

He rolled up his window, got out, and locked the door. He crossed the street, looking carefully in all directions, his right hand on the grip of the .38. The entrance hall was lighted and empty. He used his key to enter, then climbed the steps to the second floor slowly, listening for any movement. There were sounds, but they were normal muffled TV sounds from other apartments.

His apartment appeared untouched. Nothing was out of place in the living room, bedroom, kitchen, or bath.

He went back to the car and escorted Athena to the apartment.

She looked around curiously at his bookshelves, his desk in one corner, and the beige leather furniture in the rest of the room.

She sat down on his leather sofa and ran her finger over the polished wood of his coffee table. It was dusty.

She said, "Your housekeeper has not cleaned carefully."

He laughed. "I've been staying with Strang. His place is almost as well fortified as yours. Also, I have no housekeeper," he said.

She got up and inspected the rest of the apartment, beginning with his almost monastic bedroom, furnished only with a double bed, not for two but because he rolled around a bit in his sleep, a dresser, and a night table.

He brought out a new bottle of Johnnie Walker Red

Label. He did not have the Black Label; it was much more expensive and he wasn't that much of a scotch aficionado.

Athena accepted the scotch on the rocks with water.

"Are you poor?" she asked. "I mean, I've heard that professors are not well paid."

Michaelis smiled. "Poor by your standards. Rich by thc standards of most people."

"What does that mean?" she asked.

He sipped his own drink. "You want specific figures?"

She nodded.

He said, "My income is about two hundred and fifty thousand a year. Since I don't spend quite one fifth of it, by the time I'm a very old man it will probably be close to a million a year. You see, I live very simply."

"Professors make *that* much?" she asked.

He took another swallow of scotch. Was she trying to find out whether he was a fortune hunter? To hell with her if that was on her mind. He said, "I *earn* about seventy-five thousand. The rest is from royalties and investments of inherited capital." His voice was a bit testy.

She said, "Now you're angry with me."

"No, I'm not," he said.

She moved closer to him. "I was just curious. It doesn't make any difference to me whether you're rich or poor. I inherited everything I have. If I was on my own, I probably couldn't earn ten thousand a year, much less seventy-five thousand."

He put his arm around her. "I thought maybe you were wondering whether I was after your money. I don't even have much use for most of my own."

She said, "I can see that you live very simply."

He sipped more of his drink. "I'm comfortable with my own life-style."

She leaned over and kissed him hard, then pulled away quickly. "I wanted to come here because at the castle 'big brother' watches my every move," she said.

"Carbin?" he asked.

She nodded. "He's quite conscientious. And of course he's very concerned with my safety and has good reason to be," she said.

She told Michaelis about the last break-in, and how she

and Brillhagen had been pushed from room to room by the enemy blowing the doors down and throwing grenades in until there was nowhere to retreat to. Her voice trembling at times, she described how Kurt Wessel had tried to rape her, and how she had killed him, taken his Walther machine pistol, and rescued Brillhagen from his captors.

Michaelis whistled softly. He kissed her cheek. "You're one tough little lady," he said.

She said, "I didn't grow up tough. In England I felt free and perfectly safe. I could go anywhere without bodyguards or weapons. I never had a weapon of any kind. I was very feminine and soft."

He moved his hand down, stroking her thighs gently. "You haven't lost any of your femininity, that's for sure," he said.

She sighed deeply. "Everything inside has changed. I have custody of my father's great boon or curse for mankind. It has even made me a killer."

"Boon or curse?"

She explained her father's invention, its power to destroy with one hundred times greater effectiveness than nuclear fusion, and its capability of providing the world with such cheap power that even the most poverty-stricken nations could have an abundance of it. How she had flown to many countries and hidden the secret in a place that only she and its guardian knew. And its guardian did not even know its importance. How all the intelligence services in the world were after her.

Michaelis sat stunned into silence by the enormity of her problem. But he felt vaguely exhilarated. Now he knew he could never leave her. Billionairess or not, she needed him. He would share her danger, protect her.

He hugged her. "You killed in self-defense and were perfectly justified in doing so."

He made himself another drink. Her drink was still sitting on the coffee table untouched. He wondered whether Carbin could be trusted.

He said, "Strang is a bit worried about Carbin. He says Carbin is a real bad apple."

Athena smiled. "They're both ex-mercenaries. Strang is a bad apple, too."

Michaelis kissed her.

"Strang is an honest bad apple," he said.

They both laughed.

He downed a swallow of his scotch, put the glass on the coffee table, and turned to look at her. They stared at each other in silence, Athena with a half-smile on her face.

Finally he pulled her closer and they found themselves sprawled on the sofa in a tight embrace. He kissed her on her lips, on her forehead, on her neck, on her collarbone, his right hand busily roaming over her body. Eventually it found its way into her cleavage and cupped one of her breasts.

Looking into his eyes, her eyes widened.

He stared back. "No?" he asked.

"Yes," she said.

Afterward they lay together naked, happily satiated.

She caressed his cheek, smiling. "It's only our second date. You'll think I'm promiscuous."

He kissed her breasts gently. He said, "I don't think anything except that I love you. I love you more than anything in the world."

Athena buried her face between his neck and shoulder. Love. She had been thinking the same thing. She was feeling something she had never felt before. This was a man she could spend the rest of her life with. As a lover he wasn't the finely tuned machine that Brillhagen had been, but he excited her much more with his slight clumsiness and loving touches.

She raised herself on one elbow and said, "Jonathan, I love you, too. Whatever happens, I want you to know that I love you."

He cupped her cheeks and kissed her.

"That *whatever happens* sounds ominous," he said.

She ran her fingers through the hair on his chest and down to rest on his hard, flat stomach. She said, "I'm saddled with an unsolvable problem. I don't know how to get out from under it. I may be killed. You may be killed just because of our association."

He took her hand and kissed it, then put it back on his stomach. It felt good there.

He wanted to say, "Don't worry, I won't let anyone

harm you." A man should be able to protect his woman. Of course, the cards were really stacked against them. Every powerful government in the world wanted her father's secret. The KGB, the East German SSD, probably the CIA if she tried to leave the United States; even international private interests that would be ruined by the development of her father's invention might come into the picture. A safe, inexpensive source of unlimited power would wipe out the income of most of the Middle East.

He said, "We'll survive. We'll fight them, we'll run from them, we'll hide from them. We'll do whatever is necessary. I'm not inexperienced in dirty fighting. I was in Vietnam. I've learned a lot from my association with Strang."

He told her about his life as an investigative reporter and the humiliation he had felt in backing down under the threat of Brewster Fernwald's stooge. How he had been drawn into a mission to save Thomas Swift, and gave her more of the grisly details of his shoot-out with Ingrid and her two East German associates, how he had banged Konrad's head on the concrete again and again until he was dead, how Ingrid had again tried to kill him.

He said, "So you can see I am not exactly the nonviolent professor type."

Athena had been listening with a small smile.

He suddenly had the feeling that he had been boasting like a schoolboy, talking a good game. Yet how could he reassure her? The future was bleak unless she got rid of her father's curse. Boon to mankind, hell. Her money was a problem, too. He did not want to be Mr. Athena von Dietrich. Suffocating male ego, but it was there.

Athena plastered herself against him and began whispering in his ear, telling him what she wanted him to do.

They made love again. It was a longer, more exquisite trip.

After her breathing had quieted, Athena asked, "Do you want to marry me?"

He kissed the end of her nose. "Do you want to be a professor's wife?"

"Why not?" she asked.

He thought about it. Finally he said, "Well, it's so different from what you are accustomed to."

She laughed. "My father was a Cambridge don. I grew up in that environment."

He smiled. "So we have no problem. Other than a castle, sixty armed guards, a billionaire's fortune, and a horde of enemies clamoring at the gates to force you to hand over your father's papers. How can you give up all that excitement?"

She looked down. "I suppose Crendon University would not appreciate being invaded by the KGB."

He hugged her. "One problem at a time," he said.

"Which comes first?" she asked.

"Us."

"After us?" she asked.

He rolled onto his back and put his hands behind his neck. "It seems to me that you have only two choices. One, give the plans to a reasonably reliable government such as ours and hope they never use it for war. It's doubtful that they would ever use it. The enemy would respond with nuclear devastation."

She interrupted. "I don't like the first. What's the second choice?"

He smiled. "The second is, we gather a group of say four prominent people well known for integrity, public figures preferably with liberal leanings. Say a Supreme Court judge, a famous Protestant minister, a top-drawer rabbi, and a cardinal, if possible. We then photograph you burning the plans. After they are burned we smash up the ashes in a mortar and dump them in a river. Then we issue a press release to AP and UPI. There will be photographs of you burning the papers, grinding up the ashes, and dumping them into the river. There will be photographs of the public figures witnessing, attesting to the validity of the papers being burned."

Athena said, "I like it better than the first plan. But will the KGB believe it? I could be burning up any old batch of my father's papers and your four prominent citizens wouldn't know the difference."

Michaelis reached for one of his low-tar cigarettes and groped for his lighter. "You haven't heard all of it. We then feed a story to Russian intelligence that it was a phony burning. That you have sold the plans to the U.S. government, and the U.S. government orchestrated the scene so that the Russians would not know that they have it."

Athena nodded. "Then I'm out of it?"

She was silent for a while. "My poor old father will be spinning in his grave. He will come back to haunt me."

Michaelis sat up so that he could both light his cigarette and look at Athena. She was always a delight to look at.

She stroked his cheek. "It wouldn't work. Gesellschaft Dietrich invested a fortune in the development of this monster. They own half of it. There would be screams of rage and billion-dollar lawsuits against me."

Michaelis said, "Well, we could always live on my income."

Athena glanced at her small jeweled wristwatch, the only thing she was wearing. "I'm going to ruin poor Rowena's reputation. It's almost two in the morning."

She dressed hurriedly, then reached for her red wig, which she had removed when they went to the bedroom, put it on, and rushed to a mirror to adjust it.

26

CARBIN WAS WAITING UP IN THE GATEHOUSE WHEN MICHAELIS AND Athena drove through at 2:30 A.M. He went back to his desk and chewed a Tums. Michaelis was giving him indigestion. Michaelis would undoubtedly stay the night in Brillhagen's suite. Carbin had planned some target practice in the morning, the target being Michaelis's head. Now he would have to put it off. He had gotten himself all hyped up for a dangerous, tricky job and now he had to wait another day or so. He ate another Tums.

He went to his private room, undressed, and climbed into bed. Before he dozed off, another idea occurred to him, a better way of removing Michaelis from his domain.

The next morning he drove to New York to meet an old acquaintance.

Aubrey Smith was now working as a bookkeeper in a small insurance office. Smith wasn't his real name, but Aubrey was his legitimate first name. An ex-army doctor, he had been removed from the service for sexually molesting female soldiers who went to him for treatment. Later in his career his license to practice medicine in New York State had been revoked by the State Medical Board for dispensing drugs too freely for very stiff fees. Aubrey was actually a smart, competent doctor, just morally warped.

Aubrey *looked* like a successful doctor. He had silver-gray hair neatly parted on the left side, a rather broad, solemn face, and a high forehead over black-rimmed glasses with sharp brown eyes peering through them.

As a bookkeeper he made very little, and barely got by in New York living in a shabby residential hotel. He had a fine wardrobe, however, left over from his affluent days of dispensing drugs.

They sat in a dark corner of a bar on Lexington Avenue, well away from others eating and drinking lunch.

Aubrey shook his head. "I don't know, Kent. It sounds pretty risky."

Carbin shrugged. "Nothing ventured—"

Aubrey lifted his second martini. "You know I came close to being indicted last time. I could have gone to prison."

Carbin signaled a waitress. They ordered sandwiches and beer.

After she left, Carbin asked, "Are you having any fun *out* of prison?"

Aubrey gave him a sickly little smile. "No, I'm leading a shitty, miserable existence doing work that is so boring I'm ready to climb up the wall by three o'clock in the afternoon."

Carbin nodded. He said, "There's big money in it if it works, and if there are complications I think I can pull us both out before it gets too serious."

Aubrey was weakening.

Carbin said, "Call in sick day after tomorrow and wait for my call that day or the following day. It may be several days before I need you. Don't worry about your lousy job. You can get a job as a bookkeeper anytime. The *Times* is full of ads for bookkeepers."

After lunch they made a quick trip to Aubrey's hotel. Aubrey dug around in his dusty medical bag and handed Carbin a small packet. Carbin folded up a couple of hundred-dollar bills and slipped them to Aubrey.

"Just a small advance on something very big," he said. He gave Aubrey a paternal pat on his upper arm. "And by the way, line up a practical nurse you can trust to keep her mouth shut and do what she's told."

After eating breakfast outside, in the shade of a tree near the swimming pool, Michaelis and Athena sat trying to unravel the tangle of their future plans.

Athena said, "Move in here and we'll have a quiet, secret wedding. In fact, it has to be quite secret or you won't be able to come and go freely."

Michaelis nodded. Being a prisoner in the castle would make it impossible for him to continue at Crendon University. Doing nothing would drive him out of his mind. And Athena was right. As her husband he would make a fine hostage.

"I'll have a talk with Strang and see if he can come up with any ideas. He's pretty resourceful." He thought for a minute, then shook his head. "As for keeping the marriage secret I have my doubts. Even if we get a discreet judge to come here, there will still be a public record in Crendon, a license issued, something the newspapers would certainly pick up."

Athena patted his cheek. "Then we'll have to live together in sin," she said, smiling.

He leaned over and kissed her. "Maybe we can fly to a state without residency laws. You could wear your Rowena disguise."

She laughed. "That would be fun. I'll fly us there in my jet. Bet you didn't know I'm a licensed pilot," she said.

Michaelis shook his head slowly. "No way. We fly economy class and stay in a modestly priced hotel. People everywhere have heard of Athena von Dietrich. I think your trial got almost as much national publicity as the von Bulow case."

He finished his coffee and stood up. "Even that will be tricky. Maybe if you sign as 'Thena Dietrich' on the license, no one will make the connection."

She got up and walked with him to his car. She said, "I can do better and make it 'Anna Dietrich' and it will be perfectly legal. Anna is my middle name."

Michaelis drove back to Crendon cautiously, remembering Ingrid's attack on the road. This time he wasn't riding in a heavy Cadillac, and she might be. Or she might have a truck that could bounce the Volvo right off the road into a tree. What a lying bitch. Why did she keep her word when dealing with Thomas Swift, and not with him? Maybe it had not been Ingrid in the Volkswagen. Maybe he was mistaken about the green eyes. Maybe he should quit trying to kid himself. He alternated steadily between glancing at the rearview mirror and the road ahead.

He decided to stop by his apartment and pick up some more clothes. He had packed skimpily for what he thought would be a brief stay with Strang.

He parked across the street and stared at the building and up and down the street for a few minutes, looking for any signs of unusual activity.

The building and the area nearby appeared to be safe. No one was walking by, and there were no occupied cars. What might be inside was another question.

He crossed the street, his hand on the grip of his .38, and entered the apartment building. He stood in the foyer for a while, listening. There were no sounds, not even the muffled squawks of TV.

He climbed the steps slowly to the second floor, opened the door of his apartment, and stepped inside. He stood in the entrance hall listening. The apartment was as silent as the foyer had been, but there was a smell of perfume. A rather heady floral perfume, certainly not Athena's because she used a very subtle fragrance that was hardly noticeable.

As he stood there, he began to get dizzy. He stumbled back out into the hall, his ability to move fading. With an agonizing effort to keep going he started down the stairs, thinking he must get outside to fresh air. He had staggered down only three or four steps before he passed out and tumbled backward, his body bumping and sliding down the metal-rimmed treads.

When Michaelis failed to return to the castle for dinner, Athena called Strang, expecting to find him there. Strang immediately went into action, first calling Lieutenant Goudenough.

Michaelis was in Crendon Memorial Hospital, unconscious from either the effects of the mysterious perfumed gas or the crack on his head when he tumbled backward. Fortunately the woman in the apartment across the hall had heard the loud thump of Michaelis's falling and had opened her door to see what was happening.

Toxic gas experts from the army and the New York P.D. had been in Michaelis's apartment with gas masks taking samples. Both the woman across the hall and the ambulance attendants had experienced symptoms of dizziness and fading consciousness.

Strang called Athena. She hastily put on her Rowena makeup and wig and summoned Carbin to drive her to the hospital.

Crendon Memorial was a new, modern hospital with none of the harsh antiseptic smells of older hospitals. A large T-shaped beige brick building six stories high, it was set in the center of several acres of beautifully landscaped lawns, shrubs, and trees.

Carbin parked near the emergency entrance and they hurried in. Strang was already there talking to Dr. Blankenship, the hospital's chief surgeon. Blankenship was a plump, short man with rosy cheeks and a comforting bedside manner. He was wearing a navy blue suit with discreet silver pinstripes, a white shirt, and a maroon tie. After introductions were made he turned to Athena and recited his information as though giving a classroom lecture.

He said, "As I have been telling Colonel Strang, your friend is probably going to be all right. His vital signs are excellent, though he may have a mild concussion. At this time we do not know whether there will be any permanent damage from the gas because we do not know what it is.

Various tests are being made and we may be able to tell you more within a few days."

Michaelis was still in a cubicle in the emergency room area, waiting for a bed upstairs. They were allowed a brief visit. Michaelis was still unconscious. Donald Tarboy sat on one side of the curtained entrance and a Crendon policeman sat on the other.

Athena found this protection reassuring, though she grieved at seeing the bandage on Michaelis's head and the stillness of his body that was not sleep. She bent over and kissed him gently.

Carbin stood in the doorway looking grim and sympathetic. Inwardly he exulted. Luck was on his side. Now, if the sonofabitch would only have a relapse and die. Unaware of Michaelis's dealings with the von Dietrich trial jurors and Ingrid, Carbin was puzzled over the attack. Who wanted Michaelis out of the way other than himself? Maybe it could be a team effort.

Driving back to the castle, Carbin said, "Cheer up. Mr. Michaelis is going to be okay, I'm sure of it."

Athena dabbed at her eyes with a tiny handkerchief. "We're going to be married," she said.

Carbin turned for a quick warm grin. "Say, that's wonderful! Let me wish you every happiness," he said. "He seems to be a first-rate chap."

Athena said, "Thank you. He is and I love him very much."

They drove in silence for several minutes.

Carbin finally asked, "I wonder why he was attacked. Who in the world would want to harm him?"

Athena knew about Ingrid, Thomas Swift, and the bribed jurors, but decided that she had better not discuss them with Carbin, even though she trusted him.

She said, "It may date from when he was an investigative reporter. He made a number of enemies then." She sighed deeply and continued. "He helped send a few powerful people to prison, including a Mafia chief or two."

Carbin said, "Sounds like quite a guy."

They turned into the castle grounds.

After escorting Athena to her suite, Carbin paused at the door and asked, "May I offer some avuncular advice?"

Athena smiled. "Certainly."

"Keep working at your writing. You have too good a mind to waste being merely a wife. Jonathan Michaelis is an achiever, and he'll respect you more if you develop some kind of creative talent."

She stared at him silently, then grinned. "That's not bad advice, Uncle Kent."

He unlocked the door and held it open for her. "Speaking of writing, I have three pages I'm not happy with. Would you take a look at them?"

"Sure. You can bring them up now. I'll order coffee for us."

Ten minutes later Rowena arrived with coffee. She giggled at seeing Athena still in her Rowena costume. Athena remembered and removed her wig, then went to the bathroom to remove her makeup. She had been absorbed in her thoughts, which were mainly of Michaelis.

Carbin arrived with his manuscript.

Athena poured coffee, then took Carbin's three pages and began to read.

While she was concentrating, Carbin got up to pace. As he passed the table, his palm floated quickly over her coffee cup. A small cube dropped in with hardly a ripple.

27

ON HIS THIRD DAY IN THE HOSPITAL MICHAELIS APPEARED TO BE fully recovered, though the experts had not yet found out the nature of the gas in his apartment. He had a very sore bump on his head, but no concussion.

Strang drove him home. Michaelis had heard about Athena's visit to the hospital while he was unconscious and wondered vaguely why she had not been back or telephoned. As soon as he got to Strang's house, he called Athena. The operator switched his call to Carbin.

"Ah, Mr. Michaelis, Mrs. von Dietrich is ill and cannot speak to you."

"What's happened? What's wrong?" asked Michaelis.

Carbin cleared his throat. "I'm afraid she has had a bit of an emotional breakdown. Her doctor is with her now. Perhaps I could have him call you."

"A psychiatrist?" asked Michaelis.

Carbin said, "Yes, well, he's her regular therapist."

Michaelis said, "Never mind having him call, I'll be right over."

Michaelis replaced the phone, bowing his head in despair. Poor Athena, carrying the burden of her father's deadly gift to the world, living in fear of her life, attacked by vicious hoodlums, tortured, her husband murdered right before her eyes—

When he told Strang, Strang insisted upon accompanying him. He said, "I wouldn't trust this guy Carbin with his own mother, much less Athena von Dietrich. He's about as straight as a corkscrew."

Michaelis nodded and stood up. "Let's go."

Carbin had left word at the gatehouse for Michaelis to come up to Athena's suite. Strang tagged along.

When Carbin unlocked the door and opened it, he took a quick look at Strang and frowned. "Colonel Strang, would you kindly wait in the hall. The doctor says family only, and I'm stretching a point for Michaelis. I've heard that they are engaged, but it has not been officially announced," he said.

Strang gave him a sour look and plopped down in the night guard's chair.

Michaelis went into Athena's living room. The bedroom door was closed, and *Dr.* Smith lounged in an easy chair. He got up and held out his hand as Carbin introduced them.

Smith said, "No relation to the famous Sir Aubrey Smith, unfortunately."

Shaking hands, Michaelis did not smile. "I'm naturally very concerned about my fiancée," he said.

Smith patted his shoulder. "Well, don't be, old boy.

She's going to be quite all right. She has these flare-ups once in a while, but she usually comes out of it in a week or two. Little Thorazine and other medication, you know."

Michaelis nodded. "She's been under tremendous stress in recent months, I'm sure."

Smith shrugged. "Stress or no stress, these upsets do occur."

Smith strolled over to a large sofa and sat down. He patted one of the cushions and said to Michaelis, "Come over and sit down a minute and I'll tell you the situation."

Michaelis followed him and sat on the sofa.

"Athena has had a somewhat unstable personality since she was a young girl in London. When she came over here to live, her physician, Sir Oswald Ferguson, recommended me and forwarded her case history to me," said Smith.

Michaelis nodded.

Smith stared at him silently for a few seconds, then said, "I gather you plan to marry?"

"Yes," said Michaelis.

Smith said, "Let me suggest then that when and if you do, you refrain from having children."

"Why?" asked Michaelis, a slight belligerence creeping into his tone.

Smith frowned. "Because pregnancy and childbirth frequently push women in Athena's condition into the land of no return. As things are now she can lead a normal life with occasional treatment. Push her over the line and"—he shrugged—"it can mean a sanitarium for the rest of her life."

Michaelis stared down at his shoe tops, desolate. He had always wanted a family. So they would adopt some kids, he decided, his spirits lifting a little.

He said, "I would like to see her."

Smith slapped Michaelis's knee. "She probably would prefer that you didn't, but if you insist—"

"I want her to know that I'm with her all the way, whatever happens. Seeing me may get that through to her," he said.

Smith stood up. "Right-o," he said. "Give me five minutes to prepare her, and then come in. A woman in that condition usually wants to look her best."

He went into the bedroom and closed the door.

Michaelis waited about five minutes and then stood up. Smith opened the bedroom door and motioned for him to come in.

Athena was sitting in a chair by the windows. She was wearing a dressing gown of very light lemon yellow. Her hair was immaculately groomed. When she saw Michaelis, she stood up slowly and came to him.

"Jonathan, how kind of you to come," she said, stopping about three feet from him.

He moved closer to take her in his arms.

She moved back quickly, then changed her mind and rushed to hug him.

After a long kiss she pushed herself away and said, "Your eyes are burning me. Turn them off."

She backed up a few feet, staring at him.

"There's a window in your head, and there are beautiful little birds flying around inside. Some are blue, some are red, some are yellow, some are pink. Are you a birdbrain?"

Michaelis tried to smile.

She clutched her dressing gown. "You've brought bugs. They're crawling all over me," she said, her voice rising.

Her right hand frantically searched under her dressing gown, then using both hands she tore it off and stood slapping her body, now only clothed in a thin nightgown.

She screamed at Michaelis, "You've got bugs all over me! Get out, dammit! Get out!"

Smith touched Michaelis's arm. "Better leave, you're upsetting her."

He headed for the door, Michaelis following him.

Smith suggested to Michaelis that he refrain from visiting Athena for a week. "Give her time for her treatment to really work. When she goes off this way, it makes it harder to bring her back," he said.

Smith and Carbin sat in the castle's first-floor library sharing a bottle of scotch.

"Suppose you could make her dopey enough to sign a general power of attorney?" Carbin asked.

Smith nodded. "Probably," he said.

Carbin sipped his drink. "And thinking further down

the line, could she maybe die in a way that an autopsy would say *natural causes?"*

Smith shook his head slowly. "Now you're talking pretty heavy stuff. I'm not sure I want to be involved."

Carbin took another swallow of scotch. "It could mean a fortune for both of us," he said.

"How?" Smith asked.

Carbin smiled. "Well, say I have her transfer two million dollars to a numbered Swiss account for me, and two million for you. Hell, the woman is worth over a *thousand* million dollars."

Smith, visibly nervous, set his glass down with a thump. "It would look very suspicious to her heirs," he said.

Carbin asked, "So what? If there is no suspicion about the cause of her death, the heirs can whistle Dixie. She has a perfect right to reward loyal and very important employees generously. With her fortune, four million would be a generous but not unbelievable sum to give away."

Smith poured himself another drink. He said, "I suppose it could be done with one of these powerful muscle-relaxant drugs that don't show up in an autopsy."

He poured a little water into the scotch and sipped it, then said, "But I don't think I want to take part in a murder."

Michaelis paced the floor in Strang's huge living room, his footsteps silent on thick Persian rugs. Strang looked up from time to time. He was trying to read the *Times.* Finally he said, "Will you for God's sake sit down? I can't concentrate."

Michaelis sat down. "I don't like the setup there at the castle. There's something about it that—" He paused, then continued, "A hunch, I don't know why."

Strang folded the paper and put it down. "I would be damned careful about anything that Carbin had his sticky fingers in," he said.

Michaelis bent over, cupping his head in the palms of his hands. He had a monstrous headache. Daggers pierced his brain at intervals of four a second. Looking up, he said, "I have one hell of a headache. I don't like Athena's doctor. I want a second opinion."

Strang said, "I agree with you there. Take three aspirin while I call another doctor."

Strang strolled over to his living room telephone, which sat on an end table next to his favorite leather recliner. Dialing, he switched on his speaker system for Michaelis's benefit.

Michaelis came back with a glass of water and three aspirin, which he immediately downed.

"Dr. Daniel Slocum, please, Horace Strang calling," said Strang. He was switched to Slocum. "Dan, this is Strang. I want the name of the best psychiatrist in New York."

The other voice laughed. "Horace, I could give you ten names, including my own, but the *best,* forget it."

Strang said, "You'll do. I want you to examine my good friend's fiancée. We're not satisfied with the progress she's making with her present therapist."

Slocum's voice said, "Hmmmm. That's a bit ticklish. Not like a second opinion on surgery. Much more complex." He paused, then asked, "Who's taking care of her now?"

"The doctor's name is Aubrey Smith," said Strang.

Slocum said, "I'll check him out and let you know whether I can ethically step into the picture." He paused and said, "I'll call you back as soon as practical."

Michaelis leaned back and waited for the aspirin to do something, he hoped.

28

AUBREY TOSSED DOWN THE REMAINING SCOTCH IN HIS GLASS, HIS fifth drink, and stood up creakily.

"Going to hit the sack, Kent old buddy," he said.

Carbin nodded. Smith was staying in the castle to be on hand whenever needed.

Carbin said, "Before you go, that stuff you gave her, how long will it affect her?"

Smith's mouth turned down. "Not long. She's probably pretty normal by now."

He stumbled off to his room.

Carbin poured himself another drink and sat mulling over his situation. If he was Athena's lover, his control would be greater, not to mention the addition of sheer, exquisite enjoyment. He thought of her as she lay on the grass in her bikini, and of the night he had burst into her bedroom to warn them of an attack and she had sat up, the sheet falling down to reveal her lovely breasts.

Why not give it a try, old boy? he asked himself, mimicking Aubrey Smith.

He rode the elevator to the third floor and unlocked the door to Athena's suite, entered, and locked the door from the inside.

He opened the bedroom door an inch and knocked, saying, "It's me, Athena."

She called for him to come in.

Athena was sitting up in her bed, reading a book. She turned it facedown on her lap.

"How are you feeling?" Carbin asked. "You seemed a bit upset this afternoon."

She stared at him. "What was wrong with me this

afternoon? I seem to remember that Jonathan was here, but—"

Carbin smiled. "Don't worry about it. Just a bit of hysteria, I think," he said.

Athena shook her head. "What have I to be hysterical about?"

"Stress, probably. You certainly have had enough problems to worry eight people," he said.

She nodded. "Well, I feel all right now," she said.

Carbin sank into an easy chair and stared at her, smiling. He sensed a certain reserve, a certain distance she was trying to put between them. This was not the time to pursue her amorously. He would be burning his bridges if he made a forceful pass. She might even fire him.

He stood up. "Well, just wanted to be sure you were okay. Anything I can do for you before I turn in?"

She smiled. "Thanks, no."

They exchanged good-nights and Carbin left. He drove to Crendon to see his mistress. When it came to screwing, one woman was about as good as another, he told himself.

While Michaelis, Angie, and Strang were having a late breakfast, Dr. Daniel Slocum called to speak to Strang.

He said, "I've checked out this Aubrey Smith. Strange situation. He has no office listed anywhere in the area—Manhattan, the other boroughs, Crendon, Westchester, Long Island, or Connecticut. He is not a member of the American Psychiatric Society. He is not listed in any medical directories."

Strang whistled. "A complete phony?"

Slocum cleared his throat. "Not exactly. From looking at the medical directories I think we have a clue as to who he is. Quite a lucky coincidence." He paused for a small cough. "There is an Aubrey Smedilis, which we happened to notice looking for Aubrey Smith. Smedilis had his license revoked, for, in effect, becoming a high-class drug peddler."

Strang said, "I'll be damned."

"This could be a dangerous situation for Mrs. von Dietrich if he is feeding her drugs indiscriminately," said Slocum.

Strang mopped his forehead, looked pityingly at Michaelis, and made arrangements for Dr. Slocum to accompany them to the castle that afternoon for a visit with Athena.

Michaelis spent part of the morning pacing, then went down to Strang's shooting gallery in the basement and practiced with a .45 automatic. He could shoot the buttons off an assailant's shirt with a .38, but the .45 was something else.

Slocum arrived as they were about to sit down to lunch. Short, about five feet six inches tall, middle-aged, with a round face and neat brown hair combed down over his forehead, Slocum had a large mouth and lively blue eyes. He was wearing gray slacks, a light blue shirt with a black knit tie, and a herringbone sports jacket.

"Never eat lunch," he said when invited to join them.

Strang persuaded him to sit down and have coffee.

"You're the only shrink I've ever known," Strang said to Slocum. "Is it true that being a little nuts themselves attracts psychiatrists to the profession?"

Slocum gave a one-syllable laugh. "Totally untrue," he said, managing an exaggerated twitching of his eyebrows.

Strang guffawed. Michaelis managed a smile.

Michaelis endured the lunch impatiently. Athena's condition, which had worried and disheartened him, was now a matter of frightening urgency. She was being drugged by a quack.

They finally finished lunch and drove to the castle.

Carbin intercepted them at the gatehouse. "Mrs. von Dietrich does not wish to see you," he said to Michaelis. He turned to Strang. "And most certainly not you, Strang."

"I'll speak to her on the telephone," said Michaelis. "I don't believe you."

Carbin said, "She does not wish to speak to you."

Michaelis clenched his fists. "Then she'll tell me that. And she's the only one who will tell me that."

Carbin glared at him. "Her doctor does not wish for her to be disturbed."

Strang said, "Her doctor is a drug pusher who has had his license revoked. We'll bring Goudenough over here and have him arrested."

Carbin paled slightly under his tan. He did an about-face, went in the gatehouse, and slammed the door.

He said to the guards on duty, "The people outside are not to be admitted under any circumstances. Mrs. von Dietrich does not want to see them."

The three men on duty in the gatehouse eyed him curiously and nodded.

Carbin hurried up to Athena's suite.

He handed her the Uzi he was carrying. "There are some people trying to get in the grounds! I think we had better hide you," he said.

"Where?" she asked, glancing around in a mild panic.

Carbin said, "The attic is too open. How about one of the lockers in the basement?" He started out the door, motioning for her to follow him.

They took the elevator to the basement. The lockers were really small closets. Carbin quickly located one that was almost empty. He pushed an old wooden chair into it and hustled Athena in, then locked the door on the outside.

He rode the elevator back to the first floor smiling.

Michaelis and Dr. Slocum waited in front of the gatehouse while Strang drove back to Crendon to try to fetch Lieutenant Goudenough.

"This is going to take a while," said Michaelis. They found a grassy spot across the road from the gatehouse and sat down.

In less than an hour Strang returned accompanied by Goudenough.

Goudenough strode up to the gatehouse and banged on the door.

Carbin opened it and stepped out.

Goudenough said, "Mr. Michaelis and Colonel Strang believe you are holding Mrs. von Dietrich incommunicado."

Strang laughed, turning his palms up in a gesture of helplessness. He said, "Ridiculous. She has ordered me to tell him that she does not wish to speak to him. She doesn't wish to speak to *anyone.*"

"I want to hear that from her," said Goudenough.

Carbin shrugged. "Come in," he said. "We'll see if she'll talk to you."

As they walked up the driveway to the castle, Carbin said, "Mrs. von Dietrich has had a nervous breakdown. The pressure of continuing danger, the constant fear of attack. I'm afraid these worries have made her a bit paranoid. She even hides from me, even though she knows that I and my men are her twenty-four-hour-a-day protectors."

Goudenough turned to give Carbin a skeptical glance.

They rode the elevator up to the third floor and went to Athena's suite. Goudenough checked that it was empty. Carbin led him through several of the other suites, calling out "Mrs. von Dietrich" from time to time.

Finally he turned to Goudenough in disgust and handed him his key ring. "I'm sick of playing hide-and-seek with the lady. You look for her," he said.

Carbin strode away, Goudenough staring at his back uneasily.

The keys were all neatly labeled. Goudenough searched systematically, starting with the attic and working downward. He skipped opening the cobweb-draped doors of the empty rooms on the fourth floor. Obviously none of them had been opened by Athena. He went into all the rooms on the third, second, and first floors calling loudly in each, "Mrs. von Dietrich, are you in here? This is Lieutenant Goudenough."

By the time he got to the basement his voice was hoarse from shouting. He stood in the center of the huge, cavernous room and yelled, "Mrs. von Dietrich, are you down here? This is Lieutenant Goudenough."

Athena sat quietly in her locker. The hoarse, raspy voice did not sound like Goudenough. Cradling the Uzi, her forefinger hovering near the trigger, she remained silent.

Goudenough went back to the gatehouse disgusted. He crossed the road and spoke to the waiting group.

"Carbin says she is having a nervous breakdown and hides from everyone. I searched the entire building but couldn't find her."

He turned to Michaelis. "You have a psychiatrist with you. You must be aware that she is having a breakdown?"

Strang said, "That defrocked drug-pushing doctor probably gave her something to make her slaphappy. Why didn't you arrest him while you were going through the place?"

Goudenough wheeled to face Strang. "I didn't see him. I didn't see anybody but servants in the whole damned building, and they are all local people I know."

Led by Michaelis, the group crossed the road to the gatehouse and trooped in.

Carbin came out of his office.

Michaelis asked, "Where is Mrs. von Dietrich?" He stared hard at Carbin, aching to grab him by the neck and wring the answer from him.

Carbin smirked. "Hiding. She does not want to talk to you."

Strang asked, "Where is that phony drug-pushing doctor, Aubrey Smith, aka Aubrey Smedilis?"

Carbin straightened his shoulders. "I dismissed him when I learned that his license had been revoked. After all, it was Mrs. von Dietrich who asked me to call him in."

Michaelis said, "I'm going in and search for Athena."

Resting his hand on the grip of his holstered revolver, Carbin stepped in front of Michaelis. "My orders are quite definite. She does not wish to see you or talk to you. I have given Goudenough free run of the place and *that* is enough."

Michaelis looked at the lieutenant. "Does he have the authority to stop me from going in?"

Goudenough nodded. "He does. He's in charge of security here. And perhaps Mrs. von Dietrich really does not wish to see you."

Strang said, "Ridiculous! They're engaged to be married."

Goudenough smiled. "Perhaps she doesn't want him to see her in the upset condition she's in. Second-guessing a woman is not easy."

Strang grasped Michaelis's arm and muttered, "To hell with this. Let's go."

They walked slowly to Strang's car, Dr. Slocum following with a somewhat bemused look on his face.

29

ATHENA'S NEPHEW, HANS KASSENBACH, APPEARED AT THE GATE-house accompanied by two men, probably lawyers, Carbin thought. He was aware of Athena's legal problems involving Kassenbach and Gesellschaft Dietrich. She might wish to see them. In any event, he didn't dare turn them away without calling her. He picked up the phone and said, "Herr Kassenbach is here, Mrs. von Dietrich. He is accompanied by two gentlemen from Gesellschaft Dietrich and wishes to see you."

Athena sighed deeply. "Let them come in," she said.

Kassenbach stumbled into Athena's living room. He had been shoved by one of the hard-faced men accompanying him.

"Tuh-tuh-tuh-Tante Athena," he stammered. "I am so sorry. They are threatening to kill me."

One of the men shoved him down on a sofa. The other one locked the hall door.

Athena stared at them, horrified. The one who had shoved Kassenbach had iron-gray hair cut short in a military brush, and under it a long face descending to a pointed chin. He was wearing a navy blue jacket, gray slacks, and a white shirt with a red tie. The other unwelcome visitor was round-faced and plump, with thick flaxen hair sculpted to cover his ears. He wore an oxford gray suit with a pink shirt and black tie. He smelled faintly of Chanel No. 5.

The gray-haired man said, "I am Rudolf. This is my associate, Gerard. We have serious business to discuss with you, Frau Dietrich."

He reached inside his jacket and brought out a Luger automatic, then strolled over to the sofa and held the muzzle close to Kassenbach's head. "You will do as I say or I will splatter the few brains that this idiot has over your carpet."

There were tears in Kassenbach's eyes.

"What do you want?" asked Athena.

Rudolf said, "You will call your security chief and tell him that you forgot to inform him, but that some time ago you agreed to permit a group from the New York Society of Architects to tour the castle. They will arrive this afternoon and he is to admit them."

Athena said, "I see."

Rudolf jabbed the muzzle against Kassenbach's forehead. Kassenbach squealed.

Athena went to the phone and dialed the gatehouse. When Carbin answered, she said, "Kent, it was stupid of me to forget, but several months ago I promised the New York Society of Architects that a group could tour the castle and grounds today. I just noticed it on my calendar."

Carbin was flustered. "I can't believe this," he said.

"Don't, please," she said.

Rudolf snatched the phone from her. "Don't please *what?"* he asked.

She said, "My security chief wants to come here and discuss it. I don't want you shooting at each other."

Rudolf handed her the phone.

Athena said to Carbin, "There's no need to discuss it, Kent. They are a very respectable group and no danger to me. And when I make a promise I keep it." She slammed the phone back onto its cradle.

Carbin sat rubbing his chin. Could she be having a breakdown? There was nothing wrong with her. The stuff Smith had slipped her had long since worn off. Kassenbach had looked very nervous. The two men with him were probably not kosher.

It was a hell of a sticky situation. He could pull his whole staff down to the gate and shoot it out, but the thing might go the wrong way and he might end up dead or certainly without a job. Not only that, the two bastards in the castle had Athena. That alone was going to be a hell of a problem.

The group should be stopped before they got anywhere near the castle. That would at least throw the monkeys holding Athena off balance.

He needed help, big help, and where in the hell would he get it?

Lover boy, Michaelis! Strang was his pal, and he could get Strang. Strang could line up plenty of men in a hurry. As much as he hated Strang, the sonofabitch, he was hell on wheels when it came to organizing a war.

He telephoned Michaelis and explained the situation. It was too tough for his men to handle alone. Then there was the danger to Athena.

Michaelis switched the speaker system on so that both he and Strang could talk and listen.

Carbin said, "They have to approach on the road from Crendon. It's a dead end a half mile past the castle. If we can ambush them before they get to the castle, the people inside will be less likely to harm Mrs. von Dietrich."

Strang agreed on this strategy, and they settled on a rendezvous point for the ambush. Strang said, "I suggest you send half your men to hide in the basement of the castle, leave one man on the gate, and bring the rest to our rendezvous point."

"I don't know how much time we have," said Carbin.

"We'll be there as fast as we can. Michaelis and I will leave immediately. Angie will remain here telephoning, trying to hurry some of my people out to help. You call Goudenough."

"Right," said Carbin, replacing the phone with a plastic clatter.

He picked up an Uzi and hurried to find Wayne Betz. After twenty-five men were dispatched to the castle's basement, twenty-five more were squeezed into station wagons and available cars. They roared off toward Crendon.

At the half-mile point the road was flanked by wooded areas some fifty feet back, with grass and shrubbery filling in the stretch bordering the road.

Carbin's group arrived almost simultaneously with Strang and Michaelis. Six men recruited by Angie arrived ten minutes later. Under Strang's direction the men quickly blockaded the road with two old station wagons, and then took up positions in the shrubbery on the right side, most of them lying prone, ready with weapons ranging from submachine guns to carbines.

Strang, Michaelis, and Carbin squatted at the rear of the troops. The hot summer sun wafted glassy waves, vaguely distorting vision.

Strang wiped perspiration from his forehead and stood up.

He yelled, "All right, men, listen. When the bus approaches, the driver will turn left off the road to go around the blockade. During his approach, give him everything you can. Aim for windows and tires. When and if he succeeds in turning off the road, throw everything at the rear end, try to hit the gas tank."

Michaelis jabbed Strang. "They're coming!"

Strang, Carbin, and Michaelis dropped to prone positions and readied their weapons.

A hundred yards away a huge yellow school bus was rounding a curve into view. As it rumbled closer, children could be seen peering out the windows.

Strang yelled, "Hold your fire!"

As the bus slowed to turn off the road to go around the roadblock, Michaelis could see the frightened face of the young woman driving it, and the long creamy yellow tresses of a young woman standing next to her holding a Walther machine pistol, the muzzle only a few inches from the driver's right temple. Busy Ingrid never slept.

There was nothing Strang's army could do but watch the bus as it detoured slowly around the station wagons, wheeling back onto the road and off to the castle.

Strang was apoplectic. "Of all the damned smart-assed tricks! You've got to hand it to those fucking krauts," he said.

Lieutenant Goudenough came puttering up in his police cruiser.

He leaned out the window. "Now you see what we're up against. I hope to hell they are not going to take the kids into the castle."

Strang nodded. "Guess we'd better follow at a safe distance," he said.

Strang shepherded his men back into the cars that

brought them there and the procession wound its way slowly back to within a hundred feet of the gatehouse. The bus was backing out to head in their direction.

Strang, leading convoy, waved the cars behind him to a halt.

The bus pulled up next to them and stopped. The children and the young woman driver were still in it. She was having a mild case of hysterics.

Strang said, "Well, thank God the kids are all right."

The children were jumping all over, wild with excitement.

The driver wiped her eyes, blew her nose, and tried to smile.

She said, "They killed the guard on duty at the gatehouse. Two big red-faced brutes are there now. They didn't want the children around, so they let me go. I wouldn't go near the place if I were you. They have machine guns." It all spilled out hastily in a jumble of words that were hardly understandable.

Goudenough strolled up and stood between the bus and Strang's Eldorado. "I'm going to escort the bus back to Crendon. I guess we'll need the U.S. Marines to get those bastards out of there. I sure don't have the manpower," he said.

A wave of fear swept through Michaelis. "Don't bring in the military," he said quickly. "These people are East German fanatics. They may decide to kill Athena rather than give her up. They'd rather *no one* had Sir Yirmi's plans if the alternative was a Western power having them."

Goudenough chewed his lower lip thoughtfully. He asked, "Well, what the hell are we going to do? I can't allow this kind of ruckus to go on. I can't turn my back on this situation."

Strang said, "We'll take care of it. We'll get Athena out unharmed."

Goudenough shrugged. "Better make it soon. I can't look the other way for too long." He grinned. "Get a stiff neck if I do."

With a wave of his hand he turned and went back to his patrol car.

30

INGRID SAT IN THE LIVING ROOM OF ATHENA'S SUITE, HER WALTHER machine pistol resting on her lap.

Athena sat facing her.

Ingrid said, "Heavens, how I have moved up in the world. My father was a poor Hamburg dock worker, and here I am associating with the billionaire princess of Gesellschaft Dietrich!"

Athena stared at her silently.

Ingrid shrugged. "Your lover isn't so hot, is he? I've had him and I found him quite mediocre. Only four or five on a scale of ten, I would say."

In spite of her fear Athena managed to smile inwardly. Michaelis had told her all about Ingrid's invasion of his bedroom. Ingrid hated Michaelis because he had bested her a number of times and she couldn't have him either.

Athena continued her silence.

Ingrid asked, "What's the matter? Am I too low on the social scale to speak to? Did you know that I am a Ph.D.?"

Athena smiled faintly. "What is there to say when one is a prisoner?"

Ingrid smiled. "We could be friends, you know. I admire a woman with your courage and intelligence. I know more about you than you think."

Ingrid remained silent for a while, smiling. Then she said, "I know how you handled Kurt Wessel. He tried to rape you, didn't he? I know Kurt. Can't keep his mind on the job when a pretty woman is involved."

Athena shivered inwardly. She did not cherish the memory of plunging the knife into Kurt Wessel. But it was the kind of thing Ingrid would gloat over. Ingrid was probably tougher than she was.

Ingrid said, "We will be friends, very good friends."

Athena nodded slowly. She said, "So we can be friends, though I can't give you the one thing you want from me."

Ingrid frowned, then lowered her eyes to study the Walther on her lap.

She looked up quickly, almost as though reading Athena's mind. Athena had been considering a quick leap to immobilize Ingrid's weapon. The distance was too great, she decided.

Ingrid said, "It is possible that we can educate you. Our ideals are the *future.* The American constitution says all men are created equal. As you well know, they are not equal in any way anywhere in the Western world. We shall make them so."

Athena smiled. There was no point in arguing with her about the oppressive regimes in the Marxist countries. The ready answer would be that the corrupt capitalist countries were always trying to undermine the true democracies.

"I see you don't believe me."

Athena shrugged. "I've never been in your country. Obviously I can't judge intelligently."

Ingrid nodded. "You have been brainwashed by corrupt propaganda," she said. "You will learn."

They sat silently looking past each other for several minutes.

Ingrid finally said, "As for your father's great secret, if we cannot have it, we will see that no one else gets it."

Returning from her weekend off, Rowena McGrath slowed her black Ford Escort down at the gatehouse, then drove on past. Something was wrong. The two red-faced men on guard were not familiar, and this was not the way guard duty was normally handled. The security men did not stand outside. They came out of the gatehouse when a car pulled up to enter. She drove on to the dead end, turned around, and drove back past the estate at a good clip.

In Crendon she stopped at a drugstore, looked up Michaelis's number, and called. His answering machine gave her Strang's unlisted number. Michaelis gave her directions to Strang's house.

Angie took a distraught Rowena up to a spare bedroom

and put her overnight bag on a table. Rowena sank into a chair and buried her face in her hands, sobbing.

"My poor lady, what are they doing to her?" she moaned, tears rolling down her cheeks.

Angie put her arm around Rowena's shoulders and comforted her. The tears finally subsided. Angie persuaded her to wash her face and come downstairs for a drink.

Michaelis, Strang, and Carbin sat glumly sipping scotch on the rocks. Carbin had twenty-five armed men hiding in the basement of the castle, and twenty-five more in rooms at Crendon House, the city's largest hotel. Something had to be done in a hurry or the men in the basement would be discovered and there would be an abortive shoot-out. The East Germans might kill Athena.

As much as Strang despised Carbin, a partnership of convenience had to be formed.

Rowena accepted a glass of white wine.

Michaelis stared at Rowena, remembering how Athena looked with her red wig and makeup.

He said, "Now, if we could only disguise you as Athena, Rowena, we could really throw confusion into their ranks."

Angie said, "Forget it. Too dangerous for Rowena."

Rowena perked up. "Why? If they discover me, what are they going to do? I'm a simple Irish girl who has been taken advantage of," she said.

"Sure an' the modom wanted me to do it for a lark," she whined in a thick Irish accent.

They all laughed.

Angie said, "It might just work. How would you get into the grounds?"

"Easy," said Strang. "She goes in as Rowena with her disguise in her overnight case. All she needs is a black wig similar to Athena's long, straight hair, and cosmetics to cover her freckles and change her very white redhead skin to creamy white."

Michaelis drained his drink. "They may let Rowena in, but I doubt that they will let anyone leave, servants or whatever."

Strang nodded. "The best we can hope is to give Athena more freedom within the grounds. She can put on her red wig and Rowena makeup and have the run of the place. It will be much easier for us to rescue this Rowena than Athena heavily guarded in her suite."

Carbin glanced at his watch. "Somebody better hightail it into New York right now and get that wig and makeup. My men in the basement are liable to be discovered at any minute."

Angie volunteered and left hurriedly.

Michaelis got up and paced. "I don't know. When they find out they've been had, Rowena is going to be in pretty bad shape. Knowing Athena, I don't think she would cooperate in a plan that would put Rowena in mortal danger."

Rowena laughed. "So what are they going to do with a silly Irish maid who has been duped? Kill her? I doubt it."

Carbin said, "They might use you as a hostage. Athena must come back or Rowena dies. And Athena *would* go back."

Rowena shrugged. "Nothing ventured, nothing gained." She got up and poured herself another glass of wine. She was obviously enjoying the idea of this super acting assignment.

She said, "I could probably carry on my act for some time. Until you get Athena out. Then you could blast them while I hide in the kitchen, once more Rowena McGrath."

Strang laughed. "You're a very brave young lady. I could use you in my army," he said.

"It's a deal," said Rowena.

Michaelis poured another drink. He had some doubts about the plan, but Rowena was eager to try it. He rationalized that she understood the danger. But did she really? She thought her act of stupid innocence would carry it off, and probably she could with anyone but Ingrid. Ingrid was a shrewd bitch. There was a good possibility she would see through Rowena's disguise immediately. She would also be brutal and sadistic in her revenge. The men would be softer and more willing to accept this pretty Irish girl's innocence, but Ingrid—

He said, "Rowena, I must warn you that there is a woman in the group who's probably tougher than any man. Her name is Ingrid. You'll have to have an awfully good act to fool her. And the bias that men have for a pretty young woman won't help with her."

Rowena grinned. "Your warning is noted, sir. If she's a lez, maybe I can seduce her."

Michaelis smiled. This little Irish girl was much more sophisticated than he had realized.

He said, "I'm fairly sure she's not a lez."

Then, in thinking it over, he asked himself why he should be sure of that. The act Ingrid put on in his bedroom really had no bearing on her sexual preferences. A lesbian could have done it. There was no desire there, only a deadly motive.

He said to Rowena, "I shouldn't have said that. I have no evidence that she is or isn't."

Rowena shrugged. "Whatever. It's a long shot, anyway, isn't it?"

31

ROWENA BROUGHT UP DINNER FOR MRS. VON DIETRICH. AS SHE rolled the cart in, Ingrid stopped her at the door and frisked her for weapons. Then she uncovered the dishes one by one, checking even the thermos of coffee.

Smiling, Rowena spread a tablecloth on one of the small tables, then arranged the silverware and the various dishes.

When she finished, Athena asked Ingrid, "Would you care to share this meal?"

Ingrid stood up. "No thanks, I will go and eat with my own people. Don't try to leave. I have a rather uncouth guard on your door. He will probably maul you around and grab a few feels in the process of putting you back inside."

Rowena snickered.

As soon as the door closed, Rowena grabbed Athena's arm and whispered, "Quick, in the bedroom."

In twenty minutes Athena came out wearing Rowena's uniform, her freckles, and the red wig. Rowena now had a creamy complexion, almost waist-length straight black hair tumbling down her back, and was wearing Athena's pink Pierre Cardin jumpsuit.

Athena turned off the overhead light, leaving only two lamps burning. She said, "Someone should eat. I'm too nervous; can you eat something?"

Rowena said, "Sure." She stood by the table and hastily ate Athena's small steak, holding it in her fingers.

Athena ate a roll, gave Rowena a quick kiss, then began to collect the dishes and put them back on the cart, leaving the coffee at Rowena's request. She rolled the cart to the door and opened it.

The guard said, "You cannot leave until Fraulein Ingrid returns. It is verboten."

Athena backed into the room.

Ingrid returned in another ten minutes. Athena-Rowena, who had been sitting, jumped up. Trying to imitate Rowena's speech, she said, "Madam told me to sit. The guard would not let me leave until you returned."

Ingrid smirked. She carefully inspected all the dishes and then dismissed the maid.

Ingrid said to Rowena-Athena, "You didn't eat much."

Rowena said haughtily, "The steak was more than sufficient. Would you care for coffee? There's another cup here."

Ingrid strolled over and filled the cup, then carried it back to the chair she had been sitting in. She stared at Rowena.

"Your voice sounds different, higher-pitched," she said.

"It gets that way when I am on the verge of hysteria."

Ingrid put her cup down hurriedly. "Now don't, for God's sake, get hysterical. No one is going to harm you," she said.

Rowena put her hand on her forehead. "I don't feel at all well. I think I would like to go to bed," she said.

Ingrid's mouth turned down. "I have no objection. I find you rather boring, frankly," she said.

Rowena gave her a cold stare, got up, and went to the bedroom. Closing the door, she let out a big sigh of relief.

Athena wheeled the cart into the kitchen. She turned and started to leave.

A fat old lady yelled, "Hey, you! Scrape those dishes and put them in the dishwasher, you lazy Irish mick."

Athena hastily scraped the plates with food in them and put everything in the dishwasher. She slipped out the door into a corridor that led to the back of the castle.

A guard sitting in a corner holding a Walther stared at Rowena without interest as she left the kitchen.

The back stairs to the basement were metal and spiraled around a large pipe enclosed by a circular wall just large enough to accommodate the steps. Athena went down them slowly, each foot placed so carefully that there was not the faintest noise. The hall light above dimly illuminated part of the way, but by the time she neared the bottom of the steps it was almost totally dark.

A bright light suddenly beamed at her eyes and temporarily blinded her.

In a husky whisper a voice said, "Holy Jeeze, it's Rowena. Rowena, what the fuck are you doing down here?"

Athena-Rowena said, "Don't use that kind of language in Madam's presence."

"I won't, you sweet, frozen-ass little bundle of goodies," the voice said.

"Who's in charge here? And would you mind lowering that light?"

The flashlight beam dipped to the floor. "Wayne Betz is in charge," said the voice. "Follow me." The guard slipped his revolver back in its holster.

He led her to the center of the basement where most of the men were sitting on the concrete floor, their weapons beside them, backs leaning against the lockers.

Wayne Betz pulled himself to his feet.

Athena told him how the East Germans had gotten into the grounds using the schoolchildren as a shield, that Madam was a prisoner in her suite, and that Carbin and Strang, with the rest of the security force, would raid the estate at the crack of dawn tomorrow.

Wayne Betz nodded as she talked.

"Couldn't be better!" he said. "When the action starts, we go upstairs and they get hit from the back as well as the front."

Athena said, "The first thing you do is storm Madam's suite and save her."

"Right," said Betz. "She's the lady who pays our salaries."

Athena had thought of revealing her identity to them, but then decided the job would be more desperately important to them if they thought they were rescuing Madam von Dietrich. She had been worried to the point of nausea about the danger to Rowena. If anything happened to Rowena during this deception, she would never forgive herself.

She said, "Oh, yeah, I forgot. I'm supposed to tell you that when they start their break-in they'll fire three shots, then two shots, then one. At that signal you can start heading upstairs."

Betz laughed softly. "Glad you remembered that one," he said.

The men had found some dusty old blankets in one of the lockers. Athena folded one to sit on, lowered herself to the floor, and leaned against one of the locker doors."

"Anyone have a weapon they can spare for me?" she asked.

There were some snickers. Someone in the darkness said in a low voice, "You'll shoot your foot off, Rowena."

"I *would* not. I have fired everything from a thirty-eight to an Uzi."

The guard sitting next to her said, "Here's my forty-five. Show me what you would do with it." He handed her the automatic, then said, "Duck, men, watch your ass."

There was a ripple of quiet laughter.

Athena quickly removed the cartridge case, checked it, and shoved it back into the grip. She slid the cocking mechanism back, then let it go forward to put a shell into the firing chamber. She put the safety on and handed the automatic back to the guard.

The guard grinned. "Keep it, sweetie. I have my Uzi, and you seem to know what you're doing."

The long unending night crept toward dawn. The concrete floor became harder with every hour. Athena got up and walked from time to time. Fortunately Rowena's shoes were rubber-soled. The men shifted uneasily, some sitting, some lying on their sides, others walking slowly and cautiously in the dark.

Finally dawn's early light began to penetrate the small barred windows that were below ground, but faced brick-lined wells open to the sky.

Betz moved around checking the men and waking those lucky enough to be able to sleep.

The signal was quick in coming. The rapid crack of a carbine barked three, two, one shots.

Half of the men went up the back stairs, half went up the front. Athena followed the group up the back stairs, ran up two more flights to the third floor. Four of the guards were cautiously crawling along the floor of the hall leading to Athena's suite.

The burly German at the door saw them and opened fire.

He winged one, but went down with a number of holes in his torso.

Athena followed them to the door and unlocked it. She said, "Careful, there may be a guard in there."

She moved to one side. She hoped Ingrid was not with Rowena. She might even kill Rowena rather than give up their prize. Ingrid's voice saying, "If we cannot have your father's great secret, we will see that no one else gets it," ran frighteningly through her mind.

Michaelis came running into the corridor, bent low over a Walther.

One of the guards shoved the door open and dived to the floor on one side.

A look of maniacal anger on his face, Michaelis brushed by them and rushed into the room. Two of the guards followed him. No one was in the living room.

"Athena, are you all right?" Michaelis yelled, rattling the locked door to the bedroom wildly.

Athena edged into the living room. She said, "Careful, Ingrid may be in the bedroom with her. She may kill her rather than give her up."

"Right," said Michaelis.

Athena unlocked the bedroom door.

A faint voice came from the bedroom. "I'm okay, you're okay, we're all okay," said Rowena, coming out of a closet.

The two women ran together and hugged.

The guards looked stunned. Two Rowenas. Rowena had sensibly shucked her wig and makeup.

Michaelis said, "Come on, we have to get you two out of here."

He ran with them down the back stairs, through the kitchen to one of the back entrances.

A German who was guarding the rear door turned and fired excitedly without aiming. Athena, who was now carrying the .45, pulled the trigger. The guard seemed to lift about an inch in the air before tumbling backward.

Michaelis said, "Strang has been wounded, but Carbin seems to have the gatehouse under control."

They ran through the woods to the wall, planning to follow it around to the gatehouse. Michaelis spotted Ingrid on a chain and wood-slatted ladder at the top of the wall, ready to go over. He fired as she disappeared over the top. He was sure he hadn't hit her. Some of the SSD crowd had obviously turned off the electricity.

Carbin was at the gatehouse, but a National Guard company was in control. Lieutenant Goudenough was standing by. He wasn't taking any more chances.

In an undertone Athena said to Michaelis, "Get me out of here. I'll explain later."

With Goudenough identifying them, Athena, Michaelis, and Rowena were allowed to leave. They hurried into Michaelis's Volvo.

Driving fast toward Crendon, Michaelis said, "I have an idea about a place where they will never think of looking for us. Give us a breather to make some plans."

Rowena said, "They won't be looking for me. Maybe you could drop me off near my home. I think I want to be with my mum and have a nervous breakdown."

Athena turned in her seat and grasped Rowena's hand. "You saved my life. You risked your *own* life for me."

Rowena smiled, teary-eyed.

"I want to do something very big for *you*. I don't want you to ever have to be a maid again," said Athena. "You're bright. I could put you through college, make you a lawyer or a doctor."

Rowena hiccoughed. "I'll talk to Mum about it."

They pulled up in front of a modest little frame house painted white with a green trim. Athena got out and walked Rowena to the front door, arm around her shoulders. At the door they paused and hugged each other, Rowena crying. Athena kissed her and ran back to the car.

32

SINCE HIS TALK WITH CINDY HARRISON ONLY A FEW WEEKS AGO, Michaelis had already received two small checks from her, payments on the $15,000 loan. Apparently her veterinary business was improving. She might be able to tuck them away upstairs for a day or so. It was not likely that anyone would think of looking for them there. And as long as Athena wore her red wig and Rowena makeup she would be reasonably safe.

He said to Athena, "After I get you settled I'll go back to the castle and check when it will be safe for you to return."

She shook her head. "I can't go back. Protection by the government will make me a prisoner of the government."

Michaelis smiled. "This is the USA, not Russia."

She lowered her head. "Where something this important is concerned, you can't trust any government," she said.

She described Ingrid's attitude. If we can't have it, no one will have it. The U.S. government could easily rationalize that national security made it absolutely necessary to control access to this information. Now that the National Guard was in, the next step would be a permanent installation of Marines or regular army. Or perhaps the CIA would take over.

Michaelis was silent for a while. She might well be right, he decided. The government had tread lightly so far. Good relations with friendly West Germany were important, and after all, Athena was half owner of Gesselschaft Dietrich, one of the world's largest megacorporations. If mistreated, she could stir up a great deal of unfavorable publicity.

Cindy Harrison was delighted to see them. She had two patients in her reception area, an ancient gray shepherd and a frisky young cocker spaniel. The owners, two well-dressed, middle-aged women, were reading magazines and appeared to be in no hurry.

Cindy ushered them back to her large kitchen, which had a comfortable dining area set up by the rear windows.

Michaelis introduced Athena as his fiancée.

Athena mentioned that she remembered Cindy as a juror in her trial. Cindy was puzzled at what she thought was Athena's dyed hair.

She laughed. "I thought you did it, but that he probably deserved it," she said.

Athena looked down, unsmiling. There was nothing funny about Karl's death and her painful, frightening interrogation.

Cindy was immediately embarrassed. "I'm sorry, I shouldn't have been flippant about something that must have been quite tragic for you."

She busied herself at the stove, insisting that they have tea or coffee while she took care of the two dogs. Both were only there for shots. Coffee was already brewed, and hot water for tea was simmering over a low flame.

Athena accepted a cup of tea, and Michaelis poured himself coffee.

While Cindy was occupied with the dogs, Michaelis told Athena about his meeting with Cindy and his lending her $15,000 to stave off bankruptcy.

Athena stared at him for a moment. She said, "She's very pretty."

"That had nothing to do with it," said Michaelis. "I liked the way she took care of a torn-up little beagle a teenager brought in. She deserved to succeed, and she was only in trouble because she was inexperienced in collecting bills."

Smiling, Athena nodded. "She's still *very* pretty," she said.

Annoyed, Michaelis asked, "If there were anything going on between us, do you think I would have brought you here?"

Athena laughed and stroked Michaelis's cheek. "Just teasing you. Maybe I am a bit jealous."

Cindy returned and poured herself a cup of coffee. She joined them at the table.

She said to Michaelis, "I can't begin to tell you how grateful I am. William, the fellow you sent over from the university, has really accomplished miracles."

She sipped her coffee. "Not only are my bills being paid, he checked around with other veterinarians and found that my fees were much lower than theirs. So I raised mine. I'm now operating well in the black."

Michaelis smiled. "That's great. You're a very good doctor."

There was a silence while Cindy stared first at Athena and then at Michaelis.

"So what's up?" she asked. "This isn't just a social visit."

Michaelis explained their immediate problem.

Cindy stared at Athena wide-eyed. She said, "What a shame you have to live this way! Of course you both can hide here as long as you like. There's an extra bedroom upstairs with furniture in it. There's a double bed in it but I could—"

Athena said, "That's all right. I'm going to make him marry me."

Cindy giggled. "Well, congratulations and everything!" she said.

A buzzer sounded loudly, calling her to the reception area where a new patient waited.

Michaelis and Athena sat silent, both preoccupied with Athena's problem. Michaelis decided that he might be a threat to Athena's disguise and safety. If word came out that she was missing from the castle, the SSD or KGB would look for him on the chance that he and Athena would be together. They might see through her Rowena disguise, even try to kidnap them both. The only answer was to change his appearance.

He said to Athena, "I've got to work out some kind of disguise. They may decide that I'm a way to find you. Also you've got to have a new persona. How does giddy blonde strike you?"

Athena laughed and put her coffee cup down. She stared at him thoughtfully. "Why couldn't you be a macho Hispanic? Black hair, big black mustache, suntanned brown face?"

He nodded slowly. "That sounds workable."

"I'll work on the giddy blonde bit," said Athena.

Leaving Athena in Cindy's care, Michaelis got in his Volvo and drove down I-95 into New York. He had to get rid of the Volvo, too. It still percolated along nicely, but was one more bit of identification to lead them to him.

In New York he traded in the Volvo on a new Ford T-Bird, gleaming black with a cream-colored soft leather interior. His bank provided a certified check and a substantial amount of cash. The Ford salesman had promised to rush through the registration and dealer prep so that he could have the car in the afternoon.

The hairstyling shop dyed his hair black. From there he went to a costume dealer and bought a bushy black mustache, which he put in his pocket. The Ford salesman might not recognize him as it was.

He thought of having lunch at the Overseas Press Club, but decided it would be unwise. He settled for a quarter-pounder, french fries, and coffee at McDonald's on East 42nd Street.

Lunch over and two hours left to kill, he sat in Bryant Park for a while idly watching the bench sitters. A bag lady with all her belongings stacked in a supermarket cart sat like a nanny tending her baby. Homeless men cadged money and cigarettes. Well-dressed Yuppies sat in the shade waiting to buy a small bag of pot or some other controlled substance. Pigeon feeders fed pigeons. Sleeping drunks dangled legs over empty wine bottles, feet bound in cardboard and rags.

Where in the hell would he and Athena go? With all her money and his ample funds they had to flee and hide like fugitives from justice. The more he thought of it the angrier he got. Who were these bastards to make their lives miserable? There had to be some way to fight back. Track the cruds down and terminate them with extreme prejudice. Talk it over with Strang, who was in the hospital with a bullet wound in his leg. Luckily it had not clipped or shattered any bones. On his way back, with his disguise and his new car, he could safely call on Strang. Talk to Leslie Greenhaven, too, if he could locate her.

He reminded himself that he should be sitting in the sun, getting the suntan he needed. It would be a slow process. He usually burned red before he became brown. Of course, he could use this fake tan cream they sold. He left the park and wandered along 42nd Street, stopping in an appliance store to buy a sunlamp, and on to a discount pharmacy to buy a bottle of fake tan.

Late in the afternoon he pulled into Crendon Hospital's parking lot, easing the T-Bird into a spot where nearby cars would not bring gouges from opening doors.

Strang was in a private room, the hall door of which was flanked by a Tarboy on each side. They were not completely sure that he *was* Michaelis. They frisked him and took his .38 away, Michaelis maintaining a smile with difficulty.

Strang was sitting up in bed reading a newspaper. The second he saw Michaelis in the doorway, a .45 appeared quickly from under his covers.

Michaelis said, "This is really great. The Tarboys don't recognize me, and you don't recognize me."

Strang laughed.

Michaelis closed the door.

Strang studied Michaelis's light brown face. "So what the hell are you up to?" he asked.

Michaelis pulled up a straight chair and sat down. "We've got a problem, Colonel," he said.

Strang shrugged. "I would say we have more than one."

Michaelis got up and strolled to the windows beyond Strang's bed. He stared out at the trees and grass for a few seconds and then asked, "So what do we do about it? I can't tolerate the idea of Athena having to live like a hunted animal."

He strolled back to the bedside chair and sat down. "I say we go on the offensive. Hunt down the lousy bastards and wipe them out."

Strang smiled. "You can count on me, old son. I'll get my army together." He pulled the sheet aside to show Michaelis his bandaged leg. "This damned thing isn't much more than a flesh wound. The doc says I'll be fully mobile in a week or two."

Michaelis nodded. "Do you think we can trust Carbin and his men to help?" he asked.

Strang pulled the sheet up, laughing. "Absolutely. That sonofabitch loves nothing better than a good fight. He's a thoroughly rotten bastard, but protecting Athena von Dietrich is his bread and butter."

Michaelis stood up, relieved to have found enthusiastic support from Strang. It would be damned tough to do it alone. Impossible, probably. He said, "In the meantime I think we had better have a meeting with Leslie Greenhaven."

33

MICHAELIS WAS AFRAID THAT LESLIE GREENHAVEN MIGHT OBJECT TO this kind of interference from a group she would consider amateurs. After all, intelligence operatives work in strange and mysterious ways.

Surprisingly she was enthusiastic, but cautious. Meeting with Michaelis, Athena, Strang, and Carbin in Strang's book-lined study, she said, "I'll give you all the information we have on this group, but you must understand you're absolutely on your own. If you are caught by local law enforcement people, you may well go to prison. We can't help you there."

Strang said, "We understand. We'll take our chances. We aren't going to be all that easy to catch, right, Carbin?"

Carbin gave him an evil grin. "Right. But no shooting each other in the back, understood?"

Strang laughed. "We'll move side by side. I don't know if I could get used to turning my back on you."

Leslie brought out a map of Florida and spread it on the table.

She explained that the group was an SSD operation working from a headquarters camp in the Everglades, ostensibly a neo-Nazi bunch composed of a core group of East Germans who entered the United States seeking "asylum" and were now legitimate citizens. With them were some bigoted crackers from the Deep South, and a number of Cubans who had also sought asylum and become citizens, but were controlled by Castro.

Leslie said, "We know they have hidden caches of weapons that are illegal, but law enforcement people who have searched the camp have found nothing but shotguns, hunting rifles, and revolvers, which are legal in Florida."

Strang asked, "I wonder if they will have time to get to their heavy weapons before we move in?"

Leslie said, "You can depend on it. The Everglades cover some four thousand square miles of the tip of Florida. Just getting through swamps and twelve-foot-high saw grass is not going to be easy or silent. Also I suspect they have some paid Seminole lookouts around their perimeter. They'll know when you're still miles from the camp."

Strang muttered something that sounded vaguely obscene.

Leslie bent over the map with a pencil. "Your best bet would be to go in via Naples. Hire a professional guide, perhaps some Seminole Indians. They will be able to advise you on the best way to get to the camp. You've got to go exactly forty-eight miles east on Route 84, or 'Alligator Alley,' then head due south through the Big Cypress Swamp. The camp is approximately thirty-two miles south. From Route 84 you'll have to make your way through thirty-two miles of water, swamp, saw grass, and mangrove roots, probably most of it on foot and by boat across some lakes."

Michaelis whistled softly. Wiping out the bastards wasn't going to be all that easy. Trust them to hole up in something like the Everglades. Slime buckets, all of them.

Leslie, who had been studying the map, looked up. "Alligator Alley. Speaking of alligators, keep in mind that they own all the creeks in the Everglades. They made them. They are in them even in the dry season, buried in the mud."

Michaelis asked, "Why don't we go in the dry season?"

"You want to wait until November?" asked Leslie. "That's when the dry season starts."

Michaelis shook his head. "No way. By September I want to be back at Crendon University leading a quiet life with my *wife.*" He turned to Athena and smiled.

They assembled in the outskirts of Naples, Florida, thirty-five in number, including Michaelis, Strang, and Carbin. Athena had begged to accompany them, and even though Michaelis knew her proficiency with both a knife and the Uzi, he stood firm with the others. After all, the whole purpose of the operation was to protect her from risk.

Leslie had estimated that there were fifty to seventy-five men using the neo-Nazi camp as a base of operations. Strang reasoned that even if all seventy-five were there, each one of his men was worth two or three of the resident scumbags.

Bowing to Strang's greater experience, Carbin had agreed that Strang would lead.

For public consumption, the group was a botanical expedition led by Professor Perkinson. The Everglades offered thousands of species of flora to be studied and preserved.

The men gathered outside the motel to climb in trucks that would take them to the spot on Route 84 where the expedition would enter the Everglades.

Leslie Greenhaven appeared and led Michaelis aside. She showed him a small black box about the size of a pack of cigarettes. The lid opened exposing a glass-faced clock-like instrument which had only one hand tipped like an arrow.

In a low voice she said, "When you get about ten miles south of Route 84, flip this gadget on and follow the arrow. It's a homing device." She snapped the lid shut. "When you get near your goal, it will begin clicking. At this point, look for an alligator's nest."

"An alligator's nest?" asked Michaelis.

She laughed. "You'll see plenty of them on the way. They are humps covered with saw grass. About eight feet wide and two or three feet high."

Michaelis stared at her, wondering whether she was joking.

She said, "They usually contain thirty to sixty alligator eggs, but the one you uncover will have some items that will be much more useful to you."

He nodded, smiling. He thanked her and put the gadget in his jacket pocket.

She said, "Be sure you have the *right* nest. If you start pulling the saw grass off one that has big mama in it contemplating her eggs, you're in a peck of trouble."

He laughed. "Surely you wouldn't let this gadget guide us to the wrong nest?" He said it facetiously.

She smiled. "Some big mama could have built one nearby since we loaded the fake nest. But the clicking will become faster as you approach the right one."

He pulled the box out of his pocket and gave it a more careful look. "We'll be cautious about which nest we open," he said.

She put her hands on his shoulders, raised herself on her toes, and kissed his cheek. "Thank you in advance," she said. "You're going to be doing something we should do, but we are not allowed to do it."

Michaelis's cheeks were a bit warm. He wondered whether he was blushing. "We'll give it our best try," he said.

"I wish I could go in with you," she said. "But I'm not allowed. My boss wants me back at HQ."

She left him with a smile and a brief wave.

The friendly kiss had surprised him because Leslie had always appeared to be an efficient and attractive young woman, but hard as a diamond inside and without an ounce of sentiment to spare.

Strang brought over the professional guide who would lead them. He was a knobby, bony-faced man with shifty eyes named Pete Mountain. His accent was Deep South.

After shaking hands with Michaelis he said, "Now, yaw'll understand I'm taking yaw'll in, but I'm not bringing yaw'll back. 'Fore you start trouble I'm taking off."

Strang said impatiently, "I told you that was okay."

As though he hadn't heard Strang, Pete Mountain continued. "And I want yaw'll to understand I ain't guaranteeing these here Seminoles I got to help carry the heavy stuff. Some of these people got Christian ways and some of them don't. No way of telling. If they skitter off into the swamps with all your stuff some night, don't yaw'll come blaming me."

Strang laughed. "We'll post our own guards at night," he said.

Mountain turned to go. "Long as yaw'll understand," he said.

The blistering sun felt hot enough to set fire to the straw hat Michaelis was wearing. His heavy canvas shirt and pants were soaked with perspiration but offered protection from the saw grass. Though the Indians were ahead chopping a narrow path with machetes, the saw-toothed edges still whipped out into the path to avenge this molestation. Mosquitoes and other insects buzzed his face in continuing waves. Sometimes he forgot to keep his mouth closed and had to spit them out. This was worse than Nam, or had time merely softened the memory?

From time to time they found some relief in crossing open areas of spongy, mossy ground, or wading across shallow ponds, keeping a wary eye out for alligators. In crossing one pond Michaelis stepped into a deep hole and found himself kneeling in the water, face-to-face with a one-ton manatee. A great blob of amorphous head turned to him, its features so lightly sculptured that a small child's thumb might have made them. Deciding that Michaelis in no way resembled edible vegetation, the manatee moved slowly away. Michaelis, who did not know that manatees were strict vegetarians, had a bad moment of shock.

By sundown they had traveled only an estimated nine miles.

Strang said, "Tomorrow we'll make better time. I think we've experienced just about everything this fucking obstacle course has to offer."

Michaelis shrugged. He would have liked to believe that.

Coffee was made, and cans of potted meat and fruit and boxes of crackers were passed out.

The sun gradually disappeared behind giant, hundred-foot-tall mangrove trees, leaving them in a dull red shadow.

Bone-tired, Michaelis slid into his sleeping bag and tucked his mosquito bar netting under it, hoping it would keep out various ugly and/or lethal little creatures they had seen en route. Pretty, gleaming little coral snakes, scorpions larger than any Texas ever nurtured, six-inch-long centipedes, pinkish rat snakes, and one ten-foot diamondback rattler. Panthers were said to roam only south of the Big Cypress Swamp, the area they were trekking through, which was one small consolation.

He woke before dawn, though the sky was somewhat lighter in the east. Strang was squatting next to him.

Michaelis lifted the mosquito net.

Strang said, "Rise and shine. Just a mile more and we'll find Leslie's treasure trove."

Michaelis said, "Don't give me all the good news at once."

Strang handed him a cup of coffee and a bread sandwich spread with oleo. He said, "The good news is that no one attacked us during the night. These guys must surely know we're on the way by now."

Michaelis sipped the strong, rank coffee. "Maybe it's tonight. I'll sleep with my Uzi."

Strang said, "On the other hand, they may be pretty well fortified where they are. Dry mud ramparts and all that."

Michaelis gave him a toothy false grin. "I'm sure the colonel will lead us over the ramparts with colors flying," he said.

Strang stood up. "Yeah, you bet your ass I will," he said, striding off.

Michaelis ate the bread and washed it down with the abominable coffee. At least it was wet. He pulled on his shirt and pants. The heavy canvas was still wet from yesterday, and it took some hopping around to get his feet down the pants legs.

The troops were on their way before the sun rose above the mangrove trees.

After they had trudged an estimated mile, Michaelis switched on the small direction finder. The needle moved a few points to the left of twelve o'clock. He motioned to Strang and the group veered slightly left until the arrow was back on twelve o'clock.

It was easier than Michaelis had anticipated. After walking about fifty yards they were headed for an alligator nest. When Michaelis reached it, the little gadget began clicking loudly.

Strang said, "Now hold it. Some lady alligator may have mistaken this for home."

The Indian in charge of the Seminole helpers, William Broadfeet, came up with a long tree branch. Short, stocky, and brown, he smiled at them with very white teeth.

He said, "Not likely to be an alligator in it, but we'll take no chances." From his well-modulated voice he might have been lecturing at Harvard.

He began pitching the dried saw grass aside with the branch. Some large packing cases were gradually uncovered.

The cases were dragged out and opened. One contained five bazooka rocket launchers. There were two cases of rockets. One was filled with incendiary rockets and the other with shrapnel. There was also a case of grenades.

Strang was ecstatic. "No way we could have gotten this kind of stuff! No wonder she had to have them sneak it down here and hide it in an alligator nest."

Michaelis said, "I didn't know they still used these."

"They don't," said Carbin. "Much fancier electronic stuff today. This stuff has been sitting somewhere for years."

Strang lifted one of the rocket launchers to his shoulders and aimed it. He said, "At least we know how to handle these babies."

"If the old rockets aren't faulty," said Carbin.

Michaelis said, "Come on. Leslie wouldn't give us faulty rockets."

The troops reassembled and resumed the trek.

The second day was much like the first, but now they were more accustomed to the terrain and were able to cover about thirteen miles before darkness set in. Michaelis slept with his Uzi at his side.

With the assistance of William Broadfeet and some sturdy ropes, Strang climbed high into the branches of the tallest mangrove tree they could find, which was about the height of a ten-story building. He focused his field glasses on the enemy camp several hundred yards away.

It was surrounded by a dirt rampart approximately twelve feet high. Inside were low wooden buildings forming a rectangle that enclosed a small parade ground. In the center of the parade ground a flagpole flew two flags. On top Old Glory fluttered faintly in the breeze. Underneath it was a large red flag displaying a black swastika held in a clenched fist.

Small figures in camouflage fatigues wandered unconcernedly about on the parade ground. A bugle sounded and more of them appeared and trooped into one of the long buildings, probably the mess hall, Strang thought.

He made the long climb down to the ground cautiously. The late afternoon light was fading.

He said to Michaelis, "I can't believe they don't know we're here, but it sure looks that way."

Michaelis shook his head. "Probably an act to make us careless. Maybe they plan a surprise raid tonight."

Strang grinned. "I'd like to attack *them* tonight, but we'd be at a big disadvantage. The terrain is tricky. We'd have to approach with bright lights and music."

Michaelis struck a pose. "Tomorrow at dawn, men!" he said.

Strang frowned. "Don't joke, son. Some of us may well be dead before the day is over."

Michaelis was mildly embarrassed. "Gallows humor," he said. Strang was pretty touchy. In tough situations in Nam a little joking around helped take the curse off.

Strang motioned for Carbin to come over.

He said, "We better have a strategy session."

The three men squatted on their haunches, Michaelis and Carbin facing Strang.

"The way I see it," Strang said, "if I was leading them I would leave some of my men in the fort and send another group around through the swamp to attack from the rear or on a flank."

Carbin shook his head. "You assume they know we have rockets to blast hell out of the camp. I doubt they do," he said.

Strang stared at the ground. "I believe they do. We know they have Seminoles working for them. I think it's likely that we have been watched every mile of the way."

Michaelis said, "I think Strang's right. These Indians know the Everglades so well they can move like ghosts through the swamps."

Carbin gave a skeptical shrug.

"Anyway, we have everything to lose by not assuming Strang is right," said Michaelis. "If all we have to do is blast hell out of the camp and go after those trying to escape, then it's a piece of cake, but—"

Strang said, "But we'd still better protect our ass just in case."

"Right," said Michaelis.

There was a silence while Carbin thought about it. "Yeah," he said finally.

Strang said, "Another thing. I wouldn't trust this guy Mountain as far as I could throw one of them manatees."

"Well, he made it clear he wasn't accompanying us very close to trouble," said Carbin.

Michaelis said, "I agree with Strang. He was the kind of shifty-eyed bastard who would take money from both sides. And note that he took off shortly after we found the weapons."

"Yeah," said Carbin. "Maybe you're right."

They spent the rest of the time dividing the men into four squads of eight men each: the lead, the rear, and the flanks.

Later Michaelis lay in his sleeping bag coming to terms with fear. He had had plenty of it in Nam, but it never stopped him from doing what he was supposed to do. He told himself that it would not stop him tomorrow. Of course, a man never knew for sure.

34

STRANG'S ARMY ADVANCED TO A POSITION ABOUT TWO HUNDRED yards from the SSD fortress. Mangrove trees offered good cover if a man could make his way under them without tripping or breaking a leg in the mass of aboveground roots. They were everywhere, twisted, loathsome, grabbing at feet and legs.

Strang led the attack with his squad. Wayne Betz covered the left flank with his group; Michaelis's squad moved forward protecting the right flank. Carbin's crew kept far back, watching the rear.

Two of Strang's men climbed high enough in a mangrove tree to gain a direct view of the camp. A rocket launcher and several incendiary rockets were hoisted up to them by rope.

It required only four rockets to have every building in the compound blazing wildly. Not a single man ran out of the buildings.

One of the men in the tree yelled down, "They've left the fort! Watch your ass!"

At the same instant a volley of thunder erupted in the rear.

Carbin's men were on the ground firing shrapnel rockets blindly. The enemy was there, but well concealed by the heavy swamp growth.

Crouching, Strang led his group toward the rear. He yelled, "You men on the flanks, hold your positions!"

Necessary, Michaelis supposed, but it appeared that the contingent attacking in the rear was a large one. Firing from that direction was very heavy. Carbin probably needed more firepower than the addition of Strang's squad would provide. On the other hand, to leave their flanks exposed might just be what the enemy hoped.

He saw movement in the tall saw grass about twenty feet to his left. He pulled the pin on a grenade and lobbed in into the area. The explosion was followed by some anguished screams. Two men crawled out of the high grass, machine pistols crackling. Lying on his stomach, Michaelis opened up with his Uzi. Both men stopped crawling, bloody, ripped-open wounds visible on their heads and backs. Michaelis got to his knees and hurled another grenade. The screams stopped.

Now fire was coming at Michaelis's squad from the rear. The crackle of automatic weapons became louder. Bullets slapping mangrove tree branches and leaves had the rustling sound of a hailstorm. Had they broken past Carbin's defense? Michaelis ordered four of his men to direct fire in that direction, and kept the other four monitoring the right flank.

Both Strang's and Carbin's squads seemed to be retreating under heavy fire, seeking better defensive positions behind trees or in the high, saw-edged grass.

Michaelis was so busy returning fire that he did not notice Carbin crawling toward him. Carbin was only a few feet away when Michaelis saw him. He crawled over to him.

Carbin's voice was high and strained. He said, "Get me a priest. I'm dying."

For a second or two Michaelis thought Carbin was joking. Then he saw the big red opening in Carbin's chest.

Carbin said, "I know we don't have any priest." He coughed up some blood. "But I've got to—to confess. A mortal sin. You'll—" His voice faded, then became a bit stronger. "You'll promise to give my confession to a priest? Ask him to pray for me?"

Michaelis said, "I will. Anything you want, Carbin."

Carbin groaned and more blood spilled from his mouth. In a weak, almost inaudible voice he said, "I killed men in battle, but cold-blooded murder is a mortal sin. I—I killed Wolfgang Brillhagen." He coughed up more blood.

"I—I dropped a radio in his whirlpool bath. It was playing Beethoven's Ninth Symphony."

His eyes became glassy as more blood, unnoticed by Carbin, poured from his mouth.

Michaelis looked up just in time to see the granddaddy of all alligators about three feet away, his short legs pawing the spongy turf toward Michaelis, his huge jaws gaping open. Large, curved, and pointed teeth were a steel trap about to close on Michaelis with a horrendous snap. He wheeled the Uzi around and fired into the alligator's yawning mouth. The alligator kept coming. Michaelis tried to roll away, but the jaws clamped onto his leg above the knee.

Suddenly the alligator stopped all movement, either unconscious or dead, but Michaelis's leg was still caught between the sharp teeth. He put his fingers into the slimy jaws and tried to pull them apart. They might have been set in concrete. There wasn't enough space to give his hands leverage unless he could get his fingers between the teeth, but the teeth seemed to be too close together.

He wondered if he was bleeding. He was so wet with perspiration it would be hard to tell.

Wayne Betz crawled over. "You got a problem?" he asked.

Michaelis said, "Hell no. I'm just being eaten by a dead alligator."

Betz raised himself to his knees. He shoved the barrel of his Uzi between the jaws at the rear of the alligator's mouth, then pushed the stock upward hard. The pressure lessened. Michaelis was able to ease his leg out, the sharp teeth ripping threads in his pants leg.

He said to Wayne, "Thanks a million. I need this leg for a while longer."

Betz snickered. "Don't mention it. Take that thing home with you and make a suitcase."

Strang came scuttling up in a crouch.

He saw Carbin and shook his head. "Well, we all get it, sooner or later."

Michaelis said, "He made an interesting confession before he died."

Strang turned to him. "Yeah? Well, let's talk about it

later. Right now this war ain't going nowhere. We've got to gamble and change our tactics. Firing into all this fucking swamp growth to hit an unseen enemy is for the birds."

Michaelis nodded. "Right."

Strang slumped out of his crouch into a prone position when a bullet left a burn mark on the shoulder of his canvas shirt. "What we got to do is line up all our rocket launchers and blast hell out of the whole area, then go at them with every damned grenade we have," he said.

"Yeah," said Betz. "Shrapnel can find a lot more men in the bushes than bullets."

It took some frantic crawling around, but in a short time men were positioned at wide intervals to man the five rocket launchers.

At Strang's signal the hum of rockets leaving the long, tubular launchers was soon drowned out by deafening explosions in the enemy area. The swamp was literally being blasted to bits. Roots, trees, branches, earth, and bushes shot into the sky as though propelled by a hurricane.

After the last rocket was launched, Strang signaled and the men all moved closer, lobbing grenades.

The grenades created a smaller hurricane, but still sent a storm of debris into the air. After the last were lobbed, the men moved slowly into enemy territory, automatic weapons at the ready.

Four of the neo-Nazis came out from behind trees, arms high in surrender.

Strang said, "Sorry, no prisoners."

He turned his Uzi on them and mowed them down.

The sight sickened Michaelis. But it was probably necessary, he told himself. The law would not punish them, and leaving them alive would make them available to testify against Strang's group.

The bloody carnage was over. Mop up and count your losses. Five of their own were dead, including Carbin, and burying them in the spongy, water-permeated earth was difficult. Strang said a prayer over the large, single grave.

What was left of the enemy they tossed into the creeks for the alligators. Strang was damned if they were going to dig graves for them. Not for that kind of scum.

The cleanup took all day, requiring another night in the swamp. At dawn they started their trek west to the coast, some thirty-five miles south of Naples, where Strang had, they hoped, a chartered yacht waiting to pick them up.

Michaelis leaned over the rail watching the white, moonlit wake. The yacht was traveling southeast in the Gulf of Mexico, headed for the Florida Keys. So far all was well. No challenges from the Coast Guard. No attempt to intercept them by the law in any form.

The Seminoles had wisely taken off when the fighting began, and obviously had no reason to involve themselves by reporting what they thought was going to happen.

If all went well, a bus would be waiting for them in the Keys. A chartered plane would be ready for them at Miami Airport. A few hours later he would be with Athena.

What had they accomplished, anyway? The KGB and every other major intelligence agency would still be after Athena. They had wiped out a paramilitary operation of the SSD, stooges of the KGB. That was something of an accomplishment. Maybe it would discourage other paramilitary operations of the neo-Nazi groups. More than one state in the country harbored them, but most were probably not SSD operations. But ripe for takeover?

But face it, the battle hadn't done much to change their situation. He and Athena would still have to live on the run, hiding like major criminals who have committed such atrocious acts that society can never forget them, never let them relax.

35

ATHENA WAS WEARING JEANS, A MAN'S BLUE WORK SHIRT TOO LARGE for her, and feeding dogs in Cindy Harrison's boarding kennels. She still wore her red wig and freckles.

She put down her sack of dog food and ran into Michaelis's arms. They stood together long enough to be embarrassing.

"How are you doing?" he asked, his lips kissing an earlobe.

"I love it," she said. "I'm going to become a vet."

He laughed. It was exhilarating to see her so cheerful. It would be truly great if they could shrug off their voluminous problems without even discussing them.

She said, "I've been so worried about you. Don't you ever do anything like that again." She pulled away from him and gave a no-nonsense frown.

"You were the lady who made such a fuss to go with us," he said.

She kissed him. "I wanted to be there to keep you out of trouble," she said.

They went inside to Cindy's large kitchen. Cindy gave Michaelis a hug and dug a bottle of champagne from the refrigerator.

They sipped champagne in silence, the atmosphere sober.

"I'm not sure I want to hear what happened," said Athena. "But I must."

Michaelis shrugged. "We wiped them out. We lost five men. Two of Strang's group and three of Carbin's group, including Carbin."

Athena bowed her head. "Poor Kent," she said.

Michaelis downed the rest of his champagne. "No loss to humanity. He was a thoroughly evil man."

Athena looked up. "I wouldn't say that. He had his good side. He saved my life, in a way, when I was in a deep depression."

She finished her glass of champagne. "I doubt if I would ever have come out of it if he hadn't devised this Rowena disguise. He brought me back into the world of the living."

Michaelis looked down. Should he tell her about Carbin? She would probably find out from Strang or Angie anyway.

He said, "He put you there to begin with. When he knew he was dying, he confessed to me that he murdered Brillhagen. He dropped the radio in the whirlpool bath."

Athena stared at him shocked, her eyes wide. "I—I can't believe it!" she said.

Michaelis shook his head. "He was a Catholic of sorts. Probably grew up in it, then drifted away. He couldn't confess to a priest, so he told me and asked me to tell a priest and ask the priest to pray for him. Murder is a mortal sin."

Cindy said, "My God. How weird."

Athena had a tear in the corner of her eye. "Poor Wolf! That inhuman bastard!" she said, her voice breaking.

Michaelis moved close to her and hugged her.

Cindy decided to check on one of her patients. She left the room, her eyes cast down.

Athena wept silently. It was the first time Michaelis had seen her cry.

Her almost soundless sobs finally diminished. She dabbed at her eyes with a handkerchief and said, "I feel so guilty. My father's great boon to mankind. Power at less than a hundredth of the cost. No more dependence on oil from erratic Arab states."

She laughed with a trace of hysteria.

"Karl and Wolf are dead, and you're in constant danger. You could have been killed down there, or crippled for life, or blinded," she said.

He tightened his grip around her shoulders and shook her slightly. "Come on. I'm not going to let anything bad happen to either of us. My parapsychic powers tell me we both have charmed lives."

She gave him a woeful smile.

He filled her glass and his own with more champagne. He handed her glass to her, then clicked his own against it.

"You have my guarantee. The future is going to come up all roses," he said.

She nodded and took a sip. "While we keep an eagle eye out for thorns," she said.

They were lying together in Cindy's spare bedroom, temporarily satiated. The room was silent except for the rustle of summer wind in the tall evergreens. Occasionally a dog with insomnia gave a puzzled bark.

Athena said, "I have a confession to make."

Michaelis rested his hand on her stomach. "Okay, confess," he said. He moved his hand down to rest on her pubic hair.

She moved it back up to midstomach. "Be serious and listen to me," she said.

"All right," he said. "I am serious."

Athena said, "I have arranged with a man from the State Department to give us completely new identities. New passports, new everything," she said. "His name is MacVeagh Pratt. He called on me once to ask me to give Father's secret to the United States."

Michaelis sat up. "You mean the sort of thing they do for criminals who are testifying against their old colleagues?"

"Yes."

He rubbed his chin. "Hmmm," he said. "Sounds good, but—"

"But what?" she asked.

He shook his head. "I'm just trying to figure out how John Doe instead of Professor Michaelis is going to lecture on political science at Crendon."

She said, "It's just a temporary expedient. You have well over a month before classes begin."

He turned on his side and kissed her neck. "So what do we do with our new identities?" he asked.

She looked at him, smiling. "I've decided to do what you suggested. I will burn the damned papers publicly before an impeccable collection of witnesses. Gesellschaft Dietrich will sue me, but I don't care if they get *everything.*"

Michaelis hugged her. "No more running and hiding! God, how wonderful!"

She said in his ear, "You'll have to support me in the style to which I have become accustomed."

"I will, I swear it. Even if I have to turn to crime."

The matter settled, they turned to the serious business of making love for a third time.

36

THE EXPERT MAKEUP COSMETOLOGIST SUPPLIED BY MCVEAGH Pratt looked at a portrait photograph of Michaelis and decided that his black hair, mustache, and fake tan provided sufficient disguise. He supplied a cheap suit, gray and so pearly it would probably glow in the dark. To further remove him from the upper crust, the suit was a bad fit, too tight across the shoulders, and had trouser legs that dragged slightly on the ground at the heels.

Michaelis asked, "Aren't you overdoing this?"

Marcus Richy, the cosmetologist, was a short, chubby little man with long gray hair that almost touched his shoulders. He said, "With a new identity you change everything. Clothes help more than you think. If I am looking for Mrs. von Dietrich, my eye is not going to dwell quite as long on a woman wearing a cheap, tasteless rayon dress."

He settled black-rimmed, clear eyeglasses on Michaelis's nose and the transformation was complete.

Athena was fitted with her cheap rayon dress, red with

too much orange in it, a dusky complexion, a garish platinum wig which was obviously a wig, heavy eye shadow, and contact lenses that changed her green eyes to brown.

After Richy left, Michaelis asked Athena, "Have you decided when and where you're going to do your public burning?"

She said, "I've almost decided. I think it will be Ireland."

He stared at her. "Why Ireland?"

She smiled. "Because the Irish are all crazy like I am. They will understand. My mother was Irish."

He shook his head in disbelief.

"They are the most honest people I have ever known. My father had an estate near Cork and I spent many summers there," she said.

"But—" he said, then lapsed into silence.

"But what?"

"Well, security for one thing. Up until those papers are burned everyone there will be in great danger, even the broadcast people covering the event."

Athena thought about it. "They will get the whole army out if necessary. It will be an international event with worldwide publicity. The Irish will love the excitement of it."

Michaelis glanced at his new passport. He was now William A. Dobbs. "Don't forget to call me *Bill,*" he said.

Athena smiled. "I may be Jennifer Carstairs, but if you call me *Jenny* I'll clout you."

Michaelis said, "Jennifer, I love you."

They were not traveling first-class this time. Bill Dobbs and Jennifer were on Magna International Airlines seated about halfway back in coach.

Michaelis bought a scotch for himself and a white wine for Athena from the drinks wagon. He sipped his scotch and began to read a paperback. Athena finished her wine and leaned back to doze. The flight was so smooth one could have stood a dime on end and it would have remained upright.

The captain's voice rumbled over the loudspeaker. "We

shall be making an unscheduled stop at Gander. There will be some delay." His voice sounded cheerful but puzzled.

A woman nearby squawked, "There's something wrong with the plane!"

A stewardess said, "Please be calm. We are merely making an unscheduled stop. That's all there is to it. There's nothing wrong with the aircraft."

A man yelled, "Oh, yeah? Well, if there's nothing wrong with the aircraft, *why* are we making an unscheduled stop at Gander?"

"Because Gander has requested it!" said the stewardess. "It could have something to do with the weather over the Atlantic."

Michaelis leaned forward. Something was definitely wrong. But Athena should be safe enough with her new identity. Nevertheless, it was worrisome. He glanced at Athena, who was now awake and looking a bit frightened. He clasped her hand and squeezed it. "Everything is going to be okay," he said in a low voice.

The no-smoking sign finally went on and the plane made a smooth descent. The dime would still be upright. The flaps came down and the plane rolled gradually to a stop. Though it was night, the plane was in a section of the airport that was well lighted. Glancing out the window, Michaelis could see that a number of men on the ground were armed with automatic weapons.

A door was opened loudly. In a few seconds Ingrid appeared at the front of the tourist cabin. She was cradling a submachine gun.

A woman passenger began screaming.

Ingrid said, "Shut up or I will blow your head off."

The woman stopped screaming. A deathly silence blanketed the cabin, and a smell of fear permeated the air. Perspiration generated by fear smelled different, Michaelis decided. They *were* in a hostage situation.

Ingrid said, "There are two passengers on this flight who are well disguised and are traveling under false passports. We want them. If they will come forward, the rest of you will be left in peace to continue your flight to Shannon."

The passengers began muttering and looking around.

Athena bent over almost double, then straightened up.

Ingrid said, "If you think those armed men outside are police, you're wrong. They are *our* people." She shifted her submachine gun slightly. "All right, Athena von Dietrich and Jonathan Michaelis, you will stand up and come forward."

Michaelis put his hand on Athena's thigh to keep her from rising.

Ingrid said, "I see our friends are reluctant to reveal themselves. Perhaps this will hasten their decision. We shall take passengers one by one to the ramp and shoot them until you come forward.

"Or get shot anyway," she added.

There was a long silence.

A woman shrieked, "For God's sake, give yourselves up! Must all of us die for your sins?"

A man said to Ingrid, "How do you know they are even on board? Are you going to kill us all to prove you're wrong?"

Ingrid said, "If necessary, yes. But we know they are on board."

She stared around at the distraught faces of the passengers. "Last call," she said.

Michaelis kept his hand on Athena's thigh, holding her down tightly.

Ingrid said, "All *right.* The executions start."

She pointed to a pretty teenaged blonde with a backpack on her lap. "All right, you. You're first. Get up."

The girl struggled to her feet, stark terror on her face, her mouth trembling but speechless. She stepped into the aisle.

Michaelis took his hand away.

Athena stood up. "I am Athena von Dietrich," she said.

Michaelis stood up and moved into the aisle ahead of her. "I am Jonathan Michaelis," he said.

The teenager scurried back into her seat, white-faced and on the verge of fainting.

Athena pushed in front of Michaelis and marched down the aisle to Ingrid.

Ingrid said, "What a great disguise! What a cute little billionairess you are!"

She moved closer and snatched off Athena's platinum wig.

Athena's knife was now in her loose-fitting sleeve. It slid down into her hand, and all in one motion it was plunged into Ingrid's chest.

Ingrid gasped and crumpled to the floor.

Athena wrenched the submachine gun away from her as she fell.

Michaelis said, "Careful! There'll be another one in the cockpit with the pilot, and maybe one hiding in first class."

Athena had a look of weary horror on her face. She handed Ingrid's Walther to Michaelis. "You take over. I've done my killing for today," she said, tears running down her cheeks. They left white trails through her light brown makeup.

Cradling the Walther, Michaelis pulled aside one of the curtains separating the first-class cabin from the tourist cabin. One of Ingrid's men stood at the head of the aisle in the first-class cabin. He was also armed with a Walther.

Michaelis fired a quick burst. The man's body leaped backward, as though hit by a flying boom.

The door to the cockpit flew open. Another of Ingrid's men stepped out cautiously. Michaelis fired another burst, sending him reeling back inside the open door, his head half-blown away.

Michaelis collected the two Walthers and handed one to Athena. "Ingrid claimed the armed guys outside are theirs."

The pilot came out of the cockpit, stepping around the dead man. His hands were up.

Michaelis said, "Put your hands down. The good guys are in control." He walked up to the pilot and handed him the third Walther.

The pilot grinned. He was a young man with very red hair and a big mouth. He said, "Jesus, God, and what in hell is going on?"

Michaelis said, "The deceased were setting up a hostage situation. She"—he pointed to Ingrid—"said the armed men outside are theirs. So we're still in trouble."

The pilot nodded thoughtfully, his tongue running over his lower lip.

"I suggest you get on your radio and see if you can't get

the Royal Mounties or the army or something out here fast," said Michaelis. He wiped his forehead. It was wet with perspiration. "If the bastards outside find out their people in here are all dead, they may try to storm the plane or blow it up."

"Holy shit, man!" said the pilot, hurrying back into the cockpit.

Michaelis followed him. The copilot, a gray-haired man in his early fifties, sat unconscious but still breathing with a sonorous snore.

"They cracked him on the head," said the pilot. He slid into his seat, put on his earphones, and began speaking into the tiny microphone he had been wearing.

After a minute he turned back to Michaelis and said, "I'm not getting any response. They must be in control of the tower."

He began to speak into his microphone again. "This is 252 Magna on the ground at Gander. We have a hijack in progress. Hijackers have control of tower. Alert Canadian police. Alert Canadian police." He took a deep breath and then said, "I say again, this is 252 Magna on the ground at Gander. We have a hijack in progress. Hijackers have control of tower. Alert Canadian police. Alert Canadian police."

He turned to Michaelis and shrugged.

Michaelis asked, "How fast could you get this thing off the ground? And do you have enough fuel to make it to another airport?"

The pilot squinted at him. "Not so fast that they wouldn't have time to shoot at us. And yes, I have enough fuel to make it to another airport."

Michaelis bit his lip. If they started shooting at the plane, it might blow up or catch fire, incinerating everyone on board.

He asked, "Could you do something crazy like wheeling around in small circles?" He paused. "You know, make them jump for their lives. Keep them too damned busy to shoot."

The pilot grinned.

He thought it over. "Maybe, just maybe." He slapped the top of his head sharply, as though jostling his brains might help the decision. His engines were still running at idle power.

Michaelis said, "You'll be a hero if it works."

The pilot shook his head. "Or unemployed. Or dead. Or both."

Michaelis picked up the microphone used for speaking to the passengers and said, "We are about to take off. Fasten your seat belts loosely if possible, then bend forward and put your head between your knees until we are airborne. Some shots may come through the windows. Try to keep your body below window level."

The pilot increased power and made a sharp right turn. There was a loud clang as the wing knocked over the passenger ramp. His immediate target was three armed men. There were two loud thumps as he clipped them with the jet engines. He continued circling to the right. The men scattered, some running, some throwing themselves on the ground. The plane reeled around in a complete circle and headed for the runways. One more gunman went down on the last turn.

The pilot said, "I can't believe I'm doing this."

The sound of gunfire behind them sent a shock of fear through Michaelis. He left the cockpit to see if Athena was all right.

She was sitting safely on the floor in the aisle. She had replaced her platinum wig and fixed her facial makeup. She was trying to comfort the teenager who had been chosen for execution. The girl was having a quiet case of hysteria.

Michaelis went back to the cockpit.

Clanging noises resounded as bullets hit the plane.

The pilot worked on some of the controls.

He said, "Oh, shit! I can't take off. The damned ailerons are jammed."

My God, what next? Michaelis asked himself.

He said, "Taxi as far away as you can go on the field, then get the passengers out with the emergency chutes."

The plane speeded up.

Michaelis picked up the passenger cabin microphone. "Pay careful attention," he said. "We're going to take you as far away from the gunmen as we can. You will then leave the plane by emergency chutes and *disperse.* There are only two people aboard that these criminals want. Run or walk in different directions. They will probably not harm you. Stewardesses, prepare the passengers for emergency exit."

The pilot stomped the plane to a skidding halt about two miles from Ingrid's gunmen. They were in the farthest corner of the huge airport. A wooded area was nearby.

The emergency chutes worked. The passengers slid down and tumbled out and headed for the woods. Michaelis and Athena went last, helping the pilot hold his unconscious copilot while the four slid down.

Michaelis and the pilot carried the copilot into the woods.

The pilot said, "I'll stay with him. You two take off. You're the ones they are after."

Michaelis went back to the plane. Athena had stayed behind to help two old ladies who had canes and walked with difficulty.

Michaelis said to the old ladies, "I wouldn't go into the woods. Help will surely be along shortly, and these gangsters won't be interested in hurting you two."

One of the old ladies shook her cane at him. "No, they want you, you bum!" she said.

Jeep lights were approaching. Friend or enemy?

The flash of automatic weapons firing at them beat the noise by a fraction of a second. Not friends. Michaelis pulled Athena to the ground, waving the old ladies to do the same.

Michaelis and Athena opened up on the jeep with their appropriated Walther submachine guns. The jeep careened to the left and tilted over, flames briefly illuminating the three bodies that rolled out.

They got to their feet and ran into the shelter of the dark woods. Once among the trees they had to move very slowly, the moonlight providing only the dimmest help in avoiding walking into the black shapes of tree trunks.

Deep in the woods, they stopped and listened. The silence was reassuring. It was broken only by the almost inaudible rustling of small animals.

A large raccoon descended from his perch. He sat on his haunches, fat and grandfatherly, and stared at them.

Michaelis laughed silently. Athena said in a low voice, "They must not see many humans in these woods. Isn't he cute!"

Michaelis spoke close to her ear. "Don't try to pet him. They have sharp teeth and claws, and are vicious fighters."

He took her arm and guided her in a direction that bypassed the raccoon.

The raccoon went back to his tree, apparently satisfied that the intruders were no danger to his turf.

Fall comes early in Newfoundland. The air was cold, with a penetrating dampness. They had only the summer-weight clothes they were wearing and light raincoats they had grabbed before entering the chute. Athena began to shiver. It was going to be some night, Michaelis thought. There was no way they could expect to find their way out of the forest in the dark. They had gone some distance, possibly in a circle, and he was wondering whether they shouldn't try to dig in somewhere and try to keep warm. The possibility of enemy searchers finding them was no greater than the possibility of their walking right into them in the dark.

He leaned close to Athena and said in almost a whisper, "I think we should try to hole up somewhere and keep warm. We'll never find a way out of here until daylight."

Athena nodded, her teeth beginning to chatter.

If there were only some kind of debris to cover them, Michaelis thought. The leaves had turned color, he was sure, but evidently they had not yet fallen. The ground offered only dead branches and a mossy, moldy leaf surface.

He could easily make a fire from the dead branches, but that, of course, was out. The branches were no help as cover.

In the end they simply found a soft spot and lay on the ground, locked in a tight embrace, sharing body heat, warm in front with chills running up and down in back.

Michaelis asked, "Is your back as cold as mine?"

Athena said, "Probably not. Women have an extra layer of fat."

He asked, "Where is it? You're so slender and shapely." He groped around her body hunting for the extra layer of fat.

She grabbed his nose and twisted it.

She said, "Women are superior to men in many ways. For instance, we can grow babies."

His mouth close to her ear, he said, "The thought occurred to me just now. Wouldn't it be a story for our grandchildren if our first child was conceived in a forest in Newfoundland where we were hiding in danger of our lives?"

She giggled softly. "One doesn't discuss such things with one's grandchildren. And anyway, the poor babe might be born frightened like his mother."

She pushed him over so that his back was on the ground, then lay partially on top of him, her breath warm on his neck. It helped.

After a few minutes he shifted, turning her on her back and partially covering her, keeping most of his weight on his side.

There was little sleep for either of them, and they continued this alternating of positions, their motions resembling a wrestling match carried on in ultra-slow motion. The activity helped keep them somewhat warmer, if nothing else.

Early morning sunlight finally crept through the treetops. At least they now knew where east was, with a fair guide to west, south, and north. Unfortunately they had no idea which direction they had taken from the airport.

Chilled, with his muscles stiff, Michaelis limped a discreet distance away and relieved himself.

When he returned, Athena asked, "Where to now?"

He said, "Well, if we walk due east we might walk right to the Atlantic Ocean. Then we could turn right and walk south."

Athena nodded.

She tried to brush the dirt and leaf mold from her beige raincoat. Much of it stuck wetly.

She said, "Along the shore we may come to a fishing village or someone's summer home."

They started walking in the direction of the rising sun.

The sun was taking the chill from the air and they were beginning to feel more comfortable. They trudged along, each carrying one of the Walther submachine guns that had saved their lives and, in Athena's case, from a fate much worse.

When they finally came out of the woods, they found something more useful than the Atlantic Ocean, a road running north and south.

Michaelis lit one of his no-tar cigarettes. "Now what? Are we north or south of the airport?"

Athena said, "Flip a coin?"

He laughed. "Let's try south," he said.

The road was a narrow, two-lane blacktop. It provided much easier walking than the soggy undergrowth of the woods.

They had walked hardly a mile when they saw a police car approaching in the distance, red light on top flashing.

As it neared them, Michaelis waved.

The police car picked up speed and roared past them.

Athena and Michaelis stared at each other.

The police car squealed to a halt about a hundred yards away, then made a screeching turnaround and came back to within fifty or sixty feet of them, swinging to a stop at right angles, blocking the road. Two officers slipped out, both carrying shotguns. The officer on their side of the car scuttled for the protection of the other side.

One of the officers yelled, "Drop those weapons!"

Michaelis took Athena's Walther and carried them both to the roadside and placed them on the ground.

The police officers approached, shotguns at the ready.

One was short and wide and had a red face and bushy black eyebrows. The other was about six feet tall and had a flourishing brown mustache.

Michaelis yelled, "Hey, we're the victims, not the hijackers."

The tall officer said, "Well, that remains to be seen. Victims carrying automatic weapons frighten us."

The short one said, "Turn your backs. We're going to have to handcuff you until we get this sorted out."

Michaelis and Athena turned their backs and held their hands together.

"This is damned humiliating," Michaelis muttered.

After they were bundled into the back of the police car handcuffed, the short officer went to the side of the road and retrieved the Walthers.

On the way back to the airport Michaelis explained what had happened, and suggested that they check with McVeagh Pratt of the U.S. State Department with regard to their true identities.

"Have patience," replied the tall officer, who was driving. "We'll get it all sorted out."

The reception area of the airport looked almost as drab as a shelter for the homeless. Passengers from the ill-fated plane were waking from uncomfortable sleep in chairs and on the floor. The room was too warm. An odor of unwashed bodies, perspiration, and cigarette smoke lay heavy in the air.

Michaelis saw the redheaded pilot in the crowd and let out a yell.

The pilot hurried over and took one look at their handcuffs.

"Why do you have these people handcuffed?" he asked the tall officer. "They're the heroes of the hijacking. They saved the passengers and the plane, for God's sake!"

The tall officer looked disconcerted. "They were carrying automatic weapons," he said.

"Which they wrestled from the hijackers," said the pilot.

The officer blushed. "Come in the office and we'll get this sorted out."

They crowded into the security office. The handcuffs were removed.

The pilot and one of the male passengers who had been sitting near the front in the tourist cabin described what had happened. The passenger, a senior citizen with snow-white hair, was so excited that he kept wriggling in his seat.

The pilot made a speech. "Do you realize that this will go down in history as the most successful aborting of a terrorist attack of all time? There were twenty terrorists involved. Eight of them are dead, and twelve are behind bars. Not a single passenger was injured, and very little damage was done to the aircraft. *And,* it was all due to the quick thinking of these two."

The white-headed passenger said, "Everything he has told you is the truth, so help me. It's absolutely fascinating what happened."

The tall officer glanced at Athena and then at Michaelis. "It seems that we have made a natural mistake. You'll probably be receiving gold medals." He cleared his throat. "However, for the record I will check with the person in the U.S. State Department. His name was?"

"McVeagh Pratt," said Michaelis. He spelled *McVeagh* for him.

The officer turned to Athena. "Not to quibble, but would you mind telling me how you got this very lethal knife past the security screening?"

Athena asked, "You haven't seen it?"

She had left it, plunged to the hilt, in Ingrid's bosom.

He shook his head.

"It's made of heavy, strong plastic, with a very sharp point and blade edges," said Athena.

The officer sat, his mouth partly open. He rubbed his chin, then shook his head vigorously, as though trying to rattle his brains back into some kind of order.

He said, "What a Pandora's box you have opened. Now we'll have to body-search everyone."

37

ON THE NEXT TRIP TO IRELAND THERE WOULD BE NO SECURITY problems, Athena decided. She borrowed a private 747 from a friend who was an international banker. It had two bedrooms, a very large lounge, a comfortable dining room, kitchen, and two baths. Before boarding, every inch of the plane was checked for bombs, incendiaries, and any evidence of tampering with the food. The tanks that provided drinking water and bathing water were drained and refilled with chemically tested water. Mechanics checked the engines so thoroughly that it took them all night to put them back together.

Leslie Greenhaven supervised the inspection. Both she and Thomas Jonathan Swift planned to be aboard. Strang and Angie were also to be Athena's guests.

The five- or six-hour flight to Dublin did not require all this comfort, but they enjoyed it.

For the moment Michaelis and Athena were alone, sitting on a luxuriously soft sofa in the lounge. Tom and Leslie were conferring in the dining room. Strang and Angie were napping in one of the bedrooms.

Athena took a sip of white wine and said, "When Gesellschaft Dietrich gets through with me, we shall not be able to afford this sort of thing."

Michaelis rattled the ice in his scotch. "Tough," he said. "How can you bear the thought?"

"I'll be a kept woman," she said.

He reached over and patted her thigh. "A kept wife," he said.

She drained her small glass of wine. "You know, it's so wonderful to be sure I'm not being married for my money," she said.

He felt a bit hurt. "Even if you managed to keep your fortune, wouldn't you still be sure that I was not marrying you for your money?"

She leaned over and kissed him. "Of course I would. Your life-style is simple and you have no desire for great wealth. It has been obvious to me."

"So why are you so relieved?" he asked.

She smiled. "Marriages are really not made in heaven, you know. Even the most loving couples have their differences, have their small personality clashes and hurts. It is only human."

He poured himself more scotch and filled her glass with chilled wine.

He said, "I'm still not sure what you are getting at."

She kissed him again. "Picture one of these situations of minor conflict. I become snotty Mrs. Moneybags to you, and the suspicion comes to my mind that my great wealth is what attracted you to me. In other words it can turn a minor conflict into a major bad feeling."

He nodded. "You should have been a psychiatrist," he said.

She giggled.

He hugged her. "How could we possibly have any conflicts?" he asked.

She patted his cheek. "Jealousy, for one thing. Your pretty, nubile girl students."

He held up his hand. "Never have I touched a nubile student."

She pulled it down. "I'm just teasing you."

He was silent for a while, drinking his scotch. Finally he said, "If you think this is going to be a problem, we might as well face it. Gesellschaft Dietrich's suit will not make you penniless. You'll still have millions."

He laughed, and paused to light another cigarette. "They'll probably settle out of court for a miserable couple of hundred million."

Athena smiled. "You could be right."

He pulled her to him. "We'll have to live in sin."

She shook her head. "I will not have illegitimate children."

He kissed her.

"Then have your lawyers draw up a prenuptial contract. If we separate or divorce, I will only sue you for visiting rights to see my kids."

She pushed him over on the sofa and lay partially on top of him. She said in his ear, "Jon, I love you. I trust you implicitly. I'm sorry I started this discussion."

The steward came into the lounge to ask if they would like lunch served. They untangled with some minor embarrassment.

Five of Ireland's most distinguished citizens were gathered on the banks of the Liffey River some distance from the bridge that crossed it in the center of Dublin. A large platform had been constructed about twenty feet from the river's edge. Seated in folding chairs on the platform were the President, the prime minister, the lord mayor of Dublin wearing his gold chain of office, the Chief Justice of the Supreme Court, and a cardinal, the chief cleric of Ireland.

A sixth witness was a tall, gaunt-faced man in his seventies. From Cambridge, his name was Horace Carr, and he was considered one of the world's leading physicists. He had been one of Sir Yirmi's closest friends.

Behind the witnesses were crowded television crews from the major networks of the United States, England, and Europe. Some of them spilled off into the damp soil near the river.

Behind the television crews a battalion of armed soldiers stood shoulder to shoulder. Across the river another battalion of soldiers, also armed and in battle dress, stood shoulder to shoulder. Behind the soldiers, units of the Guarda, Ireland's police, patrolled in jeeps.

Michaelis had wondered where Athena had hidden Sir Yirmi's plans. On the way to the ceremony it took her only ten minutes to retrieve them from one of her father's old friends, a curator of Trinity College's famous library.

When the witnesses were all seated and the hubbub of voices was quieted by the cardinal raising his hand and asking for silence, Athena stepped out onto the platform.

She handed her father's plans to Horace Carr.

He flipped through the pages quickly, then stood up.

He said, "I can testify that I recognize Yirmi's handwriting, and that this material pertains to his antimatter discovery, and includes the details of construction of the necessary equipment needed to produce the results described."

He sat down.

Athena took the plans from Carr and gave them to each of the witnesses in turn. Since the material was Greek to them, each gave the pages only a cursory glance.

Holding the papers, Athena stepped to the front of her audience and gave the speech she had prepared and memorized.

"Ladies and gentlemen. As you know, I am here today to destroy the only documents in existence relating to my father's invention. It is a relatively inexpensive method of producing antimatter. Antimatter can convert one hundred percent of mass to energy. An explosion one hundred times greater than nuclear energy can be achieved with it. The first nation to have it will rule the world through fear. They will be tempted to use it. Greed and the desire for power, the differences between political systems and values may easily combine to produce the kind of devastation the world has never known. I cannot contribute to this. I will buy a few more years for a world free of this horror. Unfortunately, Fermilab and other research centers are already producing minute amounts of antimatter at a cost of millions. Let us hope that it will be many years before they can do it cheaply."

Tom Swift stared at her, his face reflecting a mixture of great sadness mixed with horror. An enormous coup for the USA would never be. Leslie Greenhaven's eyes were teary. Swift had even contemplated some kind of last-minute operation that would relieve Athena of Sir Yirmi's papers. Sentiment won. Michaelis and Strang had saved his life. Plus the fact that messing around with the Irish would be tricky indeed.

Athena bowed her head as the group began applauding. The loudest claps came from the TV reporters and cameramen from networks that would broadcast this message to the world. Represented or not, almost every country would videotape the scene and put it on the air.

A metal washtub had been placed about two feet from the river's edge. Athena placed the papers in the tub, then uncorked a pint bottle of gasoline. She poured the gasoline carefully over Sir Yirmi's papers, making certain that they were thoroughly soaked.

Smiling, she lit the end of a long taper. She stood back from the washtub and touched the flame to the papers.

A *plop* followed by a rush-of-wind sound came from the tub as the papers ignited and flames leaped high above the edge.

There was more applause.

She turned back to Michaelis, who had been standing by. He hugged her, stroking her hair while tears ran down her cheeks.

After the flames had died down, Michaelis broke the

ashes up with a stick. They waited until the washtub was cool enough to handle.

Michaelis picked it up, and wading a few feet out into the river, dumped the ashes into the sluggishly moving stream.

More applause followed as the videotape cameras recorded this scene.

A Rolls-Royce flying the flag of Ireland carried them back to the Royal Hibernian, where they had two suites in deference to Irish sensibilities. They were not married yet.

Tomorrow they would be. In St. Patrick's Cathedral, which strangely enough is not Catholic, but Protestant.

In the Royal Hibernian's lobby they were besieged by microphones shoved in their faces while fatuous questions were asked.

Athena kept repeating, "I've said all I have to say," and managed to scuttle into an elevator, leaving Michaelis surrounded.

Pushing his way through, Michaelis said, "Yes, we're being married tomorrow. I hope you won't make a circus of it."

"Yes, I imagine Gesellschaft Dietrich's directors will be furious."

"Yes, I love Ireland. We plan to honeymoon here."

"Yes, I'm a professor at Crendon University."

"No, I will not give up teaching."

"No, I'm not marrying her because she's one of the richest women in the world. And how would you like a punch in the nose?"

Red-faced, he managed to elbow his way through to an elevator.

There was to be a reception at the Presidential Palace in Phoenix Park. He wondered how they would ever get through it.

In his suite Michaelis removed his wet, muddy shoes and took off his sodden trousers. He cleaned the mud from his brown shoes and tried to dry them. They were probably ruined. He wouldn't need them. He had black shoes for the reception. Tuxedo required, dinner jacket. In Ireland this was informal dress.

There was a tap on the door and Athena came in.

He took her in his arms.

She giggled. He looked funny standing in his shirt, boxer shorts, and wet socks.

He said, "Laugh away. You didn't have to wade into the muddy waters of the Liffey."

She said, "You were superb. I've never seen a more efficient ashes grinder-upper."

A waiter arrived pushing a large cart containing two huge buckets of ice-packed champagne and enough hors d'oeuvres to feed a large party.

Michaelis hurried to the bedroom to finish dressing.

Athena said to the waiter, "We didn't order anything."

A voice behind the waiter said, "Didn't order anything, eh? You think we're going to take all this stuff back?"

Strang, Angie, Swift, and Leslie trooped in. Leslie hugged Athena. "You were really great, absolutely super. Now give us the Xerox copies, dammit."

Athena laughed.

Angie hugged Athena. Swift and Strang kissed her.

Angie asked, "Where's our hero who braved the dangerous, turbulent waters of the Liffey?"

"Changing his socks, shoes, and wet pants," said Athena.

Michaelis came out to join them. They applauded. He bowed, then stared at the champagne and hors d'oeuvres. "All this and the reception at the Presidential Palace, too? Tomorrow I'll be creeping down the aisle holding my head."

Athena said, "I'll brain you with an ice pack if you do."

Strang started singing "Get me to the church on time" in a hoarse, unmelodious voice.

Angie grabbed him and shook him.

He stopped singing. "This is the first time I've ever been asked to give away a gorgeous dame. I'm entitled to celebrate."

They drank champagne and toasted the bride to be and the groom. Swift raised his glass to Michaelis and Strang, thanking them for saving him from the KGB. Michaelis and Strang toasted Thomas Jonathan Swift for being a superbrave guy for even messing with the KGB.

They were all becoming mellow when Angie called a halt. "Time, gentlemen! The bar is closed!" she yelled.

Their marriage took place in one of the small chapels in St. Patrick's.

Dressed in a gray suit with a white shirt and maroon-and-black-striped tie, Michaelis waited at the altar for Athena.

She entered the chapel holding Strang's arm. She hesitated for only seconds at the door. Her mauve blouson dress of silk crepe de chine shimmered in the light from the colored windows. Buttoned demurely at the neck, the blouson with full push-up sleeves clung to her. As she walked slowly forward, the full skirt, falling halfway down from her knees, moved in graceful waves as though hurrying to meet Michaelis.

Michaelis thought she was the most beautiful woman he had ever seen.

Swift stood in as best man, with Angie as maid of honor. Attendance was limited to government officials and their families. Both the President and the prime minister sat in the front row. Newsmen were kept at a distance outside.

The ceremony proceeded with Michaelis in a happy daze. He finally heard the words "now pronounce you man and wife," and turned to kiss Athena.

Shaking hands with the dignitaries, they slowly made their way through the chapel to the door. Outside the newsmen had converged and more microphones were shoved at them.

Athena just smiled and shook her head. Michaelis repeated, "Yes, I'm gloriously happy," and leading Athena, pushed and elbowed through the crowd to their rented Lincoln, which already contained their luggage.

Strang, Angie, Tom, and Leslie threw rice.

Grinning, Michaelis drove very slowly through the crowd, which opened up reluctantly for the car. Finally free of it, he made it onto clear streets, remembering to drive on the left side of the road, and worked his way out of Dublin. They drove south toward Cork, planning to stop there overnight and then head west across Ireland to Galway.

• • •

Their itinerary had been kept secret and there was no mob of newsmen to greet them in Cork. The hotel manager recognized them, having seen them on television. He agreed to protect their anonymity. Putting his finger to his lips, he said, "Mum is the word."

Michaelis noticed a priest sitting in the lobby and remembered his promise to Carbin.

He said to Athena, "You go ahead up. I want to have a word with the priest."

She stared at him. "Your promise to Carbin."

He nodded. "If I believed in hell, which I don't, I would be inclined to think it isn't going to do him a bit of good. But a deathbed promise . . ."

The priest, a slender gray-haired man with a weather-ravaged, craggy face, was friendly and invited Michaelis to sit down.

Michaelis explained his obligation to the dying man. The priest listened, interested and somewhat puzzled.

After Michaelis finished, the priest brought out a small notebook and wrote Kent Carbin's name in it, and scribbled some notes regarding the circumstances.

Finally he said, "This is a most unusual request, but I see no reason why I cannot pray for this man's soul."

They both stood up and shook hands. Michaelis pressed a folded fifty-dollar bill into the priest's hand. "For your church's good works, Father," he said.

He went upstairs to his bride, overcome with euphoria. Now that the hullabaloo had died down and the quiet beauty of Ireland could be enjoyed, he had time to think about and revel in his married state. Athena belonged to him, and he belonged to her, in sickness and health and until death do us part. He had never been so completely happy.

About the Author

Franklin Bandy was the author of the Edgar Award-winning novel *Deceit and Deadly Lies*, *The Blackstock Affair*, and other novels of suspense. He was twice elected executive director of the Mystery Writers of America. He died in 1987.